THE LOVER
In which Lieutenant A␣
♦ 36 hours to solve the murder of the slain sun-worshipper
♦ a second murder to solve when the victim's boyfriend is also stabbed to death
♦ a bevy of beautiful suspects who all seem to revere the mysterious cult-leader known as The Prophet

THE MISTRESS
In which Lieutenant Al Wheeler must find—
♦ the murderer of Sheriff Laver's niece
♦ the missing $70,000 that the Syndicate would like back
♦ a new job if he doesn't arrest Lavers' favorite suspect, a Las Vegas gangster who just moved to town

THE PASSIONATE
In which Lieutenant Al Wheeler has to solve—
♦ the mystery of the corpse that appears in a coffin on a local TV horror show
♦ the dilemma of the mysterious caller who keeps offering warnings and clues
♦ the confusion caused by two beautiful twins who both married the wrong men

The Lover
- - - -
The Mistress
- - - -
The Passionate
- - - -

Three Novels by
Carter Brown

INTRODUCTION BY NICHOLAS LITCHFIELD

Stark House Press • Eureka California

THE LOVER / THE MISTRESS / THE PASSIONATE

Published by Stark House Press
1315 H Street
Eureka, CA 95501, USA
griffinskye3@sbcglobal.net
www.starkhousepress.com

THE LOVER
Originally published and copyright © 1958 by Horwitz Publications,
Sydney, Australia. Reprinted in the U.S. by Signet Books, New York, 1959.

THE MISTRESS
Originally published and copyright © 1958, 1959 by Horwitz
Publications, Sydney, Australia. Reprinted in the U.S. by Signet Books,
New York, 1959.

THE PASSIONATE
Originally published and copyright © 1959 by Horwitz Publications,
Sydney, Australia. Reprinted in the U.S. by Signet Books, New York, 1959.

Reprinted by permission of the Estate of Alan G. Yates, and licensed via
publishing representatives, Brio Books Pty Ltd, Australia. All rights
reserved under International and Pan-American Copyright Conventions.

"Carter Brown's Crooks, Cadavers, and Phony Prophets"
copyright © 2021 by Nicholas Litchfield

ISBN-13: 978-1-951473-26-6

Book design by Mark Shepard, shepgraphics.com
Cover design by Jeff Vorzimmer, ¡caliente!design, Austin, Texas
Cover art by Al Brule
Proofreading by Bill Kelly

First Stark House Press Edition: March 2021

Contents

Carter Brown's Crooks, Cadavers, and Phony Prophets

by Nicholas Litchfield

Launched in Australia in 1951, the swift-paced, tongue-in-cheek crime fiction tales by the incredibly prolific Alan Geoffrey Yates (1923-1985), writing under the house name Carter Brown, appeared with regularity for over thirty years. Close to three hundred titles emerged, with the series comprising roughly 215 novels and around 75 novella-length stories. These books, published in thirty-five countries and twenty-seven languages, purportedly sold more than one hundred million copies, making the author one of the top-selling mystery writers of the 1960s and Carter Brown one of Australia's most successful literary exports.

Set the daunting task of producing one novel and two novelettes per month, Yates strived hard to come close to meeting the punishing work schedule, even churning out one million words during his first year as a full-time writer. That included a 50,000-word novel in 72 hours straight. (Bolton, 1983).

By 1965, at only 41 years of age, he had penned 115 mystery novels since 1950 and was still averaging about six 50,000-word novels per year. (*The Sydney Morning Herald*, 1965). Surprisingly, the popularity of the books never waned and, despite the grueling publishing schedule and pressure to deliver inspired variation to familiar plots, the author's reliable, machine-tooled consistency stayed true throughout the series.

Interestingly, rumor has it that John F. Kennedy was a keen reader of Yates' work, and Marlene Dietrich was fond of his stories, too. According to Australian author John Baxter, when the iconic German actress' Paris apartment was cleared after her death, a collection of Carter Brown paperbacks was discovered. (Johnson-Woods, 2009, p.53).

The mystery series also had a life beyond the traditional book publishing industry. A spin-off comic book series was produced, as well as a Japanese TV series, a radio series introduced by Yates himself, titled *The Carter Brown Mystery Theatre*, and a musical written by Richard O'Brien, creator of *The Rocky Horror Picture Show*. All in all, two Carter Brown books were adapted to the screen: *The Body*, titled *Touchez pas aux blondes* (1960), directed by Maurice Cloche (an honorary Academy Award winner), and *Curtains for a Chorine*, titled *Blague dans le coin* (1963), starring Fernandel, Perrette Pradier, and Eliane D'Almeida.

The history of the Carter Brown Mystery Series (CBMS) makes for fascinating reading. Australian scholar Toni Johnson-Woods depicts the series as "a literary pandemic" spreading virulently to other countries and generating international bestsellers through "uniformly bland appeal and its ability to fit benignly into multiple book markets throughout the world." (Johnson-Woods, 2008, p.164). Intriguingly, the books achieved the highest distribution in France, which released 159 unique titles and twenty-seven reprints, more than any other country. As Johnson-Woods cautiously notes, it is unclear if the popularity is "due to the wonderful writing or innovative narratives" or merely the result of a dubiously extravagant publishing contract. (Johnson-Woods, 2009, p.68).

The success of CBMS was more about marketing than content, with the right cover art essential to promoting the series and Signet crucial in expanding foreign sales. How much of its success is owed to the collectability of the Robert McGinnis covers is anyone's guess.

With a portfolio comprising 1,500 paperback covers since the 1950s, and iconic movie posters including *Breakfast at Tiffany's*, *The Odd Couple*, *Barbarella*, and several James Bond films, few midcentury commercial artists were as prolific or influential. McGinnis produced almost one hundred of the CBMS covers, and he still paints to this day, often contributing sublime covers to the Hard Case Crime paperback line. Novelist and editor Charles Ardai said of his work: "Leggy, serene, aloof, unruffled, coiled, and deadly or enigmatic and sensuous, Bob's women are like otherworldly creatures, breathtaking and perfect." (Kingston, 2019).

Unquestionably, McGinnis's eye-popping images of provocative, seductive, elegant women have helped sell many books over the decades. Art Scott, the co-author of *The Art of Robert E. McGinnis*, phrased it this way: "The women were easier to remember than titles, and the customer's 'I don't think I've seen *her* before' sold the book." (Kingston, 2019).

If, in other countries, cover artists mimicked the style of the McGinnis covers to help sell the CBMS books, in Japan it was quite the reverse, with publisher Hayakawa Shobo not deviating from their established practice of publishing crime novels at higher prices and using quality paper and elegant abstract cover art. (Johnson-Woods, 2008, p.173). They didn't need McGinnis-style covers to market the Carter Brown books, as the books sold very well.

Often overlooked by critics, the series didn't rely on reviews to boost sales. Nevertheless, many of these novels received very encouraging reviews in dailies like the *St. Albans Messenger* and from Anthony Boucher of *The New York Times*, who was a keen fan of the "wisecracking, oversexed, irresponsible Lieut. Al Wheeler," finding the character's humor "really funny." (Boucher, 1958). He even selected *Until Temptation Do Us Part* as his "Best in the Field" among crime novels of 1968, praising it for its "nice blend of humor, sex and clever plotting." (Boucher, 1968).

In more than three-dozen reviews, Boucher wrote admiringly of the series, relishing Brown's "light and deft" touch and the "fast action and agreeably intricate plot twists." (Boucher, 1964). As for the stories contained in this Stark House volume, Boucher was complimentary of all three, remarking of the decent plotting and "nicely ironic ending" to *The Lover*, and the plentiful action and "well-constructed dénouement" in *The Mistress*. (Boucher, "Report on Criminals at Large" 1959). He enjoyed the "macabre and even ghoulish tone" of *The Passionate* and observed an improvement in the author's knowledge and understanding of American culture. (Boucher, "A Report on Criminals at Large" 1959).

Although written at a breakneck pace and published in rapid succession, the plots are varied, and each of these tales pleasantly distinctive. Surprisingly, in the opener (*The Lover*), the murder suspect actually outdoes Al Wheeler in lechery and general wackiness. Calling himself the Prophet, a handsome, brawny sun-worshiper, who parades around in only a loincloth, gathers one hundred thousand dollars in donations to build a shrine on top of Bald Mountain. His plans begin to unravel when a naked corpse turns up on his altar, leading Wheeler to investigate the members of his congregation and discover what sort of racket the man is running.

Naturally, plenty of tan, beautiful females occupy Wheeler's time, and there is a generous serving of murdered bodies in this frenetic story. Happily, the wry finale is as gratifying as Boucher claimed.

Arguably, the subsequent novel (*The Mistress*) is of an even higher caliber, with more impressive supporting characters. Here, Wheeler investigates the murder of County Sheriff Lavers' niece, whose body was dumped on the sheriff's doorstep, apparently as a warning to Lavers to stay away from her boyfriend, Howard Fletcher. Fletcher is a casino owner who has been pushed out of Las Vegas by the syndicate, and Lavers had threatened to run him out of town if he started "operating" in Pine City. However, the more Wheeler digs, including a visit to Vegas to explore Fletcher's syndicate connections, the surer he is that Fletcher has been set up as the fall guy.

Alas, Lavers hampers Wheeler's investigation by arresting Fletcher, leading the reckless detective to manufacture an alibi for the murder suspect and, as a result, put his police career in jeopardy.

Notable characters include the smart alec Johnny Torch, a vicious hood with "reptilian eyes" and lips "thin enough to cut bread with" who trades barbs with Wheeler, and the hot-tempered Gabrielle, a strip-tease artist at the Vegas gambling house Snake Eyes. Amusingly, having appeared completely naked on stage at the commencement of her set, Gabrielle then puts her clothes *on* for her routine, much to the audience's chagrin. Few—Wheeler included—appreciate the "brevity" of her performance, which she has mockingly whittled down to its bare essentials.

The original book cover to the concluding tale (*The Passionate*) promises mischievous twin temptresses, shrunken heads, corpses, and lady killers. The story, perhaps the zaniest of the three, lives up to its promise. First, a cadaver disappears from the morgue, and then a different body turns up in a fake coffin on a cheesy horror show. Finally, the missing corpse appears in the prop room of the television studio. And that is just the first chapter.

The elaborate plot centers on Penelope and Prudence Calthorpe, a pair of high society twin sisters: the former, a fresh TV actress whose debut is spoiled by the discovery of her murdered husband, and the latter, a notorious practical joker, disliked by police because of her foolish pranks. Rich, eccentric, and ill-behaved, Prudence, a woman who keeps shrunken heads on top of her bureau, as well as the mummified hand of Kubla Khan and Lizzie Borden's blood-stained dress, is the star of this macabre tale. The moment she asks Wheeler if she can purchase her sister's deceased husband's heart after the autopsy, the reader knows they are in for a wild and fanciful story.

As with other Carter Brown stories, the tone remains jokey. The focus is not on bullets and bloodshed and grisly violence but Wheeler's wisecracks, comebacks, and witty banter. The global appeal of Wheeler can be attributed to Yates' innate ability to engage and amuse his reader. "Though contemporaries and imitators may have equaled his knack of anticipating social trends and fads and using them as the basis for crime novels, few can match his talent for typing with his tongue permanently in his cheek," wrote Wayne Harrison of *The Sydney Morning Herald*. (Harrison, 1982).

Buoyed by sun-soaked settings and fine-looking gals, the light, short and snappy tales of cops and crooks, gangsters and gun molls, blackmailers and phony prophets offer an abundance of action and excitement and breezy humor. Undemanding and never dull, Al Wheeler's pleasing and surprisingly addictive adventures retain their charm and vigor to this day.

—November 2020
Rochester, NY

Works Cited:

Bolton, M. (1983, November 22). "The literary gin and tonic." *The Age*, p. 11.

Boucher, A. (1958, December 7). "Reports on Criminals at Large." *The New York Times*, BR50.

Boucher, A. (1959, August 30). "A Report on Criminals at Large." *The New York Times*, BR20.

Boucher, A. (1959, March 8). "Report on Criminals at Large." *The New York Times*, BR22.

Boucher, A. (1964, February 2). "Criminals at Large." *The New York Times*, BR32.

Boucher, A. (1968, February 25). "Crime." *The New York Times*, BRA22.

Harrison, W. (1982, August 21). "Sex and Violence: Broads and bullets make bucks." *The Sydney Morning Herald*.

Johnson-Woods, T. (2004). The mysterious case of Carter Brown: or, who really killed the Australian author? *Australian Literary Studies, 21* (4), 74.

Johnson-Woods, T. (2008). The Promiscuous Carter Brown. *Journal of the Association for the Study of Australian Literature*, pp.163-183.

Johnson-Woods, T. (2009). Crime Fiction's Cultural Field: Carter Brown in France. In A. (. Rolls, *Mostly French: French (in) detective fiction* (pp. 53-70). Oxford: Peter Lang.

Pierce, J. Kingston. (2019, February 2). "Robert McGinnis: A Life In Paperback Art." *CrimeReads*. https://crimereads.com/robert-mcginnis-a-life-in-paperback-art/.

Smith, Charles M. (1958, July 6). "Australian Detective Story Writer In America for Lowdown." *The Morning Call*.

The Sydney Morning Herald. (1965, April 3). "Author Plans Novel on Australia." *The Sydney Morning Herald*, p. 22.

Nicholas Litchfield is the founding editor of the literary magazine *Lowestoft Chronicle*, author of the suspense novel *Swampjack Virus*, and editor of nine literary anthologies. He has worked in various countries as a journalist, librarian, and media researcher and resides in western New York. Formerly, a book reviewer for the *Lancashire Evening Post* and syndicated to twenty-five newspapers across the U.K., he now writes for *Publishers Weekly* and regularly contributes to Colorado State University's literary journal *Colorado Review*. You can find him online at nicholaslitchfield.com.

THE LOVER

− − − −

by Carter Brown

"... without honor in his own country."

Chapter One

"If you promise to wear your handcuffs and let me keep the key, I'd love a date with you tonight, Lieutenant," Annabelle Jackson said firmly.

"I'd look silly in just a pair of handcuffs," I said. "I was planning on wearing my new suit."

The Sheriff's secretary flushed slightly. "There are times, Al Wheeler, when I ... what's the use! The Sheriff wants to see you, anyway."

"It's nearly five o'clock," I protested. "Doesn't he know I work union hours? I'll pick you up at seven tonight."

"With handcuffs," she reminded me.

I walked through into the Sheriff's office, remembering to knock on the door before I entered. Lavers looked at me through a cloud of smoke. He was back to a pipe again, I noted. That meant he was in a political mood, all benign and baby-kissing. Other times he's his normal repulsive self, smokes cigars and makes life uncomfortable for guys like me.

"Sit down, Wheeler," he said. "There's something I'd like you to take care of for me."

"What's her name?" I asked carefully.

"Can't you think of anything else but women?"

"You wouldn't have me thinking about schoolgirls?" I asked reproachfully. "There's a word for that."

"There's a word for you, too," he said shortly. "But I won't use it here in case my secretary hears it."

I looked at my watch again. "Speaking of your secretary, Sheriff, I have a date with her tonight."

"You did," he said briefly. "I've got something else for you to do."

"We haven't had a murder in a month," I said reflectively. "You had me detached from Homicide to your office to take care of the murders.... What do you want me to do, create one?"

"I want you to shut up and listen to me," he said heavily.

This was the Lavers I knew. "Yes sir," I said. "Why don't you have a cigar?"

"California is blessed with a climate that brings out the worst in some people," Lavers went on, ignoring my suggestion. "We have more screwballs to the square mile than any other state."

"I agree, sir," I said, looking at him thoughtfully.

"There's a new one," he said. "Calls himself the Prophet, Lover of the Sun. No other name. Just the Prophet. He's set himself up about twenty miles out of town on top of Bald Mountain."

"Selling hair-restorer?"

Lavers winced. "Sun worship and sex is what he's selling and he's selling it very well. He's got a bunch of society people up there, among others, and I don't like it."

"Sun worship?"

"I don't like any of it. These screwball religions have a nasty habit of blowing up in your face and leaving a corpse or two. I want you to go up there and take a look at it right away."

"Why tonight?"

"Because it's Friday, the best night of the week. This Prophet proposes to build a shrine up there on the mountain. It's to cost a hundred thousand dollars and a lot of people are subscribing to it already."

"You want me to make him give the money back?"

"I want you to ..." Lavers took a deep breath and thought better of it. "It could be a confidence trick on a grand scale. I want to know whether it is or not. I want you to find out for me."

"I'll ask him," I said dully. "What do I do if he says no?"

"You always seem to know what to do when a woman says that," Lavers growled. "Apply your experience in reverse, or something! Call me in the morning and let me know, but make it early. I'm playing golf."

"That's another screwball religion that's gotten hold here in California," I said. "Which is your fetish, Sheriff? The club or the ball?"

"Get out of here," he said shortly. "Before I return you to Homicide, D.O.A.!"

I got. I told Annabelle that there was a slight change of plan, that this was a "come as you are" party, and that she'd have to swallow her disappointment at not seeing my new suit this time. I smoked five butts while she wound up things in the office—one cigarette while she cleared up her desk work, four while she did all the lily-gilding she didn't need.

When she finally emerged with her new face, I hustled her out to my Austin-Healey and told her we were going up to Bald Mountain to take a look at the Prophet. I started to explain about him, but I didn't need to.

"I've heard a lot about him. He's a real dream-man, everybody says."

"An open-air Freud no less?"

"You don't have to be sarcastic," she said coldly. "My girl friend says he's the most, well, *masculine* man she's ever seen."

"She should see me in my handcuffs," I said brightly.

"I'd almost forgotten about those," Annabelle said. "Thank you for reminding me." It was strictly my error.

I drove up the winding road that led to the top of Bald Mountain and parked the Healey in between a bunch of other cars. We got out and made our way toward the large crowd of people standing close to the edge of the long, sheer drop. They were facing due west into the setting sun and I had to squint to see what was going on.

We reached the outskirts of the crowd, then I did see what was going on. There was a brunette standing with her back to the sky, facing the crowd. She wore a long white robe. I took another look and then, even without sunglasses, I was sure. "Dig that!" I said enthusiastically. "She's not wearing a thing underneath that robe."

"How can you tell at this distance without glasses?" Annabelle asked stiffly.

"When I need glasses at any distance to tell about something like that, I'll get married," I told her. "The fun will have gone out of living, anyway."

I concentrated on the brunette again. She was certainly worth the effort. She stood poised, motionless against the sky, and for a moment longer the dying rays of sunlight held that breath-taking silhouette.

Then the sun slowly slid away from the mountain top and the silhouette vanished. The statuesque brunette bent forward slowly, bowing in supplication, and the crowd of watching people bowed also.

"What happens now?" I asked Annabelle. "They serve cocktails?"

"Do keep your voice down," she hissed. "I think the Prophet will speak in a moment."

"No cocktails?"

"Be quiet!" she snarled. "I'll die with embarrassment in a moment if you keep on. These people take all this sun worship very seriously."

"The way I take cocktails?"

"Shut up!"

"I can take a hint," I said, wounded.

Slowly the brunette straightened up again, her arms dropping back to her sides. Then she turned and raised her right arm in a gesture that was both welcoming and dedicated at the same time. The sort of gesture I use to summon a bartender.

The Prophet appeared.

A white loincloth straddled his hips, in startling contrast to the deep tan of the rest of his body. He stood a couple of inches over six feet tall with wide shoulders and a deep chest. His muscles didn't bulge like those of a Mr. America candidate, but they were sinewy under his skin. He had thick, coarse black hair brushed straight back from his forehead, and a short black beard. He stood beside the brunette in the white robe and looked at the crowd without moving.

You could feel the crowd's reaction as well as hear the half-hysterical sigh that came from the feminine majority.

"Does he play a guitar, too?" I asked Annabelle.

"He's more of a man than you'll ever be, Al Wheeler!" she said shortly.

"You won't give me a chance to prove that," I said. "And besides, you haven't seen me in my new Hawaiian trunks yet."

"Be quiet!" she ordered. "He's going to speak."

The Prophet raised one hand and then spoke in a low resonant voice. "My people." His eyes widened a fraction. "Worshippers of the Sun God! Once again we have witnessed his departure. Once again he has left us to the powers of darkness and evil. But at dawn, he will return and throw his loving mantle of light and warmth over us that we may be safe again...."

There was a lot more in the same vein. I stifled a yawn and wondered if the Sun God was against smoking.

Around ten minutes later, the Prophet was building up to his climax. "Worship is not enough," he proclaimed in his deep voice. "The Sun God demands more than worship if he is not to desert us and leave us to the powers of darkness. The Sun God demands sacrifice."

His right hand balled into a fist as he raised his arm slowly. "Sacrifice! Only thus can the Sun God be appeased. We have built an altar worthy of him and now we must make the greater sacrifices worthy of him!"

His right arm was now outflung behind him, the index finger pointing toward the spur of rock that tapered away to nothing behind him. It was the topmost point of Bald Mountain. From there to the floor of the valley below was nothing but eight hundred feet of clear space.

I looked at the spur and saw something I hadn't noticed before. The altar. It stood some four feet high from the ground, neat and somehow aseptic-looking with its clean rectangular lines.

"Greater sacrifice," the Prophet repeated slowly. "We must all give for the building of the new shrine." His voice dropped to a deeper, quieter tone. "Time is running out now. There are only two days left."

His voice rose again in a crescendo. "Two days from now I shall be called to join the Sun God! When this glorious event has happened and I am one in everlasting light and warmth, then you, my followers, must build the glorious shrine in commemoration of this magnificent event."

"I have one further prophecy for you. I shall join the Sun God at sunset on Sunday evening. Between then and now, a great sacrifice will have to be made to the Sun God!"

The silence grew over the next ten seconds.

"I have spoken," the Prophet said simply.

The brunette turned to face the crowd. "Tomorrow is Saturday," she announced in a clear liquid voice. "There will be no worship at sunrise.

But at sunset, the Sun God calls you again to worship."

She bowed her head and seemed lost in thought. Or maybe she was wondering if she could make more in Minsky's burlesque in Vegas. I could have told her she could.

The crowd began to break up slowly. I lit a cigarette, inhaled deeply, and wondered where I could get a drink. Someone tapped me gently on the shoulder. I turned around and saw a man of medium height, wearing an impeccable suit of iridescent blue. He had nice wavy brown hair and a trim mustache.

"Lieutenant Wheeler?" he asked politely.

"That's right," I said.

"Allow me to introduce myself, Lieutenant. My name is Ralph Bennett. I am the business manager here."

"You mean you're the guy who watches the profit for the Prophet?"

He didn't wince. "You could put it that way if you like," he said evenly. "I thought while you're here you might care to take a look around. I imagine that's what you came for?"

"A date he said!" Annabelle said loudly. "Is this what you call combining business with pleasure, Lieutenant?"

"I'm sure it won't take the Lieutenant very long," Bennett said smoothly. "I'll have Eloise show you around while you're waiting, Miss ...?"

"Jackson," I filled in for him. "I do hope Eloise is not a damned Yankee?"

"I'm from Boston, if that's what you mean," a liquid voice said behind me. It was the brunette.

At close quarters she was even more breath-taking, the white robe even more inadequate, I was glad to see.

Bennett made the introductions and Eloise escorted the reluctant Annabelle away.

"Now, Lieutenant," Bennett took my arm persuasively, "what would you like to see first?"

"A glass," I said. "Scotch on the rocks, a little soda."

He laughed gently. "I think that can be organized. Why don't we go on over to my office?"

Two minutes later we reached his office. It was furnished modern style in that blend of expensive simplicity you can usually find wearing a skirt and standing on the corner of Hollywood and Vine.

"Please sit down, Lieutenant," Bennett said.

I sat down. I looked at my chest to see if there was a neon sign that flashed "Lieutenant" at intervals. There wasn't. I asked him the inevitable question.

"You certainly don't look like a police officer," Bennett said graciously. "I recognized you from a newspaper photograph I saw a few months ago."

"You must have a photographic memory," I told him. "Tell me about the Prophet."

"Certainly," he said, "I—"

The door swung open and a man lurched into the office. He stood there, swaying gently on the balls of his feet. He was short and fat and cherubic. An empty rye bottle hung loosely by the neck from the fingers of his right hand.

"Not now, Charlie," Bennett said impatiently. "Beat it!"

"I'm all out of firewater," the fat man said in a slurred voice. "The Sun God wouldn't like that, would he?"

"Beat it!" Bennett repeated.

Charlie drew himself up to his full height of around five feet nothing and looked at me. "That's the way he treats a pal," he said thickly. "Now he's making money he's got no time for his old buddies anymore. Now he's making dough out of this racket, he—"

"You will please excuse Charlie, Lieutenant," Bennett said stiffly. "Charlie is a lush."

"I don't like being called a lush," Charlie said indignantly. "It sounds kind of soggy. Likewise, I don't care to be called an alcoholic because that sounds kind of sterile or something. Call me a bum if you want!"

Bennett shrugged his shoulders helplessly. "Charlie is a bum," he said. He opened a drawer of his desk and took out a fifth of rye. "Here." He held it out toward Charlie.

The fat little man grabbed the bottle eagerly, dropping the empty one to the floor. "You're O.K.," he said warmly. "I guess you're not really the sort of bum to forget a fellow bum. That's what I like about you." He turned around, opened the door, and weaved his way out into the night again.

"I'm sorry about that," Bennett apologized. "Like Charlie said, he's a bum."

"I was glad you gave him that fifth," I said. "It kind of restored my faith in mankind. I wouldn't like to see you not helping him ... now that you're making dough out of this racket."

This time Bennett did wince. "That's Charlie's way of putting things. As the Prophet's business manager, I take a small percentage of the subscriptions, that's all. I understand it's perfectly legitimate, Lieutenant?"

"If they can make money out of TV commercials, I don't see why you shouldn't make money out of the Prophet," I said generously. "Tell me some more about him."

"Sure," Bennett said. "But I think I'd better make that drink first."

"It's a progressive thought," I agreed.

He pressed a button and a section of the wall swung back revealing a small bar. He made the drinks and handed me mine, then sat down again. I was happy to see the bar didn't disappear again.

"The Prophet is a wonderful man," Bennett said slowly. "A man with an incredible faith."

"Incredible is the word," I agreed. "But he was born about ten thousand years too late. Why doesn't somebody tell him that sun worship is for the makers of suntan oil, if not the birds?"

"He is a very sincere man," Bennett said reprovingly. "A man with a passionate belief in his mission as the Prophet of the Sun God. You heard him speak at sundown, Lieutenant. Could you doubt his sincerity?"

"Sure I could," I said.

Bennett drank some of his Scotch. "Anyway, Lieutenant, this is a free country. We are doing nothing illegal. The people who come here to worship with the Prophet do so entirely of their own free will. The donations they make are absolutely voluntary. The money is subscribed simply to further the movement. For specific things such as the shrine. The Prophet himself receives no income whatsoever."

"I think you should buy him a suit anyway," I said. "One of these nights he's going to catch cold."

There was a brief knock on the door and then someone walked in. I could tell right away it wasn't Charlie. Charlie would never wear a halter-bra.

She was tall and generously built. She had close-clipped white blonde hair, very blue eyes and very red lips. She looked around thirty at first glance. It was only the hard lines at the corners of her eyes that told you she was probably ten years older.

But then the full generous curves, hardly restrained by the halter-bra and so-short shorts, took over and you wouldn't have given a damn if she was somebody's grandmother just so long as it wasn't yours.

"Ralph," she said in a crisp voice. "I told you we're having cocktails in my cabana. You're late."

"I'm sorry, Stella," Bennett said easily. "I'm tied up right now."

The white blonde looked at me briefly. "Can't it wait?" she asked. "What's he selling?"

"Sun-kissed vitamin tablets," I said. "They stop the Prophet's beard falling out on rainy days."

"Is this meant to be amusing?" she asked coldly.

I looked at the halter-bra. "You should try some yourself," I suggested. "The Prophet finds them very uplifting."

"This is Lieutenant Wheeler," Bennett said quickly. He looked at me. "Lieutenant, this is Mrs. Stella Gibb."

"You're married to Mr. Stella Gibb?"

"His name is Cornelius," she said. "But for all practical purposes he's Mr. Stella Gibb."

I lifted my eyebrows. "Just how practical can he get?"

"Did Ralph say 'Lieutenant'?" She thawed noticeably. "What sort of lieutenant?"

"There are a number of theories," I told her. "My mother denies most of them."

"A lieutenant of police," Bennett filled in the gap.

"How wonderful!" she said enthusiastically. "You must certainly join us for a drink, Lieutenant."

"What are we going to drink to?" I asked her. "The departure of the Prophet? I thought the sputniks were something, but he's way out ahead of them. Did he get a new rocket fuel or something?"

Neither of them answered. They both gave me the sort of look a worm gives its other end when it finds they're both traveling in the same direction.

"I'd keep a sharp eye on that hundred grand," I told Bennett. "I'd make sure before the count-down on the Prophet zeros, that the money doesn't orbit with him, too."

The frigid silence was finally broken by Bennett. "I'm afraid, Lieutenant," he said in a cold voice, "that you don't really understand the Prophet at all!"

"Anyway," Stella said, a hint of impatience in her voice, "are you coming for a drink or aren't you, Lieutenant?"

"Give me one good reason," I said.

She took a deep breath, pulling her tanned midriff taut. The halter-bra slipped an inch, showing a thin line of soft, untanned flesh. "Me," she said simply.

I got onto my feet and headed toward the door.

"I'm ready," I said.

Chapter Two

"They used to say the punishment for sin is death," I said. "I have a better theory which I'm prepared to sell to the Treasury for a staggering sum. Sin is the one thing they haven't gotten around to taxing yet. I never could figure out why—syntax, a sort of death sentence."

There was a nasty silence which lasted for around three seconds.

"This is the first time I've met an educated slob," Stella Gibb said. "And speaking of slobs, maybe you'd better meet the rest of the people."

I was confronted with a natural blonde. There seemed to be a confusion of blondes at this party. But then if I have to be confused I'd rather it be by a blonde.

"This is Julia Grant," Stella said. "She is rich, idle, and sometimes vicious."

Julia was young, beautiful, blonde like I said. She wore a skirt and a transparent excuse for a blouse. "Hi, Lieutenant," she said in a cool voice. "Did somebody kill somebody or what?"

"I'm just relaxing," I said. "Stella promised me she'd teach me how."

"That's one promise you can rely on," she said. "Stella is an expert."

"Did I say 'sometimes vicious'?" Stella said. "Whatever made me use that word?"

"I would like another drink," I said hopefully. "Or do you two girls want to draw and get it over with first?"

"The bar is over there," Stella said. "Would you mind making your own drink? There are a couple of things I should talk over with Julia."

"I'm sorry, darling," Julia said easily. "But I don't have any leftover men for you right now. Call me in the fall. I should have a couple of worn-out models for you then."

"If one of them is the Prophet," I said helpfully, "you could probably fix it with a sunlamp. Or give him a robe, anyway. His suntan can't be all that thick."

There was a stony glare in both blondes' eyes and even my sensitive nature could detect I wasn't making a hit. I smiled wanly at them and beat a quick retreat to the bar.

I poured Scotch over some ice cubes and was adding a little soda when suddenly I wasn't alone at the bar any more. The first thing that hit me was the perfume ... a sort of documented version of "My Sin."

I turned my head slowly and looked into liquid amber eyes. I tried to swim for a moment, then gave up and let myself sink slowly and deliciously.

"Surely," a throaty voice inquired, "you've seen a girl before?"

"It's not the building that counts," I said huskily. "It's the construction."

Slowly I absorbed the whole construction, point by point. She had a tiptilted nose, creamy white skin. She was a brunette with a fringe, her hair cut short and straight so that it accentuated the oval shape of her face.

She wore a sheath of blue silk that clung to her like it was frightened of getting lost. Maybe it had good reason. She had full, high breasts, a waist that was almost impossibly slim, and nicely-rounded hips. I never yet met a dame with square hips come to think of it, but on her they would have looked good.

"You can pay the guide on the way out," she said gently.

"Can I drix you a mink?" I stuttered.

"I'd prefer mink, naturally," she said. "But I'll settle for a martini. Very dry."

"That's the cute name for straight gin."

"You could make a pass at it with the vermouth bottle," she said. "A twist of lemon."

I made the drink and handed it to her.

"Thanks," she said casually. "I hear you're a police lieutenant. From the crime lab I imagine—the X-ray division?"

"If I look stupid it's only because I am," I explained. "Al Wheeler is the name."

"I'm Candy Logan," she said.

I looked at the slim gold band on the third finger of her left hand. "Is your husband here, too?" I asked dejectedly.

"He may be in spirit," she said. "I don't know, I can't sense him here, can you?"

The blankness must have showed on my face.

"He died six months ago," she said. "I'm a widow."

"I'm sorry," I said brightly. "Wait a minute. Logan ... the real estate Logan?"

"That's right," she nodded. "Fortunately he left all his estate to me—for real! To be honest, I can't say I miss him. He was seventy-six when he died."

"Oh?"

"He dropped dead on the third day of our honeymoon," she said. "Could I have another drink please, Al?"

"Sure." I took the empty glass from her hand. I couldn't let the conversation die there too, I had to go on. "What did he die of?"

"A heart attack," she said simply. "You won't forget the twist of lemon peel will you?"

Candy Logan smiled at me as I gave her the new drink. "You look worried, Lieutenant. Is something bothering you?"

"I was just thinking," I said. "The real estate business must take it out of a guy."

"Let's talk about you," she said. "Are you a disciple of the Prophet?"

"Do I look like a—" I stopped myself in time. "No, not me."

"Neither am I, really," she said. "Although he's a terrifically sincere man. But I like the fun I have meeting other people up here. It's fun in a macabre sort of way. You meet the most revolting people."

"You go for revolting people?"

"They're different," she said. "Most people are only sordid. I never thought I'd get bored with a million dollars of real estate in my hot little fingers, but I am."

"Have you thought of trying—"

"Sex?" She pouted. "I thought you would have come up with something more original than that, Lieutenant!"

"I'm not an ambitious character," I said. "What was good enough for Adam is good enough for me. Although I prefer a less restricted field of operation, of course."

"You disappoint me," she said. "I was hoping for a nice macabre touch. I thought at least you'd like to hit people across the face with your handcuffs or something."

"I never get to feeling like that," I said. "That's the trouble with me, I'm abnormal."

"You're not abnormal, Lieutenant," she said regretfully, "just disappointing. Goodbye."

She drifted away with the glass in her hand. Watching her drift gave me a taut feeling in my throat. I don't give up easy but that "goodbye" had a certain finality about it. I thought I would give it ten minutes anyway.

"Lieutenant Wheeler?" a voice asked. "I'm delighted to meet you."

I turned around and saw a tall, slightly overbuilt character with short graying hair and the profile of a Greek god—that's what they would have said in those magazines my mother used to read, anyway.

"I am Edgar Romair," he said and looked at me expectantly.

"Hello," I said back to him.

He blinked twice. His eyelashes could have fringed a Persian rug. "You've heard of me, of course," he said. "Broadway."

"Oh, sure," I said. "Broadway, Wisconsin, isn't it?"

"That's really very funny," he said from between his teeth. "Do me a favor, Lieutenant. Cut your throat!"

He turned on his heel and walked away from me in step to a soundless overture. I thought about making myself another drink and then realized I would have to finish the one I already had first.

Ralph Bennett reappeared. "I see you just met our famous Broadway star."

"Romair?"

"Sure. You've heard of him, naturally."

"I have now," I said. "What's he playing in?"

"Well, nothing right now." Bennett cleared his throat gently. "Edgar is retired."

"His own idea—or Broadway's?"

"He thought he needed a rest."

"I see just what he means," I said.

It was about time we changed the subject. I lit a cigarette and looked around the room, then back at Bennett. "How did all these highly modern conveniences come to get built on top of a mountain?"

"Somebody had the idea of building a country club up here," he said. "They went broke about halfway through. We took it over."

"Does Stella Gibb own a piece of it?" I asked him.

"We have an arrangement whereby she has the use of this cabana," he said carefully.

"A cabana!" I said. "What does she call home—the Beverly Hilton?"

"The guy who was building the country club had very ambitious ideas," Bennett grinned faintly. "Maybe that's why he went broke."

"Don't let it happen to you," I said. I gave him my empty glass. "Make me a drink—you're nearest."

"My pleasure, Lieutenant."

There was a brittle sound from over the other side of the room. It sounded like someone getting her face slapped. I looked and saw Stella and Julia facing one another, motionless. Julia Grant's cheek was a flaming red.

"All right," she said in a clear voice. "That fixes it, Stella. Fixes it good!"

Stella Gibb took a deep breath that nearly broke the strap of her halter-bra and slapped Julia's face again. I shuddered at the sound; it must have hurt.

"All right, Stella," Julia repeated in a low, even voice. "You certainly asked for it and now you're going to get it—with both barrels!" She turned slowly and walked out of the cabana through the heavy silence.

"Your drink, Lieutenant," Bennett said.

I took the glass from him. "What was that about, do you think?"

He shrugged his shoulders. "I wouldn't know, Lieutenant. Just girls' talk, I guess."

"And what a nice couple of girls they are," I said appreciatively. "It's a wonder somebody hasn't signed them up for television. The kids' shows ... they would be strictly educational."

"You got a great sense of humor, Lieutenant," he said with an expressionless voice. "Every time they hold a show for the police fund, I bet you lay 'em in the aisles."

"Policewomen don't go to those shows," I said. "There's a city ordinance or something. You keep books of account?"

"Sure," he said. "They're in my office safe. Would you like to go on over and have a look at them?"

"I guess not," I said. "I never did really care for those kind of figures. I was just curious, that's all."

"Anything you want, you only got to ask," he said.

"I've seen enough, I think, Bennett. I'll pick up my blonde and go home."

"Nice to have seen you," he said. "Drop around any time you like."

"When the sun shines I'll think of you," I assured him.

I started off toward the corner where Annabelle and the actor seemed much too deep in something—conversation I hoped. I got about halfway when somebody grabbed my arm.

"You aren't leaving, Lieutenant?" Stella Gibb purred in my ear.

"If it isn't the new champ," I said, carefully disengaging her arm from mine. "It was a great fight, champ, and you deserved to win. A technical knockout in the first round, huh?"

"She asked for it, she got it," Stella said cheerfully. "I rather enjoyed it. It was getting to be a dull evening."

"It's been a wonderfully dull evening," I said. "I didn't enjoy it, thanks to you. I hope you won't ask me again. Can I go now?"

"You know, honey"—her eyes glittered as she looked at me—"men just don't walk out on me like this. I like you, Al. Isn't that enough?"

"It's almost too much," I said. "Good night. Give my love to Cornelius."

I finally made it to Annabelle, turning a cozy twosome into a gruesome threesome. "Did you have a hat or something?" I asked Annabelle. "We're leaving."

"Don't let me stop you," she said crisply.

"Come on, I'm hungry. We can grab something to eat on the way back."

"What's the matter, Al?" Annabelle purred nastily. "Don't tell me you didn't help yourself to the hors d'oeuvres! And they were for free, too!"

"I don't like to clutter up good Scotch," I said. "One thing at a time. You coming?"

"It so happens, Lieutenant," Romair said coldly, "that I own an automobile. I'll be very glad to drive Miss Jackson wherever she wants to go."

"Thank you," Annabelle said. "Good night, Lieutenant. It's been so nice, not being with you, I mean."

"That's the second fight tonight somebody else has won," I said, beating a retreat toward the door.

This time I made it without anyone trying to stop me. In a way I was disappointed. I stepped out into the darkness and stopped for a moment to light a cigarette. Then I saw a vague, shadowy shape in front of me.

"Going someplace, Lieutenant?" a cool, husky voice asked.

"Home," I said.

"Without that cute little blonde with the southern accent?"

"She just seceded," I explained.

"I have a cabana over there," she said. "Would you like one for the ride down the mountain?"

"You mean a drink?"

"That depends, Lieutenant," her voice had somehow got more husky. "What do *you* have in mind?"

I knotted my tie, ran my hands through my hair, and hoped my head wouldn't fall off. I picked up my coat and shrugged my arms into it.

Candy looked at me lazily. She lay in a foam of black lace on the couch. "You going somewhere, Lieutenant?"

"It's been wonderful," I said. "I'm sorry I forgot to drink my drink."

"I didn't even notice," she said dreamily. "Would you like some real estate to take with you?"

"What's the use?" I asked. "Sooner or later Conrad Hilton would make me an offer for it. What would I do with all that money?"

"You could buy more real estate," she said. "Call me, Al?"

"I call you beautiful," I said. "Next time I'll use a phone to do it. What's the number?"

Candy gave me the address of a swank building in town, and her number. Then she yawned gently and stretched her arms languidly above her head. The level of the black foam sank sharply down to her waist. I looked at her for a long moment. "I may change my mind," I said. "There could be a storm out there."

"Just so long as it isn't that southern blonde, I don't care," she said. "See you, Al."

"In Technicolor," I agreed.

I stepped outside and closed the door gently behind me. The dawn's pale light was all around, growing stronger by the minute, in strict contrast to Al Wheeler. I remembered I'd left the Austin-Healey somewhere close to the spot where the Prophet had made his spiel.

I lit a cigarette and started walking slowly. It had turned out to be a good party after all. I reached the Healey and slid into the front seat and put the key into the ignition. I took a look at the topmost spur of Bald Mountain, and then I looked again.

Like I said, the light was getting stronger by the minute. The sharp, aseptic lines of the altar stood out clearly against the sky. Only the top line wasn't clean and aseptic-looking anymore. It was blurred and kind of bumpy.

I got out of the car and climbed up to the altar. I looked down at what had destroyed the clean silhouette and took a deep drag on the cigarette, pulling the smoke way down into my lungs.

The nude body of Julia Grant was stretched out on the altar, her eyes staring blankly at the sky. Just below the gentle swell of her left breast, the hilt of a knife protruded, surrounded by the stained ugliness of congealed blood.

As I looked, the sun pushed its rim up over the horizon and its first rays touched her, turning the soft blonde hair into spun gold.

Chapter Three

"I sent you up there," Sheriff Lavers said in a strangled voice, "just to find out what sort of racket that phony religious screwball is running. And now you tell me you've got a murder!"

"I didn't do it," Sheriff," I said. "Cross my heart."

"Whenever you're around there's a murder. What are you—a magnet?"

"That's what all the girls ask me," I agreed. "Who knows, maybe it's true."

"Just try and see nobody snatches the body before I get there," Lavers said heavily. "Have you called Homicide yet?"

"Bald Mountain is outside city limits," I reminded him. "Or don't you think your department can handle it?"

"All right," he snarled. "Just wait around until I get there. Where were you when the murder was committed anyway?"

"In bed," I said truthfully.

"I guess that makes two suspects less," he said. There was a crunching sound in my ear as he hung up.

I returned the phone to its cradle, lit another cigarette, and looked at Bennett hopefully. "Coffee?"

"Sure," he said. "I ordered it. Should be here any time now. Lieutenant, why in hell would anybody want to murder Julia Grant?"

"I was hoping you could tell me," I said.

A bleary-eyed maid arrived with the coffee, dumped the tray on the desk, and departed. I helped myself after Bennett, at my suggestion, had put a bottle of Irish whisky on the tray.

"I can't think of anybody who would want to kill her," he said finally. "Unless there's a maniac wandering around here."

"After seeing them last night, there's at least six by count," I said. "What about the fight she had with Stella Gibb?"

He shook his head. "That goes on all the time. It didn't mean anything special. Stella Gibb is that sort of woman. She likes it that way."

I drank some of the coffee; the whisky tasted good.

"I was thinking of the publicity," Bennett said tautly. "It isn't going to do us any good."

"Are you kidding?" I said. "It will be wonderful for you. I'll take an even bet that two days from now you'll have that altar painted brick red and be selling souvenir postcards at two bits a card!"

"You've got a nasty mind, Lieutenant!"

"So have you," I said. "And I want a royalty on those postcards."

He grinned slowly. "Maybe we could make a deal, at that."

"Don't forget the Prophet's prophecy, either," I said. "I want to talk to him about that—now."

Bennett looked worried. "He's probably still sleeping. I don't know whether I can disturb him."

"Don't worry about it," I said. "I can disturb him with no trouble at all."

"I'll do it," Bennett said hastily and went out of the office at a fast trot.

I poured myself some more Irish whisky while I waited, and diluted it with a touch of coffee. It took about five minutes for Bennett to return with the Prophet in tow.

The Prophet was dressed in his usual uniform—the loincloth and sandals. He stood in front of me, his arms folded across his chest, his face impassive. "You wished to speak with me?" he asked.

"Sure," I said. "Why don't you sit down, have some coffee?"

"I prefer to stand," he said curtly. "I do not drink coffee, it is a stimulant."

"The Irish don't think so," I said. "Bennett's told you about the murder?"

"The sacrifice," he corrected me. "It was written."

"You mean you know the author?"

"The Sun God ordained a great sacrifice," he said. "It has been made."

"You mean you think the Sun God reached down and put that knife into her chest?"

He shrugged his powerful shoulders. "I do not know the instrument of his will."

"Where were you last night?"

"I have a small cabin here," he said. "Enough for my simple needs. I slept."

"What is your real name?"

"I am the Prophet of the Sun God."

"They couldn't have christened you 'Prophet Prophet'! You must have a real name."

"If I have, it is forgotten," he said. "I am merely the tool of the Sun God.

Through me he speaks."

"And he doesn't waste many words, either," I said. "What did you mean exactly when you prophesied you would join the Sun God come Sunday night?"

"I shall be called to join him then," he said. "How, I do not know. That it will happen, I do know."

I lit myself another cigarette. Right then I wasn't sure who was crazy—me or the Prophet. I tried again. "Do you know of any reason why Julia Grant should be murdered? Do you know anyone who would want to kill her?"

"No," he said flatly. "You do not understand this, Lieutenant. You are a worldly man, seeking worldly reasons. This is something beyond your comprehension!"

"I'm with you," I admitted. "What did the Sun God have against Julia Grant? Maybe she didn't tan so well, huh?"

"Do not mock that which you do not understand," he said angrily, "lest the wrath of the Sun God strike you down as well!"

"Do you mean that as a threat?"

He shook his head slowly. "I threaten no one. Neither the believer nor the disbeliever. It is given to me to lead the way that others may follow the path of glorious light and warmth into everlasting—"

I looked appealingly at Bennett. "Take him away," I said. "It's too early in the morning for commercials."

The Prophet walked slowly and serenely out of the office. Bennett had an apologetic look on his face. "You know how it is with him, Lieutenant," he said, "The Prophet is a—"

"If you say he's a sincere man again—"

There was a knock on the door and Sergeant Polnik walked in, a happy grin on his face. "Beautiful morning, Lieutenant!" he said brightly. "I hear some dame with no clothes on got herself knocked off up here and right away I said to myself, 'Lieutenant Wheeler!' I said."

"This is Sergeant Polnik," I said wearily to Bennett, "when he dies, he's going to be a strip-teaser's G-string."

"I don't believe in reincarceration, Lieutenant," Polnik said seriously. "I figure when you're dead, you're dead so you got to live it up while you're living."

"You should swap philosophies with the Prophet," I told him.

"Who's he?" Polnik looked at me blankly. "A company director?"

I reached out automatically for the whisky bottle again, but Bennett had sneaked up on me and put it away.

"I got a message for you, Lieutenant," Polnik said. "The Sheriff changed his mind about coming up here, sent me instead. He says he wants to see you right away in his office. I brought the doc with me and the experts." He made the word "experts" sound like a dirty word. "The Sheriff says I should take over from you up here." He lowered his eyes modestly.

"Fine," I said. "You get one sane answer to any question and you're ahead of me already."

I got onto my feet and pointed a finger at Bennett. "This is Ralph Bennett; he knows everybody up here. I've talked to the Prophet and he made no sense. See if you can do any better with the others."

"I'll start with the dames first," Polnik said promptly.

"What dames?"

His jaw sagged. "Lieutenant! There's got to be dames, beautiful dames. It just ain't a Wheeler case without beautiful dames."

"He wants to interview Eloise," I said to the goggle-eyed Bennett. "And don't tell me the Sheriff's department is full of maniacs, because I know it!"

I walked out of the office and back toward the Austin-Healey. The corpse was still there on top of the altar and a small knot of men, headed by Doc Murphy, were making their way toward it. I got into the car and started the motor. I rubbed the stubble on my chin and wished I'd been the bartender my old man always wanted me to be. That way I would have got to shave every day at least.

My watch said nine-thirty when I stepped into the Sheriff's office. Annabelle Jackson looked up from her typewriter and her nose wrinkled as she looked at me.

"You look dirty, unshaven, and repulsive," she said. "In other words ... normal!"

"You look good, too," I said.

"Did she say no?" Annabelle asked tightly. "Was that why you had to kill her?"

"She reminded me of you," I explained. "I couldn't stand the thought of two of you walking around. It would be living a nightmare with no hope of waking up."

"The Sheriff is in his office if you wish to see him, Lieutenant. I fixed the rug in there this morning. If there's any justice, you should trip and break your neck!" She banged her typewriter viciously to punctuate the sentence.

I knocked on the door, opened it and stepped carefully over the edge of the rug into the Sheriff's office.

"What have you got, Wheeler?" Lavers growled at me.

"Typhoid, I wouldn't be surprised." I slumped into the chair with the good springs. "Nothing worth speaking about. What have you got?"

"I've been talking to the doctor, and Polnik," he said. "That knife went straight into her heart. Death, as they don't say, would have been painful but fast."

"No prints?"

"No prints. No nothing, except the knife."

"What's with the knife?"

"It's an antique. Oriental. I've got a couple of men out with it now, trying to trace it with the dealers around town."

"Shame it wasn't a hatchet," I said. "That way we could have known it was a tong war. All we'd have to do would be call Charlie Chan and the rest of us could quit."

"If your cop routine was one third as good as your comic routine, I wouldn't be getting this ulcer of mine," Lavers said gloomily. "What did you find out up there on the mountain?"

"Nothing," I said. "What else did the doc have to say?"

"He figures she was murdered somewhere between one and three A.M.," Lavers said. "According to Polnik, she left the party around eleven last night."

"Check," I agreed. "I saw her go."

"The party broke up just before one," Lavers went on. "Do you check that out, too?"

"I left the party before it broke up," I said.

"Like that, was it?" Lavers sniffed heavily.

"How about alibis?" I asked him quickly.

"Nobody has one. They broke up the party, they didn't see anyone else until this morning."

"I can give Candy Logan an alibi," I admitted. "I guess she can give me one."

"I'm disappointed," Lavers said sourly. "I thought you'd taken to creating your own murders now."

"Anything for a laugh, that's me," I agreed.

"You met these people last night," Lavers persisted. "How many suspects have you got?"

"There's the Prophet himself," I said. "His Girl Friday—Eloise. She's his Girl Friday through Monday I shouldn't be surprised. Then there's Stella Gibb, Bennett ... Romair the actor, a couple of others. I'll get the complete list."

"Now listen to me. Without starting to believe in things that go squawk in the night, we've got to face up to the fact that one of the Prophet's predictions has come true already. And the second one is due to happen on Sunday night. Maybe he's figuring on disappearing then along with the hundred thousand bucks they're collecting for the shrine.

And maybe if he disappears, the murderer disappears with him."

"You have a gift for putting things clearly, Sheriff," I said. "What you're trying to say in your own subtle way is that we have to solve the case before Sunday night?"

"For once you're right," he agreed.

"This being Saturday morning, I don't know what I'm worrying about," I said. "I have all of thirty-six hours to clean up the case."

"That's exactly right, Wheeler," Lavers said, a nasty coldness in his voice. "That's why I brought you back here, just to make sure you fully appreciated the position. You'd better get out of here and start work again."

"Why not?" I said resignedly. "If I drop dead, who'll miss me?"

"Why ask me?" the County Sheriff snapped. "How would I know?"

I went out of his office, past the still-typing Annabelle. I shoehorned myself into the Healey and drove home to my apartment.

I put some Ellington on the hi-fi machine, had a shower, a shave, some fast fried eggs. Then I had a drink while I got dressed in clean clothes. I put the pickup back for "Requiem for Hank Cinq," and heard it through.

If Shakespeare could inspire the Duke, he could inspire me. "Once more into the breach ... when taken on the spur ..." So, feeling like a crisp version of a guy named Bacon, I stepped out of the apartment into the big world again.

I was going calling on Mr. Stella Gibb.

Chapter Four

It was the sort of house anybody could buy so long as he was in the one-fifty, one-seventy-five-thousand bracket. Parked in front of the porch was a new Continental in virgin white. Parked directly behind it was a new Continental convertible in exactly the same color. My Austin-Healey parked last in line made it a two and a thirdsome of cars.

I put the top up on the Healey in case it got an inferiority complex just standing there. My car has feelings the same way a Continental has feelings, even if they are scaled down a little.

I turned away from the car and saw a guy walking across the lawn toward me. He was around twenty-five, with neat black hair slicked back from his forehead and a nice tan. He wore a pair of white shorts and nothing else. The tan was evenly spread all over his muscles. He was the cigarette man, short of nothing but the tattoo.

"What did you want?" he asked in a brittle voice.

"I wanted to see Mr. Gibb," I said. "I'm Lieutenant Wheeler from the Sheriff's department."

"I'm Gibb," he said.

"I guess it's your father then I want to see. Mr. Cornelius Gibb."

"What sort of crack is that? I'm Cornelius Gibb!"

"My mistake," I said.

"You want to talk about the murder? I heard about it."

"That's right," I said.

"Maybe you'd better come inside."

I followed him across the porch and into the house. We came into a living room with about the same space as the county hall. It was furnished in this year's style which is modern oriental.

I sat down on a white leather couch and looked at the two oxblood vases on the low carved whitewood table. I looked away quickly and the mandarin on the wall opposite seemed to twitch his sixteen inches of mustaches at me.

"You like a drink, Lieutenant?" Gibb asked me.

"I would," I agreed. "Scotch on the rocks, a little soda."

I watched him make the drinks and hoped that the Scotch hadn't been made in an upturned coolie hat by a couple of oriental gentlemen. Gibb brought the drinks back and sat beside me on the couch. "What do you want to know?"

"Did you know Julia Grant?"

"I met her a couple of times here. Stella knew her better than I did."

"But you knew her."

"I just said so, didn't I? But Stella knew her better. Why don't you talk to her?"

"I'll get around to it," I said. "Right now another cop is talking to her up on Bald Mountain."

"That's where she spends most of her time these days," he said, "with that screwball Prophet character or whatever he calls himself."

"You aren't one of the faithful?"

"Me—go for that line of crap?"

"You look like a sun-worshipper," I said.

He looked down at his tan and unconsciously flexed his muscles a little. "That's as far as I go," he said. "That Prophet guy gives me a pain. I sit here and listen to Stella yack-yack about him until I think I'll go crazy sometimes. Hear her talk, you'd figure he was the only guy alive."

I finished my drink and got to my feet. "You mind if I take a look around while I'm here?"

"Help yourself," he said.

I looked around vaguely. "A nice place you have here," I said. "I go for the oriental furniture; it's kind of cute."

"It was Stella's idea," he said. "This year. Next year it'll be voodoo or something."

"She certainly went for it in a big way," I agreed. "Paintings and everything. It must have cost a fortune."

"Not to Stella," he said bitterly.

"Any genuine antique stuff go with it?" I asked him. "Swords or stuff like that?"

"There's a couple of daggers in the dining room," he said. "Go take a look if you're interested. I'll pour us another drink."

"That sounds a good thought," I said. "But I'd like you to show me."

"Hell!" he said. "I just told you to help yourself."

"Leave us not spoil the Gibb reputation for hospitality," I said. "You show me."

He dragged himself off the couch and led the way into the dining room. "Right up there.... Hey! There's one missing!"

"And that's the one that killed Julia Grant," I said very obviously.

Gibb turned toward me, his mouth dropping open. "But how in hell did it—"

"It's an interesting question," I said. "When did you last see the two daggers up there?"

He scratched his head for a moment. "I don't exactly remember. After a while you get so damned used to things, you don't really see them. You don't know if they're there or not—you know how it is, Lieutenant."

"Sure," I said. "Wives can even get that way about their husbands so I hear."

His lips tightened. "You don't have to get so smart!"

"This is the first time you've noticed it missing?"

"Sure. I guess I wouldn't have noticed it at all if you hadn't made me come in here with you. How did you know?"

"I wasn't that clever," I admitted. "Julia Grant was stabbed with an oriental dagger. All that oriental stuff in the living room ... it was a natural."

I reached up and lifted the remaining dagger down from the wall, handling it carefully by the blade. "I'm taking this with me."

"Sure," he said. "Anything you say, Lieutenant."

I wrapped the dagger in my pocket handkerchief and walked out of the house, back to the Healey. Gibb walked with me and stood beside the car as I got into it.

"I don't know how in hell that knife got out of the house, Lieutenant," he said, "and that's for sure."

"Tell me something you do know," I suggested. "How does it feel to be a kept husband?"

His face whitened under the tan. "Why you dirty, lousy ..."

I backed up the Healey then so maybe I missed the best part of his description. I drove around the two Continentals and back down the driveway to the street, wondering whether the cars ever got used or if they were for display purposes only.

I drove back to the Sheriff's office and found Polnik with Lavers. I put the dagger down carefully onto Lavers' desk top and his eyes widened as he looked at it. "Where did you get that?" he grated. I told him where I'd found it.

"Some guys are just born lucky," he said. "And some guys just never do get lucky."

"I wouldn't let it worry you, Sheriff," I said generously. "You weren't born fat, but you got lucky." I looked at Polnik while Lavers' face was still purpling. "How did you make out with the Mountain, Mohammed?"

"I didn't get very much, Lieutenant," Polnik said regretfully. "I had to quit and let 'em go home. I got their addresses, of course. The Prophet—now there's a nut if I ever met one—and Bennett and that doll, Eloise, they all live up there. And so does the lush, Charlie."

"Anybody else?"

"A couple of maids and a cook, but they all alibi each other. They were playing blackjack most of the night."

"Who won?"

"Who cares who won!" Lavers shouted.

"I do," I told him. "I might get into a game up there sometime. You need to know these things."

Polnik's face brightened up again. "I got something that's maybe a lead, Lieutenant. I searched the Grant dame's home. What a joint! You should see it! She must have been loaded! Anyway, I found this." He took a matchfolder out of his pocket and handed it to me. It had "Harry's Bar" across the folder.

"There were three or four packs like that around the place," Polnik said proudly. "So maybe it means something, huh, Lieutenant?"

"You could find out," I said. "Maybe she used to go there regularly with some guy. Call me at home if you get anything."

"Sure, Lieutenant," he said. "Anything else?"

"You could ask Stella Gibb how that dagger got out of her house and into Julia Grant, but I don't think it's going to do you any good."

"Just a minute, Wheeler!" Lavers roared. "What are you going to do?"

"Go home and sleep," I said.

"You know tomorrow night is our deadline!"

"Sure," I said. "I should live that long! Don't work too hard while I'm gone."

I walked out of his office at a fast run in case he changed my mind for me. If he did, I had the door shut before he could yell. I got into the car and went home.

Inside the apartment, I climbed out of my clothes and into bed. The next thing I knew, the phone was ringing. My watch showed I'd had five hours sleep. I lifted the receiver and said, "Wheeler Sleeptite Mattresses. We're testing right now. Why don't you call back in the morning sometime late?"

"Lieutenant," Polnik croaked. "You said to call you."

"I guess I did," I admitted reluctantly. "What have you got, so long as it's not catching?"

"The guy Julia Grant used to drink with in that bar," Polnik said proudly.

"Who is he?"

"Name's Harry Weisman, but he doesn't own the bar. He just drinks there."

"Address?"

"1658 Glenshire. The apartment number's 8B."

"Did you get anything from Stella Gibb about that dagger?"

"What a character that dame is!" Polnik's voice had a touch of awe in it. "She says it must have been stolen, she says!"

"O.K.," I said. "I'll go talk to Harry. What are you going to do?"

"Whatever you say, Lieutenant?"

"Why don't you go home?"

"You haven't met my old lady yet, Lieutenant, have you?"

I got up. I made the shower-and-dress routine in fifteen minutes. On the way downtown I stopped for a quick steak sandwich. In another twenty minutes I pulled up at the Glenshire address.

It was a walk-up apartment so I walked up. The door was opened by a sharp-looking character with a cerise shirt and a black bow tie. His suit was a color indescribable, but sharp, man, sharp! A cigarette dangled from his lips.

"I got all the insurance I want," he said.

"You could cover that shirt," I told him, "and make me happy."

"You're wild, Jack," he said. "Real wild!"

"I'm also a cop," I said and showed him my shield to prove it.

"What do you want?"

"Ask you some questions."

"All right, but make it fast, Jack, will you? I got me a date tonight."

"What with—a color harmony chart?"

I followed him inside the apartment. It must have been furnished by the landlord. The furnishings matched.

"You're Harry Weisman?" I asked him.

"Sure. So what?"

"You know a girl named Julia Grant?"

"Sure, she's my date tonight." He did the sort of double-take they used to do in movies just after sound hit—the ones you see on television now. "Say, Jack! She's not in trouble, is she?"

"Didn't you read the papers tonight?"

"I don't get time for the papers."

"Where were you last night?"

"All over. What's the beef? Something Julia did?"

"Were you all over between one and three o'clock this morning?"

"I was in the one place from midnight till around four-thirty when we quit."

"Quit what? If it's not too delicate a question?"

"The poker game. Me and four of the boys got in a game here last night. What do you want to know for, anyway?"

"Julia Grant was murdered last night," I told him.

The bow tie jumped convulsively and his mouth fell open suddenly like the string had busted. "Murdered!" he repeated vacantly. "Murdered ... Julia?"

"If you want to pour yourself a drink, that's all right," I said generously. "You can make me one, too."

"Murdered!" He sat down abruptly in an armchair. "I don't get it!"

"Julia got it," I said patiently. "You remember just who was in this poker game?"

"Sure!" He gave me a list of four names and addresses. I wrote them down. The sharp cop always carries a blunt pencil.

"Tell me about Julia and you," I said. "The dates you had."

"She was a nice dame," he said in a shaken voice. "Real nice. I went for her, she went for me. That's the way it was. Why would anybody want to murder her?"

"Everybody gets to my question first," I said. "So you went for each other. What with—tomahawks?"

"That isn't funny, Jack. I was real gone for her."

"And now she's real gone."

He took the limp butt out of his mouth and substituted a limp cigarette for it. His hands shook as he struck the match. "I don't see why anybody would want to kill Julia," he said. "She was a great girl, real great! Where did it happen?"

"Up on Bald Mountain."

The cigarette dropped from his lips to the floor. He bent down and picked it up again. "Up at that screwball Prophet's place?"

"Sure."

"I told her to stay out of it," Weisman muttered. "I told her no good could come from monkeying around with a setup like that."

"So she didn't listen to you. Did she ever talk about it?"

"Sure, she was crazy about it. Sun worship! It's for the birds, I told her, but she wouldn't listen."

"Too bad," I said. "So now you don't have a date and you're not going any place. So tell me all about it. From the first time you ever met her."

"Sure, Jack," his voice shook slightly. "Whatever you say."

"And for the record, my name is Al," I said. "But you can call me Lieutenant."

"Anything you say, Jack."

I slumped wearily into a chair. "All right, you win. Just tell the story."

It took him thirty minutes to tell the story. The way he told it, it wasn't worth listening to. He'd made a pickup in Harry's Bar one night. A gorgeous blonde job and her name was Julia Grant. So after that first night he'd started dating her regularly. What they did on their regular dates I couldn't figure out exactly but one thing was for sure, they didn't talk much. Harry Weisman was a mine of information that petered out before I'd struck one nugget.

"O.K.," I said finally. "So you don't know anything."

I got up from the chair and walked toward the door with Weisman tagging along behind me like a toy poodle looking for a sidewalk but scared of the fine.

I stepped out into the hall and looked back at him for a moment. The cigarette waggled in the corner of his mouth, the bow tie had slewed to one side.

"I hope you have business in Pine City that will keep you here," I told him. "If you didn't, you have now."

"What do you mean?" he croaked. "You think I killed her?"

I looked at him for a moment, then shook my head regretfully, "I don't think so. I don't think you got the strength—Jack!"

I walked down from the walk-up apartment wondering why I'd bothered to walk up.

Chapter Five

The two Continentals were gray ghosts in the night air.

I left my Healey parked behind the convertible and walked up onto the porch. The door was opened by Stella Gibb. She was wearing something cool for a hot night and the light behind her silhouetted her curves neatly, right through the something cool. I hadn't realized before just how warm the night was.

"Hello, Al," she said softly. "I thought you were avoiding me. Sending that little man with the ridiculous name to ask me all those ridiculous questions. I thought maybe you were just a little scared of me?"

"I've been busy," I said. "I'm not scared of you. I just like to make sure I have my gun, whip, and chair with me when I call."

"Maybe you'd better come inside," she said.

I followed her inside the house, into the Stella Tang dynasty of the living room.

"Scotch on the rocks with a little soda," she said. "As I remember?"

"You're so right," I agreed.

She busied herself making the drinks. Cornelius Gibb came into the room and stopped suddenly when he saw me.

"Have you met my husband, Lieutenant?" Stella asked indifferently. "I expect you have, he's around here most of the time. Are you going out now, darling?"

Cornelius wore a white sports coat, a silk shirt, and dark slacks. He nodded briefly at me, a look of annoyance on his face. "I guess I won't be back till late," he said to Stella. "I'm going to drive downtown, see if I can find any of the boys."

"Enjoy yourself, darling," Stella said. "Did you want any money or anything?"

A dark flush spread across Gibb's face. "Nobody's invented a name for you yet," he said thickly. "But I'm getting around to it!" He walked quickly out of the room and a few seconds later the front door slammed behind him.

"Poor Cornelius," Stella said placidly. "At times he's so sensitive."

She made the drinks and brought them with her to the couch. She sat down beside me and smiled warmly. "I'm glad you called tonight, Al. I was getting bored. I couldn't think of anything exciting to do at all."

"What about a drive downtown with your husband? Wouldn't that have been exciting?"

"All Cornelius' friends are like him," she said. "None of them could be called exciting. Not even at a spinsters' convention."

"Do you call him 'Corny' for short?"

"I never call him," she said. "He calls me, whenever he needs money. Which is most of the time."

I drank some of the Scotch and remembered this was a business call. "I wanted to ask some questions," I said.

"I'll probably say yes automatically to all of them," she smiled. "I hope you won't mind."

"Julia Grant had a boy friend," I said. "Harry Weisman is his name. Do you know anything about him?"

"I think I heard her mention the name a couple of times," she said. "Do you think he killed her?"

"He has an alibi," I said. "I haven't checked it yet but I do have a feeling it will be good. I was interested. He wasn't one of the Prophet's faithful?"

"I've never met him," she said. "Perhaps I should. He'll be lonely now that Julia's gone."

I drank some more of my drink. "What about that fight you had with Julia?"

"Fight?" She shrugged her ample shoulders. "I don't remember any fight."

"You slapped her a couple of times," I reminded her. "I saw it, I was there."

"Oh, that! That wasn't a fight, just a disagreement. We used to disagree all the time. About men, mostly."

"Was that disagreement about men, or about one man in particular?"

"Julia could be so boringly moral where other people were concerned." Stella yawned daintily. "She had some quaint idea that just because I was married to Cornelius, I should be faithful to him."

"That was why you slapped her?"

"No, that did happen to be an argument about another man. She thought I was poaching on her reserves. She didn't like it because the man preferred me to her."

"Which man was this?"

"Edgar Romair. I think you met him, didn't you?"

"The guy who closed down Broadway after he left? Sure, I met him. Did you see Julia after she left your cabana last night?"

"No, I have no idea where she went. As it happened, I didn't see Edgar last night." She giggled suddenly. "I had a little too much to drink at the party and I passed out cold. I didn't know a thing until that sergeant friend of yours woke me up. And me sleeping in the natural!"

"He'll recover," I said.

"Come to think of it," Stella said archly. "Maybe Julia did get to see

Edgar last night, after all. Have you asked him, Al?"

"I'll make a note of it," I said. "Just what exactly did Julia mean when she threatened you? She said something about fixing it and this time she'd get you good."

"I think she meant she'd tell Cornelius I was making time with Edgar," Stella said simply. "As if he'd give a damn!"

"Uh huh," I said. "Do you know anybody who'd have good reason to murder Julia?"

"Lots of them," she said promptly. "Me, for example. But I didn't. She was always sticking her nose where it wasn't wanted. I have to be honest about this, don't I, Al?"

"If it's possible," I agreed.

"Well, I don't think any of us liked her very much. She was always spreading malicious gossip, rumors and lies! I think she got what was coming to her."

"You know something?" I said. "You're a subtle woman—like a boa constrictor."

"I've never squeezed anyone to death yet," she smiled. "But it could be fun trying. Are you doing anything important tonight, Al?"

"I'm trying to solve a murder," I said. "But I'm not making any headway."

"I think you should go talk to Edgar," she said. "I think maybe he could help you."

She moved closer along the couch toward me, her heavy thigh pressing hard against mine. I felt like the walls of Jericho waiting for the last blast of the trumpet. "Yes," she murmured. "I think you should talk to Edgar ... later."

"Why not now?"

"Don't you like me or something? We're all alone in the house. Cornelius won't be back until morning. I thought at least you'd spend a couple of hours here with me and keep me amused. I've never made love with a police officer before. It would be a new experience, Al."

"Are you sure?" I asked her. "There's a rumor the cop on the beat around here walks on his knees."

"Now you're being crude!"

"I guess I am," I said. "You bring out the worst in me." I saw the quick welcoming smile on her face and moved away hastily. "Not that sort of worst. I think I should go talk to Romair."

"If you insist," she said. Her voice was suddenly bleak. "Maybe that's a good idea, Al." Then she got hopeful again. "Why don't you go and do that right away, then hurry back here? Then you won't be fretting about duty all the time or whatever it is you're fretting about. It would be much better that way. I hate a man who's always in a hurry!"

"I bet you do," I said.

She walked with me to the front door.

"Polnik tells me you don't know how that dagger jumped off your wall and into Julia's heart," I said.

"I don't have the faintest idea," she said casually. "I didn't know it was missing until he told me about it. I think someone must have stolen it. Maybe Julia did. She was always green with envy about my furnishings. I suppose it isn't possible she committed suicide, is it?"

"It's possible," I said. "If she left the dagger hanging in the air and took a running jump upward at it."

"I only asked," she said.

"I only answered."

I stepped onto the drive and walked toward the Healey, Stella following. I saw that only one of the Continentals was standing there. The convertible was missing. So they did use the cars after all.

"Hurry back, Al," Stella said as I got into the Healey. "Aren't you going to kiss me goodbye?"

"I don't think so," I said. "Where does Romair live? Polnik has a record of the address, but it means calling the office."

She told me the address. "It's not too much of an apartment," she said. "Sometimes I wonder if the poor boy has been resting too long."

"His loss is Broadway's gain," I said.

I reached Romair's apartment block some thirty minutes later. Like Stella had said, it wasn't much. He had a first floor apartment and that was about all you could say for it.

I pressed the buzzer and he opened the door a few seconds later. He was wearing a bright blue robe and his hair was combed artistically to offset the Greek profile.

"Lieutenant Wheeler," he said warmly. "Stella called me and said you were on your way over. Stella is quite a girl, isn't she?" He gave me a leer which was obviously meant as a man-to-man smile.

"She certainly thinks of everything," I agreed.

"Won't you come in?" He opened the door wider.

"Sure," I said, following him inside the apartment. "What else did Stella say?"

"Nothing, nothing at all. Just that you were dropping over to have a chat about poor Julia and that awful fellow she was going around with—Weisman, you know."

"That was very thoughtful of Stella," I said. "Did she tell you what to say or what not to say to me as well?"

"My dear fellow! Of course not. I intend to be absolutely frank with you.... By the way, you've met Peter Pines, haven't you?"

I looked at the guy with the heavy hornrims who was sunk in a deep armchair. A so-called poet who had been at Stella's party. "Sure, we've met."

"So it's you again, Lieutenant," Pines said.

"Don't be rude, Peter," Romair said firmly. "I'm sure the Lieutenant is doing his very best. Would you care for a drink, Lieutenant?"

"Thanks," I said.

"China or Indian?"

I blinked at him slowly. "China or Indian what?"

"Tea, of course. You can have either."

I sat in a chair that had seen better days around the time Romair had been on Broadway. "I think I'll skip the tea," I said. "What do you know about Harry Weisman?"

"A most unsavory character," Romair said primly. "Not that I do know very much about him. Julia was infatuated with the man. Excuse me a moment while I pop the kettle on, will you? I know Peter would love a cup of tea."

Romair disappeared into the kitchen. I lit myself a cigarette and looked around the room. There were four framed posters on the walls, each a playbill announcing Edgar Romair as the lead in a different play. One of them I vaguely remembered, a hit from around ten years back.

That was just after I'd quit the Army Intelligence job in London, lost my reason, and became a cop in Pine City. I've often wondered why; I guess it was the thought of all those beautiful oranges. It couldn't have been the thought of all those beautiful, man-hungry starlets they have in California.

I looked across at Pines. "You live here?"

"I do," he said. "But you can take that look off your face, Lieutenant. There's no delicate, effeminate relationship between us. Both Edgar and myself are normal men."

"You could have fooled me," I told him.

Romair came back into the room briskly. "Yes, as I was saying, Lieutenant, Weisman is a most unsavory character. A man who lives by his wits and—"

"I didn't come here to talk about Weisman," I said patiently, "I came here to talk about you. Last night, a couple of hours before she was killed, Julia Grant had a fight with Stella over you. That's what I want to hear about."

"You flatter me, Lieutenant." He smiled uncertainly. "There must be life in the old dog yet, eh?"

"Can the corny dialogue, Edgar!" Pines said brutally. "It might have been a riot in Sardi's around the late twenties, but it's not getting you anywhere with this bloodhound. Just talk plain English at him. As long as you keep it simple, he'll probably understand."

Romair's face reddened slowly. "Well ... I ... I don't understand where you could have got that idea, Lieutenant. I mean that the girls were fighting over me."

"I got it from Stella," I said. "And she should know. Just what did you do after you left Stella's party last night?"

"I told your sergeant that," he said defensively. "I left just after midnight and came straight on home here and went to bed."

"You have your own car?"

"Of course."

"And you deny the two women were fighting over you?"

"The very idea is ridiculous, Lieutenant! Julia was infatuated with this Weisman and Stella is already married."

"That doesn't seem to make any difference to her love-life."

"That's something I wouldn't know about," he said firmly. He straightened his back consciously. "I know things have changed quite a bit from what they used to be, but I was brought up to live by a certain code and that code—"

"Edgar!" Pines said in a murderous voice.

"Sorry!" Romair muttered.

"I know the finish to that spiel, Lieutenant," Pines said wearily. "In another five minutes he'd be standing at attention and singing 'Stars and Stripes Forever.'"

"A wild exaggeration!" Romair said bleakly.

"Do you have any idea why somebody would want to kill Julia Grant?" I persisted.

"I have." He smiled for a moment. "But it's nothing I can prove of course, Lieutenant. I can only make a suggestion. Why don't you talk to Candy Logan?"

"Stella Gibb suggested I talk to you and that hasn't got me any place," I said. "Now you suggest I talk to Candy Logan—why?"

"I just think she might be helpful, Lieutenant, that's all."

A shrill whistling noise came from the kitchen. "Ah!" Romair smiled happily. "There's the kettle. You sure you won't have a cup of tea, Lieutenant?"

"Sure, I'm sure," I said.

"Then you'll excuse me while I make it," he said and hurried back to the kitchen.

I looked across at Pines. "While we're on the subject, where were you last night between one and three?"

His eyes gleamed behind the thick lenses. "I have an alibi, Lieutenant. An almost perfect one, if I may say so."

"Say so, and I'll give you a rating," I told him.

"Do I have to give her name? It was one of the girls at the party."

"Just how far does this alibi take you?"

"Further than I'd care to say," he said modestly. "But I can give it to you in time, if you prefer, Lieutenant. Till just after three-thirty."

"I know there's some rap I can pin on you," I said thoughtfully. "I just have to think of it, that's all. Corrupting juveniles with obscene publications, maybe. Who publishes your stuff, Pines?"

A deep blush spread across his cheeks. "I haven't ... er ... actually been published yet."

"Oh," I said. "You're that sort of poet."

"It's only a question of time," he said hurriedly. "Two or three New York houses are very interested at the moment."

"They've cleaned up New York," I said. "Those sort of houses don't operate anymore."

"I wish you'd keep your cheap gibes to yourself, Lieutenant!" His face flushed a deeper red. "It makes me sick when I'm confronted by an uncouth—"

"Police lieutenant?"

Romair bounced back into the room carrying two cups of what I presumed was tea. If it wasn't, I was being cheated. He gave one to Pines, then sat down opposite me and stirred the dark liquid vigorously. "Did you have any other questions for me, Lieutenant?"

"Not really," I said. "I'd like you to remember something, though. Withholding evidence from a police officer is a criminal offense."

"Just what do you mean by that?"

"It's simple enough. If you aren't telling me everything you know about the facts surrounding this case, you can go to jail for a long, long time."

I watched the tea spill into his saucer.

"Don't let him needle you, Edgar," Pines said. "This is an old gag. He's just trying to frighten you into saying something you don't really mean."

"Sure," I said. "And I can frighten you right behind bars if you're holding out on me, both of you."

Pines sneered audibly. "He's only trying to—"

"Shut up!" I told him. He looked at me, opened his mouth again, then thought better of it. "Now," I said to Romair. "If you know anything, now is the time to say it. Tomorrow could be too late."

More tea spilled into the saucer. "I don't know," Romair said miserably. "I ... I really don't know. Lieutenant, is there such a thing as protection for a witness? I mean ..."

"Edgar!" Pines said sharply. "For everybody's sake, keep your damn mouth shut!"

I thought I'd had enough of Pines for one night. I got to my feet and walked over to where he sat. "Shut up," I told him.

"You can't ..." He got up slowly, his eyes bulging.

"Hold your hands out in front of you," I told him crisply.

He did as he was told and I took the handcuffs out and snapped them over his wrists.

"You can't do this to me!" His voice became faintly hysterical. "Why are you arresting me? What's the charge? I demand to know! I demand the right to call my lawyer! You can't treat me like a common criminal!"

"March!" I told him. "Out into the kitchen." I gave him a tap on the shoulder to help him on his way.

He staggered out into the kitchen, still protesting shrilly. I unlocked the cuffs, freeing his left wrist, then looked around the kitchen. The sink looked as if it would do. I locked the cuff again around the pipe leading to the faucet. "I'll leave you to meditate," I told him. "Maybe you can dream up a couple of poems."

I walked back into the living room, closing the kitchen door carefully behind me and closing out Pines' passionate protests about justice and the rights of man.

I got back to my chair and sat down again. Romair looked at me with wild eyes. "What on earth was that for?" he asked.

"So we don't get rudely interrupted anymore," I said. "You were saying?"

He gulped down some of his tea, then looked at me almost pleadingly. "Lieutenant, I was asking, isn't there some protection for a witness under certain circumstances?"

"Sure there is," I said. "Under any necessary circumstances. What are you afraid of? Somebody will kill you if you tell what you know? We'd be happy to give you full police protection if that's—"

"It's not that exactly," he said. "Well, to be honest, Lieutenant, I was thinking more particularly of blackmail."

"It certainly would apply where blackmail is concerned," I said. "The biggest mistake a blackmail victim can make is to keep quiet. You must know that."

"I suppose it is," he said. "But it's not that easy when you're faced with ..." He shook his head despairingly. "I'm a desperate man, Lieutenant. I only have a certain income. When I retired from the stage I had enough money invested to realize me a reasonable income for the rest of my life. But within the last two months almost a third of the capital has gone!"

There was a note of horror in his voice. "If it continues, I shall be destitute within the next six months! It can't go on anymore. Whatever happens, I don't think I could stand—"

"Who's blackmailing you?" I asked him.

"Weisman, of course," he said. "I thought you would have guessed."

"I don't have the Prophet's gift of an all-seeing eye," I said. "Why is he blackmailing you?"

"Well, really Lieutenant. I'd rather not say, I mean, is it absolutely necessary? Can't you deal with him now I've told you?"

"We need a little something called evidence," I said.

"Oh," he said limply. "I hadn't realized that. Then you couldn't protect me, could you?"

"Of course we can," I said. "We can—"

"But you can't," he said. "If I tell you, it means you will tell your superiors and that means it will come out in court and the newspapers will ... I'm sorry, Lieutenant. I've been most rude to you. I ... I was only joking."

"Look, Romair," I said. "We're talking about motive for murder. You can't—"

"I'm sorry, Lieutenant." His face was chalk-white. Slowly he held out his hands in front of him, wrists together. "Arrest me if you will, but my lips are permanently sealed!"

"Ah, nuts!" I said disgustedly. "I'm all out of cuffs, anyway."

I opened the front door of the apartment to the frantic accompaniment from the kitchen of handcuffs beating against a faucet.

"There is just one point, Lieutenant," Romair said nervously from behind me. "What about Peter. I mean those handcuffs? Aren't you going to free him?"

"Tell him I'll drop the key in the mail," I said and slammed the door shut behind me.

Chapter Six

She lived in the penthouse, of course. You came into the building through an aluminum grille and into a foyer that must have made some interior decorator ten thousand dollars. The gray-uniformed flunky escorted me to the elevator. I pushed the button marked P and was carried upward with speed and silence.

The penthouse had a foyer, smaller than the one downstairs, but no less expensively decorated. I pushed the buzzer and waited.

The door opened and Candy Logan stood there, looking at me. She wore a man's shirt—white, long-tailed. The front of it came down as far as the top of her thighs.

"Hi," she said. "I thought you were going to call me?"

"When did pants go out of fashion?" I asked hoarsely.

"It's cooler this way," she said casually. "Why don't you come in and see what I call home?"

"You mean there's still more to see?"

"Why don't you step inside and find out?"

I followed her inside. I noticed vaguely that the living room was furnished modern style, expensive but not oriental. That was something, anyway. But with Candy walking in front of me, and that shirt-tail twitching from side to side, I didn't really have time to notice much of anything else.

She walked over to the bar in one corner of the room and I sank breathlessly onto the couch and watched her make two drinks. She poured some Chivas Regal and added a squirt from a fancy seltzer bottle.

"There's a beautiful view from the window," she said conversationally.

"There's a magnificent view from right where I'm sitting," I told her. "And if you think I'm going to trade it for a lousy window, you're crazy."

She brought the drinks back with her to the couch and sat down beside me. I took the glass gratefully and drank.

"It's nice of you to find time to come and see me, Al," she said. "I thought you'd be so busy with the murder, I wouldn't have a chance of seeing you for a while."

"What did Romair tell you when he called?" I asked her.

"Romair?" She lifted her eyebrows. "What are you talking about?"

"I'm getting the run-around tonight," I said. "If you hadn't been next in line, I would have quit."

"Why don't you relax?" she said. "Take it easy, Al, and try to make some sense."

"Save it for the peasants, honey," I told her. "Stella Gibb told me I should talk to Romair and then called him to say I was coming. Romair suggested I should talk to you and my bet is he called you to say I was coming."

"You don't trust anyone, do you?" She sighed.

She crossed her legs casually and the shirtfront rode up a little. Enough to make me wonder what she was wearing underneath that shirt, if anything. I felt that was something else again that needed investigating.

"I trusted a dame once," I said. "Before I knew what happened, I was nearly married."

"That could have been a smart move, if she owned any real estate," Candy said.

"Don't change the subject," I told her. "What about Romair, huh?"

"As a matter of fact, Edgar did call me."

"What did he say?"

"He thought I should tell you the truth about Stella and Julia. He said he didn't think you'd believe him now, whatever that meant. He was going to tell you, but the conversation got crossed up or something." She frowned at me. "And he said something about Peter was going crazy trying to get away from the faucet!"

"Pines is paranoid," I explained. "He thinks the kitchen faucet is out to get him all the time. All the faucets are—he hasn't had a bath in three weeks—but the kitchen faucet is the gang-boss. It's a sort of patient and surgeon thing. Peter put a new washer in the kitchen faucet a week ago and he thinks he handled the operation a little too rough."

Candy leaned back against the couch with her hands behind her head. "All right, if you don't want to hear about Stella and Julia!"

"I want to hear."

"Edgar said you might believe me if I told you the truth about them."

"So I might. Try me."

"They hated each other," Candy said easily. "They were man-crazy and Stella was always stealing the men Julia already had."

"This I know already," I said. "I have heard this song before, the melody is turning a little sour."

"The fight they had last night in Stella's cabana wasn't over Edgar, it was over Harry Weisman."

"This is beginning to get like a Chinese juggling act," I said. "Seven little Chinamen on the stage and one of them is always pulling hats out of rabbits. But you're never sure if it's the same one or not."

"You're making with that double-talk again," she said. "If you don't believe me, I'll stop wasting your time and shut up."

"Go on," I said.

"Julia was crazy over Weisman and Stella happened to see them together in a bar one night. It was a challenge to Stella; any new man Julia had was a challenge. She set about seducing Weisman away from Julia. It would be her idea of fun to take Weisman out of Julia's bed and into her own. Afterwards she'd brag about it to Julia."

"And did she?"

Candy shrugged her shoulders expressively. "I wouldn't know. But that was what the fight was really about. Julia was warning her to lay off."

"Do you think Stella killed her?"

"I wouldn't know for sure," Candy said. "But I do know this, she was capable of it. I've never met a woman so thoroughly evil as Stella!"

"You don't think the Prophet is improving her? All that suntan and everything?"

Candy laughed harshly. "That's the funniest thing I've heard in a long time. Improve her! Don't you know that—" She stopped abruptly. "Never mind."

"Go on," I said. "I'm interested. This is better than even the scandal mags used to be."

"I mean I just don't think anything could improve Stella, except a coffin, maybe," Candy said. "Would you like another drink?"

"Sure," I said. "I'd also like to watch you walk across the room and get it for me."

"I can do both," she said and took the empty glass out of my hand and walked slowly across to the bar.

Her hips were a symphony in free movement. She came back again with the refills and sat down beside me. Her legs were long and suntanned all the way—the best advertisement for sun worship I'd seen yet.

"So that's it," she said. "Do you have any more questions, Lieutenant? I do have an alibi for the murder, you know. It just so happens that I, well, spent the night with a man. Of course, if you insist I can give you his name, but I'm sure he wouldn't want that to happen. You see, I happen to know he has a wife and eight starving children and if he loses his job as cleaner in the Sheriff's office then he'll—"

"I was wondering," I said, "if you're wearing anything at all underneath that shirt?"

"Don't pant when you ask a question like that," she said. "You remind me of my late husband. It was all that panting that started his heart trouble and—"

"I don't have any real estate," I said. "So I don't have to worry."

"That could easily be fixed," she said casually. "Why don't you marry me?"

"Oh, sure," I said. "And in no time at all we'd have a houseful of little split-levels."

"I'm serious, Al," she said in a low voice. "Why don't you marry me? I think I'd like to marry again. You're the sort of guy I'd like to marry second time around. There's enough real estate left over to take care of both of us. You could stop being a cop and working all hours and I could—"

"This is the first time any dame made me a moral proposition," I said. "I'm overwhelmed. I'm not even sure I like it. Tell me something, did you ever go on a date with Harry Weisman?"

"Don't try and change the subject!" she said sharply.

"Nobody likes Harry Weisman," I said. "Nobody cared much about Julia Grant, either. And if nobody cared about Julia, why should they worry about what sort of guy she was going around with?"

"I wouldn't know," Candy yawned. "I don't want to play cops and robbers with you. I want to get married."

"You should register with an agency," I told her. "For twenty-five bucks they'll give you a set of ten pictures of ten guys who all look different but they all have the same thing on their minds."

Candy got to her feet and stood in front of me. Slowly she peeled off the white shirt. Then she let the shirt drop to the floor and just stood there, looking down at me.

It proved one thing, if nothing else. She hadn't been wearing anything underneath that shirt. "Are you sure you don't want to marry me?" she asked softly.

"That's about the only thing I'm sure of," I said. "I'm confused, otherwise."

"We could get a special license almost right away," she said. "Would it be so tough, being married to me?"

"You must take this sun worship seriously," I said. "You have a tan all over."

"You still keep on changing the subject," she said. "This is your last chance, Al Wheeler. Are you going to marry me?"

"I don't think so," I said.

She bent down and picked up the white shirt and pulled it on over her head. It was a woman's way of getting into a shirt. She wriggled it down over her breasts and down across her hips. It was the sort of act that put vaudeville right back on its feet.

"I'm sorry you have to go so soon," she said in a brittle voice. "But suddenly you bore me, Al Wheeler!"

I finished my drink and stood up. I started walking toward the door slowly. Candy stood where she was, watching me. I reached the door and looked back at her. "I can tell you what Romair is scared of. Weisman is blackmailing him and Edgar doesn't like paying. But he likes the idea of telling what the blackmail is about even less. Is that the way *you* feel?"

"Get out!" she said from between clenched teeth.

"Julia Grant was murdered," I said. "Maybe you should tell me what's scaring you. I'd do it soon, otherwise it might be too late."

"Get out!" She picked up a bottle from the bar and threw it at me.

So I got.

It was the night of the guided tour but I didn't have a guide. One more call would finish the tour anyway. I was going to call on Harry Weisman,

Jack. It was getting to be late again and even if I did have less than twenty-four hours to Lavers' deadline, I thought I might as well be in bed for all the value I was getting out of the night.

I parked the Healey outside the walk-up apartment and walked up. I pressed the buzzer and lit a cigarette while I waited. Nothing happened for a few seconds. I pressed the buzzer again, playing the first two bars of the "William Tell Overture." I thought if that didn't waken Weisman, he'd have to be dead.

Right on cue, I heard a faint moaning noise from behind the door. Then it swung open slowly and Harry Weisman stood there, staring at me.

His eyes bulged nearly out of their sockets and both hands were clasped tight against his stomach. The hilt of a knife protruded from between his clenched fingers. I couldn't be sure whether he was trying to pull the knife out or hold his intestines in.

He groaned again, then his knees buckled slowly and he slid forward onto the floor. He jerked once convulsively before his face banged against the floor and he lay still.

I got the .38 out of the holster and closed the front door behind me. I didn't think there was much I could do for Weisman, but if whoever had killed him was still inside the apartment, there was quite a lot they could do for me.

It took around thirty seconds to check the apartment and find there was nobody else there. The bathroom window was wide open, the curtains swaying gently in the breeze. I looked out and saw the window opened onto the fire escape. The murderer must have gone that way while I was playing tunes on the buzzer.

I walked back into the living room slowly and checked Weisman's pulse. He was dead. The hilt of the knife looked familiar. It looked like the second of the pair that had hung on the wall of Stella Gibb's dining room.

I stepped across Weisman's body and walked over to the phone. I checked the directory, then dialed Stella's number. I let it ring for maybe a minute. Nobody answered. I checked Candy Logan's number, then dialed that. She answered on the third ring.

"Candy?" I made my voice as husky as I could.

"Yes," she said sharply. "Who's that?"

"Harry Weisman."

"What do you want?"

"That cop's been asking questions again."

"Can I help it?" Her voice sounded indifferent. "That's not my worry, it's yours. You can afford to worry, Harry, can't you?"

"What's with that crack?" I said in a muffled voice.

"Don't be cute! I'm paying you enough as it is, let alone the rest of them. You must be getting to be a rich man. Harry. You worry all by yourself, will you? I hope you drop dead with worry. Please don't call me again!" There was a sharp click as she hung up.

I put the phone back and lit myself a cigarette. I tried the Gibb house again and there was still no answer. I found Romair's number and dialed that. He answered almost right away.

"Wheeler," I said. "Is Pines still attached to that faucet in the kitchen?"

"He certainly is, Lieutenant," Romair said in a strained voice. "I think he's going to have hysterics any minute. Do you have any message I can give him?"

"I sure do," I said. "You can tell him from me that a close attachment to a faucet like he's got shows an unhealthy mind. Ask him why he doesn't try thinking about *girls* once in a while."

I hung up quickly, then dialed Lavers' home number and waited around twenty seconds until someone answered.

"Hello?" a sleepy voice said.

"If it isn't my favorite wife," I said. "When you're all through with the iceman, you know you just have to call me, honey."

"This would be Lieutenant Wheeler," Mrs. Lavers said patiently. "And it would be trouble too, I don't doubt."

"Just one little ol' corpse," I said. "It breaks my heart to disturb the Sheriff at this hour of the night but I think he'll want to know."

"I'll call him," she said. "When are you coming over to dinner?"

"The next time the Sheriff's out of town," I said. "I'll rig a mantrap outside the back door in case he's forgotten something and comes back for it."

"You make me feel young again," she sighed heavily. "Are you serious about that corpse?"

"I could never get serious about a corpse," I said coldly. "I am a more or less normal, more or less young, man."

"I'll tell the Sheriff that. He'll never believe it." I waited maybe another thirty seconds, then Lavers' voice bellowed in my ear. "What the hell is this about a corpse? In the middle of the night, too!"

"While you've been sleeping, I've been working," I said in an injured voice. "Such is the fate of a cop. I've been calling on people. I just called on Harry Weisman and he opened the door, but he wouldn't talk to me."

"Get to the point!"

"That's exactly what Harry did. He got to the point—got it right through his stomach. He's dead."

"Did you get the murderer?"

"He got out the bathroom window onto the fire escape."

"What were you doing while he was getting away?"

"Playing the 'William Tell Overture.'"

"Look!" Lavers said in a strangled voice. "Stop horsing around, Wheeler! If you mean you let a murderer slip through your fingers—"

"Bathroom window, not fingers," I corrected him. "I was pressing the buzzer outside the front door. I just don't have X-ray vision, Sheriff. I can't see through doors yet but I'm working on it."

"I would have thought you'd had enough practice by now," he grunted. "Weisman was knifed?"

"With a dagger that looks like the twin of the one that killed Julia Grant."

"But that's impossible. You brought that one into the office, it's locked up in my safe right now."

"Maybe the daggers were triplets and not twins," I suggested. "Anyway, will you send Polnik up here?"

"Of course," he said. "The boys in City Hall are going to die laughing over this! Me, the Big White Sheriff of Pine City who said he could handle a murder case on his own without calling on Homicide. And now we've got another murder! And that damned Prophet is due to disappear at sunset tomorrow and maybe take a hundred grand along with him!" His voice became almost pleading. "Tell me something, Wheeler. Are you making any progress on this case at all?"

"No," I said helpfully.

"For God's sake! The papers are going to roast me over this second murder as soon as it breaks. Don't you have any ideas at all?"

"I have a couple," I said. "But they don't amount to much. I'll wait here till Polnik arrives, then I'm going calling."

"Can't your women wait until you've done something about these murders?" he shouted.

"I wasn't going calling on a woman," I said reprovingly.

"Whatever you're going to do, make it fast," Lavers said. "If we don't have this case sewn up by tomorrow evening, I'm going to have to ask Homicide for help even if my face is red."

"What about mine?"

"I don't care what color your face is!" he snarled "Green, blue or purple. Any color, it would be an improvement!"

Chapter Seven

It was nice and cool on top of Bald Mountain in the early hours of the morning. I parked the Healey beside a white Continental hardtop and figured my hunch was right. There was a light burning in Bennett's office so I walked across to the front door and knocked. His voice told me to come in.

He looked up at me from across his desk top with an expression of surprise on his face. "Lieutenant Wheeler! What brings you here at this time of the night?"

"I wanted to talk to Stella Gibb," I said. "Now."

Bennett looked doubtful. "It's pretty late you know, Lieutenant. After midnight."

"I know," I said. "You have to be able to tell the time before they'll let you become a cop. You even have to know which day it is. Where do I find her?"

"Well, if it's important, I'll call her."

He reached for the phone, dialed a two-figure number and waited. "Stella," he said finally, "I hate to interrupt you, but Lieutenant Wheeler is here and he wants to see you right away.... What's that? I couldn't possibly tell him to do that! This is serious, you'll have to ..." He looked at the receiver helplessly for a moment then put it back onto the cradle.

"What did she say?" I asked him.

"She said to tell you ..." He gestured vaguely. "She says she's busy."

"Who with?"

"Honest, Lieutenant. I tried!"

"Sure," I said. "She's in that outsize cabana of hers?"

"Yes, but you can't—"

"You watch," I told him.

I reached the door a moment too late. It was already open. Charlie stood there, weaving around on the balls of his feet.

"Hiya, cop." He smiled idiotically at me. "What's new? You come up here for the sunburn? Wrong time of day ... It's night out there."

"Beat it, Charlie!" Bennett said impatiently. "The Lieutenant is busy. We're busy, we're having a private conversation, so beat it!"

"Sure, sure!" Charlie waved his arms wildly in the air and nearly lost his balance at the same time. "Just one little thing, Ralph. I don't have a drink."

"O.K." Bennett sighed heavily and pulled a new fifth out of a desk drawer. "Here you are."

"Thanks, pal," Charlie said thickly. "Can always rely on my old pal, Ralph."

"You stay right where you are, Charlie," I said. "You're in no condition to make it to that desk. I'll get it for you."

"Thanks," he beamed at me. "That's kind of you, Lieutenant. Real kind."

I walked over to the desk and picked up the bottle. Bennett made an apologetic face at me. I turned around and said, "Here, Charlie. Catch!" I lobbed the bottle fast, straight at his head.

He caught it easily and surely with one hand.

"Well, Charlie," I said. "That was a fast reaction for a guy who's loaded."

He stared at me, his face expressionless.

"What gives here?" Bennett asked blankly.

"You should ask Charlie," I said. "I've been wondering about him since the first time we met. He's just too lush a lush to be true. If he really drank a bottle of liquor as fast as he pretended, he'd be dead. So it had to be an act. I was wondering why. You tell us, Charlie."

"Yeah," Bennett said softly. "I'd like to hear the answer to that, too."

Charlie looked at both of us for a long moment. Then he grinned faintly. "Like the man says," he spoke in a normal, sober voice, "you figure it out."

He walked outside, closing the door behind him. Bennett stared at me blankly. "I don't get it."

"Neither do I," I agreed. "It might be interesting to find out. Why don't you ask him?"

"I'll ask him all right," Bennett said coldly. "He must have been taking me for a sucker for a long time now."

"I guess it wasn't too hard," I said pleasantly.

I walked to the door and let myself out of the office into the night. I was going calling on Stella Gibb to ask a few pertinent questions and, if I chose the wrong moment, the embarrassment would be all the other guy's, not mine.

The door of a cabana opened suddenly about twenty feet away from me and someone stepped out. For a moment he was framed in the light from the room behind me. Long enough for me to recognize that beard and loincloth. Who said a prophet was without honor in his own country?

Then the door closed again and the Prophet vanished swiftly into the night. I made another five feet toward the cabana, then realized with a sudden jolt that I'd also made a mistake. The cabana the Prophet had just left didn't belong to Stella Gibb at all; it was only about half the size.

I stopped for a moment to think about that and suddenly the night caved in on my head. I fell to the ground and dimly, from a long way away, I heard a voice snarl, "That should fix you for a time, wise guy!"

How long I was blacked out I didn't know. The first thing I knew was the coolness of the night air against my face, but my head was resting against something soft and warm.

I opened my eyes slowly and realized my head was cradled against an adequate bosom, much softer than Mother Earth's. I lifted my head slightly and saw dark, liquid eyes looking down into mine.

"Are you all right?" she asked softly.

"I'm fine," I mumbled. "Just let me lie here a couple of hours longer until my head stops hurting."

"I really think you must be feeling better," she said. "My cabana is just over there. Do you think you could make it?"

"Sure," I said. "If you let me hold you real tight on the way."

I got onto my feet and the horizon tilted violently, first one way, then the other. I put my arm around her shoulders and we staggered over to the cabin. She switched on the light as soon as we got inside and I slumped into a chair.

She wasn't wearing the white robe I'd seen her in the last time. She was wearing a white sweater and a pair of black shorts. They didn't reveal any less that the robe, I noted gratefully.

"Your head is bleeding a little," Eloise said. "I'll bathe it for you. What happened?"

"Somebody hit me," I said. It seemed a logical answer.

She went into the kitchen and came back a minute later with hot water, towels, and antiseptic. I winced when she bathed the cut, but by asserting my manhood I managed to cut down the volume of my screams.

Then she poured me a drink and gave me a cigarette. I began to feel better, apart from a splitting headache.

"The cut isn't too deep," she said. "I don't think you need a stitch in it, or anything."

"That's fine," I said. "Thanks, Eloise."

She smiled. "It was lucky I found you. I nearly tripped over you. I went over to the office to see Ralph—or I was going to see him, then I tripped over you."

"I'm eternally grateful that you did," I said. "You didn't see Charlie around by any chance?"

She shook her head. "No, were you looking for him?"

"He was looking for me, I think. He found me all right."

"You mean it was Charlie who hit you?" Her eyes widened as she stared at me.

"With a full fifth of rye," I said. "He's getting reckless; he just doesn't care what he does with his liquor these days."

"Why would Charlie want to do a thing like that?"

"I don't think he likes me," I said. "But it's a long story and it reminds me I have things to do. So if you'll excuse me, I'll—" I got to my feet and the room swayed violently the same way the night had done outside. I sat down again suddenly.

"Don't be stupid," Eloise said firmly. "You can't possibly move around yet. You're suffering from shock, maybe concussion. I think I should get a doctor."

"No," I said. "No doctors. I'll be O.K. in a minute. You don't mind if I sit here for a while?"

"Of course not," she said. "I'll make some coffee. Do you think that might help?"

"I guess it would," I said. "Next to just sitting here and looking at you."

She smiled vaguely and went out into the kitchen again. She was back ten minutes later with the coffee. It was good and strong. She sat opposite me, her dark-tanned legs neatly crossed, watching me drink the coffee.

"You're a wonderful girl, Eloise," I said. "The only thing I can't figure out is what you're doing up here."

"Why not?"

"How long have you been on this sun worship kick?"

"From the time I first met the Prophet," she said. "When he first came to Bald Mountain."

"Is the pay good?"

She smiled and shook her head. "You have it wrong, Lieutenant. I don't get paid anything for what I do. You see, I believe in him."

"You're kidding," I said. "The stuff he spouts is for the birds."

Her lips tightened a little. "Everyone is entitled to their own opinion, Lieutenant. I happen to believe in the Prophet. He is an immensely sincere man. Surely you've been impressed by his sincerity even if you don't agree with his beliefs?"

It was my turn to shake my head. "The only thing that impresses me around here is the money you collect from the suckers."

"You're hopelessly wrong, Lieutenant," she said stiffly, "But I don't suppose it's any use me trying to argue with you."

"Sure," I said. "I'm not the sort of guy to abuse hospitality. I'll believe you. Could I have some more coffee?"

"Of course." She refilled my cup and gave it back to me.

"And I bet the Prophet isn't the sort of guy to abuse hospitality, either," I said.

She raised her eyebrows a fraction. "I don't quite understand you, Lieutenant?"

"You're his helper, aren't you?" I said. "A sort of priestess? Familiar is another word for it. I imagine you're both really familiar with each other."

"Please don't be insulting!"

"I saw him leave your cabana just before Charlie slugged me," I said. "Did he drop over for a cup of coffee?"

"I don't see it concerns you in the least," she said icily. "But I have nothing to be ashamed of, nothing to hide! The Prophet is a wonderful man and a very virile one. I'm proud to be his handmaiden. Does that satisfy you, Lieutenant?"

"It's not me you should ask," I murmured. "It's the Prophet."

She stood up quickly. "Are you feeling well enough to leave now?"

"I guess I am," I said.

I finished the coffee and stood up. This time the room stayed in the one place. Apart from the headache, I felt all right.

"There's just one thing that still bothers me," I said to Eloise. "Is it the Prophet's sun-loving sincerity that appeals to you, or his virility?"

"Damn you!" she said. "I hope next time somebody breaks your skull!"

I guessed that Dale Carnegie would have given me a black mark. I left Eloise's cabana and walked back to Bennett's office. He was still there, sitting at his desk. He had a drink in his hand, a worried look on his face.

"Did you find Stella all right, Lieutenant?" he asked. "Can I get you a drink?"

"No and yes," I said. "I never made Stella's cabana, but I could certainly use a drink."

He turned around to the small bar and started to make the drink.

"Have you seen Charlie any place?" I asked him.

"No," he said. "I've been looking for him but he seems to have vanished—and so has my car along with him!"

"What make of car?"

"A new Thunderbird, royal blue," he said. "It beats me, Lieutenant. How in hell did he ... I mean, why did he ... what reason did he have, for crying out loud! He didn't have to pretend he was a lush to freeload on me. He could have done that anyway. He had it coming."

"That's a strong sentiment you're expressing there," I said. "What did Charlie do you owed him so much? Run away with your wife?"

"Charlie saved my life about a year back," Bennett said soberly, handing me my drink. "I had one of those crazy ideas—uranium prospecting. Me—that always figured Disneyland was out in the sticks!

So I got me a Geiger counter and went out into the desert with a jeep and a tent.

"I don't need to make a production out of it. I got lost, I ran out of water. Around the second day, Charlie found me. I was half-crazy then. I'd been staggering around in circles for six hours before he came along. I had sunstroke, heat exhaustion, the works. If Charlie hadn't nursed me like he was my mother, I would have died. He wouldn't take a dime for it, either."

"So he was your Man Friday ever after?"

Bennett shook his head. "That was the crazy part. He went back into the desert after he'd delivered me safely back into the arms of civilization. I didn't see him again until about three months back. He turned up here one day."

"And put the bite into you?"

"He said he was flat broke but he didn't want a handout. He wanted a job, he said. Not much of a job, just something that would let him eat. So I gave him a job as watchman up here. He didn't do any watching, but I didn't care about that."

"Charlie was a very reasonable guy," I said.

"He had a cabin to sleep in," Bennett said. "He got all the food he wanted and I gave him forty bucks a week spending money. It took a couple of weeks before I found out he was a lush—or he was acting a lush." Bennett shook his head in bewilderment. "Just why the hell would he do that?"

"Your guess is as good as mine," I said. "But I want to talk to Charlie. I have a personal interest in him now. He just slugged me—with that fifth, I imagine."

"Slugged you!" Bennett's mouth sagged open. "Now why in hell would he—"

"You're repeating yourself," I said. "What's his last name?

"Elliott."

"I'll use your phone," I said. I picked up the phone and dialed the Sheriff's office. Polnik answered. "Put out a general alarm for Charles Elliott," I told him. "He's around forty, about five-two; weighs a hundred and sixty, sandy-haired. Wearing a blue denim shirt and pants. Driving a new T-Bird, royal blue in color. License number ..." I looked at Bennett who gave me the number. I repeated it into the phone.

"I got it, Lieutenant," Polnik said. "What's he wanted for?"

"Assaulting a cop," I said.

"You?" Polnik asked breathlessly.

"Me," I agreed. "Of all the people who could have a good reason for slugging me, he had to with no reason."

"Maybe he just didn't like the way you looked at him, Lieutenant?" Polnik suggested helpfully. "Sometimes I get the same feeling!"

"I'll remember that," I said. "What's happening down there?"

"Nothing much," he said. His voice sounded wistful. "I'd like to be with you and all those beautiful dames, Lieutenant."

"I wish you had been," I said. "If there's any justice, it would have been you who got slugged over the head."

"I guess you're feeling O.K. now, huh, Lieutenant?" He said after a long pause. "You sure sound like your usual self."

"What about that dagger that killed Weisman?" I said.

"No prints," Polnik said dully. "The dagger matches the other two all right."

"There are a couple of things you can do," I said. "Grab this Elliott character as soon as you can. It's important. And run a check on Weisman's bank account. Get a full statement over the last three or four months. How did his poker-playing alibi for the Grant dame's murder check out anyway?"

"It checked out O.K.," Polnik said. "He was playing poker last night. Everybody who was there alibied him. A couple of them were respectable citizens, even."

"All right," I said. "I'll be around here for a while. I'll call you later."

"Sure, Lieutenant." He hesitated for a moment. "The Sheriff sure is mad at you right now. You got any red hot leads, Lieutenant?"

"I got it made," I said tersely. "This Weisman was a bad loser at poker, see? He loses a pot to the Grant dame and he gets so mad, he stabs her. Then last night he loses again and he gets so mad with himself, he kills himself."

"Yeah?" Polnik said happily. "How about that! Wait a minute, Lieutenant. If you've got it made, what are you worrying about this Elliott character for?"

"I'm just throwing him in to make it more difficult for the Sheriff," I said and hung up sharply.

I looked at Bennett. He wasn't looking so hot. Maybe he was still worrying about Charlie or maybe he was just a natural worrier. I decided I didn't care very much.

"I'm going over to talk to Stella Gibb," I told him. "If any calls come for me, you can switch them over to her cabana."

"Sure, Lieutenant," he nodded absently. "One thing still worries me— how do you figure a guy like Charlie?"

"I'd like to figure him with a torsion wrench," I said feelingly.

I left his office again and walked over to Stella's cabana. This time I didn't get slugged on the way. Eloise's cabana was in darkness when I passed it, and so was Stella's when I finally reached it.

I knocked loud enough to waken the dead, but it didn't waken Stella Gibb. I tried the handle and found the door wasn't locked. I pushed it open and stepped inside; found the light switch and flicked it on.

The cabana was deserted. The bed was still made and obviously hadn't been touched. I switched off the light and closed the door behind me on the way out. I walked back to the parked cars and saw the Continental was missing. I climbed into the Healey and started the long drive down the mountainside.

I wished I knew where I could find Charlie Chan.

Chapter Eight

The two white ghosts were back on the driveway. The hood of the hardtop was hot; the hood of the convertible warm. I walked up on the porch and pressed the button. I heard the chimes softly inside the house. I lit a cigarette and closed my eyes, trying to remember what a bed looked like.

I heard the door open so I opened my eyes as well. Stella Gibb stood framed in the doorway, wearing something even cooler than she had the last time I called.

She wore a shortie nightgown affair with lace-edged pants peeping out below the hem of the gown. It was a little too cute for a woman who was all grown-up the way Stella was.

"Is it my irresistible attraction?" she asked in a faintly mocking voice.

"I have some more questions that need answers," I said. "I was going to ask them up on Bald Mountain but I got delayed and you'd left by the time I got over to your cabana. What did you go up there for, anyway?"

"The drive," she said easily. "It was such a beautiful night and everything. I felt restless. I knew I wouldn't sleep if I went to bed early."

"Did Cornelius find any of his friends downtown?"

"I wouldn't know," she said. "He was in bed, drunk, when I got in. He still is. Aren't you coming inside? It's cool out here."

I followed her into the living room and slumped onto the couch.

"I can make you a drink, I guess," she said. "That's about your only vice, isn't it, Al?"

"Right now that's for sure," I agreed. "If you're still feeling cool, why don't you put some clothes on?"

She looked back at me over her shoulder, a slow smile widening her lips. "Does it bother you?"

"No," I said. "Maybe it would if I wore a beard and a loincloth. Then again, maybe it wouldn't?"

She turned her head away quickly but I had time enough to see the smile vanish from her lips. She made the drinks and carried them back with her to the couch and sat down beside me. I took the glass out of her hand and sipped at it.

"What kind of questions did you have, honey?" she asked. "You want to know about my love-life or something?"

"Harry Weisman was murdered tonight," I said.

She sat like a movie-still. "Murdered?" She said finally.

"To death," I agreed. "Stabbed with another dagger. Just how many of those daggers have you got?"

"What do you mean?"

"One was used to kill Julia," I said patiently. "I took the second one from your dining room wall. Now somebody used a third one to kill Weisman. Do you have a manufacturing plant in the basement?"

She bit her full lower lip, adding another bruise to the one that was already there. "I ... I'm not sure I know what you're talking about, Al."

"You can call me Lieutenant," I said. "I'll put it on the line for you, Stella. You told me to talk to Romair. He told me to talk to Candy Logan. I played along with the gag, that's exactly what I did. You know what she told me—what Romair had asked her to tell me?"

"Whatever that witch said about me wouldn't be good!" Stella said tautly. "Go on!"

"She told me the fight you had with Julia last night was over Weisman," I said. "That once you knew he was Julia's boy friend, you just had to take him away from her—even if it was only for laughs."

Stella finished her drink, got up off the couch, then walked over and poured herself another drink.

"Julia was stabbed to death with a dagger that came off the wall in the next room," I said evenly. "You don't have any alibi for the time she was murdered. You got drunk at your own party, you said. You passed out. Weisman was murdered tonight with another one of those daggers. I walked in on him just as he was dying. I called you almost immediately afterwards. You weren't home."

She turned to face me, the new drink held tightly in both hands. "I ... I guess I was on my way to Bald Mountain then ... Lieutenant."

"You guess?"

"I must have been," she said firmly.

"You called Romair and told him I was coming to see him—at your suggestion," I said. "He called Candy Logan and told her I was coming to see her. I got the run-around tonight. Why?"

"I don't know what you mean," she said.

"I've got enough reasonable suspicion to book you as a material witness right now, Stella," I told her. "I've got a strong enough circumstantial case to put you into court on a double-murder rap."

"You wouldn't!" she said in a breathless voice. "You couldn't do that to me. You know I never killed either of them!"

"I got slugged over the head tonight," I said. "I have a headache. I'm tired and I'm disenchanted. I want to go home and sleep. Right now I've got an easy solution to all my problems—take you in and book you. The Sheriff would welcome you with open arms."

"Al!" Her eyes widened as she looked at me. "You wouldn't do that to me. You know I'm innocent!"

"The hell I do," I said.

"You have to believe me," she said quickly. "I didn't kill Julia or Harry Weisman. I swear I didn't!"

"I'm a soft-hearted character," I said, "if not stupid. Maybe I could start believing you if you stopped lying and told me the truth for once. What's the story about those daggers?"

She sat down on the other end of the couch and looked at me without speaking for a few seconds. Then she made up her mind I wasn't kidding.

"There were three, originally," she said. "I picked them up at an auction the last time I was in L.A. Two were perfect but one wasn't quite so good. I had the two perfect ones mounted and put on the wall. The other one should be in that bureau drawer." She nodded toward the bureau that stood against the far wall.

"Why don't you take a look and see if it's still there?" I said.

She walked across the room and opened the drawer. She looked down at the drawer for a couple of seconds then retraced her steps back to the couch. "It's gone," she said dully.

"Now tell me some more," I said. "Tell me about Harry Weisman and Julia. Tell me the truth."

"Candy Logan told you the truth," she said dully. "I heard about Julia's new boy friend and I was curious." Her lips twisted down at the corners. "I always was curious about new men. Very curious if they were Julia's new men. We had a sort of unfriendly rivalry. So when I heard about Harry, I made it my business to meet him. It wasn't hard. He didn't try to resist. I never heard him protesting."

"He must have been a lot tougher than he looked," I said wonderingly. "Dating you and Julia at the same time!"

She nodded absently as if she hadn't really heard what I said. "I had to tell Julia about it, of course," she went on. "It was the nicer side of my personality coming out. She was so mad about it, she told Cornelius."

"I wouldn't have thought that would worry you," I said. "He's Mr. Stella Gibb, isn't he?"

"I made a mistake with Cornelius," she said softly. "He was young, fifteen years younger than I am—and he had nice muscles. He was a lifeguard when I grabbed him and married him. I thought he'd be fun to have around the house and so long as I gave him plenty of spending money, he'd do as he was told."

She shook her head slowly. "It's frightening how wrong you can be! As soon as we were married, he developed a jealous streak. He goes crazy when he loses his temper! He ... frightens me. Julia told him about me and Harry Weisman."

"So?"

"He blew his stack completely. He really terrified me. I've never seen a man so completely berserk before. He hit me with his fists—he tore the clothes off my back and beat me. I was bruised for days afterwards. I thought he was going to kill me. But afterwards he cooled down and then a funny thing happened."

"Why don't you tell me and we can both laugh," I said. "Right now I could use a laugh."

"He seemed to be all right as far as I was concerned," she said. "He suddenly seemed to switch all his hate and fury against Julia. I think maybe beating me up satisfied his ego, and he started hating Julia for telling him about it in the first place. I stopped seeing Harry after that. I was too scared to risk it. But Julia didn't believe I had stopped."

"That was what caused the fight between the two of you last night?"

Stella nodded. "She said I was still seeing Harry and I denied it. She told me I was lying and she'd fix me good. She knew Cornelius had beaten me up the first time. She said she'd tell him I was still seeing Harry."

"So if she did," I said, "then maybe Cornelius could have taken that first dagger from the wall and killed her. Maybe he even took her body back up to Bald Mountain and left it on the altar. Maybe, if he was crazy enough to kill her, he was also crazy enough to kill the man he thought was still your lover—Harry Weisman?"

She buried her face in her hands and started to sob. "Oh. God!" she said in a muffled voice. "I've been trying so hard not to believe it. These last twenty-four hours I thought I'd go crazy myself. But it couldn't have been anyone else—it must have been Cornelius!"

I heard a scraping sound in the doorway. I looked up and saw Cornelius Gibb standing there in his pajamas. There was a savage, burning hatred in his eyes as he stared at Stella.

"You dirty, lying whore!" he said thickly.

Then he started across the room toward her, his hands held out in front of him, the fingers crooked. "I'll get the truth out of you," he shouted, "if I have to break your neck to get it!"

It looked like a busy night for all lieutenants.

I stuck my leg out in front of me as he passed and he tripped and fell flat on his face. He scrambled onto his feet again, his face distorted with fury, and went after Stella again. But this time I had the .38 in my hand to dissuade him. He stopped reluctantly about four feet away from her.

"Don't do it, Cornelius," I told him. "You wouldn't look pretty anymore with a hole through your face."

"The lying bitch!" he said thickly. "She's lying, I tell you. It was all lies. I stood behind the door, listening. I heard everything she said. It was all lies."

"Maybe," I said. "You tell me the truth, Cornelius. I've got plenty of time. I'll listen."

"Would I worry about her and Weisman?" He almost spat the words at me.

"You tell me," I said mildly. "It's your story."

"Weisman!" he repeated. "He was at the end of a long line that started forming to the right of Stella years before I even met her. Maybe Julia was worried about Stella hooking her new boy friend, but I wasn't. If I worried about any of the other men in Stella's life I would have gone crazy the first month we were married!"

He looked at Stella again, his mouth working. "You!" He said in a curiously slurred voice. "You're a meal ticket to me, nothing more or less. I knew that as soon as I felt your hot little eyes digging into my biceps that first day on the beach. I played along because you stank of money! You didn't have any class, you were old enough to be my mother—but so long as the folding money was pressed into my hand every month, I'd play along!"

Stella's face seemed to crumble. Suddenly she looked tired and ten years older. She averted her head quickly.

"Me—be jealous of you!" Cornelius laughed coarsely. "If it wasn't for the dollar signs I see in your eyes every time I look at them, I'd wear dark glasses around the house all the time!"

He took a deep breath, then looked at me. His voice was calmer when he spoke again. "You asked me how it felt to be a kept husband once, Lieutenant. I'll tell you. It feels fine just so long as you don't have to see your wife very often!"

"Are you all talked out now?" I asked him.

"I guess so," he mumbled.

"Then maybe you'd better go back to bed."

"I'm not—"

"I could lock you up for the rest of the night," I said. "For your own protection. You please yourself, Gibb."

"O.K.," he said. "I'll go back to bed. And you needn't worry about anything happening to Stella. Any beatings you hear about will be strictly mythical like those others she was telling you about."

He walked slowly out of the room. I helped myself to another drink, lit another cigarette.

Stella still sat on the end of the couch, looking down at the floor. Slowly she lifted her head and looked at me. Her eyes were bleak. "I guess I asked for it," she said. "I should have known he'd have his ear to the nearest keyhole! He was lying, of course."

"One of you is," I agreed. "I have to figure out which one. Right now I'm not laying odds."

"You couldn't possibly believe him!" she said. "That dirty little ..."

"Lifeguard?"

"How I hate men!" she said passionately.

It was the statement of the week.

Chapter Nine

I pressed the penthouse buzzer and waited. I seemed to wait for a long time so I pressed the buzzer again and left my thumb there for about ten seconds. Finally Candy opened the door.

"Don't you ever sleep?" she said. "It's after two in the morning."

"Wheeler, the bloodshot bloodhound," I said.

"I didn't know I was running a policemen's convention," she said unenthusiastically.

"Life is full of surprises," I said. "We have the dinner all planned. We're going to serve a huge cardboard cake and you're coming out of the top of it, right there on top of the table and everything."

"Wearing a bright smile and a bikini, I imagine?"

"You'll be wearing a worried look and a fig leaf," I corrected her. "Just how worried you look will be in direct proportion to how securely the fig leaf is attached."

"I've often wondered how you attach a fig leaf," she said.

"You should ..." I thought better of it, "... ask a fig."

"I suppose I'd better ask you in," she said. "You might as well live here and pay rent."

"Thank you," I said politely and followed her inside the penthouse.

Candy was wearing a shirt like she had been before. Only this time the shirt was blue silk with golden palm trees growing all over it.

"You've changed," I said.

"For the better?"

"Your shirt."

"This one is for sleeping," she said. "Or it was before you came into my life."

I sank down gratefully onto her couch. She sat down beside me but not too close. "Have you been having a busy time?" she asked politely.

"Nothing but good clean fun," I said. "What is that, incidentally?"

"I always thought it was a couple taking a bath together," she said.

"Harry Weisman was murdered tonight," I said evenly.

She shivered suddenly. "Who did it?"

"I'm still trying to find out," I admitted. "That's two murders we have to worry about now. I got there just in time to see him take his last breath. Coincidence, you sending me to him and me finding him that way."

"I must have been psychic or something," she said woodenly. "Or are you, in your obvious way, trying to suggest I knew it was going to happen?"

"I wasn't suggesting anything," I said. "I like the way you wear that silk shirt. It has a slow impact technique, like nuclear fission."

"Thanks," she said.

"You don't seem your usual bright self somehow," I said to her. "You haven't even asked me to marry you yet."

"You're a cop all the way down the line, Al Wheeler," Candy said in a cold voice. "I'd trust you the way I'd trust a window cleaner when I'm taking a shower!"

"I never knew you cared so much," I said. "And you were rude to me on the phone a few hours back as well."

Her forehead furrowed slightly. "Phone? I don't remember talking to you on the phone tonight."

"But you did," I said. "You told me I could worry all by myself, you'd paid this month already. You even said you hoped I'd drop dead with worry and not to call you again."

She swallowed once. "So it was you, and not Harry Weisman I was talking to," she said huskily. "That's just the sort of lousy trick you would pull!"

"Sure," I said. "What did you pay Harry for—window cleaning?"

"I was paying him for ... services rendered."

"I didn't think you'd need to pay a gigolo."

"Then you were wrong!" she said tautly.

"I know you were paying him blackmail," I said. "Why?"

"I still say it's none of your business."

"I could book you as material witness," I said.

"To what?"

"Murder."

She lay back against the couch and laughed. "You'd find that difficult, honey! You're my alibi for the first murder, remember? Tonight you went straight to Weisman's apartment from here, and you called me as soon as you found him dead. I answered the call, Al. So I couldn't have left here after you, murdered Weisman, and got back here in time to answer your phone call, could I?"

"I guess not," I said. "But I could book you for withholding evidence."

"What I was paying Weisman for has nothing to do with either murder, Al," she said. "Believe me."

"I'd like to," I said. "Can I afford to?"

"Now he's dead and I don't have to pay anymore," she said happily, "it's finished."

"It gives you a hell of a good motive," I said.

"I know." She grinned at me impudently. "If I didn't have a hell of a good alibi, I'd be worried."

"All right," I said. "I'm out of my league—you win."

"Goodbye, Al," she said casually. "You know your way out, don't you?"

"I am definitely losing my grip," I said. "No offer of marriage. All you do is tell me goodbye."

"I didn't think you were interested in me that way any longer, Al," she said softly.

"Are you kidding?" I asked incredulously.

She came off the couch and into my arms in one movement. "Al, darling!" she said. Her lips found mine hungrily; her arms wound around my neck fiercely. I wondered vaguely whatever happened to that thing they used to call male prerogative.

Then I stopped wondering. I picked her up and carried her back to the couch. She lay there, looking up at me for a moment, a half-smile on her face. "Al," she said softly, "are you really sure you don't want to marry me?"

"I'm quite sure," I said as I undid the top button of the silk shirt. "The only real estate I'm interested in is right here with only one sub-division."

The buzzer sounded sharply and we both jumped. Candy stared at me blankly for a moment.

"Are you expecting somebody?" I asked her.

"No," she shook her head.

"Have you paid your taxes?"

"Don't be ridiculous, Al!" She got onto her feet quickly. "I can't open the door like this. You go and see who it is while I put some clothes on."

"This is a new kick," I said. "Seduction for three and as a starter the girl puts some clothes on. I must tell the beat generation about this."

The buzzer squawked again impatiently.

"Answer it!" Candy said and ran into the bedroom.

I walked across the room to the front door and opened it. The hard barrel of a .38 jabbed into my stomach and I backed off automatically. The gun came with me and the guy holding it closed the door behind him gently.

"Charlie," I said to him reproachfully, "you're spoiling my average. Here I am with a beautiful dame and you have to come busting in. Didn't anybody tell you three's a crowd?"

"I see I didn't slug you hard enough," he said softly.

His eyes were watchful and the gun was steady in his hand. He held it like he was used to guns. That was a break, anyway; it meant he wouldn't shoot me accidentally. If he killed me it would be because he meant to.

"Sit down on the couch, copper," he said. "Move slow and easy, huh? You wouldn't want me to get nervous, would you?"

"I guess I wouldn't," I agreed.

I backed up to the couch and sat down, facing him. "What do you want, Charlie?" I asked him.

"Where's the dame?" he asked.

Right on cue, Candy came out of the bedroom. She'd put on one of those things they call a peignoir, which sounds exciting but isn't, and covers a girl from neck to ankle.

She looked at Charlie and then she looked at the gun in his hand. Her eyes widened. "Who are you?" she whispered.

"You don't know me," he said. "But I know you all right. You're Candy Logan. Come over here and sit down beside the cop. Do anything foolish and I'll let you have it!"

"Don't be nervous," I told Candy. "He only means a bullet."

"That's a death worse than fate, isn't it?" she asked as she sat down beside me. She sounded nervous all right. I didn't blame her. I knew exactly how she felt.

I looked at Charlie expectantly. "What would you like to do now?" I asked him. "Shoot craps?"

"I was a dope," he said. "I lost my temper and slugged you. I shouldn't have done that."

I touched the back of my head gingerly. "I'm with you, Charlie."

"But I did it," he said. "I figured it wouldn't be long before there was a call out for me. I took Bennett's car and I knew it wouldn't be long before he found that out, either. So I didn't have much chance of making time out of Pine City before I'd be picked up."

"Do you mind if I smoke?" I asked him.

"No—don't try anything smart though."

I took cigarette pack and matches out of my pocket carefully. I lit two cigarettes and gave one to Candy.

"So I got to figuring," Charlie went on. "Where is the one place that Lieutenant and the rest of the cops won't think of looking for me? And I got the answer. In somebody's apartment right here in town. Some classy joint like this one."

"Why pick on my apartment?" Candy asked in a small voice.

"Because he knew of it," I said. "He knew all about you too. He knew you'd let him stay here and you'd keep quiet about it."

"Are you crazy?" she asked me.

"Sure," Charlie said. "The Lieutenant's crazy all right, like a fox."

"I still don't get it," Candy said.

"Harry Weisman had a partner," I said. "You're looking at him right now."

The color drained out of Candy's face as she stared at Charlie.

Charlie grinned at her unpleasantly. "The copper's wise, doll. With me knowing what I know about you, I don't have any worries about you keeping your mouth shut!"

"Tell me about it, Charlie," I said. "It must have started with Bennett, I guess. What happened out there in the desert? He told me you saved his life. Were you sick or something?"

"He told you that, did he?" Charlie sneered. "The slob! I had nothing to lose and I figured he might come in useful sometime and he did."

"He did?" I said encouragingly.

"He was unconscious there for awhile," Charlie said. "And he was babbling all the time. All about his future plans. He had a lot of interesting plans and they got me interested when I listened to them. That was when I figured Bennett was worth saving. Saving him took care of my future all right."

"Just what was your future, Charlie?"

"I'm thirsty," he said. "You can make me a drink."

"I thought you only drank by the bottle?"

"Lay off!" he said bitterly. "You had to go and louse the whole deal up!"

I got to my feet and went over to the bar. I made three drinks, handed the other two around carefully, then took my own drink back to the couch.

"I could have pulled out with my nose clean if it hadn't been for you,"

Charlie said. "You had to go and throw that bottle at me."

"I still don't understand any of this," Candy said in a bewildered voice.

"A blackmail racket," I said. "Weisman was the front man, the guy who put the squeeze on the victims. He got his information from somebody on the inside of the Bald Mountain setup—Charlie."

"Oh," Candy said softly and looked away.

"Why did you have to kill Julia Grant and Weisman?" I asked Charlie.

"You can't try that on me, copper!" His voice was ugly. "I never killed anybody and you know it."

"I don't know it," I said. "Whatever your blackmail racket was, it had to be centered around something that went on up at Bald Mountain. You were blackmailing the people close to the Prophet, the Inner Group or whatever they call themselves. Romair, Pines, Candy here. Who else?"

"Find out!"

"I guess I will," I said. "Maybe Julia refused to pay anymore and was going to talk to the police, so that's why you had to kill her? Then maybe Weisman got cold feet and wanted out, so you had to kill him to shut him up permanently?"

"You're way off base, copper!" he said thickly. "I never killed nobody."

"That's nice to hear, but hard to believe," I said.

"I had a nice little racket," he said in an injured voice. "Everybody was paying off. Why should I blow the whole setup and risk the gas chamber?"

"You tell me," I suggested.

"Get me another drink!" he said. He tossed the empty glass at me and I caught it with my free hand in an automatic reflex.

"Fill it right up this time," he said. "And skip the soda. You want to louse up a Scotch on the rocks with soda, that's your business, but don't louse up my drinks that way!"

"Anything you say, Charlie," I told him.

I finished my own drink and took the two empty glasses over to the bar. "Tell me about the racket, just to satisfy my own curiosity."

He looked at Candy who still held her face averted, and that nasty grin spread across his face again. "Sure—why not? She looks like butter wouldn't melt in her mouth, don't she? You'd be surprised, copper! I've seen her up there with the rest of them. That nut with the beard talking away at them and they're all pretending to believe him."

"You mean the Prophet?"

"Who else? He's telling 'em it's O.K. by the Sun God—as if they give a damn about the Sun God! All they're worrying about is having a good time. You should see the dame with the long black hair! Looks like an iceberg, but she warms up more than any of the others. She seemed to be the leader."

"Does he have to go on?" Candy said in a muffled voice.

"I think I dig you," I said to Charlie. "Sort of organized outdoor sport with the Prophet giving his blessing?"

"'Fertility rites of the Sun God,' he called it," Charlie guffawed. "You should have watched 'em! Dancing around naked in the moonlight! It was worth seeing."

"I can imagine," I said. "With the Prophet, Eloise, Candy, Romair, Pines ... Julia and Stella?"

"Yeah!" Charlie stopped laughing suddenly. "Where the hell is that drink?"

"I was just pouring it," I said hastily.

I put ice into the two glasses and then poured a liberal dose of Scotch over the ice. "Tell me, Charlie," I said. "What are you going to do now?"

"I been thinking about that," he said. "I figured on hiding out here for a couple of days. But finding you as well has kind of loused things up."

I picked up Candy's seltzer bottle and looked at him hopefully.

"Maybe the three of us could spend a couple of days here together?"

"You're a riot, copper!" he said sourly. "I figure I got no choice. The broad don't dare talk, so I don't have to worry about her. But I do have to worry about you. I think I'm going to have to take care of you on a long-term basis, copper. I got to say I'm happy about that in a way. You loused up my nice little racket and now I'm taking care of you!"

"I was afraid you'd say that, Charlie," I said regretfully.

I pressed the plunger on the seltzer bottle. The squirt of soda hit him neatly between the eyes. He jerked backward and the gun exploded, the slug chipping plaster from the ceiling. I kept my finger on the plunger for a split-second longer, then launched myself at Charlie.

I figured I had just one chance of hitting him, so the hit had to be good. I hit him with the stiff-fingered jab to the throat with all my weight behind it. Charlie went over backward with me falling on top of him.

We landed on the floor in a mix-up of arms and legs. I disentangled myself frantically and rolled clear, coming up onto my knees. Then I relaxed a little. Charlie lay peacefully on the floor, not moving. His face was a mottled blue color.

I picked up his gun and put it into my pocket. I began to feel a little better then. I took another look at Charlie, and then a much closer look. I had been right the first time. Charlie wasn't breathing any more. My fingers still ached a little. Maybe I didn't know my own strength.

"Is he dead?" Candy asked hoarsely.

"I guess you could call it that," I said. "He's not breathing."

I walked over to the phone and called Polnik. I told him where I was and what had happened, and he said he'd be right over. I hung up and looked at Candy. "It's been a long night and it looks like it'll be still longer," I said. "How about making some coffee?"

"All right," she whispered and vanished into the kitchen.

Somewhere down the line my headache had gone. It reappeared fifteen minutes later and its name was Lavers. He bounced into the penthouse with the eagerness of a landlord come to take up the matter of the overdue rent with the young and innocent blonde. "All right, Wheeler," he snarled. "I hope you can explain this!"

"Two words," I said. "Self-defense."

"You'll have to do better than that."

Behind him, Polnik was sniffing the lingering trace of Candy's perfume and looking around hopefully. Behind him leered Doctor Murphy.

I told Lavers the story of what had happened. By the time I was through, Doc Murphy had finished his examination of the body.

"What did you figure out, Doc?" I asked him. "He's dead?"

"I didn't think you were so tough!" Murphy snorted. "He's got all the signs of a heart case to me. Maybe even that squirt of soda was enough to do it."

"The hell!" I said. "You're just jealous. For a couple of hundred bucks you too can have a body like mine, Doc."

"There's only one place your body belongs," he said sourly, "and that's in the morgue. I don't doubt it will be my pleasure to do an autopsy on you one day soon."

"Not a chance," I told him. "You're an old man now."

"I'm fifty-four!" he said in an outraged voice.

"That's what I said—an old man."

Murphy grunted explosively and looked incapable of speech for a moment. It gave the Sheriff a chance to get back into the conversation. "What about this Elliott anyway, Wheeler?"

"He was the inside partner on a blackmail racket," I said. "Weisman was his front man."

"You think he killed the Grant girl as well as Weisman?"

"I don't think he killed either of them, sir."

"Then who did?"

"I don't know yet."

"You don't ..." He took a deep breath and looked ready to explode.

I closed my eyes and waited for the explosion. It didn't come so I opened my eyes again to see why. Lavers was staring at something over my shoulder, his face a complete blank. Polnik and Murphy had matching expressions.

I turned my head slowly and saw Candy was standing just behind me, a tray in her hands. She smiled sweetly at us. "Coffee?" she asked gently.

"And who is this?" Lavers asked in an awful voice. "Florence Nightingale?"

Chapter Ten

Finally Lavers and the crew left, and it was a nice bright Sunday morning outside the windows. I looked at my watch and saw it was eight-thirty. Candy came in from the kitchen, bringing hotcakes, maple syrup, and coffee with her. She wore a terry-cloth beach jacket that came down to the top of her thighs. She could have been on a beach, except she wasn't wearing a swimsuit underneath.

Candy put the tray down on a small table in front of the couch and then sat down beside me. "What a night last night!" she said.

"You can say that again," I agreed solemnly.

She almost blushed. "I mean what with that Charlie Elliott, and that awful Sheriff. I thought he was going to bust a blood vessel when he saw me come out of the kitchen!"

"Who knows he didn't?" I said, helping myself to more food.

"Anyway," she said, "you managed to explain things all right to him, didn't you?"

"And it only took twenty minutes!" I shuddered at the memory. "If I hadn't convinced him you were the prime murder suspect, he'd never have let me stay here."

"I'm glad he did," she said softly.

"I have a confession to make," I said. "I'm normal. I'm one of those guys who's content with sex the way it was first invented. There are only a few of us left now, and we don't talk about it very much. We wouldn't want people thinking we were queer or anything."

"You're so wonderfully refreshing, Al," she said huskily. "You don't have any inhibitions at all."

"You're so right," I agreed.

"That's another thing I like about you. You act so tough and cynical all the time but underneath you're nothing but a crusader really."

"You mean one of those guys who invented the chastity belt?" I looked at her blankly. "You must be out of your mind."

There didn't seem to be any hotcakes left. I poured myself another cup of coffee and lit a cigarette. "I guess should make tracks for the office," I said.

"When will I see you again?" she asked.

"Tonight or never," I said. "If I don't find a murderer, singular or plural by tonight, the Sheriff will probably toss me in jail for impersonating a police officer."

"I wish you luck, Al," she said soberly.

"Thanks." I finished my coffee and got to my feet.

I picked up my hat from the bar and started toward the front door.

"Al?" Candy said.

"Yeah?"

"The truth about why we were all being blackmailed—will that have to be made public?"

"I don't know," I said. "Maybe not. Both Weisman and Charlie are dead.... Depends whether it was a motive for Weisman's murder or not."

"I don't think I could stand it," she said tearfully. "I'd die if the newspapers got hold of it."

"I can see it in headlines now," I said. "Fertility rites of the Sun God! Socialites prance naked under the lights of the moon!"

I started to laugh and I couldn't stop. The more I thought about it, the funnier it got. I staggered over to the couch and collapsed beside Candy, still screaming with laughter.

I stopped laughing suddenly about ten seconds later when Candy slapped my face. I looked at her blankly. "What was that for?"

"Here I am with my life ruined!" she said hysterically, "and you're dying with laughter!"

"Honey," I said, "it really isn't as terrible as all that. It's rather funny when you start to think about it."

"You cretin!" she said disgustedly.

"Huh?"

"Don't you see, that was the strength of their blackmail. The fear everyone has of being laughed at. You can get along with the reputation of a home-breaker or a femme fatale or something. It could be almost exciting to have your reputation destroyed; there could be some glamour attached to it. But to be made a laughingstock! Don't you see what would happen if the newspapers did get hold of it? It would make coast to coast headlines. Wherever any of us went afterwards, for the rest of our lives we'd be tagged with that 'Fertility rites of the Sun God' routine! And you, you big ape! You sit there and laugh!"

"I'm sorry," I said humbly.

"Get out of here!"

"Yes, ma'am."

I got nearly to the door when the coffeepot hurtled through the air toward me. I ducked in time and it bounced off the door panel, laying a coffee trail back across the white carpet toward the couch as it rolled.

"Now see what you've done!" Candy screamed. "You've ruined my carpet!"

I got out of the penthouse quickly and rode the elevator down to the foyer. My feet sank down to the ankles in carpet as I walked to the door.

"Can I get you a cab, sir?" the flunky asked as he opened the door for me.

"That's a very nice thought," I told him sincerely. "And it isn't even Christmas yet."

I drove the Healey across town to the county sheriff's office. When I walked into the office I saw a dejected figure sitting on Annabelle Jackson's desk, his shoulders slumped. Annabelle was busy typing. I wondered who were the people that Lavers wrote to all the time. Maybe I should ask Annabelle—but then the look on her face told me we weren't speaking again.

"Good morning, Sergeant," I said brightly.

Polnik made an effort and raised his head half an inch, then squinted at me through red-rimmed eyes. "Good morning, Lieutenant," he said huskily. "Did you get any sleep last night?"

"No," I said. "But it was worth it."

"Get him!" Annabelle Jackson said to nobody in particular. "The passionate lover from the penthouse!"

"How's the poetry coming?" I asked her. "Found anything to rhyme with Peter yet? How about 'purple people-eater'?"

She didn't bat an eye. Well, they can't all be winners. "Hey, how come you're working on a Sunday?" I asked her.

"Sheriff Lavers asked me to come in as a special favor," she said. "And I also get paid for it."

"Sounds reasonable," I said. "Are you sore at me about something?"

"Me?" She laughed on a high-pitched note. "Why should I be sore at you? I had a wonderful time on Friday night when you took me out and left me. I believe you're also having a wonderful time in penthouses and everything. Why should I be sore at you?"

"I just wondered," I said lamely.

"It's just that I've made a decision," she said brightly. "I've decided I shouldn't go out with older men anymore. From now on I'm going with men more or less around my own age. You know, about ten years younger than you, Al."

"Ouch!" I winced.

"Let's see," she said, "you're around forty now, aren't you?"

"I'm nowhere near forty!" I yelled.

"Aren't you?" She blinked her baby-blue eyes at me in surprise. "Well, I must say, you certainly look it!"

"When I think of all that beautiful fried chicken they have down there in the South," I said. "And they had to send us one half-baked!"

"The Sheriff is waiting in his office to see you, Lieutenant," Annabelle said coldly. "He said if you weren't here by nine-thirty that you didn't need to bother going into his office—you could turn in your shield out here. It is now nine-twenty-nine."

"Ask not for whom the bell tolls," I muttered and made a dive for Lavers' office.

Lavers sat hunched over his desk like a bird of prey—an overweight bird of prey that might have just gorged itself on a meal of Homicide lieutenants. "How nice of you to drop in, Wheeler," he said gently. "I trust I didn't spoil your morning for you?"

"No, sir," I said cautiously.

"Such a lovely morning," he said. "What with the sun shining and a blue sky. Most people are taking advantage of the glorious day. You perhaps noticed, Lieutenant, that the town is almost deserted?"

I thought maybe I should humor him. "Yes, sir," I said.

"Perhaps you wondered where they'd all gone to on this lovely Sunday morning, Lieutenant?"

"Why ... yes, sir. I did, sir."

He came up out of his chair and his fist smashed down onto his desk top, sending pens and papers flying.

"I'll tell you where they've gone!" he shouted. "They all went up to Bald Mountain at sunrise, that's where they went! And they all heard that Prophet screwball welcoming the sun! And the damned fools all dug deep in their pockets and gave their hard-earned money toward that damned shrine of his that he's never going to build. That's what they did!"

He collapsed back into his chair and looked at me malignantly. "I told you before any trouble started, Wheeler, remember? I said this Prophet is a phony! I said it's a confidence trick, I said! I said he's going to disappear with that hundred thousand dollars. We've got to stop him!"

"You said."

Lavers glared at me. "Stop interrupting me when I'm speaking. I happen to be the County Sheriff and you work for me. Is that clearly understood?"

"Yes, sir."

"Shut up! Listen to me, Wheeler. I don't care what you do today or how you do it. But by sunset tonight you're going to produce the person or persons who murdered the Grant girl and Weisman. You understand that?"

"Yes, sir."

"Shut up! And by sunset tonight, the Prophet is still going to be up there on top of Bald Mountain and so is all that money! Carry out my orders and the rest of the day is your own."

"Thank you, sir."

"Well? What are you hanging around my office for? Haven't you got enough to do?"

I tottered out of his office and closed the door behind me.

"Polnik." I tapped him on the shoulder and he nearly fell off the desk.

"Lieutenant?" He groaned.

"We have a bright busy day ahead of us," I said.

"I heard, Lieutenant."

"You heard already?"

"They heard in City Hall and that's six blocks away," he said mournfully. "The Sheriff has a powerful voice when he's excited."

"He wasn't excited, just insane," I said.

"Yes, Lieutenant," Polnik said. "Where are we going?"

"Out into the sunshine, brother," I said. "Into the glorious fresh air."

"Lieutenant," Polnik said bleakly. "Have you gone crazy, too?"

"We're off to beard the bearded Prophet in his den," I said. "We're off to Bald Mountain and the fertility rites of the Sun God."

Polnik straightened up alertly. "You mean there might be some sex in this thing, Lieutenant?"

"Let's go find out," I told him.

"We riding in your car, Lieutenant?"

"Sure."

"You sure it will take two, Lieutenant?"

"You get out there and try it," I told him. "My car is custom-built for two people—like a girdle."

Polnik goggled at me. "You mean they're building girdles for two now?"

"Leave us leave now," I said. "Before you end up with a two-way stretch."

We went out of the office to the Healey and Polnik sat beside me reluctantly as I gunned the motor.

"Take it easy, huh, Lieutenant?" he pleaded as we started. "I got enough trouble with my old lady already!"

"You have nothing to worry about," I told him. "Just so long as you don't open your eyes."

We got to the top of Bald Mountain just after eleven. All the way up the road, cars were jammed fender to fender. It could have been the Fourth of July.

When we finally made the Prophet's headquarters, I found a parking space and switched off the motor. Polnik heaved a sigh of relief, then heaved himself out of the Healey. "Like you said, Lieutenant," he grunted, "custom-built is the word!"

I led the way toward Bennett's office with Polnik lumbering along behind me. The door was closed. I knocked and tried the handle and found the door was locked. A few seconds later there was the sound of a key turning in the lock and then the door opened a couple of inches. I got a sectional view of Bennett's nose and one eye.

"Open up," I told him. "Who were you expecting—the cops?"

He opened the door wider and grinned feebly. "Hello, Lieutenant. Come on in."

I stepped inside the office with Polnik following me. Bennett closed the door again carefully.

"Sorry about that," Bennett said cheerfully. "I was just putting away the donations we received this morning. I always lock the office door when I have the safe open."

"Sounds like a sensible precaution," I said. "I hear you got a large number of donations this morning."

"It was very gratifying," he said. "Yes. I was even amazed myself at the number of people up here at sunrise this morning."

"You getting close to your hundred thousand dollars target for the shrine?"

"We're getting in sight of it, Lieutenant," he said. "Up close to the eighty thousand mark now."

"And you keep it all in that safe?" I nodded toward the floor-safe beside his desk.

"We do," he said. "But that's a very modern safe, Lieutenant. They assured me the combination is absolutely burglarproof."

"How many people know the combination?"

"Just myself and the Prophet, naturally."

"Why naturally? I thought he wasn't interested in money."

"That's true," Bennett admitted. "But we're partners in a sense."

"He puts on the show and you take in the money?"

"I don't think that's very amusing, Lieutenant!" Bennett said stiffly.

"I can't be funny all the time," I admitted.

"Ain't that the truth!" Polnik muttered behind me.

Bennett walked around his desk and sat down on the chair behind it. "Was there anything particular you wanted? Anything I can do for you gentlemen?"

"Sure," I said. "I want to talk to the Prophet."

"He's busy right now," Bennett said regretfully.

"He can talk to me here or he can talk to me in the Sheriff's office downtown," I said easily. "I don't care much either way. But he'll look kind of stupid on the front pages of tomorrow morning's papers, don't you think? I mean photographed in a loincloth and handcuffs?"

Bennett's face blanched. "I'll see if I can contact him right away!" He picked up the phone and dialed a number. After a few seconds he spoke, telling the Prophet I was in the office and I wanted to see him. Then he dropped the phone onto the cradle.

"The Prophet will be right over, Lieutenant."

"Fine," I said.

I lit myself a cigarette and looked at Bennett. He smiled vaguely at me, then snapped his fingers suddenly. "I almost forgot, Lieutenant. I got my car back this morning. Thank you very much."

"A pleasure," I said. "You should thank the Sheriff's Department."

"I certainly will," he said. "By the way, did you find Charlie as well?"

"Sure," I said.

"Oh?" He looked interested. "How is he?"

"Dead."

"Oh!"

I sat back and smoked my cigarette, reflecting smugly that there are two jobs which allow you to be really nasty to people. One is a cop's and the other is a newspaper columnist's.

The office door opened and then I didn't hear anything so I guessed it was the Prophet in his sandals. He walked up to the desk and then turned around, glaring down at me with light blue eyes, his beard bristling aggressively. "You wished to speak with me?" he asked in his resonant voice.

"Sure," I said. "I wanted to ask you some questions."

"More questions?"

"We still have two unsolved murders," I reminded him. "And I want to ask you about Charlie Elliott. Lots of questions. Won't you sit down?"

"I prefer to stand," he said. "Please come straight to the point. My time is valuable."

"Maybe the County will pay you for it," I said. "Why don't you put in an expense account to the Sheriff?"

"Please!" he said flatly. "Am I to be forced to stand here and listen to your trivial attempts at humor?"

"I gave you the chance of sitting down and listening to them," I said. "Did you know that Charlie Elliott was blackmailing some of your followers?"

"No."

"He wasn't blackmailing you?"

"The Prophet of the Sun God?" He stared at me blankly. "You dare to insinuate that I would be guilty of conduct that would render me liable to blackmail!"

Bennett cleared his throat. "Lieutenant, you have to appreciate that the Prophet is, well ... a dedicated man."

"I'm also a dedicated man," I said. "I'm dedicated to women. What's he dedicated to?"

"I am dedicated to the Sun God!" the Prophet said, his eyes shining. "I am his prophet here on earth. I am here to spread his word among the people!"

"And to spread his seed?"

He looked down at me again. "I do not understand."

"The people Elliott was blackmailing were the people who attended your little ceremonies," I said. "You know the one I mean? The fertility rites of the Sun God?"

He folded his arms across his chest impassively. "They are sacred rites of the Sun God. How dare he defile the ritual with—"

"They might be sacred to the Sun God," I said. "To most other people they'd simply be immoral."

"But not illegal," Bennett said quickly. "Those who participated in the fertility rites did so of their own free will and they were all adults over twenty-one years of age."

"Did you get their autographs as well?" I said.

"The Sun God demands obedience," the Prophet said. "Those that would follow him must worship him and take part in his rituals and ceremonies. He demands sacrifices of them. He demands their full allegiance! If they will not give of themselves to him, then he will cast his wrath upon them."

His voice swelled like a Hammond organ with all the stops out. "And if they will not give of themselves to the Sun God, then will come the day of no dawn when darkness shall cover the earth and everything thereupon will wither and die!"

"We've had a couple of people wither and die already," I said. "That's why I'm here now."

The Prophet didn't seem to have heard me. He stood there, immobile, a look of rapture on his face.

"Speaking of sacrifice," I said, "you prophesied a great sacrifice would be made, and the next thing that happened was we found Julia Grant's body stretched out on that altar of yours. How do you explain that coincidence?"

"When the Prophet talks of sacrifice, he's talking of personal sacrifice," Bennett said hastily. "That is, I mean, financial sacrifice to help build the shrine."

"Do tell," I said coldly.

Bennett shifted around in his chair a little. "The Prophet isn't the same as you and me, Lieutenant."

"That's right," I agreed. "He's the only one out of the three of us with a beard. Do me a favor, Bennett. When I ask the Prophet a question, let him answer it."

"Oh, sure," Bennett said. "I was only trying to help."

"You're kidding," I said wearily.

I looked at the Prophet again. "You're going to join the Sun God at sunset this evening?"

"So it is written," he said.

"You really believe it will happen?"

"I know it will happen."

I gave up. "O.K. No more questions."

The Prophet walked lithely toward the door of the office.

"There is just one thing," I said. "If that eighty thousand dollars disappears out of that safe at the same time you disappear, I'll catch up with you if I have to walk up a rainbow to do it!"

The Prophet opened the door and stepped outside. Bennett looked at me and shook his head sorrowfully. "You shouldn't have said that, Lieutenant. He could be offended!"

"You think I care?" I snarled at him.

I pressed the flat of my hand against my forehead for a moment and closed my eyes.

"You feeling all right, Lieutenant?" Polnik asked anxiously. "You're not sick or anything?"

"Just confused," I said. "Let's get out of here." I got up off the chair and walked toward the door.

"What are we going to do, Lieutenant?" Polnik asked.

"You look for nuts and I'll look for bolts," I said. "Then we'll spend the afternoon fitting them together."

"The heat's got you, Lieutenant," he said dubiously. "The same way it's got that Prophet guy!"

"You could be right," I agreed as we got outside Bennett's office. "Look, I want you to stick around for a while. Keep an eye on that office. You see anybody come out of there with a suitcase, you nail him!"

"Sure, Lieutenant," Polnik said confidently.

I was halfway to Eloise's cabana when I heard him panting along behind me. I turned around and waited until he caught up with me. "What now?"

"Lieutenant," Polnik gasped for breath. "What sort of suitcase was it you're looking for?"

Chapter Eleven

Eloise opened the door of her cabana and looked at me frostily. "Yes?" she asked.

"I wanted to talk to you," I said.

"You'd better come in."

I followed her inside the cabana. She was wearing a white bikini which contrasted nicely with her dark tan. She gestured toward a chair. I sat down in it and she sat in a chair opposite me.

"What did you want to talk to me about, Lieutenant?" she asked in that cool, remote voice.

"I talked to Charlie Elliott last night," I said. "He was the inside man of the blackmail racket. Harry Weisman was his front man."

"Blackmail?" She raised her eyebrows. "I don't think I understand."

"The fertility rites of the Sun God," I said. "Charlie told me about them, all about them. He and Weisman were blackmailing the people who took part. You were being blackmailed too, weren't you?"

"No."

It was my turn to raise my eyebrows. "You weren't?"

"No, I wasn't." She smiled aloofly. "But don't put the wrong construction on that, Lieutenant. No one could blackmail me because I would have nothing to pay them with."

"You expect me to believe that?"

"You can check on it," she said. "The Prophet provides me with a home here. I have all I need."

"And you're content with a cabana and being the Prophet's girl friend?"

She flushed. "Yes ... if you want to put it that way."

"Charlie told me you were the life and soul of the fertility rites."

The flush deepened across her cheeks. "Did he?"

"That's what he said. What are you going to do for a home after tonight—and a boy friend?"

"You don't make any sense, Lieutenant!" she said impatiently.

"At sunset the Prophet joins the Sun God, doesn't he?" I said. "That means he won't be around tomorrow. Of course he may turn into a little ray of sunshine but that won't be any comfort to you in the long winter evenings."

"I think I'll get by," she said easily.

"Do you have any plans?"

"None at the moment."

"Maybe you don't believe the Prophet is going to disappear?"

"I most certainly do," she said. "If he says he is going to join the Sun God at sunset, then he will."

"When I first came up here I used to think everybody else was crazy," I said. "Now I'm becoming convinced it's just me."

"You're probably right, Lieutenant," she said sweetly.

I looked at her again. "You're the Prophet's handmaiden. You don't think you'll be called to join the Sun God at the same time?"

"I don't think so," she said. "The Prophet would have told me, if it were to be so."

"And he hasn't suggested it, not even confidentially just to you?"

"No."

"All right," I said. "I hope it's a mild winter for you, that's all."

"It will be," she said confidently. "I have certain advantages in the battle for survival, Lieutenant."

"And that bikini is just the right dressing for them," I said appreciatively. "See you at sunset."

"You'll be here then, Lieutenant?"

"Seeing the Prophet join the Sun God is something I wouldn't miss for all the starlets at M.G.M.," I told her.

I left the cabana and started to walk back to where I'd left the Healey. I was about five yards away from it, when a car in the row ahead started suddenly, moving out toward the road.

The white Continental hardtop was a car I couldn't fail to recognize. "Hey!" I yelled. "Stella! Wait a minute!" The hardtop kept on moving forward. I started to run after it but then it accelerated, chopping off a little Volkswagen that was nosing its way out.

I stopped running and stood watching as the Continental barrelled down the roadway. I could hear the driver of the Volkswagen still cursing fluently as I walked back to the Healey. I'll catch her before she gets to the bottom of the mountain, I thought, as I got into the Healey, and the only thing wrong with that thought was that I didn't. A quarter of the way down, the traffic was solid both ways, the cars fender to fender as they had been on the way up. I had no hope of catching the Continental. I didn't even have the chance of overtaking the next car in front.

Finally I got back onto a civilized highway and bowled across town to the Gibb home. I felt annoyed with Stella. She must have damned well heard me shouting to her. If she'd stopped then, she could have saved me an hour's drive.

I swung the Healey in to the driveway and parked it behind the Continental. I got out and walked across to the porch and pushed the button. I listened to the chimes impatiently and then Stella opened the door.

She was wearing a deep blue chemise that made her look better than a French postcard. Her eyes were cold as she looked at me.

"I wasn't driven to suicide during the night after that charming scene with Cornelius," she said. "Disappointed?"

"Not really," I said. "Why the hell didn't you stop when I called you?"

She stared at me blankly. "What are you talking about?"

"You know damned well what I'm talking about," I said. "Up on the mountain. You started to move your car out of the parking lot. I was right behind you, yelling my head off. You must have heard me."

"Sorry," she said. "Wrong car—wrong girl."

"Don't give me that!" I said tersely. "I'd know that white Continental hardtop anywhere."

She moistened her lips with her tongue absently. "Wait a minute. When did this happen?"

"You know exactly when it happened. About an hour ago."

She nodded. "Now it makes a little sense. Right car, wrong driver."

"I've had enough double-talk this morning to last me the rest of my life," I said. "Don't you start."

"I'll make it simple," she said. "For some reason Cornelius took my car when he went out this morning. So it was Cornelius you were shouting at and not me."

"You can do better than that!" I said.

"Take another look," she said coldly.

I turned my head slowly and looked. The car standing on the driveway was the convertible, not the hardtop. I'd been in too much of a hurry to take a good look at it on my way over to the porch.

"I'm sorry," I apologized. "My mistake."

"That's all right," she said. "You look hot. Why don't you come in and have a drink?"

"That's the first sensible suggestion I've heard today," I said.

I followed Stella inside the house into the living room. I sat on the couch while she made the drinks.

"Why would Cornelius take your car instead of his own?" I asked her.

"I wouldn't know," she said. "But the convertible isn't his anyway. It's mine. He's got the use of it for about three weeks longer and then he'll start walking again!"

"How's that?"

"I was talking to my lawyer this morning," she said. "The divorce comes up for hearing in three weeks from now."

She walked back to the couch with the drinks and sat down, handing me a glass. "So Cornelius might as well make the most of the cars while he has the chance."

"Three weeks?" I said. "That's fast, isn't it?"

"Not particularly," she said. "It was filed a little over two months ago. My lawyer's been trying to hurry it through."

"You're divorcing Cornelius?"

"You're surprised it isn't the other way round? You don't flatter me, Al. But then, you never have in the few days I've known you. Sure, I'm divorcing Cornelius. It was easy enough to set up. A certain friend of my lawyer's handled it. Five hundred dollars for him and two hundred for the girl. The girl picks up Cornelius in a bar and I get a set of perfect pictures the next day. It was cheap at the price."

"There are all sorts of ways of making a living," I said.

"So Cornelius gets nothing!" Stella said savagely. "He can go back to his beach and wait for the next female sucker to come along. Or he can starve, for all I care. Or preferably throw himself under a truck!"

"It must give you a deep, warm feeling inside," I said, "feeling about him the way you do."

"He's only getting what he's got coming to him," Stella said.

"Does he know about it?"

She smiled again and took a deep breath which strained the tensile strength of the chemise. "He knows about it all right. I gave him a duplicate set of the photos the very next day. I wanted him to be able to appreciate his position."

"Just to think," I said, "if you'd been born a hundred years ago in the Fiji Isles, you could have been something harmless like a cannibal."

"You're a man," she said, "so you're on Cornelius' side. But you don't know the things he's done to me."

"Sure," I said hastily. "But let's not get into details. Why would he be on Bald Mountain this morning, do you think?"

"I never could figure out a reason for most of the things he does," she said.

"He must have had some sort of reason," I persisted.

Stella shrugged impatiently. "Why don't you ask him?"

"I would," I said patiently, "if I could find him. I thought it was you I was chasing, remember?"

"I took him up there a couple of times when the Prophet first started holding his meetings," she said. "He might have gone up there to say hello to them again or something."

"You never told me Cornelius had been up on Bald Mountain before."

"You never asked me," she said.

"Who did he meet up there?"

"Most of the gang," she said. "After the second time I didn't take him anymore. He's got an eye that roves just as much as mine does. He didn't get along with the Prophet or Ralph, either. All in all he was better out of it."

"Was there any particular direction his eye roved?"

"He seemed to be around Candy Logan and Eloise most of the time he was up there," Stella said. "I didn't see too much of what he was doing myself. I was busy at the time." Her lips curved into a reminiscent smile.

"I heard about the fertility rites," I said casually and watched her mouth harden.

I told her briefly the story of Charlie Elliott and what he had said before he died.

"That dirty little lush!" Stella said coldly. "He was faking the whole time, huh? I wish I could have got my hands on him!"

"It's a little late for that," I said. "Unless you want to go down to the morgue?"

She shuddered. "You don't have to take me literally. But when I think of the money I paid Weisman! With Charlie getting half of it all the time!"

"It's a logical thought that one of the people being blackmailed could have killed Weisman," I said. "Thinking they'd stop the blackmail then. But why kill Julia—and why kill her before Weisman?"

"You're the cop," Stella said indifferently. "Why ask me?"

"I have a theory," I said. "Weisman was friendly with Julia Grant, yet he must have been blackmailing her at the same time."

"Having a boy friend who's blackmailing you at the same time would have appealed to Julia," Stella said, "The way it appealed to me when I took him away from her!"

"Sure," I said. "But maybe Weisman had a better reason for cultivating Julia. Once the blackmail started, everybody being blackmailed must have suspected that one of them had tipped off Harry Weisman."

"I guess they did," Stella admitted. "There was a time when people weren't talking to each other very much."

"Charlie might have worked an angle there," I said. "He could have realized that sooner or later, one of the group might start thinking about him. So before they did, he told Weisman to make a play for Julia. Then when the others saw what was happening they'd think Julia had tipped him off."

"Could be," Stella said. "It's all history now, isn't it?"

"Not until the murderer's in the gas chamber," I said.

Stella got to her feet again. "Would you like another, drink, Al?"

"Fine," I said and handed her my empty glass. "Fun and games with the fertility rites. Did the Prophet actually take part or did he just sit on the sidelines and cheer?"

"He took part sometimes," Stella said. "He was the main reason I joined in. He's quite a man, you know."

She came back to the couch with the fresh drinks. "I guess he's the main reason for everything that goes on up there. I'm sure Candy Logan and Julia felt the same way I did."

"How about Eloise?"

"Now there's an enthusiastic girl when she gets started," she said. "Her only trouble was being the Prophet's chosen girl. She had to be very careful. He's a very jealous man—I don't mean in a small, mean way like Cornelius for instance. But with his deep convictions he believed that Eloise should only take him as a partner in the rites, as she was his chosen handmaiden."

"That could make it tough for Eloise," I suggested.

"I wouldn't have minded if I'd been her," Stella said dreamily.

I gulped down my second drink. "What do you think's going to happen at sunset tonight? You think the Prophet will trip along a sunbeam into the bright blue yonder?"

"I don't know how it will happen," she said seriously, "But I'm sure that somehow it will happen. He's that sort of man, Al. He's a very great man in some ways, I think. He's almost superhuman. If he says he'll be called to join the Sun God at sunset today, then he will."

"How much have you kicked in toward the shrine?" I asked her.

"About five thousand," she said casually. "You can laugh about that if you want to, but I feel I owe the Prophet something. He gave me something I never had before in all my life. A sort of faith in myself, I guess. A hope, anyway, that there was something bigger and better than all the physical sordidness and hysterical emotionalism. I can't quite explain it."

"You have me worried now," I told her. "I can't make up my mind who's the bigger liar—you or the Prophet."

She grinned at me. "You're beyond all hope, Al Wheeler! You won't even make a pass at me when I throw myself at you."

"That's because I'm not sure whether you're a double murderess yet," I said. "Call me later and I'll let you know. But if you're calling from the death cell, don't bother."

"I won't," she said placidly.

I finished the second drink and stood up. "Thanks for the drinks, Stella. I should be going."

"I'll walk you to your car," she said.

We got out onto the porch and walked toward the Healey.

"You're one of the most baffling women I ever met," I told her as I got into the car. "And you still have me baffled. I can't quite figure out whether you're really a screwball or just playing at being one."

"There's a difference?" She grinned at me again. "I think you worry too much, Al Wheeler. Go catch your murderer and then maybe we can talk about it."

"Are you going to be up on the mountain at sunset to wish the Prophet bon voyage?"

"I'll be there," she said. "I'm going to stick around here until late this afternoon, though, and watch developments."

"Developments?"

"I just happened to check on Cornelius' room this morning." she said. "He's packed and taken his bags with him. If he thinks he's taking my car too, he's mistaken. If he's not back before I leave this afternoon, I'm reporting the car as stolen!"

"Maybe he bought a ticket on the same sunbeam the Prophet's riding out?" I said.

"I don't think that's very funny!" Stella said in a cold voice.

"Neither do I," I said soberly.

Chapter Twelve

I stopped long enough to have a steak in a diner on my way back through town and got back to the office around two-thirty. The typewriter was still clattering away as I walked in. I stopped beside Annabelle's desk and looked at her. "The Sheriff in?"

"He's in his office," she said curtly.

"Has he cooled off?" I asked her.

"I wouldn't know," she murmured.

I stared at her a moment. "Well, if I find he hasn't, I'll send him out here to the deepfreeze, O.K.?"

I knocked on Lavers' door and walked in. He was sitting behind his desk nursing his ulcer from the look on his face. Or maybe the ulcer was nursing him. At any rate, he looked his normal self.

"Well?" he said hopefully.

"Nothing to report, Sheriff," I said. "I left Polnik up there keeping an eye on the money. Anything new with you?"

"Nothing," he said. "Oh, one thing. Doctor Murphy was right about Elliott. He did have a heart condition. The doctor thinks he was probably dead before you even touched him. He's signing the cause of death as heart failure. That means you don't have to worry about a murder or manslaughter indictment. It makes our records tidier, too."

"I'm glad it helps the records," I said. "Do we have a pair of binoculars I can borrow?"

"There's a pair in that cupboard," he said. "What do you want them for?"

"I'd like to keep a close eye on the Prophet's take-off," I said.

I went over and opened the cupboard and took out the binoculars. Lavers watched me with a look of growing irritation on his face. "The way you're going on, you'd think this was a free fireworks display or something!" he said sourly. "I hope you haven't forgotten what I said to you this morning, Wheeler!"

"No, sir," I said. "And neither has anyone else for six blocks around here."

"Hadn't you better get back up there and make sure everything's all right?"

"Yes, sir," I said politely.

I'd almost reached the door when he called me back.

"Wheeler," his voice was almost pleading. "I could still call in Homicide. Between us we could put fifty men up there and cover the road leading up there and everything."

"I'd rather you didn't, Sheriff," I said, feeling like the guy who volunteered to put the noose around his own neck.

"Why?"

"I have a sort of hunch, sir," I said feebly.

Lavers brooded over that one for what seemed like two minutes. "All right," he said finally. "I just hope you know what you're doing, Wheeler, that's all!"

"Amen!" I said.

I took the binoculars with me out of his office and past Annabelle's desk. She had stopped typing and was reading a slender volume bound in red calf. I stopped beside her desk and had a look at the title. *Poems: Peter Pines*. So Pines had been holding out on me, he had been published.

"I bet he paid for the printing himself," I said.

"You have no appreciation of the finer things of life, do you, Al Wheeler?" Annabelle said loftily.

"I have my hi-fi machine," I said. "I go out with girls. What else is there?"

She sniffed loudly. "If you don't know, it's too late for you to learn now."

"I was forgetting my age for a moment," I said.

She looked at the binoculars in my hand. "What on earth are you going to do with those things?"

"The girl in the apartment opposite mine," I said confidentially. "She keeps forgetting to pull down the shades."

"Disgusting!" Annabelle said in a horrified voice.

"Not yet," I said cheerfully. "But I'm hoping, that's why I've got the binoculars."

I went back to the Healey and drove toward Bald Mountain again. When I reached the turn-off I saw two Sheriff's Department cars parked on the side. I pulled the Healey over beside them and stopped. One of the drivers got out and came over: "Hi, Lieutenant," he said when he recognized me. "What's all the excitement about?"

"I was going to ask you the same thing," I said.

"No excitement with us," he said. "Sheriff figures there's going to be a traffic snarl here later in the afternoon. Sent us over to take care of it. Some guy's pulling off some sort of stunt around sunset up on top of the mountain, I hear."

"Is that so?" I said. "I just wondered."

"I hear they're keeping you busy with a couple of murders, Lieutenant." He grinned at me. "Never a dull moment, huh?"

"Depends where you're sitting," I said. "You haven't seen a white Continental, hardtop or convertible, go up during the last couple of hours or so?"

He scratched his head. "Sorry, Lieutenant, I haven't. We've only been here around twenty minutes anyway. What do you want us to do if we do see one?"

"Nothing," I said. "A guy I want to talk to is driving one of them, that's all. I guess I can drive up there myself and see if it's already there." I swung back onto the road again. This time the traffic going up wasn't so bad, but it was early yet.

I found room for the Healey close to Bennett's office and got out. I started walking and five minutes later I found Polnik stretched out in some long grass, fast asleep. I kicked him in the ribs gently and he grunted. I kicked him again a little harder and this time he answered. "Sadie!" he mumbled. "Can't you let a guy rest? I been working all night and ..."

The third time I let him have it and he yelled and sat up quickly at the same time. He looked up at me and blinked. A sickly smile spread across his face, wavered, then vanished. He hauled himself quickly to his feet, his face a bright red.

"Just how many guys with suitcases came out of that office?" I asked him.

"Sure sorry, Lieutenant," he mumbled. "But what with the sun and everything—That guy Bennett left the office around one anyway and he locked the door behind him, so I figured everything would be O.K."

"Eighty thousand bucks inside the office and you figure it's safe because somebody locks the door?"

"Well," he shuffled his feet together. "I guess I ..."

"Never mind," I said. "You'd better see if you can get yourself something to eat."

"Thanks, Lieutenant." Polnik brightened up a little. "I saw a guy setting up a hamburger stand over at the far side."

"I'll be around somewhere close to the office when you come back," I said.

I lit myself a cigarette and ambled slowly back toward the office. I got there just in time to see Bennett unlocking the door. He straightened up and smiled when he saw me. "Hello there, Lieutenant. How's everything?"

"Fine," I said. "Looks like you're going to do some more big business tonight."

"It certainly does," he said. "I think we'll reach the total needed for the shrine without any trouble at all."

"Where are you going to build it?" I asked him. "Up there where the altar is now?"

"That's the exact spot," he said. "You see, we built the altar as a symbol of sacrifice. Once we have the money for the shrine, the sacrifice—or the symbol of it, rather—is no longer needed. So we'll take down the altar and build the shrine in its place."

"What sort of shrine are you going to build? You have a design for it yet?"

"Not yet.... Why don't you come inside for a moment, Lieutenant? To be honest I was thinking of having a drink. Before I have to start work again."

"Thanks," I said and followed him into the office.

He opened the small bar in the wall and I sat in one of the chairs facing his desk. He made the drinks and handed me one. It tasted good.

"What work do you have to do?" I asked him.

"Well," he smiled almost shamefacedly, "after the crowds we had this morning, I felt sure we'd get just as big crowds this afternoon and I should organize for them. So I contacted a few people and we have a hamburger stand and a few people selling pop and stuff like that. We get a percentage of course. It all helps toward the shrine."

"Might even help with the design," I said. "You could have a bottle of pop rampant on top of a hamburger done in bronze. It would look very effective—wreathe the whole thing with a platinum sunbeam."

"You will have your joke, Lieutenant!" Bennett said coldly.

"A humorist is like a prophet," I said, "without honor in his own country."

Bennett concentrated on his drink without saying anything.

"I remembered something I forgot to ask you about this morning," I said. "When did you first meet the Prophet?"

"Some six months ago," he said.

"Where?"

"I forget the exact location. Carmel, it could have been. Yes, I think it must have been Carmel. We stayed at the same hotel. He told me of his beliefs, his ambitions. I was impressed. I'm a businessman primarily, as you know, Lieutenant. I could see the possibilities were quite exciting."

"So could Charlie Elliott," I said.

"I'm sorry," Bennett looked puzzled. "I don't exactly follow ..."

"Charlie told me about the time he pulled you out of e desert," I said. "You were delirious and babbling. You told him all about your plans then, even if you didn't know you were telling him. He thought they sounded good enough to provide him with a future as well—a blackmail racket."

Bennett shook his head slowly. "So that's why he turned up here! Can you imagine that!"

"It would be interesting to know what exactly it was you said about your plans that made Charlie see the opportunities for blackmail, wouldn't it?"

"It certainly would," Bennett said urbanely. "Except that no such possibilities could have existed in my plans at that time or any time." He smiled at me gently. "I think Charlie was kidding you a little, Lieutenant. Why don't you ask him again about it? ... Of course! I was forgetting, you can't, can you? You told me this morning. Charlie's dead, isn't he?"

I finished the drink and put the empty glass on his desk.

"Thank you for the drink, Bennett," I said. "You know, you're wasting your talents. John Foster Dulles could use a man like you."

I walked out of the office again and met Polnik returning from his lunch.

"Everything O.K., Lieutenant?" he asked anxiously. "Nobody sneaked out with a suitcase this morning, did they?"

"I guess not," I said.

"Fine!" He sighed deeply. "What do we do now, Lieutenant? Go question some dames, huh?"

"That hamburger must have done you a lot of good," I said. "We stick around for awhile. I still want to make sure that nobody walks out of that office with that eighty grand. The Sheriff wouldn't like it."

We stuck around through the long hot afternoon. Bennett left the office around four, carefully locking the door behind him again. He didn't come back. From five o'clock on, there was a constant stream of cars arriving. A dense crowd was already beginning to form in front of the altar.

At six o'clock it was forty minutes till sunset. I had never seen so many cars jammed into the available parking space and still they kept on coming. The crowd in front of the altar was a solid mass stretching right back to the cars. Some people were beginning to scramble onto the roofs of the nearest cars to get a better view.

I lit what must have been the twentieth cigarette that afternoon and turned to Polnik. "I want you to get up to the front of that crowd—right in front of that altar."

"But, Lieutenant!" He looked worried. "How will I ever get through all those people?"

"Wave your shield at them," I said. "You're a cop, aren't you?"

"Yeah!" He grinned happily. "I forgot!"

"Be sure and remember when you want to walk, to push one foot in front of the other!" I snarled at him.

"What do I do when I get in front of that altar?" Polnik asked humbly.

"You watch," I said. "You watch that Prophet like your life depended on it. He says he's going to join the Sun God. I want you to watch him all the time. Don't let anything distract your attention—you got that?"

"Sure, I got it, Lieutenant."

"You watch the Prophet and nothing else," I said. "You don't watch Eloise, either!"

"O.K.," Polnik said sadly. "If a dame takes off all her clothes right next to me, I don't even peek!"

"That's right," I said. "When it's all over I want to know just exactly where the Prophet is, and I'll expect you to tell me."

"Sure, Lieutenant. I can watch a guy—that's simple!"

"I hope you're right," I said. "You'd better get there now."

"Sure, Lieutenant. What are you going to do?"

"I'm going to ponder the science of levitation," I said.

"Yeah?" Polnik said wistfully. "I wish I was a lieutenant, Lieutenant. That sure sounds great!"

"You'd better hold your shield so you can read it," I said wearily. "In case you forget what it says on the way."

"Thanks, Lieutenant. That's a swell idea."

I watched him go until even his bulky figure was swallowed up and lost in the crowd. I checked my watch again and it said six-fifteen. Twenty-five minutes to sunset. I walked over to Stella's cabana casually. I looked around when I reached the front of it. Nobody seemed to be watching me—they were all going the other way toward the edge of the mountain. I walked around the back of the cabana and the ground there was deserted.

I put one foot on the window sill and heaved myself up so that I got a grip on the eave. I gave another convulsive heave and then I was sprawled across the flat roof of the cabana.

I sat up and took the binoculars out of the case, then pointed them in the direction of the altar and started to focus them. The altar sprang up with startling nearness as I found the right focus. I saw there was a microphone standing just in front of it. I swept the crowd with the binoculars, seeing there were half a dozen amplifiers installed at strategic spots. It looked like some more of Bennett's organization. The Prophet's last words were going to be heard by everyone present.

I put the glasses down and lit a cigarette. The sun hung low in the sky now, directly behind the altar and the cliff-edge just beyond, but it still burned with a brilliant, dazzling intensity.

Checking my watch again I saw there were still sixteen minutes to go. I looked across the huge crowd and saw a small ripple passing slowly down it. I lifted the glasses and picked up the cause of the ripple. It was the crowd making way for Eloise and the Prophet as they moved slowly toward the altar.

The Prophet strode majestically, his arms swinging freely, his fists clenched. Behind him, Eloise walked, her face cold and remote, the white robe swinging.

I let the glasses fall again. Faintly I could hear the low continuous murmur of the crowd, punctuated by the hoarse cries of the vendors still selling their hot dogs and pop up till the last minute.

A bee droned aimlessly past, its hum suddenly loud in my ear. The sun still beat down strongly and impartially over everything and everyone.

I had a sudden, curious feeling of unreality. I wondered if this was the way the world would end. With the girls in their summer dresses sitting on the grass and eating hot dogs while a man with a beard, wearing nothing but a loincloth, was suddenly incinerated to a crisp before their eyes, and even as they watched, the Sun God himself suddenly poured forth his wrath and in one split second plunged the world into everlasting darkness, into the eternal day of no dawn where all should perish.

Then they reached the altar.

Chapter Thirteen

Slowly the huge crowd fell silent as Eloise and the Prophet climbed up to the top of the altar and faced them. I had them both in focus in the glasses and I saw Eloise take a step forward and raise both her arms slowly above her head.

"Friends," I heard that clear, liquid voice roll back to me from the amplifiers, "friends," she repeated more softly, "and worshippers of the Sun God. This is a momentous occasion for us all! Our leader, the Prophet of the Sun God, has said that at sunset of this day he will be called to join the Sun God in full view of us all."

She paused for a moment and when she spoke again, her voice was pitched lower. "This is a day of rejoicing, but also a day of sadness for us all. The greatness of the Prophet will pass from us this day. Never again will his passionate faith call us forth to worship at the departure of the Sun God in the evening and his return in the morning. Never again shall we know the warmth and comfort of his faith. But with him, we can rejoice in his everlasting union with the Sun God!"

Her voice rose again. "But when he has gone, at this place, in this very spot where I now stand ... we shall erect a glorious shrine to everlastingly commemorate this unique and wonderful event. I ask you sincerely, those of you who have not already made sacrifice, to help toward the cost of building this shrine. Give, and give freely, for never again shall we see on this earth one of such true faith as the Prophet of the Sun God!"

Eloise bowed her head in supplication for a long moment, then stepped down from the altar, and the crowd parted to make way for her.

The Prophet stepped forward, his head held high, his beard thrusting outward aggressively. "My friends," he held out both arms toward the crowd, "fellow worshippers of the Sun God! The joy, the pride, the exultation I feel this day I cannot describe to you. Within minutes now, I shall leave you forever! To be united in that glorious everlasting warmth and light that is the Sun God. I am truly fortunate!"

I turned my glasses away from his face and tried to pick up Eloise in the crowd but I couldn't. I heard the Prophet's voice droning on without listening to the words. I swept the glasses back across the crowd again and again but she had disappeared completely from sight.

I lit another cigarette and looked at my watch. There were exactly two minutes to sunset over Bald Mountain. Then I raised the glasses and focused on the Prophet again.

The dying sun behind him outlined his whole body in golden fire. I squinted as the rays hit my eyes through the glasses. It was almost impossible to see anything clearly.

"I go now, my friends, my fellow worshippers!" the Prophet shouted exultantly. "And when I have gone, you must build the glorious shrine that will forever stand on the crest of Bald Mountain that men may never forget the power of the Sun God and the meeting of the Sun God and his Prophet today!"

Slowly the Prophet turned around so that he faced directly into the sun. He lifted both arms toward the golden orb in a gesture of welcome. "Mighty Sun God!" His voice vibrated powerfully. "Fulfill thy prophesy! Take me, thy faithful Prophet that I may become as one with thee! Let this be an undying proof of your greatness!"

He dropped his hands to his sides suddenly and for a moment there was silence. The rim of the sun dropped below the edge of Bald Mountain and someone in the crowd began to scream hysterically.

There was a faint crackling sound and then a sudden pall of smoke seemed to rise from the ground and enshroud the altar and the figure of the Prophet above it.

Screams came from every section of the crowd and I crossed my fingers that Polnik could see better than I could through my glasses. All I could see was the thick pall of smoke.

For what seemed an interminable time, the smoke hung like an impenetrable curtain. Then slowly it drifted away and the clean, rectangular shape of the altar could be seen again.

A howl went up from the crowd as the last vestiges of the smoke drifted away.

The Prophet had vanished.

I watched for a moment, seeing the people nearest the altar start to run forward. I finally found Polnik in the lenses. I saw his face, red with determination, as he pounded around the altar and then on and up to the very edge of the spur. I saw him stop at the edge and look down the eight hundred foot drop to the floor of the valley below. I saw him shake his head slowly and I watched the expression of complete bewilderment creep over his face.

Then I swung the glasses away again. Polnik would have to search for the vanishing Prophet as best he could. I had other, more urgent things to do if my hunch had paid off.

The glasses picked up the front of Bennett's office and I refocused them carefully so that the door seemed to leap up and almost hit me in the face. There was something different about the door from the last time I'd seen it. Now it wasn't locked. It had swung inward a couple of inches and moved fractionally in the breeze. It looked like my hunch was right.

I returned the glasses to their case and left them on the roof. I remembered what Annabelle had said about my age, so I closed my eyes the moment before I jumped off the roof.

My feet hit the grass with a jarring thud and I sprawled forward on my hands and knees. I picked myself up painfully, and headed toward the office. The noise of the crowd was deafening, beating against my eardrums in what seemed ever-increasing waves. I thought I could hear a siren faintly a long way away.

Twenty seconds later I reached the door of Bennett's office and stopped there for a moment until I had the .38 in my hand. I'm no coward, I'm just not a hero, that's all.

I put the flat of my hand against the door and pushed gently. The door swung inward silently and I slipped into a small hall. I could see the three figures framed in a tableau in the main room, their backs toward me.

Eloise had changed out of her white robe into a dark sweater and skirt. They were more in keeping with the gun in her hand, anyway. Cornelius Gibb was wearing his white sports coat and tan slacks; the expression on his face didn't match the rest of his outfit.

Bennett's face was gray as he looked at them. "You're crazy!" he said hoarsely. "You'll never get away with this!"

"We won't if you stall us much longer," Eloise said crisply. "If we have too, we'll shoot out the lock, but I'll make sure we shoot you first!"

"Don't be a sucker, Ralph!" Cornelius said. "Save yourself some grief. Open it up!"

"You won't get to the highway even," Bennett said shakily. "The police will pick you up and—" He moaned softly as Cornelius' elbow drove brutally into his solar plexus.

"You can skip the funeral notices!" Cornelius said tautly. He raised his right hand, then brought it down in a vicious, chopping movement so that the edge of his hand smashed into the bridge of Bennett's nose.

Bennett went down on his hands and knees and began to sob harshly.

"Next time I'll do some permanent damage!" Cornelius whispered. "This is your last chance, Ralph. You going to open it or not?"

"Yes!" Bennett said feebly. "Yes! Don't hit me again."

"The quicker you open it, the less chance you have of Cornelius hitting you again, Ralph," Eloise said coolly. "I'd hurry if I were you."

Still on his hands and knees, Bennett shuffled around until he was facing the safe. His fingers shook as he started to turn the dial. The other two watched him intensely and so did I.

There was a sharp click and Bennett took his hand away from the dial. The safe door swung open slowly. Cornelius said something impatiently obscene and grabbed the handle pulling the door open wide.

The silence inside the office expanded suddenly in intensity, in strict contrast to the noise of the crowd outside. I could see into the safe over Bennett's shoulder from where I stood in the doorway. I could see the emptiness of it, except for the few folded papers and documents on the shelf.

"That's very amusing, Ralph," Eloise said in an emotionless voice. "Now tell us where the money is."

"It's ... it's gone!" Bennett said, his voice shaking. "It's not possible!"

Cornelius grabbed the lapels of Bennett's coat, pulling him to his feet and shaking him violently. "Where is it!" he almost screamed into Bennett's face. "What did you do with it! Eighty grand! It's ours, you hear! Ours! Eighty grand doesn't get up out of a safe and walk away all by itself! What did you do with it!"

Bennett gurgled in terror. "I don't know!" he pleaded frantically. "I swear I don't know! It was all there this morning. It was there at noon when I left the office! I know it was. I counted it all and then I put it away myself!"

Cornelius hit him twice and Bennett's head jerked violently from one side to the other. "I'll strangle you with my bare hands!" Cornelius said. "I'll stamp you to death! I'll—"

"Shut up!" Eloise said suddenly, her voice like a whiplash.

Cornelius looked at her blankly for a moment. "It's our money!" he said in a reedy voice. "Eighty grand, and it's all ours. And this bastard has double-crossed us! He's hidden it somewhere else!" He started to shake Bennett again.

"You fool!" Eloise said scornfully. "You never stop to think, do you? If he's hidden it somewhere else, he can always come back and get it another time. And so can we! All we have to do is take him with us. Once we get him from here, we'll have plenty of time to persuade him to tell us where he put the money." Her voice sounded like ice water running slowly. "I'm sure we'll be able to persuade him."

"Yeah!" Cornelius relaxed his grip on Bennett slowly. "Sure—that's it. I've got to hand it to you, Eloise. You've got brains."

"And you've got a beautiful body," she said drily. "If I really had brains I wouldn't let those muscles of yours throw me the way they do."

He laughed confidently. "You and me, babe," he said. "We make beautiful music together."

"Let's make some beautiful money first," she said. "Let's get him out of here for a start."

"Sure," Cornelius nodded. He grabbed hold of Bennett's arm viciously. "We're going out of here, to my car," he said. "You understand? One peep out of you and Eloise will let you have it! You got that?"

The gray of Bennett's face had gotten dirtier in color. He drew in a whistling breath and managed to nod to show that he understood.

"Fine," Cornelius said. "Then let's go!"

The three of them turned toward the doorway together.

"Hi," I said.

They froze into statues for a brief moment. I saw the sudden wild hope leap into Bennett's eyes; the hatred that was replaced by sudden fear in Cornelius' eyes. And just in time, I saw the calculated indifference that showed in Eloise's eyes, backed by hard resolve.

I pulled the trigger of the .38 a split second before Eloise pulled the trigger of her gun. By the feel of it, the slug passed between my head and right ear and hit the door, punching it shut again.

For a timeless moment, Eloise stood facing me, her mouth half open. Then her eyelids dropped slowly as if she was suddenly tired. She half-turned toward Cornelius, then dropped to the floor. It was only then I noticed that the front of the black sweater was stained a bright scarlet.

Cornelius looked down at her, his face chalk-white, then he raised his head slowly and looked at me. His mouth started to tremble uncontrollably and then he burst into tears.

"A hell of a murderer you are!" I said to him disgustedly. "You should be back on the beach, strutting your muscles to the little girls who are still excited by their first brassiere. How could you ever get so far out of your league as her?" I gestured towards Eloise's prone body on the floor at his feet.

He thrust the knuckles of his right hand into his mouth and bit down on them hard. It stopped him crying and started him whimpering. I wasn't sure whether it was an improvement or not.

I heard heavy footsteps outside and then someone's fist pounded on the door. "Open up in there!" Lavers' voice boomed in my ears. "It's the law!"

"I thought they only said that in adult westerns," I said to Bennett. "Open the door for the Sheriff, will you?"

He nodded and staggered rather than walked to the door and pulled it wide open. Lavers burst into the office like an actor late on cue, followed by three uniformed men.

"What kept you?" I said quickly to Lavers before he had a chance to say anything.

He glared at me, his face crimsoning. "You ... you ... What the hell goes on here!"

"Mr. Bennett can give you a clearer picture than I can," I said. "He was here before me."

Lavers looked inquiringly at Bennett, then saw Eloise on the floor. "That woman's been shot!" he said explosively.

"I shot her," I said. "She's dead."

Lavers straightened his shoulders and looked at me. I watched his face slowly change from fury to anger; from anger to annoyance to indifference to resignation. "All right," he said in a tired voice. "I don't doubt you had a cast-iron reason for killing her, Wheeler." He looked at Bennett again. "Tell me what happened, Mr. Bennett." Bennett fumbled his handkerchief out of his top pocket and wiped his lips. "It happened about an hour ago, I suppose," he said shakily. "Or maybe longer than that, I'm not sure. I was here in the office when Eloise called on the phone. She asked me to go over to her cabana right away. She said the matter was private and urgent." He fluttered his hands in the air for a moment. "I naturally assumed it concerned the Prophet so I went. She opened the door and I stepped inside. Something ... somebody ..." He glared at Cornelius. "You! Hit me over the head."

"When you came round, you were tied up and locked in Eloise's cabana?" I said. I felt I couldn't live that long to wait to hear Bennett tell it.

"That's right," he nodded.

"Then Eloise came back with Cornelius," I continued. "She changed her clothes, they freed you, brought you over here and tried to force you to open the safe. Finally you did."

"That's right," Bennett nodded his head vehemently in agreement.

"I waited until the Prophet disappeared," I said to Lavers. "I could see the door of the office clearly through your glasses, and I saw it had been unlocked and was slightly open. So I came over here and found them. Eloise took a shot at me and I took a shot at her."

Lavers turned to one of the uniformed men. "Carson—call my office, get them to contact Doctor Murphy and tell him to come up here with an ambulance right away."

"Yes, sir." Carson moved toward the phone.

Lavers gestured toward Cornelius. "Take him away and lock him up someplace!" he said to the other two uniformed men. "Someplace where I can't hear him snivelling. He reminds me of my son-in-law!"

I remembered I still had the .38 in my hand and put it back in the holster. I moved to one side so that the two cops could hustle Cornelius outside. Carson finished with the phone and hung up.

The Sheriff concentrated on me again. "I know you've got all the answers nicely tabulated!" he snarled. "I don't want to hear them but

I've got to—so get on with it."

"I think you'll be able to get all you want from Cornelius, Sheriff," I said. "Right now he'd happily fry his mother if he thought he was coming up before a cannibalistic judge."

"I'll confirm your story with him—or otherwise," Lavers said. "For the second time—it's your story I want!"

"Yes, sir," I said. "You remember that Elliott was blackmailing the wealthy members of the sect who indulged in the fertility rites—and Weisman was fronting for him?"

"You told me that last night," he said impatiently. "What about her?" He pointed at Eloise's body.

"Eloise didn't have any money," I said. "She was the Prophet's handmaiden—his girl. She lived for free up here and got the Prophet thrown in along with her meals and that was all. But she was a girl who liked men and she was ambitious. She wanted money, too."

"You sound just like one of those radio serials Mrs. Lavers is always listening to," he said wonderingly. "Go on!"

"Cornelius was married to a rich wife who was going to divorce him," I said. "She already had the evidence cut and dried. He'd got used to money and driving a Continental. So he was desperate for money, too. His wife brought him up here a couple of times and he met Eloise. They went for each other. She went for his muscles and he went for her brains."

"Her what?" Lavers stared at me open-mouthed.

"Among other things," I said obligingly. "So then all they needed was money. The Prophet was making money up here, but Bennett controlled that. Then the Prophet announced his shine project and the money really started to pour in. So Eloise and Cornelius decided they'd grab that."

"That makes sense," Lavers said grudgingly. "Where do the murders fit into this?"

"The Prophet was a jealous man where Eloise was concerned—so she and Cornelius had to meet in secret. It's my bet that Julia Grant caught them and said she'd tell the Prophet."

"You aren't going to try and tell me that they murdered the woman because they were frightened of this Prophet's jealousy!" Lavers thundered.

"No, sir," I said politely. "If Julia told the Prophet, he'd kick Eloise out. She had to stay on the inside, up here, if they were going to get their hands on the shrine money. If Eloise was kicked out of here, they'd never get it. That was why they had to stop Julia Grant telling the Prophet at any cost."

"What about Weisman?"

"Charlie Elliott had told him to get friendly with Julia, which he had. Charlie's reason was that when all the sect members were wondering who had talked to Weisman so he could start blackmailing them, he didn't want them thinking about Charlie Elliott. They would know Julia was friendly with Weisman and think it was her."

"So why did Eloise and Gibb kill him?"

"I'm not sure about this, Sheriff," I said. "But I think there's a touch of irony here. They knew Julia was friendly with Weisman, they were sure she would have told him she'd seen them together. So they felt that after they'd killed Julia, Weisman would suspect them of the murder and at least talk to the Prophet, if not the police. So they made up their minds to kill him before he could, and they did."

"Where's the irony?" Lavers growled.

"I don't think Weisman suspected them for a moment," I said. "He was in the blackmail business—neither of them were worth blackmailing because neither of them had any money. As far as Weisman was concerned, he'd got friendly with Julia because Charlie had told him to do it—as a cover for Charlie.

"So when Julia was murdered, my bet is that Weisman thought she'd been murdered for revenge by one of the blackmail victims."

"They weren't exactly bright using daggers taken from Cornelius' house," Lavers said.

"It was also Stella Gibb's house, remember?" I said. "I think they hoped they might be able to pin the killings on Stella. Cornelius certainly tried hard enough."

"What made you sure it was that particular pair and none of the others?" the Sheriff asked suspiciously.

"I could alibi Candy Logan," I said. "Directly after I found Weisman's body, I called Romair and Pines and got an answer, which alibied them. Neither of the Gibbs were home. It narrowed the field a lot. All the people who were paying blackmail could afford to pay without being driven to murder. Where was the big prize—the pay-off for murder? Right here in this office—the money pouring in for the new shrine. Eighty grand, as Cornelius said."

"Speaking of the shrine money," Lavers said sharply, "where is it?"

"I can tell you where it was, Sheriff," I said. "In that safe."

Lavers stared at the safe, then looked at Bennett. "Where is it!" he almost screamed.

"I don't know, Sheriff," Bennett said. "I don't understand it at all. There were only two of us had the combination. Myself and the Prophet."

"Where's that damned Prophet!" Lavers roared and charged toward the door.

"He's disappeared," I said gently. "Went to join the Sun God."

Lavers froze in midstride. He turned around slowly and ominously. "Wheeler?"

"Sir?"

"I'm a tolerant man. Now—answer me! Where is this Prophet guy!"

"He's disappeared," I said helplessly. "I saw him go. So did about two thousand other people. Suddenly there was a curtain of smoke in front of him, and when it cleared away, he was gone—vanished without trace."

Lavers licked his lips slowly. "I am surrounded by cretins and maniacs," he confided to no one in particular. "Wheeler, nobody just disappears like that. He had to go somewhere—and don't you damned well tell me again he joined the Sun God!"

"I'm sorry, Sheriff," I said. "He just disappeared."

"Taking eighty thousand dollars with him!" Lavers screamed. "Damn it, Wheeler, 1 knew this was going to happen! Right from the start I told you your job was to see it didn't happen!"

"You also gave me a couple of murders as well," I reminded him. "I got you two murderers—they're more important than the money."

"Who said so!"

"That eighty thousand is only sucker money," I said. "Anybody who gives their money away to build a shrine to commemorate the Sun God claiming his Prophet, shouldn't be allowed out alone in broad daylight!"

"Eighty thousand dollars!" Lavers moaned. "They'll never forgive me comes the election!"

"I think they will," I said consolingly. "They'll know by tomorrow at the latest that they were suckered out of their money. Who wants to remember the times he made a fool out of himself!"

The office door burst open and Polnik came charging in. He skidded to a stop in front of me, his face a mottled red. "Lieutenant!" The breath whistled between his teeth. "I been looking all over for you! Where you been?"

I thought about it. "Around," I said carefully.

"Something awful happened!" he said and gulped noisily.

Lavers grabbed his arm. "What is it?" he asked urgently. "Speak up, man!"

Polnik shook his head helplessly, then he took a gigantic gulp of air. "It's dreadful!" he said in a noisy whisper. "I got to tell you, Lieutenant ... Sheriff."

"Then tell us, man!" Lavers bayed like an emasculated wolf.

"It's the Prophet!" Polnik announced in a sudden roar of despair.

"He's disappeared!"

He was drowned out by the louder roar of despair that came from the Sheriff.

"Maniacs and cretins!" Lavers bellowed at the ceiling. "I'm surrounded!" He spun around and looked at me. "Stay out of my sight for the next forty-eight hours, Wheeler. I feel I shall go stark raving mad if I see your face again too soon."

"Yes, sir," I said happily.

"And keep him out of my sight!" Lavers pointed a quivering finger at Polnik. "Otherwise there'll be another homicide waiting for you when you get back to the office!" He stamped out of the room, slamming the door shut behind him.

Polnik looked at me blankly. "Did I say something, Lieutenant?"

"You could have told him about Abe Lincoln," I said. "Given him some news item that was a little more current."

"Huh?"

"Don't let it worry you," I said. "Go home and sleep for the next two days. I'll see you Wednesday in the office, Polnik. I think the Sheriff will be his normal ulcerous self by then—he's had a hard weekend one way and the other."

"Whatever you say, Lieutenant," Polnik said.

"Do one thing for me," I said. "I left the Sheriff's glasses on top of Mrs. Gibb's cabana. It's the biggest one of the lot, you can't miss it. Get them for me and bring them back into the office on Wednesday."

"Sure, Lieutenant." He started toward the door, then stopped.

"Forgive the question, Lieutenant. What were you watching up on that roof?"

"The Prophet," I said.

"If you was watching the Prophet ..." He brooded for a moment. "Then why was I watching him, too?"

"Even with the two of us, he still got away," I said.

Polnik's face relaxed into a satisfied grin. "Ain't that the truth!" he said and marched out of the office with a steady tread.

Bennett looked at me after the door had closed. "Lieutenant, I'd like to ask you a question, if you don't mind."

"Anything you like," I told him.

"When you first got here, had Gibb started to beat me up?"

"No," I said.

His voice trembled slightly. "So all the time he was beating me up, you just stood in the doorway—with a gun in your hand—and watched!"

"Sure," I said.

"Why?"

"I saw the Prophet disappear," I said. "And it was very well done, very well done indeed. And I saw you didn't want to open that safe. Both Eloise and Gibb obviously meant business—they were threatening to kill you and they meant it, but you still didn't want to open that safe for them. Your own life is always worth more than money—anybody would have opened that safe for them—with one exception."

"Exception?" Bennett shouted. "What do you mean?"

"The guy who already knew the money wasn't there," I said. "He'd be scared stiff of opening the safe because he'd figure that Gibb and Eloise's reaction to seeing the safe empty could easily be to vent their fury on him—kill him, even."

Bennett stared at me, his mouth working.

"So I figured right then that you and the Prophet played the whole deal between you very smoothly indeed. The Prophet vanishes without a trace and the money goes with him. You're left—the innocent party who, when he opens his safe, cries out in horror that he's robbed and the only other person who could have got at that safe was the Prophet."

I grinned at him. "A very neat deal, Ralph, very neat indeed—so long as nobody finds the Prophet, it's foolproof. So when I saw you getting pushed around I figured you were getting very well paid for it. You didn't get anywhere near a forty-thousand dollar beating, Ralph. I take it you and the Prophet will split the deal straight down the middle."

"I think you're out of your mind, Lieutenant," Bennett said in almost a whisper, and started to walk quickly toward the door.

"There's only one thing, Ralph," I said. "I wouldn't wait too long before you catch up with the Prophet. That eighty thousand as one big piece, with nothing cut down the middle, must be looking awfully tempting to him right now."

Bennett walked out, leaving the door swinging open behind him. I walked out of the office slowly and bumped into Polnik coming in.

"I thought I told you to go home," I said.

"I am, Lieutenant." He looked at me almost sheepishly. "There's just one thing, Lieutenant. This Abe Lincoln character—should I know him?"

Chapter Fourteen

Candy Logan sat beside me in the Healey and took a deep, enthusiastic breath. "It's a wonderful night, Al! Look at that great big gorgeous moon!"

"Perfect night for a fertility rite," I said.

She shuddered. "Don't remind me of that! Are you sure there won't be any mention of the blackmail and the rest of it?"

"Sure," I said. "It wasn't a direct motive for either murder. Eloise is dead anyway and Cornelius will plead guilty. There won't be any trial—he'll just be sentenced."

"It's just wonderful to be alive again," she said. "What do you really think happened to the Prophet?"

"I just don't know," I said.

"He couldn't just disappear off the face of the earth," she said.

"But that's what he did."

"Nonsense!" Candy said firmly. "There must be a perfectly simple and perfectly logical answer. All we have to do is think about it."

"Listen!" I said. "I wound up a double murder case this afternoon and missed out on a fraud and a vanishing Prophet. I got chewed out by the Sheriff, but comes Wednesday and I'm back in his office, he'll be happy to settle for the murders. So now I can relax. I am taking a beautiful brunette out driving with that very intention. I need logical problems with logical answers like I need a hole in the head!"

"I still say there's a very easy answer somewhere!" Candy said stubbornly.

"Hole in the head," I repeated. "Hole in the head?"

"Shift the needle," she said. "I never knew you had a hi-fi machine built into yourself as well!"

"Hole in the head!" I shouted. "That's it! Candy—you're a genius."

I made a screeching right turn off the freeway and found my way back onto it, heading in the opposite direction.

"Are you sure you shouldn't just go home and rest up for a while?" Candy asked.

"I told you," I said, "you're nothing if not a genius. A hole in the head. Where would you hide something if you had nothing but your head to hide it in?"

"That's a ghoulish question!"

"You'd dig a hole in your head and hide it there," I said happily. "That's exactly what the Prophet did."

"You mean he dug a hole in his own head and climbed into it?" Candy shifted as far away from me as she could in the restricted space of the Healey. "That's how he disappeared?"

"How about that!" I said. "I'm beginning to like the Prophet. That guy must have nerves made of solid steel."

"I don't know whether you should see a psychiatrist or a surgeon," Candy said helplessly. "Is this hole in your head real or just a figment of your imagination?"

"It's real all right," I said. "It was so real that nobody even noticed it."

"It was so real that ..." Candy's voice petered out. "Al, if you don't mind, let me out, I'd rather walk back to town."

"I'm going to show you the Prophet's hole in the head," I said. "You want to see that, don't you?"

"Sure," she said. "If you have any screaming skulls in your collection I'd love to see those, too. Cozy!"

I turned off the freeway and five minutes later turned off again onto the road that led to the top of Bald Mountain.

"Do we have to go up here?" Candy asked. "This place doesn't have any particularly pleasant memories for me."

"We're only going to see the hole in the head," I reminded her.

"I'll tell you something, Al Wheeler," she said in a restrained voice. "If this is starting out as a gag, it won't end up that way. If you're taking me up here for nothing, I'll dig a hole in your head with a pickax!"

"Patience, child," I said. "We're nearly there."

We came over the edge of the road into the parking area. Compared with how it had looked at sunset, it was now a ghost town. There was no other car in sight. No light showed from the windows of Bennett's office, or any of the cabanas.

I drove as far as I could, then stopped. I got a flashlight out of the car and started climbing up the spur until I reached the altar. Candy followed me up the spur and caught up with me a few seconds later.

"All right," she said. "Now show me the hole in the head!"

"You're right beside it!" I patted the altar almost affectionately.

"This?" She pointed at the altar. "You're crazy."

"He was standing on top of the altar," I said. "The smoke suddenly appeared in front of him so that you couldn't see him or the altar any more. When the smoke cleared, he was gone. But the altar was still there."

"How could he get into this thing? It's solid!" Candy said dubiously.

"We'll use some of that logic you were tossing around so freely," I said. "This is the only place he could have gone—so therefore it can't be solid, it only looks solid."

"That's logic?" Candy said helplessly.

"It has to open from the top," I said. "He was standing on it, and he'd have to able to drop straight into it."

I shone the flashlight down on the top of the altar and moved around it slowly, feeling the edges. I found it in the angle of the third corner I came to. You couldn't see it, you could only just feel it—a minute raised projection. I pressed down on it with my thumb.

"Al!" Candy screeched hysterically, "it's opening!"

The hinged lid of the altar fell inwards smoothly with no noise. "A very delicate piece of machinery," I said admiringly.

The lid stopped when it reached a vertical position adjacent to one side of the altar. "See how thick those sides are?" I said. "You'd never tell it was hollow from the outside. The Prophet certainly had a job of work done here!"

"Al," Candy sounded disappointed, "it's empty."

"What did you expect—Dracula?" I asked her. "I told you I'd show you the hole in the head—the brains left some time ago, I imagine."

"Wait a minute!" She grabbed my arm suddenly. "What's that—tucked in the corner there? Something white."

I shone the flashlight down into the corner. There was a piece of paper there, neatly folded in half. I had to climb into the altar to get it.

"What is it?" Candy asked impatiently. "Has it got any writing on it?"

I managed to climb out of the tomb again and unfolded the paper, then shone the flashlight down on it. There was writing all right. "Lieutenant Wheeler," it said across the top of the sheet.

"It's addressed to you!" Candy said excitedly.

"Probably the tomb of an ancestral mummy of mine," I grunted. "Or daddy."

I started to read the rest of it:

Lieutenant Wheeler,

I take it for granted you will be the first one to find this note. I have spent an anxious two hours wondering just how long it will take you to solve the apparent paradox. Long enough, I hope, for darkness to fall and for me to leave here complete with my precious suitcase. Bennett was so nice to bring it up here. He is to meet me in Miami. Needless to say, I shall not be there. Did you know he even cheated me on those hamburger stands?

I enjoyed your questioning, Lieutenant. Your cynicism was an excellent foil to sharpen my mysticism. I hope you find your murderer, I'm sure you will. I'm afraid that even if we do meet again, I shan't be able to afford to recognize you,

Goodbye from the Prophet (now beardless and clothed).

I folded the note again carefully and put it into my coat pocket.

"Well!" Candy said. "He certainly had nerve, didn't he?"

"He certainly did," I said. "I wouldn't say this out loud in front of Sheriff Lavers, but I hope he enjoys spending that eighty thousand. And I hope that Bennett waits a long time for him in Miami."

We walked back to the car and got in. I started the motor and drove slowly back to the road.

"I have a feeling that Bald Mountain will never be quite the same again," I said.

"Just so long as I don't have to come up here again, I don't care what happens to it," Candy said. "Al?"

"Yeah?"

"The smoke? Where did that come from?"

"I was watching him walk down to the altar through the crowd," I said. "I noticed he had his fists clenched then, but it didn't mean anything. He probably had a couple of those little smoke-bombs with him. You can buy them for fifty cents in any magic shop. You just throw them on the ground, the capsule breaks, and you got smoke. He was standing with his arms upraised and just before the smoke came, he dropped his arms suddenly down to his sides."

"What happened after he got inside the altar?"

"He just stayed there until everybody had gone. He would have put all the things he wanted inside the altar beforehand. Clothes, a watch, a flashlight. He'd know by the watch when it was dark. The one risk left for him was there might be someone around when he climbed out. But it wasn't likely. It was a good risk. It certainly paid off for the Prophet."

"And he used some of the time to write you a note," Candy said. "I think that was nice of him."

"Remind me to tell Sheriff Lavers. Just watch his ulcers jump."

Ten minutes later we were back on the highway again.

"You want to keep on driving?" I asked.

"No," Candy shook her head. "Let's go back to my place. I'd like a drink."

"Spoken like a true Wheeler woman," I said.

I pointed the Healey more or less in the direction of her penthouse and we drove in silence for about five minutes.

"When 1 think about it now," Candy said finally, "the whole deal seems crazy. How could people fall for a line that—sun worship and sun gods yet!"

"It's crazy now because the Prophet isn't around anymore," I said. "And when he was around he wasn't selling people like you and the others sun worship."

"Then what was the selling?" she demanded.

"Muscles," I said. "Glamour. Moonlight and—"

"All right!" she said quickly. "You don't have to keep on. I get your drift."

We reached her block and I parked the car on the curb directly outside the entrance. The flunky came hurrying out to open the door, then saw it was me inside the car and abruptly lost all interest.

"Well!" Candy said indignantly. "What's the matter with him!"

"He's a worried man," I said. "He's saving all his money to buy me a cab for Christmas."

We got out of the car and trekked our way through the carpet to the elevators. We left the elevator at the penthouse and Candy opened the door.

She smiled at me as we got into the living room.

"Did you bring your handcuffs?" she said softly.

"Pines!" I snapped my fingers. "I knew there was something I'd forgotten."

"Pines?"

"Remind me in the morning, honey. I have to mail him a key."

"Key?"

"If he's still attached to that faucet, with Edgar making him fresh cups of tea all the time, the boy will never think up any new poems," I explained.

"Al!" Candy looked at me solemnly. "You need rest! Go and lie down this minute!"

"I'll have a rest if you'll have a rest," I said hopefully.

"All right," she grinned. "You go and lie down now and I'll be there just as soon as I've made a couple of drinks."

I walked into the bedroom and stretched out on the bed. I could hear the comforting hiss of soda from the living room. A few moments later I watched Candy Logan walk into the room with the drinks. I didn't have to be back at the office until Wednesday.

Who needed eighty grand?

THE END

THE MISTRESS

- - - - -

by Carter Brown

"Journeys end in lovers meeting ..." —*Shakespeare*

Chapter One

The driveway of the Sheriff's house was cluttered with two departmental cars, a number of cops, and the corpse on the top step of the porch. I left the Austin-Healey at the end of the line and pushed my way through to the front of the crowd.

"Lieutenant," Sergeant Polnik said proudly, "I just got a woman's body!"

"Have you told your old lady about it yet?" I asked him. "This may change her plans for a second honeymoon."

"A female corpse, I mean," he corrected himself hastily. "I got enough troubles with my old lady already."

I took a closer look at the corpse. It was a girl, brunette, who looked somewhere in her mid-twenties but you never can tell these days for sure. They're all girls until suddenly they're grandmothers. After a second look, I decided this one really was a girl.

She wore a pink sweater and a black skirt. Someone had shot her neatly in the back, making a mess of the sweater. Even under the harsh glare of the spotlight, her face was almost beautiful.

"The Sheriff's waiting inside the house for you, Lieutenant," Polnik said. "He said he wanted to see you right away as soon as you got here."

The front door of the house was open. I walked inside and found Sheriff Lavers in the living room. His normally ruddy face was white and pinched-looking. "Glad you made it fast, Wheeler," he said. "You saw the body?"

"Yes, sir," I said. "Anyone you know?"

"My niece," he said shortly.

I lit a cigarette and waited for him to tell me more. A nervous tic jumped beside his mouth as he spoke. "Her name was Linda Scott, my sister's child. I hadn't seen her in twenty years until she suddenly arrived in Pine City a month ago."

"Did she come here just to see you?"

Lavers shrugged his shoulders, "I doubt it. I never did figure out exactly why she came here. She settled down in a very expensive apartment. She wore good clothes and she never seemed short of money."

"Was she working?"

"No. The money didn't come from her family, either. We had her over to dinner a couple of times, the first two weeks she was here. She was friendly but that was all. Kept herself to herself, you know what I mean?"

"There has to be more to it than that, Sheriff," I said.

"There is," he said bleakly. "There's Howard Fletcher!"

"The Vegas wheel?" I queried. "I didn't know he was in town."

"There was no reason to tell you," Lavers said curtly. "He got here at exactly the same time Linda did."

"What brought him here?"

"I wish I knew. So does the Commissioner. He's been keeping tabs on Fletcher the whole time, but he's done nothing illegal."

"How did your niece ever tie in with him?"

"She was his girl friend," Lavers said. "I think that's the polite word for it."

"You think the money came from Fletcher—he paid for the apartment and so on?"

"I think so," the Sheriff said wearily. "The last time Linda was here, I tried to speak to her about it. Finally she walked out. She wouldn't listen to me. I tried to tell her what sort of a man Fletcher is. It made no difference."

"That was the last time you saw her?"

Lavers nodded. "The last time I saw her alive."

"How about Fletcher?" I asked carefully.

He grinned savagely. "You don't miss a trick, do you, Wheeler? I saw him just a week ago. You could call it a delicately worded interview. He had a proposition."

"I can guess," I said. "He wants to start in operating here the way he operates in Vegas."

"I think his Vegas operations are past tense," Lavers grunted. "He was the last independent, and the grapevine says the Syndicate squeezed him out. He wants to start operating in Pine City. To be accurate, in Pine City County. I guess it's cheaper to put a sheriff in your pocket than try half the city fathers and the police commissioner."

"And you said no, Sheriff?"

"What the hell do you think I said?" Lavers got some color back into his face. "I told him to get the hell out of my office and if I caught him starting anything in my county, I'd run him into jail so fast his clothes would take another twenty-four hours catching up with him."

"How did he take that?"

"He said he meant business." Lavers' voice shook with uncontrollable fury. "He told me I'd get one final warning, and after that there'd be a vacancy right where I was sitting!"

I finished the cigarette and stubbed it in the nearest ash tray. "Anything else, sir?"

"Linda's body was deliberately left on my doorstep!" Lavers was shouting now. "That was Fletcher's last warning. I want you to go out and get him, Wheeler. He's going to the gas chamber for this and I'm going to be there to watch. He's got an apartment out on Vista Avenue; 807 is the number. Bring him in!"

"Yes, sir," I said. "I—"

"You what!" The echoes of his voice jarred my eardrums.

"Nothing, sir," I said.

I went out of the house, back onto the porch. Polnik looked at me eagerly. "What's the deal, Lieutenant? Where do we go from here? I bet you got the next move figured out already—and it's a dame."

"I have to go and see a man," I said. "What did you find here, anything?"

Polnik shook his head. "Not a thing, Lieutenant. The Sheriff and his old lady was out for dinner. When they got back they found this corpse right on their doorstep. That's it."

"No clues?" I sighed. "No signed confession left with the body?"

"Not a thing, Lieutenant!"

"You'd better stick around until things are cleaned up here," I told him. "The Sheriff might get another brainstorm."

"O.K., Lieutenant." Polnik looked doubtful. "Brainstorm?"

"If he blows another fuse, you'd better call an electrician," I said. "You ever hear of Howard Fletcher?"

"The big-time boy from Las Vegas?" Polnik blinked. "Sure, I heard of him. You want to bet, he's got it. A real operator."

I walked back to the Austin-Healey and climbed into it. I backed out of the driveway and headed in the direction of Vista Avenue. It was a little after midnight with a faint breeze stirring the palm trees, removing the last traces of perfume that clung to the lapels of my coat. The Sheriff's call had killed what promised to be an interesting evening.

It was a little after twelve-thirty when I parked the car outside the apartment house on Vista. The board said that Mr. Fletcher's apartment was on the fifth floor.

I rode the elevator up, and a couple of seconds later pressed the buzzer of Mr. Fletcher's door. The door opened six inches and a pair of reptilian eyes glared at me. "Yeah?"

"Mr. Fletcher?" I asked politely.

"Who wants him?"

I showed him my shield. "I want to talk to him."

"Maybe you'd better come in," the voice said sullenly.

The door opened wider and I could see something more than the eyes. The rest was no improvement. A kid, somewhere around twenty. He was lean but not undernourished, judging by the quality of the suit he was wearing. His lips were thin enough to cut bread with. I followed him into the apartment. "Wait here," he said curtly and walked into another room.

I had time to light a cigarette before he came back. He sank into an armchair and draped a leg over the arm. "The boss will be out in a minute," he said negligently. "What's the beef?"

"You've been playing hooky the last month," I said. "The school board wants to know why."

"Wise guy!" He rolled the cigarette from one corner of his mouth to the other. "The boss don't like being wakened up in the middle of the night!"

"You mean he slept nights in Vegas?" I said.

The door of the other room opened and a man walked briskly into the living room. "I'm Fletcher," he said crisply. "What's this all about?"

He wore a silk robe over silk pajamas. He was tall and well-built with short curly black hair. His face said he was around the forty mark, except for his eyes—they looked older than original sin.

"I'm Lieutenant Wheeler," I said, "from the sheriff's office."

"So?"

"What have you been doing tonight?"

His eyebrows came up a fraction. "I need an alibi?"

"I'd say you do," I said patiently, and repeated the question.

Fletcher lit himself a cigarette carefully. "Well, let's see now. I left here about eight ..."

"Alone?"

"Johnny was with me."

"Johnny?"

He nodded toward the kid sprawled in the chair. "That's Johnny— Johnny Torch. You haven't met?"

The kid grinned tightly. "Wheeler, huh? I heard about you, the gun-happy cop. Figures the world is one big graveyard and it's his job to fill it!"

"Where did you get him?" I asked Fletcher. "In a crap game?"

"Wise guy!" Johnny snarled.

Fletcher smiled vaguely. "Johnny is a friend of mine. Like I said, we left here around eight and went out to dinner."

"You had dinner in a restaurant?"

"Sure, the Magnifique." He grinned. "It isn't."

"Then what?"

"We got back here around ten-thirty, I guess. Another friend came up and had a couple of drinks. We've been here ever since."

"This friend," I said. "He's got a name?"

"Nina Booth. It's a she."

"Why waste time talking to him?" Johnny Torch grunted. "Let a mouthpiece do it for you. Why have a cop lousing up the apartment?"

"Shut up!" Fletcher said. "That sort of stuff doesn't impress anybody."

"It impresses me," I said. "An original line of dialogue always does."

"Now can you tell what it's all about?" Fletcher asked politely.

"Linda Scott," I said.

The grin withered and died on his lips. "Linda? What about Linda?"

"She's dead," I told him. "Murdered. Somebody shot her and left her body on the County Sheriff's doorstep."

"Linda—murdered!" His lips tightened. "When did it happen?"

"Tonight," I said.

"You got a cast-iron alibi, boss," Johnny said. "You should worry."

Fletcher took a quick step forward and brought the back of his hand down and across Johnny's face. He put his weight behind it and the kid's head swung sideways with the impact.

"I told you before," Fletcher said softly. "I told you to shut up."

Except for the angry redness of the imprint of Fletcher's hand, Johnny's face was chalk-white. "You told me," he whispered. "Don't do that again—not ever!"

"The hired help gets worse every year," I said sympathetically to Fletcher. "I wonder why you have him around—lousing up the apartment."

Fletcher's face was impassive. "Tell me the rest of it, Lieutenant."

"That's all there is to it," I said. "Or almost."

"Almost?"

"There is one other little thing," I watched him carefully ... "The Sheriff remembers a conversation with you about a week back, when you made him a proposition. He declined your offer and you told him you'd give him one final warning."

"You don't think I'd be crazy enough to do that—murder his niece and leave her on his doorstep!" He shook his head. "I don't operate that way, Lieutenant. I also have an alibi."

"Johnny?" I grinned. "The restaurant—did you have a table booked?"

"No, we just walked in." Fletcher glared at me.

"And the friend who came up for a drink," I said. "Nina Booth? Where does she live?"

"The next floor down, apartment 32. Was there anything else, Lieutenant?"

"I don't think so," I said.

"Johnny!" Fletcher nodded toward the door. "Show the Lieutenant out."

Johnny got up from his chair and walked toward the door with me following him. He opened the door, then waited for me to step out into the corridor.

"There was one thing more," I said, turning back and looking at Fletcher. "If you didn't murder the girl and leave her on the Sheriff's doorstep, then somebody else did."

"You're real smart, copper!" Johnny said.

"And that somebody else must have had you in mind for the fall guy," I added, still watching Fletcher. "They tailored it to fit you like a glove. I'd think about who else besides you and the Sheriff knew of that conversation you had in his office. Who else did you tell about it ... like Johnny, for instance?"

I stepped out into the corridor, felt a twitch between my shoulder-blades, and looked back.

Johnny Torch's gray eyes glared at me with dilated pupils.

"You're the big boy in the bush league," he said hoarsely. "Shoot a couple of guys in the back and get your name in the papers. Big deal! Watch it you don't come up against somebody who shoots back, copper!"

"Johnny," I said politely, "are you threatening me?"

"I'm not threatening nobody," he said. "I'm just telling you for your own good, copper."

"Johnny, you're a punk. A young punk and you'll be a punk all your life, but if you go on talking this way you'll never even get to be middle-aged."

The door slammed in my face.

Chapter Two

I found the right apartment on the next floor down, pressed the buzzer, and waited. I waited maybe ten seconds then pressed it again. The door opened just enough for me to see the night chain across the inside of it.

"Who is it?" a low voice asked.

"Police," I told her. "Lieutenant Wheeler, sheriff's office. I want to talk to you."

The chain chinked, then the door opened wide. "You'd better come in," she said.

I stepped inside the apartment and got my first look at Nina Booth. She was a tall redhead with big blue eyes that looked like they were beyond being surprised anymore.

She had a figure that Nature had sculptured in generous

proportions—with every portion in proportion. There was a coat over her nightgown and both were in nylon and lace. The coat was open in the front and the lace edging of the nightgown did a cute job of not concealing anything much around the bustline.

The nightgown was sea-blue in color, and the warm pink made an interesting contrast where her breasts thrust hard against the inadequate nylon. Her legs were long and they matched. I looked from the white sheen of her thighs under the sea-blue, to the bare, slender ankles. If any guy ever wanted to take her out, he was crazy. Nina Booth was strictly a girl to stay home with.

"You did say you wanted to talk to me?" she queried. "Are you all through looking now?"

"It's not often I get to see such a lot of girl in the one piece," I said. "I was just paying homage. I didn't want to miss anything. You don't have a guided tour by any chance?"

"You kill me," she said, "but it's a nauseating way to die! If you're really a cop, and you sure act like one, what do you want anyway? It's late and I'm missing my beauty sleep."

"Where were you tonight?" I asked abruptly.

"What do you mean?" she asked cautiously.

"I want to know where you went, what you did, who you were with?"

She shrugged her ample shoulders. "It's easy enough, I was right here in the apartment until around ten-thirty. Then I had a few drinks with some friends. I guess I got back here sometime around midnight."

"Who were the friends?"

"A couple of guys called Howard Fletcher and Johnny Torch. What's it all about?"

I told her what it was all about. She bit firmly down on her lower lip with nice, white teeth when I told her Linda Scott had been murdered.

She turned away from me and walked across the room to the bar against the far wall. "I need a drink," she said abruptly. "How about you, Lieutenant?"

"Scotch on the rocks," I said. "A little soda."

Nina Booth took her time about making the drinks. Finally she brought them back with her to where I stood. "Why don't we sit down?" she asked. We sat on the couch and she handed me my glass.

"You gave me a backhander there," she said. "I kind of liked Linda. She was a good kid. She was one of the very few friends I've ever had."

"She had a lot of friends," I said. "You, Fletcher, and Johnny Torch. It amazes me how she managed to get herself murdered."

"I don't know why anyone would want to murder her," she said soberly. "Linda never did anybody any harm. She was too soft, maybe that was her trouble."

"How long had you known her?"

"Around fifteen months, I guess. We worked together in Las Vegas."

"For Fletcher?"

She drank about half the contents of her glass, then nodded slowly. "Sure, for Howard. What's wrong with that? He'd rather use girls at the dice tables instead of stickmen. Gets him more business, he figures, and the suckers don't bitch so much when it's a well-stacked dame who's taken them for a ride."

"I didn't know Fletcher was a student of mankind. A philosopher yet," I said. "Is Johnny Torch his Boswell?"

"Huh?" Nina looked at me blankly.

"Never mind," I told her. "What made you and Linda come to Pine City?"

"Howard brought us with him when he left Las Vegas," she said.

"He's planning on setting you up in a dice game here?" I asked her.

"I wouldn't know what he's planning on," she said. "But he's paying good money, with all expenses thrown in. It's a vacation for me. I should worry what he's planning!"

"Maybe he had plans for Linda, too?"

"You got it wrong if you think Howard killed her," she said firmly. "He's not made that way."

"What makes you so sure?"

"You just know about things like that," she said. "I know, anyway. I've known enough men in my time to be sure about things like that."

I waited while she finished her drink. "What else do you know?" I asked.

"About Linda? I never did know much about her, now I come to think of it. She never talked about what she'd done before I met her. I do know she came from the East, originally. She had an uncle here, or something. Maybe he could tell you more about her than I can."

"I've met her uncle," I said. "You couldn't say we're friends but we know each other very well indeed."

"She had a boy friend, too."

"You mean Fletcher?"

Nina looked up at me with surprise showing in her eyes. "No, I don't mean Fletcher. He wouldn't go for Linda's type. Not those big wide eyes and all that innocence!" She giggled suddenly and shook her head vigorously. "Howard goes for a very different type from that. You must have heard of Gabrielle?"

"The horn-player?"

"The stripper."

"I can see my education has been neglected," I said. "Tell me more."

"Acts come and acts go at the Snake Eyes," she said easily, "but Gabrielle goes on forever. She's still there, and she's the only real passion in Howard's life."

"You mean he likes her more than he likes making money?" I asked disbelievingly.

Her lower lip curled a fraction. "I was talking about his hobbies."

"So who was Linda's guy?"

"Rex Schafer is his name. He's a reporter, I think."

"You know where I can find him?"

"Sorry, Lieutenant." She shook her head. "I don't even know the newspaper he works for."

"I can check and find out," I said. "Anything more about Linda?"

"I can't think of anything else right now." She held out her empty glass. "Get me another."

I got us both another drink, then came back to the couch again. "The way I heard it, Linda was Howard's girl friend."

"Then you heard wrong," Nina said confidently. "You go take a look at Gabrielle sometime. That'll clinch it for you—it would for any man."

"Maybe I will, sometime," I said.

She drank her way through half the new drink, then looked at me over the rim of her glass. "You had it all figured, didn't you?" she said. "Linda and Howard—nice and cozy. A love-nest killing, huh? Something like that?"

"Something like that," I agreed. "But now I've got to start all over again."

"Maybe I could help?"

"How?"

"I don't know...." She shrugged those shoulders again and the lace fluttered helplessly for a moment, then gave up trying altogether. "There must be something I can do," she said. "I liked the kid!"

"Tell me about Johnny Torch?" I suggested.

The glass stopped abruptly an inch from her lips. "Johnny Torch?" she repeated in a flat voice. "What about Johnny?"

"Why does Fletcher have him around?"

"Johnny is a friend of his," she said carefully. "A good friend. Was there anything else, Lieutenant?"

"He scares you," I said. "He doesn't scare Fletcher."

"I wouldn't bet on that," she said in a low voice.

"What was the name again of Fletcher's place in Las Vegas?" I asked.

"The Snake Eyes."

"That figures," I said. "And Gabrielle yet."

I finished my drink and got onto my feet. "Thanks for the drinks."

"Surely," she said, "you can pour me another before you go, Lieutenant."

I did as I was told, then handed her the refilled glass.

"Thanks." She smiled up at me and took a deep breath at the same time. "You're not a bad guy really. If I can help you any way at all, you let me know. Why don't you drop around tomorrow night and let me know how you're making out?"

"I might do just that," I said, "if you promise to wear the same outfit you're wearing tonight."

She looked down at herself complacently. "I always figure if a girl's stacked the right way, she shouldn't keep it all to herself. I don't promise to wear the same outfit, Lieutenant."

"Too bad," I said.

"But I promise not to wear anything more!"

"We have a date," I said, and walked toward the door. "If you do think of anything else about Linda, call me."

"I'll probably save it for tomorrow night," she said.

I drove back to the Sheriff's office. He was there, with Polnik, waiting for me. He looked at me, then behind me, as I stepped into the office. "Well?" he demanded.

"Well what?"

"Where is he? Where's Fletcher!"

I sat down carefully in the good visitor's chair and lit a cigarette. "He has an alibi," I said.

"What the hell do you mean, he has an alibi!" Lavers roared. "I told you to go out and get him!"

"He was with either one or two other people all evening," I said. "Since when has a gathering of three people been illegal?"

"There are times, Wheeler," Lavers grated, "when I ... Who were these two other people he claims he was with?"

I told him the story pretty much as it happened. He grunted sourly when I'd finished. "Lies, obviously! I told you once already, Wheeler, and now I'm telling you for the second and last time. You go out and—"

"Sheriff," I said. "I know how you feel about your niece. But we don't have any case against Fletcher, and when you cool off a little, you'll know it. If I bring him now, his lawyer will have him out again inside thirty minutes."

The Sheriff subsided slowly into his chair. "All right," he said finally in a strangled voice. "Then I want whoever did murder Linda and I want him fast. I still know damned well it was Fletcher and we've got to prove it, that's all. You got that, Wheeler?"

"Yes, sir."

"Polnik can tell you what's happened," he grunted. "Not that it's worth hearing. I'm going home. The doctor gave Mrs. Lavers a sedative, but I want to make sure she's all right."

"Yes, sir," I said. "Did you know Linda had been in Las Vegas the last fifteen months?"

"No, I didn't," he said. "She didn't tell me very much—I told you that before."

"Yes, sir," I said. "I'll see you in the morning, then?"

"You see me when you've got something worth telling me," he growled. "Check that alibi of Fletcher's. It's my bet it will fall apart. From what you say, it rests on the word of a gun punk and a redheaded hustler." He sneered audibly. "You still believe in fairies, Wheeler?"

"Well," I said. "There's that place in San Francisco…"

The sound of the door slamming behind him put the period to that sentence. I looked at Polnik who looked about as happy as I felt right then. "Don't keep me in suspense," I told him. "Give with what you've got."

"Nothing, Lieutenant," he said flatly. "No clues at the Sheriff's house, no tire marks or anything. We checked with the neighbors and they didn't know a thing about it. They never even heard a car stop."

"That's fine," I said.

Polnik looked apologetic. "You know what it's like out there, Lieutenant. The Sheriff's place is set right back from the street and there are trees everywhere. You could put a brass band on his doorstep and nobody would hear it! Me, I can hear the guy in the next apartment breathing."

"Lavers picked that house because he likes peace and quiet," I said. "That's a laugh, isn't it?"

"If you say so, Lieutenant," Polnik said dutifully.

I thought I was worrying him with unnecessary thoughts, so I got back to relevant facts again. "What about the girl's apartment?" I asked him. "Did you check that?"

He nodded. "Sure. Nothing there that looks like a lead, either. It don't look too good, does it, Lieutenant?"

"You're so right—for once," I said. "We might as well go home and get some sleep."

"I could use some." He looked at me enviously. "I guess you got a date waiting for you, huh, Lieutenant?"

"Only with a bed," I said.

"That's what I mean, Lieutenant. I wish I—"

"It's not what I mean," I told him. "I mean I'm going home to sleep …

alone. And I ... ah, hell! What's the use of trying?"

"You don't even have to try, Lieutenant," he said. "Every time I see you, you got a dame tagging right along. Blondes, brunettes ..."

"Shut up!" I told him, taking a leaf from Fletcher's book. "And listen. In the morning, first thing, go around to that restaurant, the Magnifique. See if they remember Fletcher and Johnny Torch being there tonight."

"Sure, Lieutenant."

"I'll find this reporter, Schafer, and go see him. Maybe he knows something about Linda Scott and Fletcher that Nina Booth doesn't."

"Anything else you want me to do, Lieutenant?"

"Check if either Fletcher or Torch has a record. You'd better try Las Vegas first."

I got onto my feet again and looked across at the Sheriff's empty desk. "Polnik, you smell something fishy around this office?"

He sniffed noisily. "I don't think so, Lieutenant. Do you?"

"I never did before," I said soberly, "But right now I'm beginning to wonder."

Chapter Three

"You don't seem very upset about Linda Scott's death," I said.

"I am not resigned to the shutting away of loving hearts in the hard ground," Schafer said softly. "That's poetry, Lieutenant."

"But no answer," I told him.

He drank some more of his screwdriver, then looked at me casually. "We all got to go some time," he said. "We all got the same mortal coil. Death and decay are the only things you can be sure of in this life. You start dying the day you were born."

I lit myself a cigarette and took another look at him. A guy in his early thirties with dark hair and a widow's peak. His face was gaunt, lit by dark, somber eyes. He looked like the guy named Joe on television who always gets run over by a truck in the first five minutes.

Only now there was a switch, it was his girl friend who'd got herself shot instead. And he wasn't in character anymore.

"Linda Scott," I persisted, "she was your girl."

"Maybe it looked that way," he said. "Maybe I wanted it to look that way."

"Maybe you could make some sense out of that for me," I said wearily. "I'm only a poor dumb cop. Spell it out."

"I was working on a story," he said. "I still am. I figured Linda was the best one to give me the story."

"It still doesn't make sense," I told him.

"Look, Lieutenant," he said patiently, "the easiest way to make dames talk is to make them. It builds their egos if they think you're crazy about them. Linda wasn't any different from any other woman. I can take them, or leave them alone."

"I'm with you on the first half," I said. "What was the story?"

He finished his drink and nodded to the bartender to refill it. "Why Fletcher's come to Pine City. Why he brought two of his stickgirls with him. And Johnny Torch."

"Go on," I said, "you interest me."

"Linda hadn't told me yet," he said. "A bullet got her and now the worms will get the story first."

"You must know something about it?"

Schafer shook his head decidedly. "That's the hell of it, Lieutenant. All that expense money I threw away on her—wasted. She was about ready to talk, I figured. Maybe somebody else knew it and decided they didn't want her talking."

"Somebody like Fletcher, you mean?"

"Could be. Like I said, Lieutenant, I wouldn't know."

I finished my own drink in time for the bartender to refill my glass as well. This was some more of that expense money Schafer was wasting, I hoped. "Why does there have to be a story in Fletcher coming here?" I asked.

Schafer grinned. "He was the last independent in Las Vegas and the Syndicate boys squeezed him out. He got paid off, plenty from what I hear. So why come to Pine City, why bring his girls and his personal protection with him? Not for a vacation, that's for sure. So he's here on business and gambling's not legal in this state. So there's a story—a big story if I can find out exactly why he's here. So I start making one of his girls, but I don't get anywhere before somebody bumps her off. Does that spell it out for you, Lieutenant?"

"I guess it does," I said. "You think Fletcher's going to try and set himself up in business here?"

"I don't see any other reason for him being here right now," Schafer said. "Maybe he's got a pull with somebody here. Maybe somebody's going to look the other way when he opens up for business."

"You have anybody special in mind?"

He shook his head again. "Not right now. That's one of the things I hoped Linda was going to tell me."

"Too bad she died," I said. "Where were you last night?"

He grinned: "I thought you were never going to ask me, Lieutenant!

I was out working on a story the other side of town."

"Alone?"

"Most of the time. Up to just after midnight when I got back to the office."

"That's not much of an alibi."

"I need an alibi, Lieutenant?"

"You might," I said. "Think about it. Think about all the other things you haven't told me yet. You might have a change of heart."

I finished my drink and stood up. He looked at me most anxiously. "You leaving now?"

"Check," I agreed.

"You going to pay for the drinks before you go?"

"No," I said. "You can write them off along with all that expense money you threw away on Linda Scott."

I walked out of the bar to the Healey at the curb. It was a little after eleven-thirty. It had taken me thirty minutes earlier in the morning to locate Schafer at the *Tribune*. Another twenty to find the bar where he was drinking. A wake for all that expense money.

It was five after twelve when I got into the office. The honey blonde by the name of Annabelle Jackson looked up from her typewriter. She doubles as the Sheriff's secretary and the frustration in my personal life. "The Sheriff is out," she said. "He doesn't expect to be back until late this afternoon."

"For small mercies," I sighed. "I was looking for Polnik."

"He hasn't come in yet," she said.

"Maybe he talked himself into a free lunch at the Magnifique. When do we have another date?"

"When I'm through my next judo lesson," Annabelle said. "I figure I'll be able to get the best of three falls then."

"Why, honey-chile," I said reproachfully. "You sound as if you don't trust me."

She laughed hollowly. "Trust is something no maiden can afford when you're around, Al Wheeler. Not if she wants to stay that way!"

The door opened and Polnik walked into the office. It saved me trying to think of an answer for Annabelle. "I checked the restaurant, like you said, Lieutenant," he told me. "Nobody remembers any two guys who look like Fletcher and Torch."

"You're sure?"

"Sure, I'm sure!" Polnik looked hurt. "I checked with the guy that runs the joint; the headwaiter, and all the other waiters. Nobody remembers them, not even the cashier."

"What does she look like?"

Polnik shuddered. "She reminds me of my old lady!" Then he beamed at me hopefully. "Anything else you want me to do, Lieutenant? Like questioning this Booth dame again in case you overlooked anything?"

"You know I never overlook anything when I question a dame, Sergeant," I told him. "You can go and talk to Fletcher and Torch. Tell them nobody remembers them at the restaurant—see how they react to that."

Polnik looked disappointed. "All right, Lieutenant. This Torch—if he gets too fresh, can I bop him one?"

"No," I said. "Ignore him. Act dignified—you know, like a gentleman."

"Uh?" he said weakly. Then he groped his way toward the door and five seconds later was gone.

I concentrated on Annabelle again. "How about lunch?"

"Too busy," she said briefly and hit her typewriter viciously just to prove the point.

"This is business," I said. "I mean it."

"I suppose I'm reasonably safe with you in broad daylight." She debated the point with herself for a few seconds. "All right, I'll take a chance."

"One thing's for sure," I said moodily. "You weren't around the South when Caldwell wrote *God's Little Acre*."

We went downtown to a restaurant I couldn't afford. Halfway through her cocktail, Annabelle looked at me severely. "You said this was business?"

"And so it is," I assured her.

"Well, then!" she said impatiently.

"I was wondering," I said. "You were in the office the day Howard Fletcher called to see the Sheriff?"

"Of course," Annabelle said. "Where else would I be?"

"I have too delicate a mind to inquire," I said. "Did the Sheriff say anything to you after Fletcher had gone?"

She thought for a moment, then shook her head. "Not that I remember. Did he say something important I should remember?"

"I just wondered," I said hopelessly.

"He was very annoyed after Mr. Fletcher left," Annabelle added. "But then the Sheriff gets annoyed so often, particularly when you're around, which is understandable, and I—"

"Shall we order?" I said swiftly.

We finished lunch around two and I dropped Annabelle outside the office, then drove on downtown to the *Tribune* office.

It took me ten minutes to get to see the editor. His name was Clinton H. Denny, according to the stencil on the door of his office. He was small and bald and looked tough enough to break rocks with.

"Sit down, Lieutenant," he said in a clipped voice. "What can I do for you?"

"You could tell me about one of your reporters," I said and sat down.

"Journalists!" he barked. "This paper stopped employing reporters around Repeal!"

"Rex Schafer is the journalist I'm thinking of," I said.

"What about Schafer?"

"He was friendly with Linda Scott," I said. "He told me he was working on a story the other side of town and got back here around midnight."

"I can check that for you," Denny said brusquely and picked up his phone. He talked to the managing editor for about a minute, then hung up. "He was sent out to do a story on the family of a guy who got killed driving his own truck on the highway the day before yesterday. Human interest story—Schafer's good at that sort of thing. He left here around six, came back close to midnight with the story. Seems a long time to get a story like that but maybe he was conscientious."

Denny linked his fingers together over his paunch, sprawled back in his chair and looked at me. "Anything else?"

"You could tell me about Schafer," I said.

He shrugged his shoulders. "He's been with us just over a year. He came from Chicago before that."

"Why did he come out here?"

"He was a good journalist. He applied for a vacancy we had, and he was the best prospect."

"I didn't ask you why you took him, Mr. Denny," I said patiently. "I asked why he left Chicago."

"Why don't you ask Schafer that?"

"I'd rather hear it from you first."

"There was a warehouse fire. Schafer and a photographer were covering it. They got onto the top floor of a building opposite. They weren't supposed to, but it gave them a better angle—particularly for pictures. The watchman was trapped on the top floor of the burning building, but nobody knew it.

"Schafer and the photographer saw the man. The photographer obviously wanted to take pictures, so Schafer went for help. But he stopped on the way down at the first phone and called in his story to his paper."

"The watchman's name wasn't Little Nell?" I asked suspiciously.

Denny didn't smile. "When they got to the watchman, he was dead. The call Schafer made wouldn't have taken more than a minute. That minute probably wouldn't have made any difference to the watchman.

But the photographer talked and one of the opposition papers ran the story. Schafer wasn't popular in Chicago for a time. He got fired from his own paper; I guess that was when he applied for the position here with us."

"You don't have any watchmen?" I asked blandly.

Denny shrugged his shoulders again. "I'm not a sentimentalist, Lieutenant. I knew by his record that Schafer was a good journalist. He'd had a bad break, that was all. He's still a good journalist. He's got the right equipment for the type of stories I give him. He's an iconoclast."

"You have to keep him away from the statues in public parks?"

"A natural cynic, a womanizer and he's always spent next month's pay check in advance!" Denny concluded.

"And I thought you said you never employed reporters!" I shook my head sadly. "I think you've been kidding me, Mr. Denny."

He grinned for the first time. "You asked me about Schafer, I've told you about him. I know he was friendly with Linda Scott and I know why."

"Why?"

"Because he knew there was a story there, a big story. Her murder's just making it even bigger. The story of why a Las Vegas gambler should move into Pine City, complete with his two stickgirls and his hired gun. I think it's going to be a beaut when it breaks, Lieutenant."

"I think maybe you're right, Mr. Denny," I said.

"I hear that Fletcher called on Sheriff Lavers a few days back," he went on. His voice was suddenly mild. "Paying his respects, do you think, Lieutenant?"

"Why don't you ask the Sheriff?"

"Because I'd rather ask you—you used that gimmick on me. Fair's fair, Lieutenant!"

"I guess it is," I said. "But I wouldn't know why he called on the Sheriff."

"The way I hear it, Fletcher had a proposition to put to the Sheriff. Something to do with a gambling house and an officially blind eye." He took a cigar case out of his breast pocket. "Cigar, Lieutenant?"

"No, thanks," I said. "I was frightened by Groucho Marx when I was a child."

He lit a cigar for himself and pushed still further back into his chair. "Another thing, Lieutenant. I understand that Linda Scott was the Sheriff's niece?"

"That's right."

"I wonder if she wanted to bring the Sheriff into Fletcher's circle, or whether Fletcher wanted to bring the Sheriff back into his own family circle." Denny smiled at me. "What do you think, Lieutenant?"

"I think you're wondering too close to a libel suit if you print any of it," I told him.

"I wouldn't print a story like that unless I had some facts to back it," Denny said easily. "Meantime, looking for the facts will keep me busy. You're from the Sheriff's office, you said, Lieutenant?"

"I am," I agreed.

"If I might offer you some advice." The cigar jutted from the corner of his mouth, pointing straight at me like a cannon.

"I know you've got a job to do and you're busy right now trying to find out who murdered Linda Scott. But we've got a job to do, too. I won't like it if any of my men are unnecessarily impeded when they're trying to earn their pay check."

"Meaning Rex Schafer?" I asked him.

"Schafer, and anybody else working on the story. I'm giving you fair warning, Lieutenant!"

Maybe that was the time to get onto my big flat feet and give him the treatment. I thought again and decided it wasn't, so I just got onto my feet instead.

"Any time I can be of assistance, Lieutenant," Denny said affably, "come into my office, or call me. Be only too happy to help, if I can."

"Thank you, Mr. Denny," I said thoughtfully, and walked out of his office.

I drove back to the Sheriff's office slowly. I thought I should check and see how Polnik had made out with Fletcher and Torch, so I went into the office.

Annabelle looked at me with big, round eyes. "The Sheriff is back," she whispered. "Polnik got back about twenty minutes ago and he's been in there ever since. The Sheriff is raving—I've never seen him like this before."

"What's he raving about?" I asked cautiously.

"You, mostly!" Annabelle said in an encouraging voice. "I think you'd better go in."

"I think I'd better leave town," I said. "I'll come back tomorrow; he might have cooled down a little by then."

I got halfway across the office when I heard the door open behind me. "Wheeler!" Lavers roared. "Come in here!"

I let my heels drop back to the floor and turned round.

"Good afternoon, Sheriff," I said brightly. "I was just going to—"

"In here!" he thundered.

He seemed to be making himself very clear and I didn't have any choice about it. I walked into his office and he slammed the door shut behind me. Polnik was standing at one side of the room, rigidly at attention, a worried look in his eyes.

"Where have you been?" Lavers snarled at me as he slumped down onto the chair behind his desk.

"Talking to the editor of the *Tribune*, sir," I said.

"Making sure you get your name in the papers, eh? You knew at midday that restaurant alibi of Torch and Fletcher's didn't stand up!"

"Yes, sir."

"Then why the hell weren't you out with Polnik to bring them in!"

"For what?"

"Murder, you fool! What else?"

I closed my eyes for a long moment, then opened them again slowly. "We've been through this routine before, sir," I said wearily. "Even if their alibi doesn't stand up, it's still not enough to arrest them."

"Are you telling me I don't know what I'm talking about?" Lavers asked in a dangerously soft voice.

"On this point—yes, sir."

"That's very interesting, Wheeler. Perhaps you have a better idea?"

"I think we have to find out why Fletcher and the rest of them came to Pine City from Las Vegas," I said. "I think the only hope we've got of finding that out is in Las Vegas."

"I see." His voice was still gentle. "And, naturally, the man who should go to Las Vegas is Lieutenant Wheeler?"

"I hoped you'd look at it that way, sir."

"We are in the middle of a murder case," Lavers said with a rising inflection. "It may be incidental to you, Wheeler, that it was my niece who was murdered, but it isn't to me! We have a solid case against Fletcher, but you don't want us to do anything about it. Having made sure you'll get your name in the papers, you now want a paid vacation in Las Vegas!"

His voice had reached top pitch by the time he got to the last few words, and the inkstand on his desk was jumping, keeping Polnik company. I lit a cigarette, taking my time about it. When I'd finished, his face was still just as red.

"I had you detached from Homicide to my office," he said suddenly in a normal voice. "It will be a very easy matter to return you to them. Accompanied by a report which should put you back to a sergeant, if not a traffic detail! You aren't popular now in Homicide, Wheeler!"

"No, sir," I said. "I think you should hear what Clinton H. Denny, editor of the *Tribune*, had to say this afternoon."

"I don't give a damn what he had to say!"

"I think you should, Sheriff," I said. I went on and told him before he had a chance to get his breath back.

When I'd finished, there was a sudden silence in the office. I watched Polnik take a brightly colored handkerchief from his pocket and furtively wipe his face.

"What do you think Denny meant exactly?" Lavers asked quietly.

"That I was mixed up with Fletcher in a deal to look the other way while he operated a gambling house?"

"Yes, sir."

"Then arresting Fletcher should quickly clear his mind of any doubts on that score, shouldn't it, Wheeler?"

"No, sir. It was your niece that was murdered. If you try and bulldoze Fletcher into the gas chamber, without an airtight case against him, it's going to look as if you had a deal and it went sour, that's all."

Lavers rubbed the side of his nose with the index finger of his right hand. "Do you believe I had a deal with Fletcher?" he asked in a flat voice.

I looked at him squarely: "I don't know, sir."

There was a faint gurgle from across the room. I looked and saw Polnik's eyes bulging as he stared at me.

"So that's how it is," Lavers said. "Thank you, Wheeler. We know where we stand now. I think you'd better leave immediately."

"Yes, sir," I said. "I'll tell Inspector Martin at Homicide that your report will follow?"

The Sheriff stared at me blankly for a moment. "Martin? What the hell are you going to see Martin for?"

"He's the boss of the Homicide Bureau," I told him. "That's where I'm going, isn't it?"

"Who the hell said anything about Homicide!" Lavers roared. "I'm talking about Las Vegas, that's where you want to go, isn't it? Well ... go!"

He bounced out of his chair and strode toward the door. Then he stopped suddenly with the door wide open and looked back at me. There was a horrible leer on his face. "And while you're gone," he said throatily, "I'll get Polnik to help me set up the slot machines in my office!" A moment later the door slammed shut behind him.

Polnik mopped his face carefully, then looked at me with wonder in his eyes. "Jeez! Lieutenant!" he said in an awestruck voice. "And I think I got troubles with my old lady!"

Chapter Four

I had a good table for the midnight show right in front of the stage. The pheasant under glass had been superb and I wasn't even worrying about the size of the tab. This was eat-drink-and-be-merry Wheeler having his final fling—in Las Vegas.

The music started, the curtains parted, and the chorus line flung their left legs at me, missed, then tried again with their right legs.

There was a blue-rinsed blonde at the end of the line, with the longest legs I'd seen in a short time. She looked interesting, but I told myself I was here on business and I couldn't afford the time. I couldn't afford a blue-rinsed blonde, either.

The waiter brought me another drink and I leaned back in my chair, starting to relax. Watching the chorus line reverse and wiggle their rear ends at me, was strictly business. I began to appreciate why business is so popular with businessmen, and why so many conventions are so unconventional.

After what seemed too short a time, the chorus line danced offstage. The announcer came to the microphone. "Ladies and gentlemen," he said. "We now have pleasure in presenting the ruination of the gambling business here at the Snake Eyes. The finest pay-off in all Las Vegas for you lucky people here tonight ... Gabrielle!"

The lights dimmed right down, leaving the stage in darkness. A single white spot hit the center of the stage—and there was Gabrielle.

She was a tall brunette; her hair was clipped short fairly close to her head. Somehow it gave her a tousled, wanton look that matched the rest of her equipment. She stood there, looking out at the audience. Under the brightness of the spotlight she seemed relaxed, almost insolent. The only thing missing was a small pair of horns sprouting from her head.

Her skin was a creamy-white color. Her breasts were twin peaks of high perfection. Below them, a narrow waist blossomed outwards into satin hips. Her legs made the blue-rinsed blonde a blurred memory.

She stood without moving in the center of the spotlight for about sixty tense seconds, wearing absolutely no clothes at all. Then the spotlight went out as suddenly as it had come on.

There was a howl of protest from the male section of the audience. It finally dropped to a subdued murmur as time went on and wives fought for and won their rights. The band played soft music but nobody was listening.

I sat there, hoping there was an electrician in the house who could fix that spotlight. When I was all through hoping, it came on again. Gabrielle was back in the center of the stage, but this time she was fully dressed.

She waited nonchalantly for the protests to die down, then stepped forward to the microphone. "Ladies and gentlemen," she said in a deep-throated, mocking voice. "I apologize for the brevity of my act. But I think you'll agree—I've stripped it of all the nonessentials!"

She waited until they stopped clapping, with that same insolent look on her face. "Now," she said blandly, "is there anything else you'd like me to do for you?"

A little, bald-headed guy in the front row started to tell her, but shut up suddenly when his wife's elbow hit him just above the heart.

Gabrielle's eyebrows lifted fractionally: "I guess I shouldn't break a habit," she said, "but I'm really an artist. I like to think my act has a message."

She wore a strapless gown which had a zipper down the side. Everyone in the audience knew exactly where that zipper was, because she unzipped it. The gown slid slowly toward the floor. She twitched her hips once, lazily, and then it had arrived. Underneath she wore a white slip. "Maybe I should sing or something?" she asked.

The slip followed the gown, and that left her in a strapless bra and a pair of panties with fantastic lace ruffles that frothed around the top of her thighs. "You don't want me to sing?" she asked in a little-girl-hurt voice. "Then maybe I should dance?"

It was so quiet in the room you could have heard a brassiere drop. Right then, that was what everyone was waiting for. Gabrielle pouted at the audience. "I don't think you're very nice," she said. "I'm not going to talk to you anymore." She turned her back on the audience, her fingers sliding behind her back to unhook the strapless bra.

The bra fluttered carelessly from her fingers, then she hooked her fingers into the waistband of the panties and peeled them off, standing on one foot to kick them free behind her. They fluttered through the air and draped themselves modestly over the little guy's bald head.

Then Gabrielle turned slowly to face the audience again. "I guess I just don't have a message after all," she said sadly.

The spotlight was killed again and there was a storm of applause. When the lights were restored, the announcer was onstage to announce the big-name act who was the main part of the show.

The big-name act was a nationally famous TV comic. Maybe he told a lot of very funny stories but I didn't hear them. Jokes you can buy in comic books, but a girl like Gabrielle doesn't happen very often. Besides, she was business.

I had to wait until the show finished because the waiters weren't allowed to serve while the big-name was onstage. It was nearly an hour later before I could get   hold of the waiter. "I'd like to see Gabrielle," I told him.

He smiled understandingly. "I'm sorry, sir, but that's impossible. She sees nobody."

"I wonder how much it would cost me to send her a cable, waiters' union?" I asked him.

His smile became a little more friendly. "Five would cover it, sir. But I've never known anybody to get an answer, even to a reply prepaid."

"I'll take my chances on that," I told him.

I scribbled on the back of the airline envelope, removed the return half of my ticket, then gave the envelope to the waiter. I also gave him a sawbuck. "That's the reply prepaid."

"Thank you, sir," he said. "I'll see she gets it."

The dining room was practically empty. I realized the cold feeling at the back of my neck was caused by the impatient stares of half a dozen waiters. I got up from the table and walked out into the main room, which was crowded.

The Snake Eyes was picking up business again fast, now the show was over. The chuck wagon was doing business but the crap tables were doing better business. So were the roulette wheels and the blackjack games. Above the steady hum of conversation, the endless chatter of the slot machines sounded.

I lit a cigarette and thought maybe I should gamble. Being in Vegas and not gambling would be like being locked in a harem and going to sleep. I walked over to the steel mesh grille that separated the cashiers from the customers.

The two beefy guys in blue uniforms stared stolidly at me as I fronted the cage. I looked at their holstered guns and their deputy sheriff's badges and wondered if the Old West had ever been like this. I thought it probably had, but not so highly organized.

"Yes, sir?" the guy behind the grille asked politely.

I put a dollar bill on the counter and pushed it under the grille. "I want the lot in nickels," I said. He blinked once, then smacked a handful down in front of me.

"They just struck oil back on my ranch in Texas," I explained. "Tonight, I'm having myself a time."

"Yes, sir," he said and cashed close to a thousand bucks' worth of chips for the guy standing beside me.

I moved over to the nearest nickel machine and started playing it. I lost eighty cents cold, then got a payout which gave me three nickels back. A warm feeling crept over me as I felt glad I hadn't let my head go and tried one of the dime machines.

Somebody tapped me gently on the shoulder, just as I was down to my last nickel. I looked around and saw the waiter standing there, a look of blank surprise on his face. "It's Gabrielle, sir," he muttered hoarsely. "She wants to see you now."

I dropped the last nickel into the one-armed bandit and it lived up to its name. "Fine," I said. "You lead the way."

"Yes, sir." He shook his head slowly. "I never knew it to happen before!"

"It's my handwriting," I told him as we moved out of the main room through a curtained doorway, and into a long corridor.

"My handwriting is irresistible to strip-tease artists and pizza pie makers."

"Yes, sir," he said over his shoulder.

"But only to female pizza pie makers," I added. "There is nothing queer about my handwriting."

He stopped outside a door and knocked on it gently. "Come in," a husky voice called from inside. The waiter stepped back obligingly and I opened the door quickly before the palm of his hand got in my way.

I closed the door equally quickly once I got inside, and leaned against it. It was a dressing-room and I was disappointed that Gabrielle was already dressed. She sat in front of a mirror, wearing a strapless silver lamé gown. I waited while she finished fashioning herself a new pair of eyebrows and watched my reflection in the mirror at the same time.

"You're a friend of Howard's?" she asked finally.

"You could call me that," I said, stretching a couple of points.

"I heard about Linda's murder," she said. She glanced down at my note on the table in front of her, "You say that Howard's in trouble. What sort of trouble?"

"Linda was the County Sheriff's niece," I said. "Howard made the Sheriff a proposition a little while back, but the Sheriff didn't want any part of it. Howard told him he'd give him one final warning—the Sheriff thinks Linda's body on his doorstep was just that."

She took a cigarette from the pack on the table and lit it. "That was stupid of Howard," she said casually. "It's not like him. But what can I do about it?"

"I'd like to talk to you about that," I said. "Why don't we go and have a drink someplace?"

"I can't," she said. "I have to see somebody else almost right now. But I could see you afterwards. Around two-thirty?"

"Fine," I said. "I guess nobody sleeps nights here, anyway."

"There's all next day for sleeping," she said.

"I'll see you in the bar here?" I queried.

Gabrielle thought for a moment, then shook her head. "I don't think so. You'd better come over to my place. You go right down to the other end of the Strip. There's a gas station there called Norman's. Make a right-hand turn beside it and my place is two blocks down on the corner. You can't miss it. It's painted blue and white."

"Fine," I said. "I'll see you there at two-thirty."

"If I'm not home go right on in and make yourself a drink," she said. "The front door isn't locked."

"That's what I call hospitality," I said.

"What was your name again?" she asked.

"Al Wheeler."

"All right, Al. See you then." She turned back to the mirror and started to add eye-shadow underneath the new eyebrows.

I walked out into the corridor and closed the door behind me. I'd gone maybe ten feet down the corridor, when two guys came through the curtained doorway and walked toward me. They were both big and wearing nice suits, and they looked like professionals. I kept on walking toward them, and they stopped to wait for me.

Just as I reached them, they moved a little so they stood shoulder to shoulder facing me. "The manager would like to see you," one of them said politely.

"I didn't really want to stay here any longer," I told him. "I've lost a dollar already."

"His office is right down the corridor," the second one said. He patted my coat expertly, then lifted the .38 from the shoulder holster. He clicked his teeth gently.

"You're supposed to have a license for these things," he said.

"I'll tell the finance company," I assured him. "Three more payments till it's mine."

"Witty," the first one said. "I like that. A guy with a sense of humor. I've even seen them die laughing."

"Let's go," the second one said, "now that we're comfortable." He slid my gun into his hip pocket. It wasn't going to do his suit any good at all.

We walked down the corridor and stopped at the door which had "Manager" stenciled on the outside. The first one knocked and then opened the door. The three of us walked into the office.

It was a big office complete with a couch to suit either casting or a psychiatrist. The guy sitting behind the blond wood desk didn't look in need of a psychiatrist. He looked in need of absolutely nothing.

"Sit down, Wheeler," he said quietly. "I want to talk to you." He looked at the other two and made a gesture of dismissal. "You wait outside."

They went out and I heard the door close gently.

The guy stared at me without saying anything for a while. He looked the picture of the successful company executive, which he undoubtedly was. He had one big advantage—he worked for a syndicate the anti-trust laws couldn't break.

"Your name is Wheeler," he said coldly. "You came in tonight from Pine City. You sent a note to Gabrielle, telling her Fletcher's in trouble and needs her help."

"That's right," I agreed. "What's that to do with you?"

"Gabrielle is a very special piece of property right now," he said. "A kind of insurance, you might say. She's not going to be able to help Fletcher, because she's staying right here in Vegas."

"I only brought a message," I said. "For a friend."

"Just how good a friend of yours is Fletcher?" he asked softly.

I shrugged my shoulders. "I've only known him since he got to Pine City. He's figuring on operating there. I figure he might be a good guy to tag along with—that's as far as it goes."

"You're working for him?"

"I wouldn't say that," I said. "I have a little operation of my own."

His lower lip curled slightly. "Knocking over banks, Wheeler?"

"Not exactly." I tried to look embarrassed. "You know how it is. Pine City is run by the cops. I pick up what I can here and there."

"I had you figured the moment you walked in here," he said contemptuously. "You don't even look like a pro. You look like a small-time chiseler to me. Knock over a candy store and run when the guy shouts 'Copper!'"

I tried to look even more embarrassed. "What's the beef, anyway?" I said nervously. "Fletcher asked me to talk to the dame, that's all. Tell her he's in real trouble with the cops over the Scott dame's murder and they're trying to pin it on him. Tell her he wants help, that's all. You don't mind me talking to the dame, do you?"

"I mind," he said.

"So all right," I said. "I don't talk to her anymore."

"I'll give you some more advice," he said. "You don't have the backbone to make even a small-town chiseler, Wheeler. What are you carrying that .38 around for? Aren't you scared it will go off and frighten you to death! Guys like you should stay honest!"

"O.K.," I said. "So I take your advice and go back to Pine City. But what do I tell Fletcher when I get back? He paid me a couple of hundred bucks to come here. I got to tell him something!"

"Tell him Gabrielle's fine," he said. "In good health and she's likely to stay that way so long as he doesn't send any more friends here to see her."

"Is that all I tell him?"

"That's all, friend." He pressed a buzzer on his desk and the two beefy characters reappeared. "Max," he said, "Mr. Wheeler is leaving town for the sake of his health. Take him out to the airport and stay with him until he gets on board the plane."

"Sure, Mr. Fulton," Max said politely.

Max was the guy who liked humor. He looked at me and jerked his head toward the door. "On your way, Wheeler!"

I looked at the other one. "Can I have my gun back?" I asked hopefully. He looked at Fulton who nodded and said, "Sure, give it to him back, but take the shells out first. The only thing he's likely to use that gun for is to blow his brains out!"

Chapter Five

Outside the rear of the place, a blue Cadillac was parked. Max opened the door and nodded to me to get in. "You drive," he said. I got in behind the wheel and he handed me the keys.

We pulled out onto the Strip and I could have admired the blaze of neon if I hadn't been preoccupied. I drove slowly, using the inside lane.

"That's right, Wheeler," Max said, "take it easy. We got plenty of time. Be a couple of hours now at least before you can get a plane."

"That Fulton," I said. "He's a rough one."

"You're not kidding there," he agreed. "He's a smart one, too. You were smart to take his advice and not try and pull anything."

"I figured he was way out of my league," I said. "This must be a tough town."

"It's a very peaceful town," Max said. "But it can be real tough if somebody tries to start something. You could call this a well-organized town and you'd be right."

The turn-off to the airport was clearly marked. I followed it obediently. Five minutes later we were there at the airport. We got out of the car and walked into the terminal building. The clock on the wall said a quarter after two. The next plane out to L.A. was at five-thirty. I checked my ticket with the clerk at the desk and got a seat on the plane without any trouble.

"Now all we got to do is wait," Max said as we walked away from the counter. "What do you want to do, Wheeler? Play the slot machines? No, I almost forgot—you lost a buck already! Want some coffee?"

"How about leaving it awhile," I said. "We got over three hours to kill before that plane. Can't we take a walk?"

"Where to—Pine City?"

"Just around the terminal," I said. "If it's okay by you."

"I guess so," he said. "But just once, Wheeler. My feet hurt."

We walked outside again slowly. I kept on walking until we were in the shadow beyond the spread of light from the terminal. I stopped, looking at the continuous blaze of light that was the Strip. "That sure is something to see!" I said.

"You get used to it," Max said indifferently.

I pointed with left arm. "Is that the Sands over there?"

"Desert Inn," he said briefly. "The Sands is a little farther down than that." He pointed obligingly, his head turned away from me as he looked.

I eased the empty .38 out of its holster with my right hand and laid the barrel across the side of his head. Max was tough all right. He sank down onto his knees slowly, his hands groping in front of him. I reversed the gun in my hand and brought the butt down hard on the top of his skull. He slid slowly onto his face and lay still.

There were no shouts, no hurried footsteps. I looked around carefully and couldn't see anybody near enough to worry about. It took me thirty seconds to reach the parked Cadillac, a little longer to drive it back to where Max was still stretched out on the ground.

He was heavy. I dragged him across to the car and bundled him into the back. He slumped against the back of the seat, then rolled off onto the floor, banging his head again as he did so. I would have felt sorry for him if I had the time. I closed the rear door, then got into the front seat of the car and drove out of the airport toward the Strip again.

Nobody was going to miss Max until a while after that plane had left. That gave me until five-thirty anyway. Meanwhile he was a problem. I had a date and three's a crowd on any date, but it would be sacrilege on a date with Gabrielle.

I reached the Strip and headed out of town. As soon as I was clear of the city limits, I pushed the Cadillac up to eighty along the highway, and held it there. After a good five minutes I took my foot off the gas and slowed to around thirty. Another minute and a turn-off showed up in the headlight beam. It was a dirt track with a faded sign that said, "2 miles to ..." The rest had faded almost completely. Maybe it led to a dude ranch or maybe nowhere.

I followed it until I came to a deserted shack that had a realtor's notice also faded which said: "This valuable property for sale, apply ..." It looked just the place.

When I opened the rear door of the car, Max groaned feebly but didn't move. I prodded his ribs with the toe of my shoe and got no reaction; so I dragged him out of the car to the side of the track and stripped him down to his shorts.

"You've got a long walk home, Max," I told him. "But it's a warm night. I hope you don't start a riot on the highway when they see you in those shorts—they're really wild." He obviously wasn't hearing me, so I got back into the Cadillac and reversed it cautiously.

Fifteen minutes later I stopped outside Gabrielle's house. I walked up the short path to the door and found it open. The lights were on inside the house.

"Al Wheeler?" her husky voice queried from somewhere inside. "I'm in the living room, come on in."

An open door led into the living room from a hallway the size of an airmail stamp. Gabrielle had her back to me, busy making herself a drink. "You're late," she said indifferently.

"I take my Scotch on the rocks, with a little soda so that I won't become an alcoholic," I said hopefully as I walked into the room. "I got detained."

"Detained?" She started to make a second drink and I resisted the impulse to snatch it away from her before she'd finished pouring the soda.

"I had to talk to a couple of guys," I said. "No problem."

She turned around and looked at me. I looked at her and got the better of the exchange. All she was seeing was one slightly beat-up cop; but what I was seeing was worth a thousand words of a Hemingway.

Gabrielle had changed her clothes again—I guess it gets to be a habit with a stripper anyway. Now she was wearing an orange-colored shirt and a pair of leopard skin print pants that fitted her tighter than they ever could a leopard, and I could see their point of view. Who wants to hug a leopard anyway? They hugged Gabrielle all the way down to her ankles and anytime they got tired I was willing to quit being a cop and take over.

"Sit down," Gabrielle said. "Tell me about it."

We sat down on the couch and she gave me the drink. The Scotch tasted good. "What happened?" she asked.

"There were a couple of guys waiting for me outside your dressing room. They said I should meet the manager."

"Fulton?"

"Fulton," I agreed. "He's a fortune-teller. He told me mine, and yours, too. Inside of five minutes."

"Just what did he tell you?"

"You're a valuable insurance policy he's carrying right now. You can't help Howard Fletcher because you're staying right here. Fulton suggested I should get the next plane right back to Pine City and tell Fletcher that. You could say he insisted on it—he even gave me an escort to the airport."

Gabrielle sipped her drink slowly. "So where's the escort now?"

"Prospecting," I said. "I think."

"You don't make any sense!" she said impatiently. "What did you do to get rid of him? Shoot him?"

"I didn't think I was out West far enough for that," I said. "I just slugged him."

She took a deep breath and thought about that. I watched her take the deep breath. "You ever wear snowshoes?" I asked her.

"In Las Vegas?" She blinked once. "Are you crazy? I'd never need them."

"You don't wear a bra for the same reason, I guess?"

"Just keep your mind on business, Wheeler," she said curtly.

"If you insist," I said regretfully. "Anyway, Fulton isn't important, but Fletcher is. Let's talk about him."

"I'd like to know a little more about you first," she said. "Just where do you fit in this picture?"

I finished my drink. It tasted good and I thought I'd earned it. I moved over to the table and poured myself another, then came back to the couch. "The fortune-teller had me all figured out. A small-time chiseler way out of my league. He figures I should stay honest, I just don't have what it takes for the rackets."

"Who was the escort he provided?"

"A guy called Max," I told her. "I thought they were all called Joe. Maybe it's the climate out here."

"If you slugged Max and got here to talk about it, you have character all right." She smiled faintly. "Tell me some more about Howard."

"You're one of the most beautiful women I ever met," I said sincerely. "And I'd say that even if you were wearing a bra."

"Let's talk about Howard!" she said wearily.

"I am," I said indignantly. "Not that he wears a ... I mean, I have a decision to make and I've made it right now. I just couldn't be a heel to a girl with the sort of figure you've got."

"Why don't you try making some sense for a change!"

"O.K." I shrugged my shoulders. "I'll give it to you straight. You don't rate with Fletcher anymore. You're not even a memory as far as he's concerned. Nina Booth has the top rating now and she has since they first arrived in Pine City."

The contents of her glass got up and hit me in the face.

"You're lying!" she said coldly.

I dabbed my face and my eyes with a handkerchief. "So I'm lying," I said. "Forget it. Make yourself another drink."

"He wouldn't dare!" she whispered fiercely. "He knows what I'd do to him the next time I see him!"

"When will that be?" I asked politely. "In the obituary notices?"

The nails of her right hand scrabbled the arm of the couch. "Nina Booth!" she said from between clenched teeth. "That redheaded, overweight hustler! Why she—You're lying!"

"Why should I lie to you?" I asked her. "There's no pay-off for me. You're a well-stacked dame and you appeal to my sense of chivalry."

"I like that!" she said. "Coming from a small-time chiseler, that's really something! Chivalry yet!"

"It wasn't me who went off with a redheaded, overweight hustler and left you here with Fulton as insurance," I said. "Was it?"

"If he thinks he can do this to me and get away with it!" she said slowly. "Give me a cigarette!"

I gave her a cigarette, lit it for her and one for myself. She sat there brooding for a few moments, and from the way that shirt stretched, she was coming up to a boil fast. "You know what that lousy rat did to me?" she asked finally, in a choked voice.

"No," I said. "Why don't you tell me, maybe I can help?"

She sucked smoke deep into her lungs and exhaled slowly. "How much do you know about Howard's operations here in Vegas, Al?"

"I know he owned the Snake Eyes," I said. "I hear the Syndicate put pressure on him until he finally sold out to them. Then he went to Pine City. That's all I do know."

"They paid him off for the place on a Monday," she said. "He had until Friday to move out. Meanwhile he still managed the place, but it was the Syndicate's money for the rest of the week, not his, you understand?"

"Something happened before Friday?"

"It happened on that Wednesday," Gabrielle said flatly. "A guy walked in and took the house for seventy grand on one of the crap tables."

"Everyman's dream come true," I said. "Was it on the level?"

"Linda Scott was running the table when the guy started," Gabrielle said. "When he got as far as thirty thousand, Howard took a look. After a while he took Linda off the table and replaced her with Nina Booth. The guy kept on winning. When he got up to seventy grand, he quit and walked out of the place."

She handed me her glass. "Make me a drink, Al." I moved back to the table and did as I was told. "Fulton heard about it," she went on. "He wanted to check on the winner. He thought he'd like to meet a guy with a nice wide streak of luck like that. So he put the word out that he wanted to see him. Finally they found him—out in the desert about two miles out of town with a hole in the back of his head and nothing in his pockets."

I handed her the new drink and sat down beside her again.

"So somebody who saw him win all that beautiful money, followed him and shot him, then took the money," I said. "People have been murdered for fifty bucks or less."

"That could be it," she nodded. "If it was, it wouldn't worry Fulton too much. It was the alternative that worried him."

"What was that?"

"That the guy hadn't won the money legitimately in the first place."

"That's crazy," I said. "He would've had to use a pair of loaded dice to do it. He couldn't have got away with that."

"Fulton looked at it another way. They'd forced Howard to sell out to them, but right then he was still managing the place and it was their money, not his. So maybe he got smart. Maybe he set the whole thing up. The guy comes in with a pair of loaded dice in his pocket and plays the table that's being operated by one of Howard's own stickgirls. Maybe she just looks the other way when he palms his dice. Howard checked the table, sure. But he could have looked the other way and so could his other stickgirl when he put her on the table."

"It starts to make a lot of sense," I said.

"The poor slob who played the dice could have been told that ten grand or so was his share. All he had to do was to meet somebody after he'd won, hand the rest of the money over, and keep his ten grand. Fulton said maybe that somebody was Johnny Torch and Johnny paid off with a slug instead of folding money."

"What I don't get," I said, "is if Fulton thought all this, why the hell did he let them leave Las Vegas?"

"The Syndicate are very careful people," she said. "Fulton would have to be quite sure about it before he did anything. He let them go, but the Syndicate can keep just as close tabs on them in Pine City as they can here. You can bet your sweet life they are. Fulton also has some insurance too, don't forget—me! He let the others go, but I had to stay. If Howard tried to make a break for it, Fulton told him it was me who'd get it."

I shook my head: "If he couldn't prove it right after it happened, how does he hope to prove it now?"

"You're forgetting the seventy grand, honey!" she said. "If it was a take, the four of them had to be in on it. They can't wait forever to split the money. That's what the Syndicate boys are waiting for. They know exactly how much legitimate money Howard and the others had with them when they left here. They make one mistake and spend any of that seventy grand and the Syndicate's got its proof."

"What would they do about it?"

She laughed incredulously: "Are you kidding? Do you think they could let anybody take them in Las Vegas, and then let them get away with it! If one person does it, others might try. If they get proof, they'll make a permanent example of Howard and the rest of the bunch!"

"There's the seventy-thousand-dollar question," I said. "Was it a take?"

"I don't know," she said slowly. "I don't even want to know. Howard said it wasn't. He said Fulton was crazy to think anybody would be so tired of living they'd try and take the Syndicate. But that's what he'd say, anyway. When I think of that lousy, double-crossing bum cutting loose on the Coast with that Nina Booth, I could ..."

"And I'd like to watch you do it, too," I said. "You know who belongs to the Syndicate in Pine City?"

"No," she shook her head. "That reminds me, what about Max? You'll be in real trouble when they find out what you did to him!"

"I'm still catching that five-thirty plane to L.A.," I said. "I don't think they'll hear from Max before then."

"I hope you're right for your sake," she said. She looked up at me suddenly. "What's your real interest in this, Al?"

"Don't ask me," I said. "It will spoil the whole evening for you."

"Tell me!" she said fiercely.

"I'm a cop," I said simply.

She looked at me for a long moment, her mouth dropping open. Then she laughed helplessly. "I have to say one thing for you," she gurgled. "You sure have a sense of humor!"

"I hope you have, honey," I grinned back at her.

Then I held out my shield so she could see it.

For a moment she just looked, then her right hand came up fast, the long nails lunging for my face. I caught her wrist and held it. "You've been in Vegas long enough to be a good loser," I said. "Smile!"

She relaxed suddenly and lay back against the couch. "A cop!" she said. Her whole body shook with laughter again. "A cop! You sure fooled me! You must have fooled Fulton, too. All the way down the line. Wait till Max hears he was taken by a cop."

"Do I rate another drink?" I asked, and looked at my watch. "There's still a couple of hours before that plane leaves."

"After that, we both rate a couple of drinks," she said easily. "You make them, Al."

I got up from the couch and walked over to the table. When I'd finished making them, I picked up the two glasses and turned around toward the couch, then I stopped. The couch was empty, Gabrielle had disappeared. While I stood there, wondering, her voice called out from somewhere. "Bring the drinks in here, Al."

There was only one bedroom in the house, I discovered, and Gabrielle was there. A reading lamp on a sidetable provided the only illumination. Draped across a chair were the orange shirt and the leopardskin print pants.

She sat up in the bed and the lavender-blue sheet slipped down to her waist. "You said you had two hours before the plane left, didn't you?" she asked in that husky voice.

I put the drinks down on the sidetable. "That's right," I said in a strangled voice. "This is the first real hospitality I've hit in Las Vegas."

"There's only one string attached to it, Al," she said tautly. "Just mention it to Howard when you get back to Pine City, will you?"

Suddenly she coiled her arms around my neck, pulling me down toward her. She kissed in a cold fury that was born of passion but carried it a stage further.

I slid my hand down the naked warmth of her back, then up underneath her breast and squeezed gently. She shivered for a moment then bit down hard on my lower lip.

I never did get around to having that drink.

Chapter Six

The little men were breaking rocks inside my skull when I stepped into my own apartment. Ten o'clock on a bright sunny morning and the hell with it. I went out into the kitchen and made some coffee.

Vegas was a memory. I'd caught the five-thirty plane with nobody trying to stop me. One hour's sleep on the plane back to L.A. and then about fifteen minutes more on the plane back to Pine City. Sleep was something I needed but couldn't afford to have, I decided. So I settled for three cups of black coffee and that woke up the little men inside my stomach.

It was just after eleven when I called on Howard Fletcher. Johnny Torch opened the door to me. He wore a black silk robe over pajamas of the same color. There were silver-outlined dancing-girls prancing with gay abandon across the front of the robe. I couldn't help shuddering at the sight.

"What's the matter, copper?" He looked hopeful. "You sick or something?"

"I felt fine until I saw that robe," I told him. "It's only for the very young."

"What do you want?"

"I want to talk to Fletcher," I said. I put the flat of my hand against the cavity where his chest should have been and pushed him gently backwards into the apartment. "Be a good boy, Johnny," I told him. Then I looked at his robe again. "Otherwise I'll book you for running a bordello."

He walked out of the room muttering under his breath. I sank into the nearest chair and lit myself a cigarette. Howard Fletcher came into the room a few moments later. He wore a sport shirt and a pair of slacks. His eyes were slightly bloodshot, I noticed.

"Sit down, Fletcher," I said, "I want to talk to you."

He sat opposite me and lit himself a cigarette. Johnny Torch reappeared and leaned against the wall behind Fletcher, watching me.

"Every cop in this damned town wants to talk to me," Fletcher said. "Don't they have anything better to do?"

"Maybe not," I said. "It's not often we get a chance to talk to a big shot like you. A guy who's tried to buck the Las Vegas Syndicate. We want to talk to you while we've got the chance, Fletcher, before it's too late."

"Just what the hell are you talking about?" he asked softly.

"The guy who got lucky at the crap table," I said. "The guy who picked up seventy grand at the Snake Eyes, and got a hole in the back of his head for his trouble."

"I had nothing to do with it," he said, his voice tired. "Sometimes a guy does get lucky. If nobody got lucky there wouldn't be any gamblers."

"The Syndicate thinks you had something to do with it," I reminded him. "A guy called Fulton in Vegas does."

"Somebody's been shooting off their big mouth," Johnny Torch said savagely.

Fletcher silenced him with a look, then concentrated on me again. "I don't see that what happened in Las Vegas is of any interest to you, Lieutenant."

"If it ties in with the murder of Linda Scott, it interests me a lot," I told him. "And I'm sure it does."

"I can't stop you talking!" He shrugged his shoulders helplessly.

"I've been thinking about this thing," I said. "Any way I figure it, Fletcher, you're right behind the eight ball!"

"What do you mean?" he asked coldly.

"You took the Syndicate for seventy thousand and

"You're crazy! I did no such thing!"

"O.K.," I said generously. "You didn't, but they think you did and that's just as bad. Let's imagine you did. Both your stickgirls had to be in on it and I imagine Johnny was with it, too."

"Why don't we get a mouthpiece up here, boss?" Johnny asked in a shrill voice. "We don't have to take this from him, copper or no copper! It's getting so I can't—"

"Shut up!" Fletcher rasped. "If you don't like to hear it, take a walk. Get lost!"

"O.K.," Johnny muttered. "I'll listen, maybe I'll get a good laugh."

"So you've got seventy thousand dollars you can't spend," I went on evenly. "You can't even split it, in case one of you spends some of it, because the Syndicate would know it as soon as it happened. Then Linda Scott gets murdered."

"What's this supposed to do to me, Lieutenant?" Fletcher asked. "Make me feel nervous or something? Confess to a murder that I didn't do?"

"I thought you might like to hear the way I figure it," I said. "I figure that Linda Scott was killed for one of two reasons. Either the Syndicate is convinced the four of you took that money and they killed her as a start and intend taking the rest of you in turn; or you killed her because you were scared she was going to talk to the Syndicate to try and get herself off the hook."

Fletcher lit himself another cigarette. "Anything else, Lieutenant?"

"If the Syndicate killed her," I said, "then you don't have very long to live in any case. But whether they did or they didn't, the case against you is strong enough now for an arrest."

"How the hell do you figure that out!"

"The whole Las Vegas story," I said wearily. "You're not a fool, Fletcher, you can see it. The four of you knew the only way you could stay alive was to convince the Syndicate you didn't take them for seventy grand. Linda Scott was the weakest link in your chain.

"She had an uncle here in Pine City who happened to be the County Sheriff. She called on him a couple of times. Her nerve was going. At any time she could tell either her uncle or the Syndicate the truth, and that would mean the finish for the rest of you. So you had to kill her to stop her from talking."

"It's a lie," Fletcher said, his face white.

"You have an alibi that depends on the word of Johnny Torch," I said. "We can laugh that out of court. The restaurant part of your alibi doesn't even stand up."

"You're trying to frame me," he said hoarsely. "That damned Sheriff has got his knife into me because I made him a proposition and—"

"I'll give you a break, Fletcher," I said. "I don't know why the hell I should. You must know a Syndicate man has been keeping tabs on you ever since you arrived here. Maybe the Syndicate did kill Linda Scott and is planning on killing the rest of you. I'm prepared to take a look at it."

"What do you want?" he asked.

"The name of the Syndicate man here in Pine City," I told him.

He got up from his chair and walked toward the window slowly.

"Don't tell him a damned thing, Boss!" Johnny Torch said anxiously. "He's only trying to take you for ride. He—"

Fletcher hit him viciously, low in the stomach with his whole weight behind the fist. Johnny doubled up, his eyes glassy. Then he stumbled toward the bathroom, making a high-pitched, keening noise.

"Maybe you ought to get him a muzzle?" I said.

Fletcher turned around and looked at me. "Maybe I should get him a psychiatrist," he muttered. He rubbed his forehead with the palm of his hand. "I just can't think with that crazy kid shooting off his mouth all the time."

"I'll tell you how it is," I said. "Just once more, Fletcher, then I'm going to be all out of patience. You tell me the guy's name or I'm booking you for homicide."

"You said that already!" His dark eyes brooded over my face for a moment. "All right. His name is Salter, Hugo Salter. He's got an office downtown in the Connington Insurance Building."

"He needs an office to keep tabs on you?"

"There's a legitimate business there as a front," Fletcher said tiredly. "Salter called the day we got here, introduced himself to all of us. Told us he'd be watching all the time. A war of nerves I guess you'd call it ... or something."

"O.K.," I said. I stood up and walked to the door. "Did Johnny put the hole in the back of the lucky guy's head that night?"

"I don't know what you're talking about," he said tonelessly.

"If I was tied to a crazy punk like him, I wouldn't sleep nights," I said. "You don't look as if you sleep nights, Fletcher."

"I sleep all right," he said. "Johnny's O.K. He just gets excited, that's all."

I let myself out of the apartment and went back to the Healey. I drove downtown and parked outside the Connington Building. Hugo Salter's office was on the seventh floor, the board said. It also said he was an importer. I wondered what he imported?

There was a blonde at a typewriter when I walked into the office. She wore a tight black dress that looked as demure as she did. "I'd like to see Mr. Salter," I told her.

"Who is calling, please?"

"Lieutenant Wheeler, Sheriff's department," I said.

Her smile became a little fixed around the edges. "I'll tell him you're here, Lieutenant. Won't you take a seat?"

"Why not?" I sat down and waited while she lifted the phone. "He'll see you right away," she said fifteen seconds later.

I walked past her to the inner office, knocked on the door, then walked in. It was a nicely furnished office, expensive in the modern manner, and the guy behind the desk looked the same way.

He had thick gray hair, a nice suntan, and a neat gray suit. He stood up and shook hands with me. "Sit down, Lieutenant." His voice was pleasant. "What can I do for you? We don't often have a visit from the police. This is the first one, as a matter of fact. I'm intrigued."

"Have you made up your mind about Fletcher and the others yet?" I asked him as I sat down.

His face became a polite blank. "I'm sorry. I don't understand?"

"I'm a tired man, Mr. Salter," I said. "I don't want you to play games. I wouldn't mind with your secretary, but not with you. You're the Pine City representative of the Las Vegas Syndicate. Fletcher and the rest of the people with him are suspected of taking the Syndicate for seventy thousand dollars. Your job, or one of them, is to try to find out for sure whether they did take the money or not. I want to know if you've made up your mind yet?"

Salter shook his head slowly. "This is the most fantastic thing I've ever heard, Lieutenant. Are you sure you're talking to the right man? I mean, I imagine there are a number of people with the name of Salter in Pine City."

"O.K.," I said. "So we'll start again. Your name is Hugo Salter and you're an importer?"

"That is correct."

"What do you import?"

"Well, all sorts of things, Lieutenant. Photographic equipment, mainly."

"You have heard of the murder of Linda Scott?"

He nodded. "Of course, Lieutenant. I read the newspapers. I couldn't avoid hearing about it."

"Where were you, the night she was murdered?"

"As I remember I was right here in the office," he said easily. "As a matter of fact we were working late. We'd just had in a new shipment and we were checking the details. My secretary was here with me, as it happens."

"I bet she was," I said.

"Really, Lieutenant! I don't care for the tone of your voice."

"You'll have to blame my parents for that," I said. "My old man was a whisky baritone and my mother always said their honeymoon was a song of love. Now. There are two theories about why Linda Scott was murdered. One is that Howard Fletcher murdered her. The other is that the Syndicate had made up its mind about them, and its Pine City representative murdered her."

"I still have no idea what you're talking about," he said carefully.

"I don't think for a moment that you do," I said. "But there is one interesting thought, Mr. Salter. If another one of them is murdered, it would sort of prove the point that the Syndicate had made up its mind about them, wouldn't it?"

He just looked at me without saying anything. I got up again and headed for the door. "I guess I must have picked the wrong Salter," I said. "If you have any ideas on the subject, you might let me know."

"Just a minute, Lieutenant!" he said crisply.

I turned around and looked at him. "Yeah?"

"You're from the County Sheriff's department?"

"Check."

"You're investigating the girl's murder?"

"Check again."

"You're not interested in the ... importing business, as such?"

"I'm only interested in finding Linda Scott's killer," I told him.

He placed his elbows on his desk, making a pyramid of his hands and rubbing the fingertips together softly. "Then I think I could answer a question for you, if it will help. The answer is no, the gentlemen in question haven't made up their minds yet."

"Thanks," I said.

"And if they had," he smiled faintly, "I'm quite sure that nothing so crude would have occurred."

"I'm glad to hear it," I said. "Goodbye, Mr. Salter."

Goodbye, Lieutenant," he said. "Wheeler, you said your name was?"

"That's right."

"I must remember to tell a friend of mine," he said. "He'd be most interested to hear there is a lieutenant by the name of Wheeler in Pine City."

"Your friend's name must be Max," I said.

"But of course." he smiled again. "He arrived back at casino about seven-thirty this morning, so I heard."

"I hope he was in good health?"

"A little too much exertion too quickly," Salter murmured, the grin broadening on his face. "And a slight case of overexposure."

Chapter Seven

"You didn't stay very long in Las Vegas," Annabelle Jackson said. "Lose all your money the first night you were there?"

"I lost a dollar," I said. "But I met a Gabrielle."

"He couldn't have picked a better place to blow the trumpet!" she said.

"This one has two *l*'s and an *e*. She's feminine and as far as I know, no relation," I explained.

Annabelle started to hammer her typewriter. "I should have known you'd get mixed up with some sordid female. It's the Wheeler routine, isn't it?"

"You know how I feel about women," I said.

"I certainly do," she said viciously. "Desperate!"

"Is the Sheriff in?"

"He's got somebody with him at the moment. You want me to tell him you're back? I don't think he'll roll out the red carpet."

"Tell him, anyway," I said. "What can I lose but my job?"

She picked up the phone and spoke into it. "He said for you to go straight in," she told me as she replaced the receiver. "He must be losing his mind, he sounded almost pleased to hear you were back."

"He looks on me as a prodigal son," I said smugly. "He'll probably kill the fatted calf next." I looked at her critically. "I hope you've been watching your weight lately?"

She made a grab for the heavy rule on her desk and I stepped quickly into the Sheriff's office, closing the door behind me firmly.

Lavers almost smiled at me from across his desk. "Glad you're back, Wheeler," he said. "This is Mr. Schafer, from the *Tribune*."

Schafer smiled at me thinly from the visitor's chair. "I've already met the Lieutenant," he said. "How's the investigation progressing?"

"We're making progress," I said.

"Something concrete?" he persisted. "I'd like any details you can give me."

"Mr. Schafer seems to think we aren't making progress fast enough," Lavers said heavily. "He's wondering why we haven't called in Homicide to help."

"The case comes under the Sheriff's jurisdiction," I said to Schafer. "We can handle it."

"You don't seem to be getting any results yet, Lieutenant," he said smoothly. "My editor is very interested in the case. He feels the people have a vital interest in it, also. In fairness to our readers, he thinks—"

"I know what your editor thinks," I said. "He told me."

Schafer shrugged and looked at the Sheriff. "We'd like to cooperate with you, Sheriff," he said. "But I take it you don't want cooperation? Lieutenant Wheeler's attitude makes that very clear!"

Lavers shifted uneasily in his chair. "I wouldn't say that at all," he hedged. "The Lieutenant, like all of us right now, is under a strain and—"

"—it's hard to cooperate with a suspect, anyway," I finished the sentence for him.

Lavers' face started to redden as he glared at me.

"That's true, isn't it, sir?" I asked him politely. "Schafer is still a suspect. We know he was very friendly with Linda Scott. It could be a crime of passion."

Schafer stood up slowly. "I guess that's one way of not answering questions," he said. "But, suspect or not, I represent the biggest newspaper in this city, Sheriff. If you're not going to answer questions and cooperate with us, my editor is going to want to know why—in print." He walked out of the office, slamming the door behind him.

I sat down in the chair he'd just vacated and lit a cigarette.

"I called you in because I thought you'd be a help," Lavers said in a resigned voice. "Haven't you ever heard of the word, 'tact'?"

"Yes, sir."

"Then why the hell didn't you use some? You know what the *Tribune* can do to me over this case. Or don't you care?"

"I don't think we can be tactful with either Schafer or his editor, Sheriff," I told him. "The only thing we can do is find Linda Scott's murderer. Tact would be taken as a sign of weakness by the *Tribune*, and only confirm their suspicions that we've got something to hide."

"Oh, that again!" Lavers grunted. "You still think I'm in partnership with Fletcher to start a gambling casino somewhere in the county?"

"No, sir," I said. "Not after Las Vegas."

"Las Vegas?" His voice showed sudden interest. "You found out something there?"

I told him the story. Lavers didn't say anything when I'd finished. He filled his pipe methodically and took his time about lighting it. "Good work, Wheeler!" he said finally. "That's all we wanted."

"All?" I queried. "For what?"

"To arrest Fletcher," he said fiercely. "Now we've got motive. If Linda was mixed up in it, I think your theory is right. She wouldn't have been able to stand up to the nervous strain. She'd crack up, and that's why Fletcher killed her. To stop her talking to the Syndicate!"

"We can't be sure the Syndicate didn't kill her, Sheriff," I said. "Salter's word that they haven't made up their minds yet isn't exactly evidence, is it?"

"The case we've got against Fletcher is good enough for me!" he said.

"It's nowhere near good enough for me," I told him

He bit down hard on the stem of his pipe and glared at me. "You seem to be very reluctant to book Fletcher," he growled. "I'm beginning to wonder why, Wheeler."

"I think we should be sure about it, sir," I said as politely as I could. "He made you a proposition about starting a casino here and you refused. He threatened you, said he'd give you one final warning. You're not going to believe that he then killed Linda and dumped her on your doorstep? He would have known it was almost as good as a signed confession."

"Maybe," Lavers said. "Maybe there's another way of looking at it, too. Supposing he did just what you said? Then when you questioned him, he could say he wouldn't be crazy enough to do what he said he was going to do, couldn't he? A neat switch."

Lavers had a point there. "A sort of double-take," I said. "I see what you mean, but I still don't believe it. Fletcher isn't the sort of guy to back long shots."

Lavers sucked his pipe for a few seconds. "If Fletcher didn't kill her, then who did? The Syndicate?"

"I don't know," I admitted. "Give me a little more time and I'll find out."

"We don't have that much time. Apart from my personal interest in this case, you heard what that newspaperman said just now. We're about to get the treatment from that paper. Don't forget that I have to think about the voters at the next election. You don't!"

"Give me another two days, Sheriff," I pleaded. "If I haven't gotten a better idea by then, we'll book Fletcher."

"Two days is a very long time right now," he grunted. "But ... all right."

"Thanks, Sheriff."

I went out of his office and found Schafer outside, sitting on Annabelle's desk, swinging his legs idly. "Waiting for you, Lieutenant." He grinned at me. "You owe me a drink." A drink sounded like a good idea.

We went out of the office and walked half a block to the nearest bar. After the drinks had arrived, Schafer looked at me. "Did you find out anything interesting in Las Vegas?"

"Who said I'd been there?"

"That sweet-talking chile from the Deep South in your office," he said almost cheerfully. "I told you I had a way with women."

"So you did." I remembered. "No, I didn't find out at anything of interest there."

"You wouldn't tell if you had, I guess," he said. "There was nothing personal in what I said back there in the Sheriff's office, you understand, Lieutenant? I'm just a working guy the same as you."

"Like you said, I owe you the drink," I reminded him. "You don't have to paint hearts and flowers on the table."

"I have an editor," he said. "He dictates the policy of the newspaper, you understand?"

"Sure," I said. "You had an editor in Chicago, too?"

His face darkened. "Just what the hell do you mean by that?"

"I mean that if the Chicago story is true," I said carefully, "you're a get-the-story-and-what-the-hell type character, and I'd trust you as far as I'd trust myself in a nudist colony."

"Could be you're right," he said evenly. "But that's no reason why we can't work together. You want to get Fletcher and I want to get the story."

"I want to get a murderer," I said. "What makes you think it's necessarily Fletcher?"

"You think it's Fletcher, Lieutenant," he said. "It's your boss who doesn't want him brought in. Sure, you'll deny it because you work for the Sheriff, but I get a feeling about these things. Am I right?"

"Do me a favor, Schafer," I said politely. "Go get yourself a job as a watchman some place. Then I can set fire to the building."

His face paled a fraction. "All right, if you want it that way. If we can bust a Sheriff, an ordinary cop is no trouble at all. And don't think we can't; the *Tribune's* broken bigger people before!"

"I must come around to your office and listen to the snapping sounds," I said. "Does it happen all the time or only on Thursdays?"

"O.K.," he said tautly. "If that's the way you want it!" He got to his feet and walked out of the bar.

I finished my drink, had one more, then went back and picked up the Austin-Healey from outside the office. I drove home and went up to the apartment. I put Sinatra on the hi-fi machine and listened to "Mood Indigo" while I made myself a drink. It was mood music for the mood I was in. I sat down in an armchair and closed my eyes. Five minutes' relaxation would do me a lot of good.

It was a noise that woke me up, an irritating, persistent noise. I opened my eyes and realized it was the sound of the door buzzer. I looked at my watch and the time was five-thirty. The five minutes had turned into three hours.

I heaved myself out of the chair and walked to the front door and opened it.

"It's about time!" Gabrielle said tartly. "I've been standing here for five minutes."

"I didn't know it could happen," I said. "A dream within a dream. Did Freud ever hear about this?"

"What are you babbling about?" she asked coldly.

"I was asleep," I said. "Then I woke up when I heard the buzzer and opened the door, and you're here. So I'm still dreaming. You're in Las Vegas."

"I'm in Pine City," she said. "Just don't stand there—let me in!"

I moved to one side obediently and she walked into the apartment, carrying her suitcase with her. She dumped it on the living room floor and turned around. "You could offer me a drink or something."

"You're real?" I queried.

She flicked the tip of my nose painfully with her thumb and forefinger. "Does that prove you're awake?"

"I guess it does," I said. "How did you ever get out of Vegas?"

"Give me a drink," she said. "I'm thirsty."

I made two drinks and gave her one. She looked at me critically. "You look like you've just been exhumed! Go and comb your hair or something."

"What have I got to lose?" I muttered. "Except hair?" I went into the bathroom, washed my face and hands, combed my hair, then came back in the living room again.

Gabrielle was sitting comfortably in the armchair, the drink in her hand. She looked nice and fresh in an off-white silk chemise that didn't come from a bargain basement. I sat down on the couch opposite her and picked up my own drink. "Tell me about it?"

"There's nothing to it," she said. "Fulton called on me this morning. He said I must have talked to you last night and he thought I should know I was free to go anywhere I liked, any time. That story about having to stay in Vegas was just a gag. He was more polite than I've ever known him. After a while I started to realize he must be on the level, so I didn't wait around for him to change his mind. I caught the next plane out."

"Why come to Pine City?" I asked, and I knew it was a stupid question as soon as I asked it.

"Why, Al!" Her voice became a throaty purr. "I wouldn't pass up the opportunity of calling on my old friends. I'm going to drop around and see Howard tonight. Howard and his redheaded playmate. I've got a couple of things to say to both of them!"

"I wouldn't do anything hasty!" I said feebly.

She glared at me. "You wouldn't maybe, but I'm different. When I've finished with that little ..."

"After all," I said, "what's done is done. Why don't you forget all about—"

"Have you seen Howard today?" she asked crisply.

"This morning," I said without thinking.

She smiled contentedly. "You told him about last night?"

"Last night?"

"Don't be bashful!" she said impatiently. "You told him about us last night, I mean! That was the one stringer I put on the hospitality, remember?"

"Sure," I said. "I remember."

"Well?"

"No," I shook my head. "I didn't tell him."

"So you're another double-crosser!"

"Let me get you another drink," I said hastily.

She threw her empty glass at me and I caught it more by luck than judgment. "Why didn't you tell him!" she stormed.

"You know how it is." I pleaded. "That sort of thing is difficult to say to a man when ..."

"All right!" She bounced onto her feet. "If you don't have the nerve to tell him, I certainly do! I'm going right over there now. Then I'm going to take him and that no-good Nina apart. When I've finished, it won't be worth anybody's while to pick up the pieces! I'm going to—"

"I wouldn't," I said.

"Why not!"

I put the two empty glasses carefully on the table, then turned to face her. "I told you I was a cop, didn't I?"

"What's that got to do with it!"

"When I was talking to you last night, I wanted some information about Howard. I knew you were his girl; you wouldn't tell me anything while you felt that way about him. So I had to change your feelings first before you'd talk, if you see what I mean?"

The expression on her face changed from bewilderment to naked murder. "You mean," she said slowly, "that story you told me about Howard and Nina was ..."

"Made up," I agreed. "A complete fabrication. No truth in it at all as far as I know."

"And to get even with Howard I let you ..." She came at me like a guided missile with a homing device. Her fist hammered a tattoo against my face while she balanced on one leg and hacked my shin painfully with the heel of the shoe on her other foot. It hurt! I put my hand against her face and pushed.

She staggered backwards across the room, fighting to regain her balance. The back of her knees hit the arm of the chair and she fell backwards across it. The hem of the dress rode up above the tops of her stockings and for a moment she was still. Then her heels started to drum into the side of the chair and she dissolved into hysterics.

The Scotch was too good to waste so I went out into the kitchen, filled a jug with cold water, and brought it back into the living room with me. Her long legs were still beating out their message against the chair and she was yelling at the top of her voice. I remembered the landlord didn't like me anyway. I poured the cold water over her head and she stopped suddenly.

There was a long five seconds where nothing happened, which gave me time to light a cigarette. Then she stood up slowly. Her hair was plastered down tight on her scalp and the chemise clung to her like one of those "Before" pictures advertising a non-shrink treatment. "The first chance I get," she said in a low, clear voice. "I'll kill you, Al Wheeler! It will be slow and painful, do you understand?"

"Yes, ma'am," I said humbly.

"Get me a towel!" she said bitterly.

I went into the bathroom and collected a towel. When I got back into the living room, the soaking-wet chemise and a slip were draped across the couch. Gabrielle stood there in a pair of panties, glowering at me. She snatched the towel out of my hand and began to dry herself.

I made two more drinks and handed her one. She stopped towelling herself long enough to down the drink, then handed me the empty glass. When she was dry, she picked up her suitcase and disappeared into the bedroom. She reappeared five minutes later, wearing a white cotton sweater and a pair of black matador pants. She looked at me and I braced myself for round two. Then she smiled suddenly. "I rather enjoyed that," she said casually. "Howard would never fight, he said it was childish."

It looked like an occasion for another drink and I took advantage of it. Gabrielle curled up in the armchair, her drink in one hand, and looked at me thoughtfully. "I cooled off a lot after Howard ran out and left me," she said. "So maybe I'm not really so mad at you after all."

"You don't have to convince me," I told her. "Just my shinbone."

"But I'd like to see him again all the same," she said. "I'd like to tell the rat just what I think of him!"

"Do something for me," I said. "Tell him Fulton let you leave Las Vegas because he said there was no need to keep you there any longer. Tell Fletcher that the Syndicate has made up their minds about him and they know he can't run out of Pine City now, so they didn't need you any more as a hostage."

"Why should I tell him that?"

"It won't hurt to tell him that, will it?"

"I guess not," she conceded. "All right, Al, since you asked me nicely."

"Fine!" I said. "I have to go out now. Can I drop you any place? Which hotel are you staying at?"

"Al!" She looked hurt. "Where is that Pine City hospitality I've heard so much about?"

"Huh?" I blinked at her.

"You certainly didn't have anything to complain about over my hospitality in Las Vegas, did you?"

"I guess not," I said.

"Then that's settled," she said brightly. "I didn't think I'd have to complain about your hospitality in Pine City!"

Chapter Eight

It was around eight that night when I called on Nina Booth again. I pressed the buzzer three times before she opened the door. That enchanted look was missing from her face as she looked at me. The first two buttons of her blouse were undone and the zipper of her skirt was two inches short of being closed. Her hair was mussed and her lipstick had a blurred look around the edges. "Oh," she said unenthusiastically. "It's you."

"I'm keeping the date I missed last night," I said. "Sorry I couldn't make it but I got detained." I went to walk past her into the apartment but she blocked the way.

"Make it some other time, will you?" she said. "I'm busy right now."

"You can't obstruct justice," I said reproachfully. "I am one arm and two legs of the law. I want to talk to you." I put my hands on her waist, lifted her out of the way, and walked into the living room.

Fletcher came off the couch in one flurried movement, pulling a handkerchief from his pocket and dabbing futilely at the lipstick smears across his face.

"So I'm psychic and never knew," I said. "There are times when I even scare myself!"

"Don't I have any privacy?" Nina asked bitterly.

"Any time but now," I said. "I want to talk to you." I looked pointedly at Fletcher. "Now you've got a postponement, why don't you retire to your corner and freshen up a little?"

He glared at me and said one word under his breath, then he picked up his coat and walked toward the door. I remembered happily that Gabrielle was calling on him one floor up. It should be quite a reunion. The door closed behind him with a bang and Nina glared at me. "What do you want?"

"Things have changed between us somehow," I said regretfully. "Night before last you were offering me a cozy chat. We were going to talk over our problems and you in your negligee and everything. Did I do something?"

"I guess I can't call a cop and have you thrown out," she said. "You might as well make yourself a drink while I get tidied up a little."

"That sounds more like the Nina I thought I knew," I said.

She disappeared into the bathroom and I walked across to the bar and made myself a drink. Then I sat in a chair and waited. Five minutes later she came back. The buttons and the zipper had been taken care of, her hair was in place, and her lipstick had a nice clean outline. She went over to the bar and made herself a drink.

"What did you want to talk about?" she asked.

"Seventy thousand dollars," I said. "Who's got it—Fletcher?"

"I don't know what you're talking about!"

"Leave us not play games," I said. "I know about the guy who got lucky playing craps and died suddenly before he could enjoy his luck."

She turned around and looked at me, her face set hard. "I don't know anything about that, Lieutenant," she said crisply. "All I can tell you is that the guy was winning fair and square while I was handling the table."

"The way I hear it, the Syndicate's made up its mind that he didn't win fair and square," I said casually. "That lets you out as a murder suspect of course, the same way it lets Fletcher and Torch out."

"What do you mean?"

"It's obvious, isn't it?" I said. "The Syndicate took care of Linda Scott, dumped her on Sheriff Lavers' doorstep to make it look like Fletcher did it."

She finished her drink and put the glass down on the bar carefully. "Then all you have to do is to find the Syndicate boys who killed Linda, Lieutenant, and the case is finished."

"Sure," I said. "I just hope we find them before they find you."

"If you really think I'm in danger, Lieutenant, you should give me police protection. Is that what you're here for?" A derisive grin curved her lips. "What sort of a dope do you think I am? Just driven in with a load of turnips, or something?"

"The load you carry has nothing to do with turnips," I admitted. "All right, so you aren't scared. But I'm telling you again, the Syndicate has made up its mind."

"I told you before I don't know what you're talking about," she said. "Would you like me to write it down for you so you don't forget again?"

"I'll remember," I said. "It doesn't make a bad epitaph at that. 'She didn't know what they were talking about.' You want to be buried with a pair of dice in your hand?"

"Why don't you get out of here?" she said. "You bore me, Lieutenant."

I was beginning to bore myself. I returned the empty glass to the bar and then walked toward the door. The buzzer blipped just before I got there. "Maybe this is the Syndicate already?" I said cheerfully.

Nina smiled contemptuously: "With you for protection, why should I worry?" She walked past me and opened the door.

Gabrielle stood there, a tigerish smile on her face. "Hello, sweetie," she purred. "Howard was still cleaning off the lipstick smudges when he got upstairs. You've been making time in Pine City, honey. But then you never were a girl to let the grass grow under your feet, were you?"

"I don't have anything to say to you!" Nina said coldly and started to shut the door.

"I only called to give you something to remember me by," Gabrielle said. She swung a roundhouse right that caught Nina squarely in the solar plexus. The redhead moaned softly and started to fold. Gabrielle grabbed her blouse with both hands and dragged her across the apartment toward the bathroom. "I won't be a minute, Al," she said as she went past. "Wait for me."

"Yes, ma'am," I said nervously.

The bathroom door closed behind them. There was the sound of a scuffle; a shriek followed by a slap, and then the sound of running water drowned the others. I walked over to the bar and made myself another drink. I wondered if another murder was going on and I should stop it. I decided I didn't have the courage.

Five minutes later the bathroom door opened and Gabrielle came back into the living room, wiping her hands on a guest towel. "Shall we go?" she asked politely.

"Do you mind if I take a look first?" I asked her.

"Help yourself," she shrugged. "But don't take too long. I'm hungry and you're buying me dinner."

I pushed the bathroom door open cautiously and took a look inside. A pile of clothes lay on the floor. The door to the shower stall was closed and the noise of the running water thundered in my ears. I had a mental vision of the water running red inside, and shuddered. I pushed the door wide open.

A goose-pimpled vision staggered out of the shower and stood there, shivering violently. I switched off the cold water and the noise ceased. "Get me out of this damned thing!" Nina said thickly.

After the first look I closed my eyes. Where in hell had Gabrielle got a straitjacket? Then I took another look and saw it wasn't a straitjacket after all. Gabrielle had pulled Nina's girdle up above her waist, leaving her arms inside. Maybe it was better than a straitjacket.

"Don't just stand there!" Nina said hysterically. "I'll die of pneumonia in a minute! Get me out of this thing!"

It was no time for modesty. I hooked my fingers under the edges of the girdle and managed to wrestle it down over her goose-pimples to her ankles. She stepped out of it, grabbed a bath towel and wrapped it around herself, then sat weakly on the edge of the bath. "I'll kill her!" she said in a shaking voice. "I'll tear her heart out! I'll ..." The details began to get a little more intimate. I would have liked to have heard the rest but Gabrielle called impatiently from the living room.

When I got back there, Gabrielle was screwing the cap back on a bottle. She replaced the bottle behind the bar and smiled at me. "That was the last one," she said. "Shall we go?"

"Sure," I gulped. "You're an active sort of girl, aren't you?"

"I'm a hungry sort of girl," she said. "Let's go eat."

We went out of the apartment house and into the Healey. I drove downtown to a restaurant I knew, where they didn't insist you buy your steak outright; they'd give you a mortgage.

Gabrielle carved her way through soup, a T-bone, and two bowls of strawberries with cream. By the time the coffee arrived, she had relaxed a little. "I like Pine City, Al," she said happily.

"It will never be the same again," I observed somberly. Then I remembered. "What did you mean about that being the last bottle?"

"Last bottle?" She batted her eyelids innocently. "Did I say that?"

"You know damned well you did—just as I came out of the bathroom."

"How was Nina?" she asked sweetly. "All cooled off?"

"Yeah," I said. "The bottle?"

"Oh, that?" The Borgia look came into her eyes again. "Nina's bar was very well stocked, Al. I counted fifteen bottles of hard liquor."

"So you can count."

"I found something else, too," she said. "A bottle of that stuff you fill cigarette lighters with, whatever they call it."

"You didn't run a fuse into it and light it just as we left?" I shuddered.

"Al!" She looked at me reproachfully. "You know I wouldn't do a thing like that. I just added a teensy-weensy little bit of the lighter stuff to all the other bottles."

"If she drinks any of it, it will probably kill her!" I said.

"I hope so!" Gabrielle agreed enthusiastically. "But I hope she gives Howard some first!"

We got back to the apartment around eleven. Gabrielle disappeared into the bedroom. I put Sinatra's "Songs for Swinging Lovers" on the hi-fi machine. It seemed an appropriate title for Gabrielle somehow. I sank into the nearest chair and started to think about Linda Scott, then I stopped thinking about her quite suddenly. Gabrielle came back into the room. "What's that you're wearing?" I asked her hoarsely.

"It's my harem outfit," she said complacently. "It's for sleeping in, and things. You like it?"

The harem outfit consisted of a short-sleeved top and a pair of baggy pants caught tight at the ankles. Below the cuff on her left ankle, two gold slave bangles jangled. There were two further pertinent facts about the outfit. It was black in color and completely transparent.

She walked over and sat on my knee, putting her hands on my shoulders. "I like Pine City!" she said huskily. She bent her head down and kissed me. It was like the chair was wired and somebody had loosed off about fifty thousand volts. The kiss started to develop into an experience. From little acorns and all that jazz.

The shrill of the phone cut across my nerve-ends like a butcher's knife. Gabrielle straightened up reluctantly on my knee.

"Whoever it is," she murmured, "tell them to go away for the week."

I eased her gently off my knee, stood up, and walked across to the phone. I lifted the receiver and said: "This is a hell of a time to call me!"

"Lieutenant Wheeler?" The voice was crisp and feminine. "This is Nina Booth. I thought you'd want to know that—" There was a muffled sound, then silence.

"Hello?" I said. "Nina? Nina!" I heard an empty humming noise, then the faint click as someone replaced the receiver.

"What did she want?" Gabrielle asked lazily from the depths of the chair. "To sue me or something?"

I replaced the receiver. "She was going to tell me something, then it sounded like she got slugged."

"Good!"

"I'd better go take a look," I said.

Gabrielle's eyes widened as she sat bolt upright in the chair. "You mean you're walking out on me ... now!"

"I'll be back," I said. "I'm a cop, remember?" I picked up my hat and headed toward the door.

"Just one thing, Lieutenant!" she said coldly. "You might be back, but I won't be here when you arrive."

"That's Fate for you," I said. "Now you got it, now you don't."

I watched reluctantly while she slipped the top of the harem outfit over her head. It came down to about three inches below her waist. She picked up the baggy pants in one hand, then looked at me impatiently.

"Well?" she demanded.

My head was shaking all by itself. "It's just that I'm crazy," I told her, and dragged my feet toward the door.

It took me twenty minutes to get across town to the apartment house I'd left a couple of hours before. I rode the elevator up to Nina's floor and then walked along to her apartment. I pressed the buzzer a couple of times, then tried the door handle and found it wasn't locked. I pushed the door open and stepped inside the apartment. It was in darkness.

I ran my hand down the wall until I found the light switch and flicked it on. The living room looked much the same as it had before earlier in the evening. Nina Booth lay face down on the floor. There was a bright wet stain on the rug, and an ice pick protruded from the back of her head. Very messy.

I lit a cigarette and forced myself to look away. There were two wet smears on the bar where two glasses must have stood recently, but the glasses themselves had disappeared. They'd been cleaned, I guessed, and so had the phone.

Whoever had killed her must have had a cool head to stay in the apartment long enough to clean up any proof of having been there at all. Knowing that I'd follow up that call of Nina's; knowing that I would arrive at any minute.

Chapter Nine

Fletcher backed up into his apartment and I followed him inside. "What now?" he asked wearily. "Not more questions! The hell with it, Lieutenant, you're wasting your time. I don't know any more answers!"

He wore a robe over his pajamas. His hair was mussed and he looked like he'd just got out of bed, but that didn't mean anything much. His right eye was discolored. "What happened to your eye?" I asked him.

"Had a visit from an old girl friend when I wasn't expecting her," he grinned faintly. "Just after I left Nina's place when you busted in there. She has a quick temper and a fast left, Lieutenant, that's all."

"What did you do after that?"

"I've been here," he said. "In the apartment. Why?"

I looked around the room; nothing was propping up the wall. "Where's Johnny Torch?"

"I wouldn't know," Fletcher said. "He went out around ten. Said he was going to have a couple of drinks some place. He was restless."

He watched me as I walked past him into his bedroom. The covers were thrown back and the bed looked untidy. I checked on the bathroom and Torch's room. Fletcher looked at me curiously when I finally got back to the living room. "Is this more trouble or what?" he asked

"Nina Booth was murdered less than an hour ago," I told him.

His face crumpled suddenly. "Nina?" he whispered "I don't believe it!" He sat down slowly and stared at me for a long moment with the face of an old man. "How did it happen?"

I told him how it had happened. He shook his head as if the words hit him with physical force. "Nina!" he whispered again. "First Linda and now Nina. Who did it, Lieutenant?"

"That's what I'm trying to find out," I said. "You sure Johnny went out just for a drink?"

There was a slight movement behind me. I turned around quickly and saw Johnny Torch standing in the doorway, looking at me with an expressionless face. He walked slowly into the center of the room, his hands in his pockets, his hat tilted to the back of his head. His eyes were slightly glazed.

"Sure I went out for a drink," he said. "I had maybe four drinks, I don't remember. That a crime in this crummy town of yours, copper?"

"Shut up, Johnny!" Fletcher said harshly. "Somebody got Nina with an ice pick about an hour back."

Torch's face drained of color rapidly. "Nina?" he said hoarsely.

"Don't let us have that routine again," I said. "I've been through it once with Fletcher. Where were you drinking?"

"A bar down the street," he said.

"What's it called?"

"I don't know. It served liquor, it was open. That was all I needed to know."

"You'll have to do better than that, Johnny," I told him. "A lot better."

"It's about two blocks south of here," he said. "Same side of the street."

"When did you last see Nina?"

"Sometime this afternoon, I guess. She was up here for about half an hour. We were talking, the three of us."

I looked across at Fletcher who nodded. "That's right, Lieutenant. That would have been around four o'clock. I went back down with her. The last time I saw her was when you called on her."

"All right," I said. I looked at Johnny Torch. "We'll check that bar. I hope somebody remembers you there, for your sake. Nobody remembered either of you at that restaurant the night Linda Scott was murdered."

"Stop riding me, copper!" Johnny said tautly. "Why don't you get after the guys that really killed her! Maybe you're too scared, huh? Or maybe the pay-off in this town's a little too big for you to go asking awkward questions!"

"Lay off, Johnny," Fletcher said wearily. "This won't get you any place."

"Shut up!" Torch snarled. "You shut up for a change! I'm tired of you pushing me around. Tired of this whole lousy setup, you hear!"

"You're not telling me," Fletcher said coldly. "Right now you're just telling the Lieutenant!"

"Go on, Johnny," I said encouragingly. "This is getting interesting."

His lips tightened until they disappeared. "I've said all I'm going to say, copper."

He sounded like he meant it, so I went back down to Nina Booth's apartment where I'd left Polnik as soon as he arrived. He had company now. Doc Murphy, the Sheriff, the boys from the Crime Lab. The apartment was a hive of industry with Lavers looking like a queen bee that's just been stung.

"Well?" he growled at me.

"Fletcher was in his apartment all night," I said. "Torch just got back. He went out around ten, he's been drinking in a bar two blocks south on the same side of the street."

Lavers made a disgusted sound in the back of his throat. "No alibi for the second time!"

Doc Murphy came out of the bathroom, drying his hands on a towel. "If it isn't the lecherous lieutenant!" he said benevolently. "Picking out your redheads now, Wheeler?"

"You know how it is," I said. "I got to thinking that if I didn't do something different, I'd end up like you. Better the gas chamber."

Murphy chuckled appreciatively. "I can give you the benefit of my long years of study and the even longer years of following my profession. She was hit with an ice pick in the back of the head and it killed her. You see the advantages of being a doctor?"

"Stop clowning!" Lavers snarled. "Time of death?"

"What's got into you, Sheriff?" Murphy looked at him with mild surprise. "When you've seen one cadaver, you've seen them all, you know that. What's so special about this one?"

"Time of death!" Lavers thundered.

"Eleven-twenty," I said. "That was when she stopped talking to me over the phone."

"A good a time as any," Murphy said. "I would have said within the last hour. Anything else you want to know that I can't tell you, Sheriff?"

"Instantaneous?" Lavers asked sharply.

"The point of the ice pick went straight into her brain," Murphy said. "It must have given her something to think about." He cackled again then stopped suddenly when he saw the cold fury in Lavers' eyes. "Sure," he nodded. "Instantaneous."

I picked up the phone directory and flipped through it. Hugo Salter had his home number listed. He lived out in Cone Hill where they roll up the sidewalks at nine every night, but they dust them first so the residents don't dirty their shoes next morning.

"Death and decay," a familiar voice said from the door of the apartment. "'Dirge without Music'—that's a poem, you know? 'Down, down, down into the darkness of the grave, Gently they go...' A woman by the name of Millay wrote it—if anybody cares."

"How did you get here?" Lavers asked harshly.

Schafer grinned at him. "You called out the Crime Lab boys from Homicide," he said. "The city cops always let us know what's going on; they're different. They don't play secrets like the Sheriff's department."

The Sheriff's face turned to a bright shade of scarlet. "You..." he almost choked.

Schafer looked down at the body. "She was a nice-looking kid," he said somberly. "Who did it?"

"That's what we're trying to find out," Lavers said harshly. "We can do it a lot quicker without any interruptions from you!"

"Go right ahead," Schafer said easily. "I'll just stick around and watch."

"Wheeler!" Lavers exploded. "Get this ... *journalist* out of here!"

"Yes, sir," I said promptly. I grabbed Schafer's arm and propelled him out of the apartment into the corridor.

"Are you arresting me, Lieutenant?" he asked coldly.

"Not exactly," I said. "But the Sheriff will if you stick around inside there much longer."

"I don't like being pushed around," he said, carefully freeing his elbow from my grasp. "Your Sheriff is going to learn that he can't push the *Tribune* around, before he's much older."

"I tremble for him," I said politely, and pushed the elevator button.

"Wait a minute!" Schafer said quickly. "Where are you going?"

"'Ask me no more '" I said gravely, "'what answer should I give?'"

"Hey!" He glared at me. "That's poetry."

The elevator arrived and the door slid open. I stepped into the cage and smiled at Schafer. "A gentleman by the name of Tennyson wrote it—if you care?" Then I pressed the button and the closing door erased the blank look on his face.

I drove out to Salter's house on Cone Hill. My watch said one o'clock when I got there, but the house was a blaze of light and there were five or six cars still parked in the driveway. This must be one night they forgot to roll up the sidewalks.

The door was half-open. I pressed the buzzer and waited. There were a lot of party noises coming from inside the house. High-pitched voices, glasses clinking; maybe it was Old Home Week for the Las Vegas Syndicate? I pressed the buzzer again and left my thumb leaning against it.

A tawny blonde moved down the hall uncertainly toward the front door. She wore a black sheath which emphasized her magnificent figure. When she got real close, I saw she couldn't have been any more than twenty. The glass jiggled in her hand as she squinted at me gravely. "What have you got there?" she asked with interest. "A riot?"

I removed my thumb from the buzzer. "I'd like to see Mr. Salter," 1 said.

"I'm Mrs. Salter," she said. "Won't I do?"

"Under almost any other circumstances you'd be an improvement," I told her. "But I have to see your husband."

"I suppose it's business," she said. "Sometimes I wish Hugo wasn't in the importing business; nobody else seems to work the hours he does."

"Las Vegas is such a big market," I said.

She looked at me blankly. "Las Vegas? Hugo imports cameras and stuff, he sells them here."

"My mistake," I apologized. "Can I see him?"

"I'll find him for you," she said. "What was the name again?"

"Wheeler," I said carefully, "Mr. Wheeler."

"I'll go find him, Mr. Wheeler," she said. "I will search high and low, to and from, near and far, up and down, there and back ..." Her voice drifted away with her as she swayed gently down the hall.

I lit a cigarette and leaned against the doorframe. Maybe a minute later, Salter came walking briskly down the hallway toward me. "Come right in," he said pleasantly. "Sorry you've been kept waiting. We're having a little celebration, my wife's birthday as a matter of fact, and she's been enjoying it." He smiled broadly. "You know how these things are. She's been celebrating a little too much, I suppose. Still, you only have your nineteenth birthday once, I guess."

"Nineteenth?" I said. "What was she, a child bride?"

"We've only been married six months," he said. "My third wife. I'm her first husband of course."

"What did you do with the first two wives?" I was interested. "Lose them on the slot machines?"

He grinned. "You have the sort of humor I appreciate, Lieutenant. Come into my study, will you? We shan't be disturbed in there."

I followed him along the hallway and then into a room off to the left. He closed the door behind him firmly. "Won't you sit down, Lieutenant? Can I get you a drink?"

"Scotch on the rocks, a little soda," I said. "Thanks."

He opened up the bar and made the drinks.

"When did your party kick off tonight?" I asked him.

"Around nine," he said. "The way it's going it will be dawn before it's through, I guess. I doubt if Angela is going to stay with it until the end."

"You've been here all the time?"

"Of course." He turned around from the bar and handed me my drink. He lifted his own glass. "Good luck, Lieutenant."

"You would have witnesses that you've been here all night?"

Salter lowered the glass slowly and looked at me. "It's like that, is it? What's happened?"

"Tell me about your witnesses first," I said. "And here's to the importing business that keeps a man working all hours!"

"You must have been talking to Angela," he grinned. "She doesn't know anything about my other interests. Witnesses, you said, Lieutenant? I guess there'd be around twenty guests who are still here now. They all know I've been here the whole time."

"Nina Booth was murdered tonight," I told him. His face blanked off automatically. "That's interesting. Do you know who did it?"

"Would I be here?"

"No, I guess you wouldn't. Stupid question. I can't help you, Lieutenant, I'm sorry. You can check my witnesses, naturally, but you'll find I haven't been out of this house since nine tonight."

"Maybe you didn't need to," I suggested. "Maybe you had somebody else do the job for you?"

"Call the local branch of Murder Incorporated—you're joking, Lieutenant!"

"And my jokes aren't very funny and their timing is all off," I admitted. "I'd still give a lot to know if your people in Las Vegas have already made up their minds about Fletcher and the others; and just when they made up their minds."

"They haven't," he said flatly. "The way things are developing, they won't need to. There are only two of them left now, Lieutenant, and one of them at least must be a murderer and you'll catch him. We'd just like to be sure about the money, one way or the other."

I finished the drink and stood up. "I should be going," I said.

"Don't you want to question my witnesses first?" Salter asked.

"I don't think so," I said. "Either way I won't get any place. If you did kill Nina Booth tonight, your guests will be hand-picked to swear you never set foot outside the house. If you didn't kill her, what do I care about your alibi?"

"That's an original way of looking at it, Lieutenant, he said. "You're so right, too."

He walked me down the hall to the front door "Well, good night ... Mr.

Wheeler," he said. "The 'mister' was your idea?"

"It breaks the monotony," I told him.

"I appreciated that," he said. "As I told you, Angela only knows that I'm in the importing business and handle photographic equipment. I appreciate your tact, Lieutenant. Maybe someday I can do you a favor in return. You've only got to let me know."

"Thanks," I said. "The next time I go to Vegas you might fix it so I can take my own roulette wheel with me."

I climbed into the Healey, backed down the drive and out into the street. I drove home gently. I wasn't going back to the office. Lavers would get along without me, I hoped. I knew what was going to happen when we talked and I still didn't want it to happen. Maybe he would have cooled down a little by normal office hours much later in the morning.

I left the Healey against the curb and went up to the apartment. I switched on the living room lights and saw there was no sign of Gabrielle in the room anywhere. A slight tinge of regret hit me but it was no use barking—ask the Hounds of Fate. I made myself a drink and slumped into a chair, hoping the phone wouldn't ring. Then I heard a scuffling sound and the door of the bedroom flew open. A slave-bangled bombshell, wearing a black harem outfit, landed squarely in my lap, knocking my drink clean out my hand. "I thought you'd left," I said somewhat dazed.

"Al, lover!" she pouted. "I've been waiting for you! Now, where were we?" She slid further down my lap and twined her arms around my neck. She felt very warm. Her lips parted slightly as they closed the gap toward mine. "I remember," she said huskily. "About here, I think?"

I got that feeling of being hit by a high-tension line whipping free, as we kissed. The kiss developed into a marathon but the big race was still to come.

For no good reason, Gabrielle suddenly broke free, pushing herself away from me. She stood up, her hands on her hips, looking down at me thoughtfully.

"What did I do?" I asked desperately. "What didn't I do? You can't want a drink, not now."

She shook her head slowly. "I'm slipping," she said. "I must be getting old, or something, Al. My memory is going!"

"Huh?" I muttered weakly.

"I asked you where were we," she said accusingly. "And you didn't tell me."

"You didn't give me a chance."

"Well, you should have known I was wrong. We weren't about here, we were a lot further on from here."

"I'm happy for us to retrace our steps," I told her sincerely.

"I like to have things right," she said.

She stepped out of the baggy pants in one swift movement, and stood there, holding them in one hand. "That's where we were!" she said in a satisfied voice. She dropped squarely into my lap again. "I like to get things right, Al," she said. Then she squealed suddenly, and her body relaxed.

"You do talk on," I said.

"But only to a man of action," she whispered huskily.

Experience is the cornerstone of living, some guy once said. If he's right, I built myself a skyscraper that night.

Chapter Ten

"You're late, Lieutenant," Annabelle Jackson said as I walked into the office. "It's five after ten."

"I know I'm late," I said happily. "But it was worth it."

"The corpse-littered Casanova!" she said acidly. "The usual situation exists at the moment. The Sheriff is waiting for you. The Sheriff is furious. The longer he waits—"

"The shorter time I have left to remain a cop," I said. "I hear you talk but it sends me no message."

"Would you like your eyes bandaged, a last cigarette?" she asked sweetly.

"'Not a drum was heard, not a funeral note ...'" I said. "Did you know that's poetry?"

"Well, well," she murmured. "Walt Wheeler yet!"

I winced. "After that, the Sheriff's going to be easy to take."

When I saw the look on Lavers' face as I walked into his office, I revised my estimate quickly.

"Why bother to come into the office now?" he asked. "It seems a pity to waste what little is left of the day here!"

"I would have been early, sir," I explained, "but I was late."

"Why don't you sit down, Wheeler?" he persisted. "You must be tired. You didn't leave that apartment until about twelve-thirty last night. Whereas Polnik and myself got away at 4 A.M.!"

"Yes, sir," I said. I sat down carefully and felt for a cigarette.

"May I ask where you went that it was so important you walked out in the middle of a murder investigation?" Lavers asked with the mincing sarcasm of a flat-footed elephant. "Not that I want to intrude on your private life, of course. I'm just curious, that's all! I mean, it will look better in my report if I can give some reason!"

"I checked with Salter out at his home," I said. "He had a cast-iron alibi."

"Why Salter?"

"He's the Syndicate's representative here."

"You aren't still fooling around with that half-baked idea!" he thundered. "We've run out of time, Wheeler."

"Yes, sir," I said and wondered what the hell he was talking about.

"Since you were too busy this morning to get here on time, I sent Polnik out to take care of it."

"Polnik? To take care of what?" I stared at him.

"Fletcher, who else?"

"You mean you're booking him?"

"What else!"

"But you promised me I could have another two days, and that takes us through to tomorrow morning."

Lavers shook his head decisively. "I told you, time's run out on us, Wheeler. Haven't you read this morning's *Tribune*?"

"I never read any newspapers," I said. "They make me worry too much about a guy called Khrushchev. I figure the State Department should have given him a vicuna coat while they had the chance."

"Read this!" Lavers snarled, and thrust the newspaper at me.

I took it from him and looked. It was a front page story which headlined Nina's murder. The story only started with that; it developed the connection between Nina and Linda Scott. Then it tore into the County Sheriff, taking him apart limb by limb. It was done very well by insinuation and by questions.

There was nothing you could hang a libel suit on as far as I could see. But after I'd finished reading the full story, it was crystal clear that the pieces it left on the floor just weren't worth picking up. The byline was Rex Schafer's.

"Well!" Lavers snapped. "Now, do you still want another twenty-four hours while we do nothing?"

"Yes, sir," I said.

"Wheeler," he said tiredly. "Occasionally you have flashes of idiotic genius. But not this time. We have to face facts; you've gotten absolutely nowhere with either murder. It screams to high heaven, on the evidence we've got, that Fletcher is responsible for both murders. If I didn't book him this morning, I'd think I deserved the treatment that newspaper's given me!"

I opened my mouth to argue some more, then closed it again. The look on Lavers' face proved he'd passed the point of no return. I remembered I still had the cigarette I'd been searching for, between my fingers, unlit. I struck a match to it and inhaled deeply.

Lavers had a look of vague surprise on his face. He'd been waiting for my counterblast and couldn't quite figure why I hadn't launched it. The answer was simple really. I didn't have one. Not right then.

"He should be here any time now," the Sheriff said in a rasping voice. "I called the newspapers—all of them. They're sending reporters and photographers down."

"Did you get the *Tribune's* permission to call the other newspapers, Sheriff?" I asked him.

"Get out of my office, Wheeler!" he said. "Get to hell and gone! I don't have to take that from you!"

"Do you want me to come back?"

"Not here," he said crisply. "If Homicide wants you back I imagine Martin will let you know. But I don't want to see you inside this office again. Never! Is that clear?"

"Loud and clear," I agreed. I stood up and walked toward the door.

"This time, Wheeler," he said quietly, "I mean it! You set foot inside this office again and I'll have you thrown out!"

I closed the door behind me gently and saw that Annabelle Jackson had company. There were half a dozen guys in the office, waiting. Schafer was sitting on Annabelle's desk, swinging his legs idly. He looked at me and grinned. "I see the Light is shining brightly all around this office today, Lieutenant."

"Shed by the *Tribune*," I said. "I guess if you can run the Sheriff's office, I can always get a job with a newspaper."

"You could run a column," he suggested. "Call it 'Poets' Corner.' Could be a big thing."

"After that watchman in Chicago, I guess burning a County Sheriff was easy?" I said, conversationally.

Schafer's eyes widened a little. "That reminds me," he said in a brittle voice. "I haven't gotten around to you yet, Lieutenant. Maybe I should do a story on you?"

Right then Polnik walked into the office with Fletcher. Schafer forgot all about me as he fought his way into the mob surrounding the ex-Vegas wheel.

"Lieutenant!" Polnik yelled in an anguished voice as he was flattened against the wall. "Help!"

"You have the wrong number, Sergeant," I told him regretfully. "Dial 'L' for Lavers." Then I walked past them out onto the street.

So it was a nice bright morning with the sun shining and no leftover smog from L.A. around, and I had absolutely nothing to do. I sat in the Healey and thought about having nothing to do and the idea came along and sat with me.

It was only a little thing, wrapped in a package labeled "Dynamite." I unwrapped it carefully and took a long look at it. Once it was free of the package, it grew a couple of feet and I took another look at it. I could try, I thought. What did I have to lose?

It was eleven-thirty when I walked into the apartment. Gabrielle looked up from the couch and frowned. "If you're going to do this often, you'd better tell me," she said. "I might have a man in here!"

"Make sure it's the landlord," I said. "He never liked me when I was respectable, even."

"You—respectable?" she gurgled with laughter. "Lover, I could believe anything of you except that."

"Don't laugh," I told her. "In college I was voted 'The Man Most Likely to Succeed!' Or was it 'Impede'? There is something I'd like you to do for me, honey."

"Al!" she said fondly. "You're such a wild, impetuous boy!"

"Don't get me wrong," I said hastily. "I just want you to say something happened last night that didn't."

"I don't remember anything that didn't happen last night," she said anxiously. "What was it?"

"Just something I want you to pretend happened, that's all," I said. "Just a little thing."

"What?"

The moisture was beginning to collect across my forehead. "Well," I laughed nervously. "There's plenty of time to get around to it. Right now, why don't we have some coffee?"

"O.K.," she said. "If it was coffee you wanted, why didn't you say so in the first place?"

"I was confused," I said. "I guess I'm way out this morning. So far out, I'm disaffiliated."

"Al!" she beamed at me. "I didn't know you were a hipster. What with that cornball stuff you were playing yesterday—vocals yet—I thought you were strictly a rinky-tink boy!"

"I go for the crazy stuff," I said feebly. "Like coffee?"

"Sure!" She came off the couch in one ripple of movement and headed toward the kitchen. Right then I realized there must have been a lot of square poets. There was one guy who even wrote an Ode to a Grecian Urn. And there were Gabrielle's hips, just waiting for a sonnet.

Ten minutes later, Gabrielle served the coffee. As she bent forward to give me the cup, the top of her blouse dropped open and I got a view worth another six stanzas at least. Then she sat down opposite me and crossed her legs carelessly. I was going to end up with an epic poem before I was through.

"What was it you wanted me to do, lover?" she asked brightly. "That we haven't done already, I mean."

"Oh, that?" I said and gulped some too-hot coffee which scalded the roof of my mouth. "Well, I just want you to say you weren't here last night."

"I know!" She laughed throatily. "It's that landlord!"

"Not exactly," I hedged. "It's not that I want you to say you weren't here so much. The important thing is that I want you to say you were somewhere else."

"What's the difference?"

"There's a hell of a difference," I told her. "It's very important to me. Will you do it for me?"

"I guess so, if it's that important," she said. "Where do I say I was last night?"

"With Howard Fletcher, in his apartment," I said, and ducked just in time.

Her cup splintered against the wall behind my head. I watched the irregular, dark brown stain spread over the new wallpaper and wondered if people would accept it as abstract.

"With Fletcher!" Gabrielle screamed. "What do you think I am—a loose woman or something!"

"It's only to help me," I said. "I have to give him an alibi for Nina's murder."

"Alibi!" she said. "He probably killed her anyway. I don't know how you have the nerve to think that I'd ..." She looked around for something else to throw and couldn't find anything, so she kicked the same old target— my shin.

Hot coffee splattered over me and I yelped with the twin agony of burned knees and a bruised shin. "All right!" I said. "Forget it. Forget I ever mentioned it. Let them bust me. I can do something else besides be a cop. I think I can, anyway ... it's kind of tough for a busted cop to get a job. Forget it! I'll find something ... maybe."

"Busted?" she said.

"Forget it," I said. "Get yourself another cup of coffee, honey. I should have known better than even to suggest it."

"Why would they bust you?"

"Because I think Fletcher didn't do it," I said. "But now they've arrested him, I'm right behind the eight ball. There's no chance of catching the real murderer unless Fletcher is free. But don't let it worry you, honey. I can always dig ditches.... Do they dig ditches anymore?"

"Al, lover!" She dropped on her knees beside me. "Why didn't you tell me it was important!"

"It isn't important," I said. "They still have relief, don't they? Maybe they've got soup kitchens set up that I don't even know about. I'll get by—and it's still summer. Sleeping out in the open won't hurt me." I coughed; a deep, hacking cough and the echo as it bounced off the far wall sounded harrowing even to me.

"I'll do it!" she said and threw her arms around my neck wildly. "I'll do it for you, Al!"

"That's my Gabrielle," I said and patted her shoulder briskly. "You got to his apartment at five after ten last night. Just before you got to the entrance to the building you saw Johnny Torch come out and walk off in the opposite direction, but he didn't see you. You left at midnight. You didn't think any more about it until this morning when you heard about Fletcher being arrested. Got that?"

"I think it might be easier to find you a job digging ditches," she said doubtfully. "But, all right! I've got it."

"Fine!" I said and patted her again. Then I got onto my feet, stepped around her, and headed for the phone.

I called the Sheriff's office first. Annabelle answered. I pitched my voice an octave lower than usual. "I wish to speak to Mr. Fletcher's attorney right away," I said. "It's urgent."

"I'm sorry," she said. "Mr. Hazelton left ten minutes ago. I believe he's going straight back to his office. You should get him there by now."

I hung up and thumbed through the directory until I found Hazelton's number. He'd just arrived, his secretary told me, but he was busy and couldn't be disturbed.

"Tell him Lieutenant Wheeler's calling him," I said. "Tell him it's about Fletcher and it's urgent; it won't wait."

"I'll tell him, Lieutenant," she said doubtfully. "But he's awful busy right now."

"Tell him the longer he takes to talk to me, the longer his client stays in jail," I said.

There was nothing but silence for about twenty seconds. Then an irritated, male voice. "This is Hazelton. Look, Wheeler, you work for the Sheriff's office. Waste his time, not mine!"

"I don't work for the Sheriff's office anymore," said. "We had a disagreement. I didn't agree with booking Fletcher."

"Oh?" His voice sharpened with interest. "Why tell me?"

"Because I've just found Fletcher an alibi," I said.

"You've what!"

"I'm at my apartment," I said. "You'd better come over and we'll talk about it then. It has to be handled carefully."

"You're not kidding me, Lieutenant?"

"I want to kid somebody, why should I pick on you?" I said. "This is on the level."

"All right," he said briskly. "I'll come right over. What's the address?" I gave it to him and then hung up.

Gabrielle had gotten us both some more coffee. She sat on the couch and looked at me pensively. "I'm beginning to feel a little bit scared about this, Al."

"You don't have to be," I said. "Just stick to the story, that's all. Make a statement and don't add anything more to it. You'll have Hazelton right alongside you. Nobody can disprove the story."

"I should have known better than to fall for a cop," she said in a resigned voice. "Las Vegas was dull compared to Pine City!"

Hazelton arrived fifteen minutes later. He looked like a successful attorney and he looked like the sort of attorney Fletcher would hire. A very well-dressed guy in his late thirties with a neat toothbrush mustache and large white teeth.

I introduced myself and then Gabrielle. He stood there, looking around the apartment like a terrier waiting to snap at the first thing that moved.

"All right," he said finally. "Where is it?"

"What?"

"The alibi!"

"You just met her," I told him. "Gabrielle."

"So?" His eyes widened a fraction as he looked at her. "That's the best alibi I've met in my whole career!"

Gabrielle smiled wanly at him. "Thanks for nothing," she said.

I made us all a drink; I thought we were going to need it. I explained to Hazelton who Gabrielle was, and the Las Vegas tie-in with Fletcher. The more I told him, the more he smiled. I figured he was a guy for smiling anyway, with those large white teeth. But now he looked as if he really meant it.

"There's the one obvious question," I said. "Why didn't Fletcher say this last night? Why didn't he say he had an alibi then? What's more, why didn't he say so this morning when he was arrested?"

"You don't have to tell me, Lieutenant!" Hazelton held up his hand smugly. "Let me tell you. It would compromise the lady in question. It was a point of honor with Fletcher. He wouldn't smear the lady's reputation, even to save himself!"

"You're crazy," I told him. "Who do you think you'll be talking to, a jury?

You've got to have a story that people like Lavers and the D.A.'s office will believe."

The large white teeth vanished for a moment. "You have a better suggestion, Lieutenant?" he asked coldly.

"I hope so," I said. "They had a fight in Fletcher's apartment last night. It was the finish, it was all over for them. During the fight Gabrielle blacked his eye for him—he's got physical proof of that. Then she stormed out of the place. The only reason Fletcher didn't mention her was because, after that fight, he was convinced she wouldn't help him. He thought if he told the police she was there, she'd only deny it to spite him."

Hazelton gnawed his mustache for a moment. "I must admit," he conceded finally, "that sounds far more feasible."

"It's good enough," I said. "They can't break it. You'll need to let Fletcher in on it first. And stay close to Gabrielle when they question her. It's a foolproof story so long as nobody tries to elaborate on it."

"I'll watch it," he said confidently.

"Make sure you do," I said. "I have a very personal stake in all this."

Hazelton looked at me curiously. "Just what is your angle, Lieutenant?"

"I like Howard Fletcher," I said, giving him my honest look. "That makes sense, doesn't it?"

He thought about that for a moment then shook his head. "No."

"I've given you an alibi for your client," I said. "You want reasons yet?"

"Of course not," he said hurriedly. "I think we'd better get downtown. Are you ready to leave, Miss ... er ... Gabrielle?"

"I guess so," she said. "Is this going to take very long?"

"A few hours at the most," Hazelton said. "You have nothing to worry about!"

"Try and convince me!" she said dubiously.

I walked with them to the door. "Goodbye, lover!" Gabrielle said, almost tearfully. "They don't still use that third degree thing, do they?"

"Only on women," I reassured her. "Like Mr. Hazelton says, honey, you don't have a thing to worry about." I closed the door behind them, then crossed my fingers and added, "I hope!"

Chapter Eleven

It was a long wait. I spaced my drinks an hour apart and even tried to make a start on my epic poem. I got as far as the first two lines....

> *"In Las Vegas, who's the Belle?*
> *Gabrielle ... Gabrielle!"*

I got discouraged after that. It didn't look at all like Tennyson somehow. When it got to four in the afternoon, I started shortening the spaces between drinks. It made the Scotch go faster, if not the time.

My watch said five-thirty when the buzzer finally sounded. I opened the door and said brightly, "Welcome h—"

"Well, thanks, Lieutenant!" Schafer grinned at me. "You sure you got the right party?"

"'Summon the weeper,'" I said. "'Wail and sing!'"

"I know," he gritted his teeth. "A woman called Millay. It was my mistake to start the thing in the first place."

"Did you want something?" I asked him.

"I thought I'd stop by and visit for a few minutes," he said. "You mind?"

"I gave up minding sometime this morning," I said. "I guess you might as well come in."

He followed me into the living room and slumped down into a chair. "Drink?" I asked him.

"Whatever you're having—but no soda!"

I made the drinks, gave him his, and sat down opposite him. "What's on your mind, Schafer?" I asked him.

"Fletcher was sprung about half an hour ago," he said. "I thought you'd like to know."

"He was?" I tried my surprised look on for size. "How did that happen?"

"You can stop clowning, Wheeler!" he said savagely. "You organized it."

"I don't think I'm with you," I said. "Dope it out for me."

"That stripper," he said. "Gabrielle. She did a real fine job and she only made one mistake."

"Mistake?" I hoped my voice didn't sound as hollow as I felt.

"It didn't hurt Fletcher any," he said. "You don't have to worry about him, he's still sprung. When they were typing her statement, they asked her the routine questions. You know, like name, occupation, address ..."

I saw it coming. "Go on."

"So she gave your address." Schafer grinned savagely. "You should have seen the Sheriff's face! It was worth a month's pay to see it ... or a cop's career, even."

"So what are you?" I asked him. "The vanguard of the mourning party?"

"You'd know about it sooner or later, Wheeler," he said. "I thought I'd like to be the first to tell you. You're washed up in this town. Maybe you're washed up any place. I guess you'll find that out soon enough. So now you can summon the weeper, wail and sing."

I finished my drink, then lit a cigarette. "Why are you gunning for Lavers?" I asked him.

"I'm not gunning for him," he said coldly. "All ever wanted out of all this is a story, and I'm getting one. I told you I'd get around to doing a story on you Wheeler, didn't I? And now I've got it. It's a good story; the grand-standing cop who couldn't take being wrong, so he manufactured an alibi for a murderer, just to prove he was right!"

"Put it into words that I can sue," I said.

"Libel?" Schafer laughed. "You have to have some sort of character to be libeled before you can take it into the courts, didn't you know that? What sort of character will you have after I run my story? The girl whose testimony sprung Fletcher today is a Las Vegas stripper, and she's living with you as your mistress. Those are facts, pal! You think you can argue you have a respectable name or character after that?"

"Well," I said, "thanks for breaking it down into words of one syllable. Is that all?"

"You were so tough that first time in the bar," he said softly. "The big-time lieutenant, the white-haired boy of the Sheriff's office who thought he could walk all over me and get away with it. You made a bad mistake, Wheeler, when you picked on me!"

He stood up suddenly. "You want to watch for tomorrow morning's *Tribune*, pal! You'll be there, all over the front page!"

"Watch you don't bust a blood vessel," I told him. "You could ruin my carpet."

He got as far as the door, opened it, then turned around and looked at me. "You know something else, Wheeler?"

"If I did," I said, "I still wouldn't spoil your exit line."

"This time, you paid for the drinks!" He slammed the door shut behind him.

I thought there was a word for Schafer and maybe it was 'paranoiac.' I thought there was a word for me, too, and any time now it was going to be 'bum.' While I was waiting, I thought I might as well practice.

"Buddy," the voice sincere but desperate, "buddy, can you spare a dime?"

Dime! I tried again. "Buddy! Can you spare a buck?" I wondered if Fulton in Vegas might consider me for Max's job?

The buzzer sounded again. "Wheeler," I said to myself as I walked toward the door. "You are only human, after all; and repressions are bad for you. If you bust Schafer right in the nose it will remain a happy memory through the lean years to come."

I flung the door open and just managed to stop my fist an inch away from Gabrielle's delicate, uptilted nose.

"Al!" She dissolved into tears. "You know! The stupid thing I said when they asked me my address! I don't blame you—go ahead. Hit me!"

"I thought you were a couple of other guys," I said. "Honest!"

We got inside the apartment and Gabrielle sank onto the couch. I made her a drink while she dried her eyes. "That Sheriff guy! He's like something out of a TV Western!"

"You did fine!" I told her. "There's nothing to worry about." I made her a drink, just to prove it.

"I felt so damned stupid!" she said. "Right after I said it, I knew what I'd done, but it was too late then. I thought the Sheriff would explode!"

"Just jealousy," I said. "He probably wished he was me, and you still had the same address."

"I feel exhausted," she said, and finished her drink. "They must have asked ten thousand questions. Not all different, but the same ones, over and over again!"

"You did all right," I repeated. "Why don't you rest for a while? I have to go out, now I know you're O.K."

"Out?" Her eyes had that steely look in them again.

"Unfinished business, honey," I said. "I'll be back."

"Maybe it's that Southern fried chicken in the Sheriff's office?" she said tautly. "How come you never told me about her?"

"You never asked," I said. "Why don't you rest for a couple of hours?"

"After all I've been through today, just for you!" she said, her face a mask of tragedy. "I've suffered, been humiliated ... for you! And now you're going out!"

"Yeah," I said, grabbing my hat. "Well, take it easy, honey." I closed the door behind me just in time. A split second later, something thudded solidly against it. By the sound of it, it was probably the couch.

It was a nice evening outside, the same way it had been a nice morning. In between times, the sky had dropped in on Al Wheeler, but nobody seemed to have noticed. I got into the Healey and drove in the direction of the Sheriff's office.

When I got there, I drove past it slowly, noting that all the lights were still on. I parked outside a bar, half a block farther on. I ordered a drink and used the phone while I was waiting. I dialed the office number and heard it ring a few times, then the clunk as the receiver was lifted.

"Sheriff's office," a hoarse voice said.

"Polnik?"

"Yeah—who's that?"

"Wheeler," I told him.

"Lieutenant!" He sounded punch-drunk. "I figured you would have left town before now."

"I'm in the bar half a block down from you," I said. "Can you make time for a drink?"

"Sure!" he said. "The Sheriff's not here, and anyway, I got to get to say goodbye, don't I, Lieutenant!"

"I'll order you a drink."

Polnik ambled into the bar a couple of minutes later. I'd taken a corner table and the two drinks were waiting. Polnik looked around until he saw me, then came over, bug-eyed. "Sure good to see you, Lieutenant," he said as he eased his bulk into a chair. "Where you going? New York, Miami ... Cuba, maybe?"

"If this works out right, I'm not going any place," I said. "And if it doesn't, I figure even the Russians won't have me. I want your help, Polnik."

"Anything I got you want, it's yours!" he said. "I been thinking about it all day. No more beautiful dames; no nothing! If you go, Lieutenant, I guess I'll feel like something's gone out of my life, like ... like suddenly there wasn't any beer anymore!"

"Well, thanks," I said. "I've been feeling like I was canned all day."

"That Sheriff!" he said in an awestruck voice. "You should have seen him, Lieutenant! When he heard that classy brunette give your address and—"

"I've been through this routine twice already," I interrupted him. "I'm willing to admit I should have seen that Sheriff."

Polnik wasn't listening to me. His eyes had a dreamy look in them as he stared into the middle distance. "Tell me something, Lieutenant! How do you make a dame like that?"

"It's easy," I said. "All you need is a do-it-yourself kit. Or talk to your old lady about it," I suggested.

"Nobody talks to my old lady," he said emphatically. "She talks to them. They got no chance of talking back—likewise me."

I finished my drink and nodded to a hovering waiter. Polnik saw him coming and drained his glass hastily. "Same again," I said, and the waiter whisked the empty glasses away.

"What did you want to know, Lieutenant?" Polnik asked suddenly. "Any way I can help, I'm glad."

"Did Johnny Torch's alibi stand up?"

"I guess it did, and then, it didn't." Polnik scratched one ear thoughtfully. "They remembered him being there all right, but nobody remembered what time he came in or what time he left."

"Were there any leads inside Nina's apartment?"

"Nothing," he said promptly. "No prints, no nothing. The ice pick belonged to the apartment."

"So the only thing Lavers had on Fletcher was a motive he couldn't prove and the fact that he had no alibi," I said. "Until Gabrielle came along."

"Man!" Polnik said, breathing heavily. "She blows her trumpet just the one time, and I'll be there!"

"I should never have brought the subject up again," I said.

I was saved by the waiter with the new drinks. Polnik got sidetracked by the beer.

"What's the Sheriff doing, now Fletcher's been sprung?" I asked.

"You ask me, Lieutenant," Polnik said unhappily. "I don't think he's doing anything else but working out how he can fix you, but good. You should have heard what he called you when he got back inside his office!" He looked suitably shocked. "You know something, Lieutenant? Some of the things he called you, I wouldn't even call my old lady!"

"I appreciate the sentiment," I said. "You know anything definite he's planning for me?"

Polnik scratched his head again. "He was talking on the phone to the cops in Las Vegas. Getting a run-down on that brunette of yours." His eyes started to cloud over again, so I joggled his beer with my elbow. That fixed it.

"Anything else?"

"I heard him talking to Inspector Martin for a time. Anybody could hear him, the walls were bending. Then he talked to the D.A.'s office. I think he talked to the Commissioner and the Mayor. He did a lot of talking, Lieutenant. Mostly about you."

"The way you talk, anybody would figure Lavers didn't like me or something," I said.

Polnik rubbed his nose thoughtfully. "None of my business, Lieutenant, but I sure hope you got that dame stashed away in a safe place!"

"What do you mean?"

"They gave her a tough time today. The way it looked to me, she came close to cracking up a couple of times. No offense, Lieutenant, but if they had her on her own for maybe an hour, without you or that attorney there to back her up ... You get the drift, Lieutenant? That's why I'm saying I hope you got her stashed away somewhere real safe!" He began to get that dreamy look again. "A small cabana maybe, out on the beach ... Even a motel isn't so bad; not with a dame like her!"

"Sure," I said. "I've got her stashed away somewhere real safe—in my apartment!" How dumb could I get?

"Lieutenant," Polnik pleaded almost tearfully. "You're kidding. Tell me you're kidding!"

"I was so busy being a mastermind, I forgot all about the obvious," I said. "I'd better get back there."

"I wouldn't do that, Lieutenant," Polnik said firmly. "Lavers talked to the Commissioner and Martin. They'd have a stake-out on your apartment for sure. They couldn't stop her walking out when she had Fletcher's attorney with her. But you bet your sweet life when they saw you leave on your own, they went in and grabbed her. Maybe she's cracked up already. You go back there, and that stake-out is waiting for you!"

"Did Lavers tell you this, or did you figure it out for yourself?" I asked him.

"I doped it out myself all right, Lieutenant," he said proudly. "The Sheriff tells me nothing; except to get the hell out from under his feet. I got a feeling he figures maybe I'm a little too close to you for him to tell me anything. And he'd be right!"

"Thanks, Polnik," I said. "I wonder whether my car's hot?"

"Where you going, Lieutenant?" he asked sympathetically. "Mexico?"

"I've got a couple of other places to try first," I said, "but that Healey's kind of conspicuous."

"My Mercury's down the street," he said. "Why don't you take that?" He dug the keys out of his pocket and dropped them onto the table.

"Thanks again," I told him as I picked up the keys.

"About a block down on the other side of the street," he said. "Green Mercury. It's got a dent in the front bumper, where my old lady backed into it one day."

"She backed into your front bumper, walking?" I asked.

"That's my story, Lieutenant!" Polnik wink hugely. "There were no witnesses. Could have been different story if the motor hadn't stalled. You'd better get going, Lieutenant. You don't have much time!"

"I guess I don't," I agreed. "Are you going back the office?"

"It don't really matter," he said. "I was just sticking around in case the Sheriff came back and wanted something doing, that's all."

"I was wondering," I said, "if they've got Gabrielle by now, whether they'd bring her back to the Sheriff's office."

"Not to question her, they wouldn't," he said. "They wouldn't take a chance on you finding out quick, and coming down there with that attorney under your arm. My bet is if they caught up with her in your apartment, Lieutenant, they'd question her right there."

"You're probably right," I said. "And worrying about Gabrielle isn't going to get me anywhere right now. You could do me one more favor, Polnik."

"Name it, Lieutenant."

"Call Fletcher's attorney for me. Hazelton is his name. Tell him what you've told me about Gabrielle. Just say you're calling for me; you don't have to give him your name."

"I got you, Lieutenant!" Polnik nodded. "It's fixed now!" He thrust a massive hand at me. "If I don't see you again, good luck, Lieutenant!" We shook hands and I winced as the bones started to crack.

There was a wistful look in Polnik's eyes. "I wish I was going with you, Lieutenant," he said. "All those hot females, those beautiful señoritas!"

"What the hell are you talking about?" I asked him.

"Mexico," he said blankly. "That's where you're going, ain't it?"

"No," I said briefly.

"Don't try the far north, Lieutenant!" he said quickly. "It's too cold up there!"

"But in winter," I told him, "one night lasts for three months."

That dreamy look came back into his eyes again. "Well," he said softly. "How about that?"

Chapter Twelve

Johnny Torch opened the door of the apartment and a sneer spread over his face as he looked at me. "You want to rest your flat feet, copper," he said, "try some place else!"

I was in no mood for chitchat. A long time back, I'd met a guy like Johnny Torch before. Only one. They don't come very often and for that I'm thankful. If you were going to take them, you took them fast or they'd put a couple of holes through you. Not out of spite, just reflex action.

I grabbed the lapels of his coat and jerked him toward me, bringing my knee up at the same time. It caught him hard in the pit of the stomach and he sagged forward. I let go of his lapels and brought my knee up again hard, so his jaw going down met my kneecap coming up.

It spun him sideways to the floor. He lay there, his fingers scrabbling on the rug for leverage, but he didn't have enough left to pull himself up onto his hands and knees. I knelt down beside him and lifted the gun out of his shoulder holster, then stuck it in my hip pocket.

As I straightened up, Fletcher came out of his bedroom. He stopped suddenly when he saw me. "Lieutenant?" Then he saw Johnny, or maybe he heard him first. Johnny was sobbing into the rug. Tears of pure rage. "What's this all about?" Fletcher asked carefully.

"Somebody will kill him one day," I said. "Nobody could like him if he tried to be pleasant. But when he gets that sneer on his face and starts shooting off his mouth ..."

"I know what you mean," Fletcher said. "He gets me that way at times. Maybe you noticed?"

"I noticed," I said.

"He'll get over it," Fletcher said briefly. "How about a drink?"

"I'd like that," I told him.

We moved across the living room. Fletcher busied himself making the drinks, while I sat down on the couch and lit myself a cigarette. A few seconds later, I heard a shuffling noise behind me. I looked over my shoulder and saw Johnny moving slowly across the room toward the nearest armchair on his hands and knees. His face was a mask of sweat and he moaned softly to himself all the time. But he kept on moving along.

He made it at the same time Fletcher handed me a drink. I watched Johnny haul himself up, slowly and painfully, into the chair. Then he sat there, crouched forward with both arms hugging his stomach. His eyes shone wildly as he watched me, without saying anything.

"I haven't thanked you, Lieutenant," Fletcher said, "for what you did for me today. I don't know how to thank you, to be honest. I don't even begin to understand why you did it; or how you persuaded Gabrielle to cooperate. But I'll never forget it!"

"It just so happens that's why I called on you, Howard," I said easily. "I thought of a way you could thank me. A nice, practical sort of a way."

"I don't understand you," Fletcher said. "What are you talking about?"

Johnny Torch started to laugh and finished with a sob of pain. "Don't be so dumb, Howard!" he said in a cracked voice. "I told you—they're all the same. Coppers are no different from any other sort of people, except maybe they aren't people! He wants dough, Howard! The folding stuff. He's come to collect. This is the big pay-off!"

"I don't know where Johnny got the words," I said to Fletcher. "But he's right."

He stared at me in open amazement. "You! You want money for springing me!" He laughed shortly. "That's really funny. I thought if there was one cop on the square, it was you, Wheeler. I figured you fixed up that alibi for me because you really believed I didn't kill either of the girls. For about the first time in my life, I figured I'd met a decent guy!"

"Now you're breaking my heart, Howard," I said. "But I can't afford the time to wait around here until it's broken. You can pay me off now."

"How much do you want?" he asked in a flat voice.

"Twenty thousand," I said. "Cash."

Fletcher laughed again. "Are you crazy? Where would I get that sort of money now?"

"You've got it, Howard," I said. "I'm being a very reasonable guy. You've got seventy thousand dollars hidden away in here some place, and I'm only asking for twenty thousand. I figure that's a cheap price to pay for keeping your neck out of the gas chamber."

"You're wasting your time," he said shortly. "I don't have any seventy thousand. The more I think about that night in Las Vegas, the more I'm convinced the Syndicate framed me. They wanted me to get out and stay out. They framed me to make sure I'd never dare try to come back. They planted the story that I'd got the money because they hoped, sooner or later, somebody like Johnny would believe it. Then maybe he'd blow my brains out trying to find what I'd done with it."

"It makes a good story," I said. "Why don't you try selling it to Schafer. He's with the *Tribune*. Maybe he could use it. There's only one thing wrong with it, Howard. I don't believe you."

Fletcher shrugged his shoulders indifferently. "Suit yourself, Wheeler," he said. "It makes no difference to me."

I slid my own gun out of the shoulder-holster and held it in my hand. "I could get tough about this," I said. "Real tough."

"Why don't you?" He sneered at me. "You think I'm some little punk who's going to faint at the sight of a gun?"

"I'm a cop," I said, and crossed my fingers that it was still a true statement. "I could shoot both of you and end up the hero of Pine City for a week."

"I hope you enjoy it!" he said curtly.

I heard Johnny cackle with laughter again, and looked at him. He'd managed to straighten up a little in the chair. From the look on his face, he was beginning to feel better. "Sure," he said. "Howard's damn right, copper. Shoot the both of us! Only one thing wrong with that. You'll never find the dough then—if Howard has got the dough!"

"I wouldn't have to kill him," I said. "I could shoot him in the arm, the leg, maybe. Somewhere painful, but not fatal."

"Be your age, Wheeler!" Fletcher said contemptuously. "So you shoot me in the arm or the leg. I tell you I just remembered I have got the seventy grand after all. I tell you I hid it under a rosebush in a park some place. Or maybe I put it into a box at the post office. Or any place. How do you know whether I'm telling the truth or not? We could play that sort of game for weeks if you really wanted to."

He walked over to the bar and stood with his back turned toward me, making himself another drink. "There's a blue silk suit hanging in the closet in my room," he said. "There's a billfold in the inside pocket. Six, maybe seven hundred dollars in it. Take it, Wheeler, and get out of here!"

"Are you crazy?" I said hoarsely. "I got to have more than that! A hell of a lot more than that! Seven hundred wouldn't take me anywhere."

Fletcher turned around slowly and looked at me again. "You're going someplace, Wheeler? What's wrong with staying right here in Pine City?"

"I can't stay here," I said tautly. "Any more than you can—not if you don't want to wind up facing a double murder rap again!"

"What the hell are you talking about!"

"Gabrielle," I said. "I left her alone in my apartment."

"So what?" Johnny asked.

I looked at Fletcher. "She nearly cracked under their questioning today, when she had Hazelton right there beside her. I didn't think about it until it was too late. They'd have a stake-out outside my apartment building. As soon as I left, they'd go and grab her. They got all the time in the world to ask her questions. She's going to crack up, Fletcher. Any time ... maybe she has already. And you know what that makes me!"

"A crooked cop!" Johnny Torch said softly. "A cop who made an alibi, strictly for money!" He began to laugh softly. "A cop on the run with nobody to go to! I dig that, Howard! Don't you figure that's worth a laugh?"

"Don't be a fool!" Fletcher said tautly. "If it puts him in jail, it puts me right back there beside him. We'll have to get out of here!"

I walked into the bedroom while they were still arguing. I took the billfold out of the suit in the closet and opened it. It did look closer to seven hundred than six. I stuffed the money into my inside pocket, then walked back into the living room. They were still arguing.

"I'm getting out of here, now!" Fletcher said. "What do you expect me to do? Stick around and wait for that County Sheriff to come and get me?"

"Not yet, Howard," Johnny Torch said softly. "We'll wait a little while."

"You can wait on your own!" Fletcher said. "I'm going now." He brushed past me and walked quickly into the bedroom. From where I stood, I watched him drag a bag out of the closet and put it on the bed. Then he started tossing clothes into it.

I looked around into the baleful eyes of Johnny Torch.

"You get your seven hundred bucks, copper?" he asked softly.

"Yeah," I said. "And now I'm getting out."

"Sure," he said. "You go. Maybe you'll get lucky and make the border in Mexico. Have you figured out just how long seven hundred lousy bucks will last you?"

He started to laugh again. "Have you got yourself a time coming, copper. I hope you make it across the border, I'd like to think about that!"

"You should be thinking about Fletcher, Johnny," I said softly. "Fletcher and that seventy grand. He's going to walk out of the door with it any minute now, and never come back."

I still held my own gun in my hand. Johnny looked down at it for a moment, then looked up into my eyes.

"How can I stop him leaving, copper? You took my gun away from me. How do you stop a guy with a gun, if you don't have a gun?"

"That's a logical argument, Johnny," I said. "You need a gun to stop him." I pulled his gun out of my hip pocket with my free hand and offered it to him, barrel-first.

He took it slowly. "Thanks, copper," he whispered. "When I got time, I'll figure out your angle."

"Just don't be tempted to take care of me first," I said, and angled my gun toward him so that he was looking down the barrel.

"Me?" he said. "Why would I want to do a stupid thing like that?"

Fletcher came out of the bedroom, wearing his hat and carrying the grip. He stopped abruptly when he saw the gun in Johnny's hand. "Relax, Howard!" Johnny told him. "You aren't going any place. Not yet, anyway."

"You crazy fool!" Fletcher snarled at me. "You gave him back that gun!"

"What did you think seven hundred bucks bought you, Howard? Protection?"

The color drained out his cheeks slowly. He looked at me for a moment longer, then he looked at Johnny Torch.

"You might as well relax ... boss," Johnny said. "Like I said, you're not going any place. You and me are going to sit around here until the cops come for you. When you've gone I'm going to sit around here on my own. A day, a week, a month even. Who knows? I'll pick the right time to blow. Nice and quiet, you know? Here today and gone tomorrow."

"You double-crossing little punk!" Fletcher said thickly.

"Now you're hurting my feelings," Johnny said.

"You, the big shot who used to tell me to shut up before I even opened my mouth. Give me the fast one-two, just to prove to yourself you really were a big shot! And now you're nothing, Fletcher! Nothing but a name in the newspapers and a corpse in the gas chamber. I'll think of you in the gas chamber, Howard. You think of me while you're there, won't you? I'll be in Florida!"

Fletcher stood there, his mouth working. Then suddenly his eyes brightened. "Wheeler!" he said quickly. "Seventy thousand dollars— yours for the taking! All you have to do is go get it. It's hidden in—"

Johnny Torch uncoiled out of the chair faster than a snake. The barrel of his gun curved through a wide arc and smashed down on top of Fletcher's head. I watched Fletcher collapse to the floor and then Johnny's cold eyes bored into mine. "It's about time you were leaving, copper," he said gently. "Or you'll never make it across the border."

"Maybe you're right," I said slowly. I backed to the door, opened it, and stepped out into the corridor. Then I closed the door shut and walked toward the elevator. I holstered my gun as I went.

Al Wheeler, the mastermind himself! I wouldn't have felt so bad if just one thing had gone the way I'd figured it would. And that got me worrying about Gabrielle again. I rode the elevator down to the street level, then walked through the foyer. I stopped just outside the entrance for a moment and looked around.

There was a black Cadillac parked at the curb right in front of me, with a guy leaning against it. "Hello there, Lieutenant," he said softly.

My nerve-ends rubbed against each other and screamed softly. I took a couple of steps toward him, then relaxed a little when I saw his face. "Mr. Salter," I said. "How are things with you?"

"Fine," he said amiably. "Coming along just fine. Can I drop you anywhere, Lieutenant?"

"No, thanks," I told him. "I have a car parked down the street."

"I think you should ride with me, Lieutenant," he said. "If you don't mind? There's someone in the car I'd like you to meet."

I looked at him and he nodded toward the rear door. "Get in, Lieutenant." For a moment I wondered if Max was vacationing from Las Vegas; I thought he couldn't have picked a better time. I opened the rear door and climbed into the car.

"Al, lover!" a husky voice said one moment before I was hit by a feminine avalanche.

The world was suddenly a beautiful place. "Gabrielle," I mumbled, and got a mouthful of her neckline. "How on earth did you get—"

"Hugo's an old friend of mine," she said. "He came to the rescue!"

The car moved away from the curb, accelerating smoothly. I managed to disengage myself from Gabrielle's clutches long enough to ask where we were going.

"My place," Salter said. "There are things I think we should talk over, Lieutenant."

Chapter Thirteen

Angela, the girl-wife, met us at the door. "People!" she said enthusiastically. "Now we can have a party!"

"I'm afraid not," Salter said. "This is business, honey. You'd better run along."

"Business!" Angela pouted. "I'm sick and tired of business! When do we ever get to have some fun?"

"That's a leading question in front of witnesses," Salter grinned at her. "I'll take that up with you later."

He led the way down to his room, while his wife obediently got lost, as he'd directed. Once we were inside he closed the door carefully.

"I think we should have a drink first," he said.

I looked at Gabrielle while he was busy making the drinks. "What happened?"

"It was wonderful," she said. "Only about five minutes after you'd walked out on me, somebody pressed the buzzer. Al, lover, I was scared! But whoever it was wouldn't go away. They kept on pressing the buzzer, so finally I opened the door. Guess who it was!"

"Salter," I said.

"If you know the story, why ask me to tell you it?" she said coldly.

"That was a lucky guess," I said. "Go on."

"Well, like I said before, Hugo's an old friend of mine. He told me the police were out front and we should go out the back way, so we did. Then he took me to dinner at a wonderful place you've never taken me to, and after that we had a couple of drinks, then we parked right outside Howard's apartment house and waited there until you came out."

Salter handed round the drinks. "I thought it better she didn't see the police again for a while," he said. "The County Sheriff in particular."

"You were so right," I said. "I didn't think of it, until it was too late to do anything about it."

"It was a pleasure to return a favor," he said easily.

"How did you know I was in Fletcher's apartment?"

"I had a man tailing you all day," he said. "I think it's time we had a talk, Lieutenant."

"Sure," I said. "Go ahead."

"You must have had a good reason for getting Gabrielle to help you fake an alibi for Fletcher. What was it?"

"He wasn't any good to me in jail," I said. "I had to get him out somehow."

Salter grinned faintly. "I'm not with you, Lieutenant!"

"I figured Fletcher was the key to everything. The money, the murders. He was a guy with a problem, one hell of a problem. Sooner or later, he'd have to make a break. If I could stick close enough to him when he made the break, I figured I'd find a murderer somewhere close."

"It sounds good when you say it," Salter murmured. "But I'm still trying to get some sense out of it. I don't get any facts, that's for sure!"

"It's kind of hard to explain," I said. "Right now, Fletcher's got an even bigger problem."

"What?" Salter asked sharply.

I told him how things were when I left Fletcher's apartment. How Johnny was keeping him there, confident that the police were coming for his former boss, because they would have broken down his alibi through Gabrielle,

"So they'll sit there forever—or until Johnny gets tired?" Salter said.

"If we let them," I said. "This talk was your idea, Salter, and I went along with it. We're both wasting our time unless we level with each other right now. Answer me one question. What exactly do you want? What exactly does the Syndicate want?"

"If they've got that seventy thousand," he said evenly, "we want to make sure they never get around to spending it. We want everybody in Vegas to know they never got around to spending it. We want them taken care of, Lieutenant. It doesn't matter to us whether we take care of them or the law does. We'll handle it ourselves, of course, if nobody else does."

I lit a cigarette. "We've got a basis for cooperation, I think," I told him. "How about it?"

"Sure," Salter said lightly. "I have nothing to lose in cooperating with you, Lieutenant. If it doesn't work out your way, I'm sure it will work out mine."

"What are you two talking about!" Gabrielle demanded.

"We're doing all right, honey," Salter grinned at her. "You be a good girl and keep quiet."

"I'll keep quiet," she sniffed. "But don't ask for the impossible!"

"You had something specific in mind, Lieutenant?" Salter looked at me again.

"I think so," I said. "How about Gabrielle calls Fletcher right now, and tells him everything is all right. She's with you and the cops have no chance of getting her at all?"

"Supposing Johnny Torch won't let him talk on the phone?"

"It doesn't matter," I said. "She could tell him the same thing. Then as soon as she's finished speaking, I want you to say a few words."

"Such as?"

"Tell them the Syndicate is now convinced they have got the money, and both of them are scheduled to die before morning."

"Melodrama?" Salter said softly. "Where will that get us, Lieutenant?"

"Straight to the money, I hope," I said. "And a direct route to the murderer if I'm right."

"You're being very honest tonight." Salter grinned faintly. "Much more honest with me than you were the first time we met, Lieutenant. So I'll be honest with you—and deny it afterwards if necessary, naturally. I'll go along with you, play it your way. But if your way doesn't produce results, then I'll play it my way."

"I'm a cop, Salter," I said. "I couldn't possibly agree to that, but I guess I wouldn't even know about your way, would I?"

"If you ever get tired of being a cop, Lieutenant," he said, "call me. We always have a place in our organization for bright young men with absolutely no scruples at all!"

He picked up the phone. "We should start moving," he said. "You know what to say, Gabrielle?"

"Sure," she nodded. "It will be a pleasure."

"You call from here," he said. "I'll take the Lieutenant into the living room. There are a couple of extensions in there and we can both listen. When you've finished your message, say that I want to talk to them, and I'll take it from there. O.K.?"

"Fine," Gabrielle said. "You don't mind if I call Fletcher a few names while I talk to him?"

"It will be a pleasure to hear them," Salter said.

I followed him into the living room and picked up one of the phones there. Salter lifted the extension phone across the other side of the room, and then we both listened.

I heard the ringing tone, which stopped suddenly.

"Yeah?" Johnny Torch's metallic voice said.

"I want to speak to Howard," Gabrielle said.

"Who is this?"

"Gabrielle. That you, Johnny?"

"Gabrielle! I thought the cops had picked you up?"

"Not me, Johnny!" She laughed easily. "I got friends in this town. Put Howard on, will you?"

"He can't talk right now," Johnny said. "You can tell me."

"I talk to Howard or I don't talk at all," she said crisply. "You please yourself, Johnny."

There was a long pause. "O.K.," Johnny said finally. "I'll put him on. But talk it up, so I can hear what you're saying. You got that?"

"Sure," she said.

Another pause, and then Fletcher's voice, taut and strained.

"This is Howard. That lousy cop told us you'd been picked up and they'd forced you to make a statement breaking the alibi, Gabrielle!"

"He was lying—as usual!" Gabrielle said cheerfully. "Like I told Johnny, Howard, I got friends in this town. The cops will never find me, so you've got nothing to worry about."

"Who is your friend?" Howard asked tightly.

"You know him," Gabrielle said. "Hugo Salter. I'm with him right now. As a matter of fact, Howard, he wants to speak to you. Hold on a moment!"

Salter looked across the room at me, a sardonic grin on his face. "Fletcher?" he asked gently.

"Yeah?" Howard's voice shook slightly.

"I thought I should tell you," Salter went on in an impersonal voice. "I've just had word from Las Vegas."

"Word?"

"They've made up their minds, Fletcher. You and Torch have the seventy thousand."

"It's a lie!" Fletcher shouted. "It's a dirty lie! It's a frame, somebody's trying to frame me!"

"I have my instructions," Salter said conversationally. "I am to take care of the details before morning."

"Wait a minute!" Fletcher pleaded. "Don't be like that, Salter! For God's sake be reasonable. Maybe we can make a deal?"

"Deal?" Salter made it sound like a dirty word.

"Yeah, a deal!" Fletcher's voice broke in the middle of the word. "Supposing, just supposing, I knew where that money is? I could tell you where you can find it. You'd have it back. The Syndicate wouldn't lose a dime!"

"You think we care about the money?" Salter chuckled dryly. "Howard! You should know us better than that. It's not the money we're concerned with, it's the principle of the thing!"

"Salter! I'm begging you—"

"Don't waste your time!" Salter said crisply. "I'll see you in two hours' time. You and Johnny Torch. I won't be alone, of course. Wait for us in your apartment. Cooperate, and I promise you it will be quick and painless. I don't have to stress the alternatives, do I?"

"Salter!" Fletcher's voice rose in a scream. "I'll do anything ... anything. You can—"

There was a thumping noise, and then the harsh metallic voice of Torch spoke again. "Salter!"

"I hear you, Johnny!" Salter said evenly.

"Well, get this. You don't scare me any. You come right over any time. I'll be waiting for you. Waiting to blow that stupid head right off your shoulders."

"Whatever you say, Johnny," Salter said. He looked across at me and I nodded. He dropped the phone back onto the cradle. "It all sounded very childish, didn't it?" he said. "What's the next move, Lieutenant? We're still handling it your way."

"We get back to that apartment house and sit outside and wait," I said.

"It doesn't sound very exciting, but all right."

We went back to his room to collect Gabrielle. I stopped at the door, to let him go first. "Thanks, Lieutenant," he nodded and walked into the room. I took my .38 out of the holster and slugged him across the back of the head with the butt. He dropped to the floor and lay there without moving.

Gabrielle's eyes bulged as she looked at me. "Whatever did you do that for?"

"I feel like a heel," I said. "Tell him I apologize when he comes round, will you?"

"But I won't be here!" she said. "I'm going with you!"

"Not this trip, honey," I said. "I'm sorry."

"Why, you—"

"You don't want to tangle with Johnny Torch, do you, honey?" I asked her.

She stopped calling me names and bit her lip. "I ... guess not."

"I'm taking Salter's car," I said. "Tell him I'll return it later."

"Will you come back here for me, afterwards, Al?"

"Sure," I said. "And you'll be safe here from either Lavers or Fletcher and Torch."

I walked down the hallway to the front door quickly, then out to the Cadillac standing on the driveway. I drove back into downtown Pine City as fast as I could. Around fifteen minutes later I parked on the far side of the street from the apartment house, and settled down to wait. I wondered who was going to walk out of the building—Fletcher or Torch?

The minutes crept past slowly and stretched into half an hour. I lit the fourth cigarette since I got there, and started to worry. Another five minutes and then I saw the figure walk out of the apartment house and stand close to the curb. It was Johnny Torch. He let two cabs go, and picked up the third. I started the motor of the Cadillac, waited until the cab was a block away, then made an illegal U-turn and followed it.

We went out of the downtown area and into the respectable but usually unexciting suburbs. Tailing the cab was no problem. The traffic was light. Finally the cab stopped on a corner of two suburban cross-streets and Torch got out. I went on past the cab, made a left-hand turn, and stopped.

I got out of the car quickly and walked back to the corner. I saw the cab move away, then make a right-hand turn and vanish with a final blink of its taillights. I turned the corner in time to see Johnny Torch walking up the driveway of a house. There seemed to be something familiar about the house. I crossed the street to follow him and then I knew where I was.

I stopped on the sidewalk, looking at the house. Suddenly there was a nasty taste in my mouth. I heard a car coming down the street and then I didn't. Quick footsteps coming toward me made me realize I had company. I eased the gun out of its holster and spun around.

"Two men with but a single thought or something?" Schafer's voice said softly. "You can put that gun away, Lieutenant, it's the story I'm after."

"How the hell did you get here?" I asked him.

"Like I said, two guys with the same idea. I've been watching that apartment house from the time I left you around six tonight."

"Why?"

"The same reasons as you had, I guess, Lieutenant. This is my story, has been from the beginning. I want to get a beat on it. Right now it looks like I'm going to."

Schafer turned his head slowly and looked at the house. "The end of the trail, Lieutenant?" he asked softly. "The home of County Sheriff Lavers!"

There was a sudden, wild shriek from somewhere inside the house that stopped as abruptly as it had started. I sprinted up the driveway toward the house, with Schafer running beside me.

Chapter Fourteen

I stopped on the porch for a moment, the .38 in my hand, remembering how Linda Scott's body had looked three nights before. Schafer stopped beside me, peering at the half-open front door. "What are we waiting for, Lieutenant—a bus?"

"You feel brave, go on in," I told him.

He shook his head. "I'm only an amateur. You're the professional. I'll follow you."

I kicked the door fully open and waited. Nothing happened. A convulsive leap brought me into the hallway, which was empty. Schafer followed me inside cautiously. The living room door was also open, so I went in.

Mrs. Lavers lay in a crumpled heap on the floor. I knelt down beside her and saw she was breathing evenly. There was a bump on her forehead and a thin red line across the center of it, where the skin had been broken. It looked as if Torch had slugged her with the barrel of his gun.

"Is she all right?" Schafer asked anxiously.

"Knocked out cold," I said. "But I think she'll be all right."

"Where's Torch?"

"Upstairs, maybe," I said. "Do you have a gun?"

"What would I do with a gun?"

"I could make a suggestion," I said. "You'd better stay here with Mrs. Lavers and look after her." I nodded toward the phone on the table. "Call the Sheriff's office. If Lavers is there, tell him what happened. If nobody answers, try Homicide."

"Sure," Schafer said. "What are you going to do?"

"Look for Torch," I said. "He must be upstairs."

"I hope you find him before he finds you," Schafer said. "He's a killer!"

"You're just as brave as I am," I said. "And that's no consolation. If you see him while I'm upstairs, scream."

"You don't have to worry about that, Lieutenant!" Schafer grinned nervously. "They'll hear me in L.A."

I went out into the hallway again and stood still for a moment, listening. There was no sound from upstairs. Maybe Torch was busy up there; or maybe he was waiting at the top of the stairs to let me have it. The sharp vision of a refrigerated drawer in the county morgue took shape in front of my eyes. I didn't mind being a hero, but a dead hero was something else again.

The stairs didn't squeak, which was some small consolation. I went up them slowly, one at a time. I had got about halfway up when I heard footsteps coming up behind me. "Don't be stupid, Schafer!" I whispered. "He'll blow your head off just for kicks. Get back downstairs."

But he kept on coming. I couldn't worry too much about him because I was concentrating too hard on the top of the stairs, in case Johnny Torch's head suddenly appeared. I made another three steps, and then Schafer was right behind me.

The next thing I knew, the unyielding barrel of a gun thrust hard into my ribs. "Drop your gun!" a voice said quietly in my ear.

"Drop it!"

My fingers relaxed obediently and the gun dropped on the carpeted stair, one above the one I was standing on. Two mistakes I'd made already. The first one was not looking around when I heard the footsteps coming behind me, and the second was presuming they belonged to Schafer.

"O.K.," Fletcher said, his voice still pitched low, a shade more than a whisper. "Now we go on upstairs. You should have been happy with that seven hundred bucks, Wheeler!"

"I should have been happy to stay home and read a book," I grunted.

We reached the top of the stairs and stopped. The door to the main bedroom was right in front of us. Off to the left was the bathroom and then two further bedrooms. "Call him!" Fletcher breathed into my ear.

"What?"

"Call him, Wheeler!" The gun barrel jabbed harder into my spine, emphasizing his words.

"O.K.," I said. I raised my voice slightly above its normal level. "Torch? Johnny Torch!"

For about three seconds, nothing happened. Then he answered suddenly. "In here, copper! You want me, come and get me!" It sounded as if his voice had come from the third bedroom, the one farthest away from where we stood.

"You heard him," Fletcher said gently. "Move!" We got as far as the door to the third bedroom, which was shut.

"Open it," Fletcher whispered. "Walk in."

"And get my head blown off!" I whispered back.

"You're expendable. Don't open it and you get a slug in your spine right now!"

The one thing I appreciated was having a choice. I could see them right now in the county morgue, opening up that drawer so it would be all ready for me.

Fletcher's gun dug painfully into my spine again. "You got about two seconds," he whispered. "Make up your mind, Wheeler!" I made up my mind. I turned the handle of the door, then pushed the door open wide. Torch wasn't visible in the half of the room I could see, so I quickly deduced he must be in the half of the room I couldn't see. The odds were he was waiting right behind the door. Mentally, I could see the barrel of the gun in his hand all ready; physically I could feel the barrel of Fletcher's gun boring into my back.

I took three paces forward and the next one would carry me beyond the protection of the open door. Instead of taking the fourth step, I threw myself forward and landed flat on the floor. There was one shot that sounded deafening in the confined space of the room, and it was followed almost immediately by two more. There was a thud as something dropped to the floor, then silence.

Either I wasn't hurt, or I was dead. I moved my head cautiously, turning it around slowly.

"Get up, Wheeler!" Johnny Torch said. "On your feet." I did as I was told. He sat on the edge of the bed, the gun in his hand, grinning at me. "You want to say goodbye to Howard?" he asked softly, then nodded toward the door.

I looked. Fletcher's gun was on the floor, which accounted for the thud I'd heard. Fletcher himself was standing just past the door, leaning forward from the waist as if bowing to some invisible personage. He bowed lower still, until he passed the point of balance and fell forward onto the floor.

"Right between the eyes," Johnny Torch said in a satisfied voice. "He should have stayed in the apartment."

"I wonder he let you leave on your own," I said.

"I slugged him, so he didn't have no choice." Johnny grinned bleakly. "He should have stayed home, copper, and so should you."

"I wouldn't argue about that," I said. "Have you found the money yet, Johnny?"

"I'll get it," he said. "It's somewhere in this house all right. Got to find it, that's all. I already checked the other two bedrooms. If it's not in this one, it's got to be somewhere downstairs. You're going to help me look, copper. You can start in that closet."

"What happens when you find it?" I asked.

"I wouldn't think about that," he said. "It would only worry you. The closet!"

I walked over to the closet and opened the door. It wasn't hard to search—except for an ancient sports coat of Lavers', it was empty.

"All right," Johnny said. "Now try the bureau."

I emptied the contents of the bureau drawers out onto the floor. There was nothing there that even looked like money. Johnny moved off the bed and watched while I stripped it. He made me rip the cover off the mattress, then he examined the stitching carefully to see if it had been renewed anywhere, but it hadn't.

"You think maybe somebody else got to it first?" I asked him.

"Not a chance!" he said confidently.

"That journalist, Schafer," I said. "He's a smart guy, maybe he figured out the money was here."

"Schafer?" Johnny repeated. "You mean the guy Linda was sweet on? What would he know about it?"

"Why don't you ask him?" I suggested hopefully.

"Don't be a wise guy, copper." he said. "It's getting so I don't need you anymore."

"I mean it," I said. "He's downstairs right now. And downstairs is the one place you haven't looked for the money, isn't it?"

Johnny Torch's mouth tightened as he stared at me. "Who do you think you're kidding?"

"It's true," I said. "You don't believe me, go and see for yourself."

"Maybe I will," he said. "But I think I'm going to take care of you first."

"You're not using your brains, Johnny," I said quickly. "If he is downstairs, it's easier to have me go first, isn't it? I can talk to him and throw him off guard when you get down there."

"You sure want to live for another five minutes!" He grinned contemptuously. "You want to live so bad, you'd shoot your own mother right now if it would help, wouldn't you, copper?"

"I admit it," I said.

"Why not?" He thought about it for a moment. "Yeah—I kind of go for that, copper. There's no real hurry to take care of you, anyway. I'd like to watch you worry a little longer. When you do get it, Wheeler, it's going to hurt awful bad. I'm going to make sure of that!"

"You want to see Schafer, or don't you?" I asked him.

"Sure," he said. "You go first."

I walked out of the bedroom and back to the head of the stairs with Johnny right behind me. Two steps down, I deliberately missed my footing and fell backwards. I thumped down six more stairs on my backside before I stopped.

"That you, Lieutenant?" Schafer called out from the living room. There was a slight quaver in his voice.

"Sure," I yelled back. "I'm O.K. Be down in a minute. Don't worry, everything's been taken care of."

I looked up and saw Johnny Torch standing right behind me, a grin on his face. "It won't hurt long enough for you to worry about it," he said softly. "That was smart of you to give Schafer the right answers. You'll live a little longer yet, copper!"

Sitting on my own .38 was highly uncomfortable—worse than that visitor's chair in Lavers' office—but it had a very soothing effect at the same time.

"Get on your feet!" Johnny said abruptly. "If you bust a leg, you can crawl the rest of the way."

I knew I couldn't get the gun out from underneath me without him seeing it. He'd have plenty of time to shoot me before I had a chance to even point my own gun at him. I hoped my reflexes were coordinating better than his.

I reached out to grab hold of the banister to pull myself up, and at the last moment I grabbed hold of Johnny's leg instead. I yanked frantically. He gave a startled yelp, and the next second his gun exploded.

The slug buried itself in the wall about six inches above my head. Johnny sailed over the top of my head, his arms and legs flailing the air wildly. He hit the stairs, two from the bottom, and rolled the rest of the way. He still had hold of his gun.

I came onto my feet with the .38 in my hand. Johnny pushed himself up onto his knees painfully, the gun in his hand weaving a little but starting to point toward me. I preferred that chivalry died before Al Wheeler. I had the advantage of Johnny for maybe another two seconds, so I took it. I put two bullets into him and he slumped forward, his face hitting the edge of the bottom stair.

I went down the stairs quickly and picked up his gun. Then I knelt down beside him and turned him over. He was still breathing—just. Both slugs had hit him in the chest and he was getting air into his lungs without inhaling for it. He was losing a lot of blood the same way.

"Wise guy!" he said faintly.

"I didn't mean for it to hurt, Johnny," I said truthfully, "but I guess you made me nervous."

"I don't figure you out at all, copper," he said feebly. "Why did you give me my gun back in the apartment?"

"It's a long story, Johnny," I said. "I don't think you've got the time to understand it. I never figured Fletcher as the killer and if I'd let him go then, he'd have picked up the money from this house and never stopped running. I wanted that money here for bait, Johnny. For you, for the real killer."

"You talk," he gasped, "but it don't make no sense."

"That's why I had Salter call you and say he was coming to get both you and Fletcher," I went on. "I wanted you to panic, Johnny, and lead me to the money and the killer at the same time."

His mouth dropped open as I said that, and for a couple of seconds I thought it was surprise. Then I realized he wasn't breathing anymore.

"Lieutenant!" Schafer's near-hysterical voice shouted from the living room. "What goes on! Was it you firing those shots?"

"Who the hell do you think it was?" I said disgustedly. "The Marshal of Dodge City?"

I holstered my .38, then walked back into the living room. Mrs. Lavers was still unconscious and still on the floor. "You could have picked her up off the floor and made her comfortable," I said to Schafer.

"With all those shots going on upstairs!" he said in a taut voice. "I was just waiting for somebody to walk in and blow a hole right through me!"

"That's the trouble with being a journalist," I said, "you have too much imagination."

"What happened, anyway?"

"Fletcher and Torch," I said. "Johnny was upstairs and Fletcher came in just as I was halfway up the stairs. He used me as a cover against Johnny, but Johnny killed him all the same. I killed Johnny, and that's the story. It was a lucky break that Fletcher arrived when he did."

"Why do you say that?"

"He came up behind me on the stairs and made me drop my gun," I said. "So it was waiting for me on the way down."

"Huh?" Schafer stared at me blankly.

"Just take my word for it," I said. "Help me lift Mrs. Lavers onto that couch."

We put her on the couch with a cushion underneath her head. Johnny must have slugged her pretty hard, but her breathing still seemed all right. "Did you tell Lavers to bring a doctor with him?" I asked.

"Doctor? Oh, sure!" Schafer said blankly. "What was Torch doing up there anyway, that was so important?"

"Looking for seventy thousand dollars," I said.

I lit myself a cigarette and sank gratefully into the nearest chair.

Schafer stared at me. "Seventy thousand dollars? Are you crazy?"

"Not me," I said. "But I'm not prepared to prove it. They took the Syndicate in Las Vegas for seventy thousand—the four of them. Nina Booth and Linda Scott were murdered, so that left only two of them interested in the money. Fletcher and Torch—and they both came looking for it."

Schafer shook his head slowly. "It's incredible! What a fantastic story this is going to make. The money really exists?"

"Sure," I said. "And it's hidden in this house somewhere. Well hidden, I'd guess. Johnny had been through the bedrooms without finding it." I looked across at the couch. "I hope the Sheriff doesn't take too long getting here. She should have a doctor."

"I guess I should phone in my story," he said. "I wish Torch had found that money, it would have wrapped up the story nicely."

"You can't have everything," I told him.

"Maybe we could get lucky?" he said eagerly. "We don't have anything else to do but wait for the Sheriff. Why don't we look for the money, Lieutenant?"

There was no reason why not. "O.K.," I said. "Let's try and be smart before we wear ourselves out. If you wanted to hide something in somebody else's house, where would you put it? It would have to be somewhere it couldn't be found accidentally. A place that doesn't get cleaned regularly, for example."

"Sure," Schafer nodded. "Keep talking, Lieutenant."

"The tops of wall cupboards," I said. "Taped under the lid of a toilet tank; behind the stove in the kitchen. Then there's always the chance it was pushed down between the arm and the seat of an upholstered chair."

"I'll go look!" he said eagerly. He tried the chairs and the couch in the living room first, then he went outside. Five minutes dragged past and then I heard him race back along the hall and up the stairs three at a time. I thought it was nice to be enthusiastic.

Another couple of minutes went by and then I heard him coming down the stairs at a much slower, more deliberate pace. I got up from the chair and walked over to the door of the living room and stood behind it, with the .38 in my hand.

Schafer came back into the room slowly, an almost dedicated look on his face. In one hand he held a bulky, brown-paper package, and in the other hand he held a gun. It looked like a .32 and his finger was tensed around the trigger.

I waited while he stopped, his eyes widening as he looked around the room and couldn't see me. Then I cracked the barrel of the .38 down hard onto his wrist. His gun dropped to the floor and he cried out shrilly in pain.

I looked into his hate-filled eyes and grinned. "You think I didn't know it was you?" I asked him.

Chapter Fifteen

I dropped the phone back onto the cradle with Lavers' voice still demanding explanations in my ear. Schafer sat huddled in a chair, looking at the pattern of the carpet between his feet. I picked the phone up again and dialed Salter's home number. I kept the .38 in my free hand because a cop can die suddenly if he gets too complacent.

Salter answered and I told him where I was and for him to come right over. He was better than Lavers, he didn't ask questions, he just said he'd be there. I hung up the phone again and looked at Schafer. "You didn't call the Sheriff of course," I said. "You were waiting for a chance to get your hands on the money and then start running."

He didn't say anything; he kept on studying that strip of carpet. "Linda told you about the money?" I asked softly.

Schafer lifted his head slowly. "She told me. I think she was around breaking-point then. She couldn't take the nervous strain of waiting until the Syndicate's heat cooled off. I guessed she would have cracked wide open to the Sheriff or to Salter, if she hadn't talked to me."

"That was her mistake," I said. "If she'd talked to either of the other two, she'd still be alive."

He didn't try to answer that. "She told me everything," he said. "Except where the money was hidden. She hadn't told the others that, so she said. She was crazy for me and I said we'd go away together but it was crazy not to take the money with us. So she said she'd get it."

"And you trusted her," I grinned at him. "You followed her to make sure she wasn't double-crossing you?"

"Of course I did," he said. "Then I saw her walk up the driveway to this house. The Sheriff's house. I remembered she'd told me that Lavers was her uncle. I thought she was going to tell him the whole story, and if she did I'd never have a chance of getting all that money. I had to stop her, the only way I could stop her was with a gun!"

His lips quivered. "Why didn't she tell me she'd hidden the money in this house!" he sobbed. "Then it wouldn't have happened. It was all her own fault. If she'd trusted me and told me where the money was, I would never have made that mistake. There would have been no need to kill her!"

I heard a car come up the driveway and stop outside the house. The front door was still open, I remembered. Five seconds later, Salter walked into the room slowly, with Gabrielle behind him. He looked at me and the gun in my hand, and then he put his own gun away. "I see somebody took care of Torch, Lieutenant?" he said evenly.

"Yeah," I said. "It's been quite a night one way and the other. The ..." I heard more cars coming up the driveway fast.

"You'd better get over on the far side of the room," I said to Salter and Gabrielle. "Pretend you're cleaning up the place or something. The Sheriff is about to ride in on his white charger."

They just made it across the room before Lavers burst into the room followed by Doc Murphy, Polnik, and a couple of uniformed men. I started talking before Lavers had a chance to open his mouth.

In nothing flat, Murphy had revived Mrs. Lavers and she was sitting up, taking an active interest in the proceedings. I could see by the look on his face that the Sheriff was trying to make a mental readjustment and he was having trouble.

Doc Murphy, having taken care of Mrs. Lavers, was waiting around hopefully for somebody to give him a drink. Polnik was just staring at me, obviously wondering why the hell I hadn't gone north while I had the chance. Schafer had his face buried in his hands and was worrying too much about what was going to happen to him to worry about what was going on around him.

Finally Lavers found his voice. "What are these people doing here?" he shouted, pointing at Salter and Gabrielle.

"I called them just after I called you," I told him. "They have a right to be here, I think."

"You shouldn't be shouting at the Lieutenant," Mrs. Lavers said firmly. "After him saving my life and catching your murderer and everything and not so much as a thank you out of you!"

Lavers' face reddened. "You've had a bad time," he said in a strangled voice. "Don't you think you should go to bed and rest, dear? I'm sure that's what the doctor would advise." He looked appealingly at Murphy.

"Your wife is a remarkable woman, Sheriff," Murphy said gleefully. "Constitution like an ox, if you'll pardon the phrase, Mrs. Lavers? If she feels fit enough to stay up, I see no reason why she shouldn't."

"Of course!" Mrs. Lavers said. "It was just a hit over the head when I wasn't looking or I'd have shown him a thing or two! Now, as I was saying—"

"All right," Lavers said wearily. "We'll get around to that later. If you're feeling that bright, how about making us some coffee?"

"Coffee?" Murphy said in a horrified voice.

"Coffee!" Lavers repeated coldly.

"Very well," his wife said and walked toward the door, "but don't you be bullying the Lieutenant while I'm gone!" She went out of the room and Lavers sighed heavily. "Even my own wife!" he muttered under his breath.

I lit another cigarette and waited, but not for long.

"I hate to do this," the Sheriff muttered. "But I suppose I don't have any choice. All right, Wheeler! You can get that smug look off your face and tell me what it's all about, but in detail this time."

When he'd first arrived in the room, I'd told him that Fletcher and Torch were dead, and that I had the murderer right there. Now was the difficult part, to fill in the detail.

It didn't take too long to tell him what had happened from the time Johnny Torch had left Fletcher's apartment, with me following him, to the point where Schafer came back into the living room with a gun in his hand.

"Why would Torch come here, to my house, anyway?" Lavers asked blankly.

"He came for the seventy thousand dollars," I said. "The money they'd taken the Syndicate for in Las Vegas."

"How could that money possibly have got here!" the Sheriff fumed. "Don't be an idiot, Wheeler!"

"The money was here because that's where Linda Scott hid it," I said.

"What safer place than the home of the County Sheriff? It must have been a hell of a problem for them. They brought the money with them from Vegas, but they couldn't touch it because the Syndicate would find out. They couldn't bank it for the same reason. It would be too dangerous to leave around in any one of their apartments in case one of the Syndicate boys got in and searched, and that could happen any time. But Linda could visit her uncle without arousing any suspicions, and while she was here she could hide the money."

I looked at the brown-paper package on the table, then I looked across at Schafer. "Where exactly was it hidden?" I asked him.

"It was taped underneath the lid of the toilet tank," he said sullenly. "One of your guesses was lucky!"

"Linda was an amateur," I said.

"What about Schafer?" Lavers asked. "How does he fit into the picture?"

"Let's talk about your niece first, Sheriff," I said. "She was different from the other three. Fletcher and Johnny Torch were professionals. Nina Booth was as tough as they come, and she was also Fletcher's new girl friend. The three of them could take the nervous tension of waiting for the heat to cool off before they touched the money. But Linda Scott wasn't built that way. She started to crack."

"Schafer!" Lavers said loudly. "I told you to tell me about Schafer."

"I was getting around to it," I said. "Don't rush me, Sheriff. Schafer said he thought there was a story in Fletcher and the rest of them coming to Pine City from Vegas. He also said the quickest way to a story was through a woman. That was why he'd gotten friendly with Linda. She fell for him, she cracked up, and told him about the money."

I looked across at Schafer. "Here's a guy with a reputation of being ruthless in his job, of being a womanizer, and always broke. That was what his editor told me. Suddenly, seventy thousand bucks is practically tossed right into his lap. He sold Linda the idea of her getting the money and the two of them skipping town together."

"Then why kill her?"

"She'd agreed to get the money, she went out to get it." I told him the rest of that story as Schafer had told it to me.

"That's almost funny!" Salter said. "She was being honest with him and he killed her because he thought she was double-crossing him."

"You have a wild sense of humor, Hugo," I said. "But you're right."

Lavers grunted. "I guess that part makes sense. What about Nina Booth?"

"It was a wonder Schafer didn't go crazy and really blow his stack," I said. "He'd murdered to get that money and he still didn't know where it was. All he knew was that it really existed somewhere. My guess is he followed up his usual routine, the quickest way to a story was through a woman.

"Only he didn't realize that Nina Booth was twice as smart and twice as tough as Linda Scott. I think he went to her apartment and tried to bluff her. Told her that Fletcher had killed Linda, and he was planning to kill both Johnny Torch and Nina, so that he wouldn't have to split the money with them."

"But why kill her, too?" Lavers prodded.

"Nina was no dummy," I said. "She knew Schafer had been Linda's boy friend. She could see that Linda must have told him the story of what happened in Vegas and the money. She wouldn't trust Schafer. She'd think he was trying to trap her for the sake of his story. If she listened to him at all, she was admitting that the money really existed.

"So she decided to call his bluff. She lifted the phone and called me. She was going to tell me what Schafer had said to her. What she didn't realize was, in doing that, she was also telling me who had murdered Linda.

"But Schafer realized that all right. He had to stop her somehow and he did—he stopped her with an ice pick."

"You make it sound plausible," Lavers said. "You have any proof of all this?"

"Schafer hounded us both from the moment, almost, that Linda Scott was murdered," I said. "He wanted us to arrest Fletcher. He even convinced his editor that you must be somehow mixed up with Fletcher because you wouldn't book him for murder right away."

"True enough," Lavers admitted. "But then that alibi of Fletcher and Torch's didn't stand up. Nobody remembered them in that restaurant."

"I think I can explain that," Salter said blandly. "That particular restaurant is an investment owned by the ... people I represent."

"You mean you told the staff not to remember them being there?" Lavers gaped at him.

"I thought it would be interesting to add a little more pressure, and see what effect it had on Fletcher," Salter said calmly. "We weren't particularly friendly, you know?"

I cut in hastily on the conversation before Lavers exploded. "Schafer came to my apartment after I'd cooked up the alibi for Fletcher and he'd been sprung," I said. "He was half-crazy with rage. His newspaper was going to break me, he was going to break me. I'd be a bum for the rest of my life and—"

"You still will be," Murphy cackled. "Cop or no cop, it doesn't make any difference to you, Wheeler."

"Shouldn't you be about your corpses?" I asked him. "Instead of fooling around here, hoping the Sheriff will give you a drink sometime?"

"That alibi you cooked up," Lavers said in a gentle voice. "I was going to ask you about that, Wheeler."

"The way I figured it, with both girls murdered and you putting the heat on Fletcher," I said, "sooner or later, Fletcher or Torch was going to pick up the money and run. When they went for the money, the murderer—whoever he was—was going to be there, too.

"It was just possible that Johnny had killed the two girls to avoid splitting the money in shares, but I felt sure Fletcher hadn't. He would have realized what a case there was against him, and he wouldn't have taken the risk. I didn't think the Syndicate had killed the two girls, either. I had it on good authority that they hadn't." I glanced at Salter for a moment, and he grinned back at me. "They would have handled it better, in any case," I said.

"So?" Lavers said.

"So I was trying to build up the pressure to the point where Johnny would run for the money and the murderer would be either him, or the person who was right behind him. Then you booked Fletcher and gummed up the whole works. With Fletcher out of the way, Johnny would be in no hurry to pick up the money, knowing it was safe where it was. I had to get Fletcher sprung somehow, so Johnny would worry about Fletcher grabbing the money and getting away with it at any time."

Lavers rubbed his nose irritably. "All right, so it's a wonderful theory. What about some facts?"

"The gun Schafer dropped is over there on the table beside the money," I said. "Ballistics shouldn't have much trouble matching up the slugs still in the gun with the slug that killed Linda Scott. And my bet is, if you really want a confession, all you've got to do is ask him."

Schafer lifted his head slowly. "All right," he said hoarsely. "I killed them. I killed both of them! I told you it was a mistake killing Linda, but what else could I do!"

"You could have read some more poetry," I suggested. "It might have kept you out of trouble."

Lavers looked across at Polnik. "Take him away," he said. "Get a full statement from him. I'll come down to the office later."

Polnik walked to the chair where Schafer sat, and heaved him onto his feet.

"Just one point, Sheriff," Salter said smoothly. "That brown-paper package on the table. It contains seventy thousand dollars, stolen from the owners of the Snake Eyes in Las Vegas. I'm sure they will bring legal action for its return, so I'll be obliged if you see good care is taken of it. Things like that can very easily get lost, you know."

Lavers gave him a venomous look, then walked over and picked up the package. "I'll see it doesn't get lost!" he growled.

Polnik slapped a pair of handcuffs onto Schafer's wrists, then hustled him out of the house. A few moments later, Mrs. Lavers came back into the room with a trayful of cups of coffee. "Here it is," she said triumphantly. "You can help yourselves."

"I have to be going," Murphy said sourly. "If you'll excuse me."

"I think I should also be leaving," Salter said. He walked over to me. "Thank you for everything, Lieutenant." He grinned suddenly. "That headache you gave me earlier tonight seems to have disappeared completely now."

"I'm glad to hear it," I said. "It had me worried for a while."

"I wouldn't worry, Lieutenant," he said. "I still owe you a favor." Then he turned around and walked out of the room.

I drank a cup of Mrs. Lavers' coffee. It was good coffee, as always. Then I looked at the Sheriff. "Is there anything else, sir?"

"You can take that girl home, if that's what you mean!" he said. "But be in the office at nine o'clock in the morning."

"Yes, sir," I said.

"And if you think I'm going to apologize, you're mistaken!"

"Yes, sir," I agreed.

"Why didn't you damned well tell me what you were trying to do!"

"Would you have believed me?" I asked politely.

"No," he grunted.

I said good night to Mrs. Lavers and escorted Gabrielle out of the house and down the driveway. Salter was waiting for us on the sidewalk. "I'm driving my wife's car," he said. "I thought I'd wait and tell you to take the Cadillac. You can return it to me tomorrow."

"Thanks," I said.

"My pleasure," he said. "You won't forget what I said about any time you get tired of being a cop, to look me up, will you?"

"I won't," I told him.

"That is," he said, "if you're not running for President."

I walked Gabrielle around the corner to where the Cadillac was parked. We got in and I drove us home. I made up a drink as soon as we got inside the apartment.

"Al, lover," she said softly. "Hugo's got me an engagement in one of the Miami hotels. It was too good to refuse."

"Sure," I said. "When do you start?"

"I have to leave on Monday," she said. "That only gives us the weekend, doesn't it?"

"I guess it does," I agreed.

"We should make it a wonderful weekend, lover!" she said excitedly. "Why don't we fly up to Vegas and really have a ball!"

"Are you out of your mind?" I said. "Where would I get the money to ... money?"

"Are you all right, Al?" she asked anxiously. "You look as if you had a sudden pain, or something."

"It wasn't a pain," I said, "I just remembered something."

I put my hand into my inside pocket and pulled out the wad of bills. Gabrielle's eyes bulged slightly when she saw them. "What did you do, rob a bank?"

"I'd forgotten all about this," I said. "Fletcher gave it to me—the pay-off for the alibi we made him. So I guess half of it's yours, honey. I mean, it's no good to him now, is it?"

"Certainly not!" she said quickly. "That's wonderful, lover! Now we can really have a ball in Vegas!"

She came close to me and wound her arms around my neck.

"Sweep me off my feet, lover!" she said. "You're a very clever lieutenant and you deserve the victory I am about to give you."

"There's just one thing about the weekend in Las Vegas, honey," I said carefully.

"What's that?"

"No crap games at the Snake Eyes!" I said, and then I swept her off her feet.

THE END

THE PASSIONATE
- - - -
by Carter Brown

Chapter One

Outside, it was a warm passionate night, and inside my apartment I'd left a warm passionate blonde. I figured by now she must have got the same damp, disenchanted feeling that I had. The morgue at midnight is not my idea of fun.

I looked at Katz, the head mortician, in disgust. "You sure you just didn't count 'em wrong, Charlie?" I asked him.

"Lieutenant Wheeler," he said indignantly. "You don't think I dreamed up this bruise on the back of my head, do you?"

"Could be," I said. "You almost live here—you could dream up anything."

"It's gone," he said flatly.

"Who wants a stiff?" I said. "Who wants to steal a stiff? What can you do with it? You can't even hock it."

"I guess that's your business to find out," Charlie said primly.

"Your trouble is you don't have a sense of humor, Charlie," I told him "And will you put your eyes back into their sockets? They worry me."

"Aren't you going to do something about it?" he asked plaintively. "In all my twenty years here, Lieutenant, nothing like this ever happened before, never!"

"There's always got to be a first time," I said, "like I told that blonde before I was so rudely interrupted by the Sheriff's call. What happened, anyway?"

"Somebody knocked on the door," he said hoarsely. "That isn't usual, Lieutenant, mostly they just walk in."

"The stiffs?"

"People!" he snarled. "You want to hear this, or don't you?"

"I don't want to, but I don't have any choice," I sighed deeply. "Go on."

"So I went outside to see who it was," he continued, "and just as I stepped out the door—pow!"

"Pow?"

"Somebody slugged me," Charlie said feelingly. "When I woke up there was nobody in here. So I called the County Sheriff's office and—"

"And it finished up with me," I said. "Then you checked the stiffs?"

"Sure," Charlie nodded. "I got a responsibility here, Lieutenant, even if you don't appreciate it. I found one of them was gone!"

"You think maybe some kid's got himself a 'Do-It-Yourself doctor kit with real scalpel supplied,' and he wanted something for practice?" I saw the look on Charlie's face. "Never mind. Just describe it."

"Came in early this morning," Katz said. "A dame, blonde and she was some looker. Dropped dead on the sidewalk outside a downtown bar, of a heart attack. It being Saturday, Doc Murphy said he'd leave the autopsy till Monday morning."

"She was a looker, you said?"

"Real nice," Charlie said wistfully. "I kind of miss not having her around the place."

"Was there any identification on her?"

"None at all. She didn't even have a purse with her. Nobody knew where she came from. She just stopped outside the bar and—"

"Dropped dead," I agreed. "There's a moral in that somewhere, Charlie. If she'd been inside the bar, a shot of bourbon might have fixed the whole thing."

The phone rang at Charlie's elbow and he reacted violently. It kept on ringing while he looked at it the way I look at Marilyn Monroe in CinemaScope. Twitching.

"You lift the receiver, it stops ringing," I told Charlie. "It's one of the newer things."

"You answer it, Lieutenant," he pleaded. "I'm nervous."

I picked up the receiver and said, "County morgue."

"I have a message for you," a cultured, male voice said smoothly. "I understand you are missing one corpse? I can tell you where to find it."

"Where?"

"At Television Studio KVNW."

"Who is this speaking?" I asked.

"Just a fellow who likes to keep things nice and tidy," the voice said pleasantly. "I hate to think that empty drawer is worrying you." There was a click as he hung up on me.

I put the phone back and told Charlie the news. His face brightened a little. "I'm glad," he said. "Be nice to get her back. You going out there to make sure?"

"I guess so," I nodded. "But I'd like to know who the guy was who made that call."

"He could have been a mortician sometime," Charlie said seriously. "He's got the right feeling for it, keep things nice and tidy. Just the way I feel about it."

"Maybe he's retired and got nostalgic for the smell of formaldehyde," I suggested. "Have you seen a psychiatrist lately, Charlie?"

"Sure, about a couple of weeks back."

"What did he say?"

"Say?" Charlie's mouth dropped open. "He didn't say anything. He couldn't. He'd cut his own throat with a nail file. Why else would they bring him in here?"

"I had to ask," I said wearily.

Thirty minutes later I parked my Austin-Healey in the alley behind the building housing KVNW. There were eight trash cans all in a row, all king-sized, and just for the hell of it I checked them—but none of them housed a corpse.

I walked around to the front entrance and told the doorman who I was. While he went looking for the manager I used the phone on the reception desk and called Sheriff Lavers.

He was home and, by the sound of his voice, in bed when I called. I told him about the anonymous phone call and that I was now inside the television studios. The Sheriff said fine, keep looking, and the next time I wanted to call somebody when I had nothing of importance to say I should call my mother. At least, I think it was mother he said.

By that time the manager had arrived. He was a small guy in a neat suit, with neat black hair and a neat mustache; the sort of guy who wouldn't wrinkle the sheets on his honeymoon.

"My name is Bowers," he said crisply. "Something wrong, Lieutenant?" There was polite disbelief in his voice as though in his world nothing would dare be. I told him what was wrong and lit a cigarette while he made up his mind to believe it. "But why would anyone dump a body in *our* studios?" he asked helplessly.

"Don't ask me," I told him. "I already checked the trash cans but they're crammed full with dead cowboys."

"The whole thing sounds ridiculous," he said, getting that executive decision back into his voice. "Absurd!"

"I'm with you," I agreed. "But I have to make an investigation, the County Sheriff tells me."

Bowers looked at his watch, then shrugged his shoulders irritably. "All right, Lieutenant. What do you want me to do?"

"Suppose we look around the studios first?" I suggested.

"Very well." He looked at his watch again and bit his lower lip gently like it was fragile, and maybe it was.

I looked at my own watch—the habit was catching—and saw it was a quarter of one. "A brand new day," I said. "You have an early appointment, Mr. Bowers?"

"The Late Late Show goes on in fifteen minutes," he said. "It's one of the old horror movies...."

"Not *Gone With The Wind?*" I asked, fascinated.

"It's called, *Stepchild of Frankenstein,*" he said coldly. "But we have a new master of ceremonies—Bruno—and I want to be on the set to see how everything goes."

"How long will it take?"

"Ten minutes," he said. "Then the movie runs straight through after that."

"No commercials?" I asked. "What are you preaching—revolution?"

"That's very amusing, Lieutenant." Bowers' voice didn't sound as though it agreed, and his face wore an expression to match. "Why don't you send it to the *New Yorker?*"

"If this thing is only going to take ten minutes," I said, "why don't we both watch it? I can start asking questions when it's finished."

He smiled at me warmly. "That's very understanding of you, Lieutenant. I'm grateful." He grabbed my elbow and propelled me toward the nearest iron door. "We're all set up in Studio Two, just through here."

Studio Two looked like Bedlam the night Adolf Hitler arrived. In front of the set there was a tight group of onlookers who kept fouling the camera cables, while the disembodied, godlike voice of the director pleaded with them to get the hell out of the way.

I just had time to notice an exotic-looking brunette; then Bowers directed my attention to the set. It was something out of a nightmare—like one of the "sick-sick jokes" come to life.

Bowers chuckled. "What do you think of it, Lieutenant?"

"One thing," I said. "Any of the kiddies who stayed up after their bedtime—this will send them to bed—or the nearest nuthouse." The set resembled the interior of a vault, a cellar, a tomb—a combination of all three. Huge plastic cobwebs glistened in the two corners, and in the middle of one web was a large glob of something black. The more you looked at it, the more you hoped it was a spider. Even a black widow would have been a relief.

In the forefront of the set was a long wooden bench fitted with a mad scientist's idea of how to make nuclear power the cheap way—or something. There were a lot of peculiarly shaped glass bottles joined together with glass tubes. A bubbling black liquid chased its own tail, wildly and unceasingly, through the whole setup.

In back of the bench, resting on two wooden horses, was a pinewood coffin, a little rough around the edges. It looked like the end result of a Do-It-Yourself project.

"This is our first introduction of Bruno," Bowers informed me. "And naturally, we want to make it a real production. Horrific hosts for horror shows are getting to be a big thing, you know, Lieutenant."

"Not in my life," I assured him.

"Bruno should be here any moment now," he said. "His make-up is really something! He has an assistant, too, a girl."

"Brunhild?"

"How did you guess?"

"It figures," I said.

He looked around, lowering his voice almost to a whisper. "I'll let you into a little secret, Lieutenant. Brunhild is really Penelope Calthorpe!"

"You don't say!"

"It's true," he whispered gleefully. "You'll keep it a secret, Lieutenant?"

"Cross my heart," I said. "Who's Penelope Calthorpe?" His face stiffened. "You're not serious! You've never heard of the Calthorpe sisters?"

Then I did remember, and wished I hadn't. "Oh, no," I pleaded. "Not *the* Calthorpe sisters! The crazy Calthorpes, the merry madcap morons of high society—playgirl Penelope and practical-joking Prudence!"

"I see you do remember them," Bowers said happily.

I shuddered. "Every cop in this country knows Prudence Calthorpe— mention her name and we all start running. She's the dame who screamed, 'Run for your lives!' in the middle of a crisis-ridden UN session, then tossed a smoke bomb into the middle of the delegates. It landed on the head of the chief Russian delegate, I remember. It took the New York police commissioner a week to try and explain why he hadn't had her shot, and even then the Russian wasn't convinced."

Bowers looked even happier. "Such wonderful publicity they get!"

"They were in Los Angeles six months back," I said broodingly. "Hired a trailer and took it out onto the Hollywood Freeway on a Friday afternoon, parked it at right angles blocking all four lanes, and then Prudence beat a drum while Penelope did an Oriental belly dance and for a climax stripped off all her clothes and threw them at the cops coming to arrest her. Dear Prudence slipped her panties into the pocket of a lieutenant as he was wrestling her into a squad car, and when the reporters met her at the station she claimed she'd been raped by the lieutenant and offered the panties as proof!"

"They do like their fun," Bowers nodded. "Two of the ten richest women in the country, you know. I'm flattered that Penelope chose these studios to try out her act."

"I'm happy for you," I said. "Why did she bother choosing? With all the dough you say she's got, it would've been easier for her to buy it."

Bowers wasn't listening. "Here they are now," he said thankfully, and checked his watch again.

Bruno was a tall thin guy, dressed in a long black robe that came down to his ankles. The make-up department had done a job on his face. They'd turned his right eye into just a socket, and given his left eye a permanent stare. His front teeth had been blacked out, but to compensate they'd given him two prominent fangs, one at each corner of his mouth, and they protruded down across his lower lip.

The final, subtle touch, was the red line right across his throat, crisscrossed with thick black lines to resemble a home stitching job done by somebody who was understandably nervous when they joined up his throat again. I had the feeling I wouldn't even have liked to know him when he was alive.

Brunhild was an almost wholesome contrast. On her head was a Viking's helmet, but instead of the horns projecting from either side of it there were two remarkably lifelike clenched fists. She wore what looked like a white silk sarong, way off the shoulder and just reaching the tops of her thighs. It was girdled around the waist with a rusty iron chain decorated with giant teeth. She was a redhead with delectable legs and maybe she was nice-looking, but you'd have to remove the make-up to find out.

Bowers checked his watch again. "One minute to go," he said.

"Who's in the coffin?" I asked him. "Charlie's Aunt?"

"It's just a prop," he said impatiently. "Quiet, please, Lieutenant!"

A sudden hush descended on the studio. Bruno took up his position behind the bench, with Brunhild standing beside him. A camera moved in for the opening close-up.

I looked across at the monitor screen and saw the titles fade from *Stepchild of Frankenstein*, accompanied by some weird music. It died away as a new slide proclaimed "Introduced by your host, Bruno," accompanied by some more weird music. Then finally, "And his assistant, Brunhild!"

The opening shot was a very close close-up of Bruno's head and shoulders. He leered out of the screen, then touched that unspeakable throat gently with his index finger. "Next time somebody shouts, 'Cut!' I'll use a safety razor," he lisped confidingly. He leaned forward, his one piercing eye staring straight at his audience.

"Don't let's be strangers," he pleaded. "Remember, just one step and I'm in your living room!"

I guess he wasn't bad if you went for that kind of stuff. Bruno did nearly all the work—Brunhild seemed to be around strictly for decoration. He made two or three references to, "Our little monster," who apparently lived inside the coffin. I made the brilliant deduction that the coffin was the gimmick climax of his introduction, and so it was.

"He's our very own," Bruno told his audience confidentially. "Our very own little masterpiece and we love him. It's just unfortunate that he turned out wrong, that's all. We didn't have the formula exactly right—but it doesn't matter. He's a lovable ... thing. It's like having a child around the tomb, so long as you don't look at him."

He turned to Brunhild with a paternal snarl on his face. "Lift the lid, dear, and let our friends see it. After all, if we can't sleep, why should they?"

"Yes, dearest," Brunhild said happily. She minced toward the coffin, then stopped suddenly.

"You mustn't keep our friends waiting," Bruno said chidingly.

She hesitated for a moment. "Dearest, shouldn't I take the ax with me. I mean, well, it might be ... awake?"

"Not a chance," Bruno said confidently. "I've given him his ration of luminous toxins for today. He'll be sleeping like a vampire at high noon!"

"You're so clever, Bruno!" she said rapturously. "You think of everything!"

"Well," he said modestly. "I can't make the werewolves sit up and beg yet—but give me time."

Brunhild bent forward over the coffin and into the camera. I wondered if Bruno had already used the ax on his assistant—she showed enough cleavage.

The camera swooped down for a close-up, showing just her hands as she removed the lid slowly. She pushed it to one side until it dropped to the floor with a sinister thud. Then there was only anticlimax.

Inside the coffin was a guy in his late thirties. An average-looking guy, running to fat a little, his features beginning to blur. He lay there peacefully, his eyes closed, looking like a commercial for someone's mattresses.

Bruno was still at the bench, chattering happily about exactly what went wrong with the formula when they made the little monster in the first place, but it didn't jibe with the occupant of the coffin.

Then another camera swooped in for a final close-up of Bruno as he said good night. I figured the gimmick had been flat, but then I saw it had gotten a reaction from somebody. Brunhild stood at the head of the coffin, her eyes glazed, her whole body rigid.

The red light on the camera winked out and the amplified voice of the director announced it was all over.

"Wonderful!" Bowers said, rubbing his hands together. "I think we've seen the start of something big tonight, Lieutenant!"

"You could be right," I told him, and walked across the set toward the coffin.

Brunhild didn't move as I reached the coffin. Her eyes looked straight through me, unseeingly. Bruno came bustling over, a happy smile on his face. "I think it went over all right," he lisped contentedly. "What did you think of our little monster? A masterpiece in papier-mâché, I call it."

He reached out toward the inside of the coffin with both hands, and looked at the occupant at the same time.

"I wouldn't touch it if I were you," I murmured. "That body's for real."

Bruno stood perfectly still for a moment while he looked at the guy's face. "But that's not ..." Then he saw what the camera hadn't shown— the bullet hole in the chest and the dried blood around it, staining the white shirt. "Blood!" he whispered, then keeled over in a dead faint.

Brunhild sighed softly, took one tottering step backward, then collapsed onto the floor beside her master.

"What a lousy pair of monsters you two turned out to be!" I said disgustedly, but they didn't hear me.

There was a wild scream from somewhere in back of the studio. I started running automatically and collided with a wild-eyed female of uncertain age. She clutched the lapels of my coat in a convulsive grip. "In there!" she said wildly. "In the property room, there's a girl and she's dead."

I unwound her fingers from my lapels and walked inside the room. It looked like the granddaddy of all the junk shops in the world. Seated motionless on a shabby gilt throne was a stony-eyed blonde. I went over to her and touched her cheek gently—it was stone cold. It looked like Charlie Katz wasn't going to be lonely any more.

Chapter Two

Sheriff Lavers puffed his pipe contentedly and leaned back in his chair. "Why don't we start at the beginning, Wheeler?" he asked.

"That's a good question," I admitted. "It gets us no place, but—still a good question."

"Someone stole a corpse from the morgue," he said. "Then you get an anonymous phone call telling you where to find the corpse, and that's where it is."

"In a TV studio," I said. "I don't think that corpse is significant."

"It is to whoever it belongs to."

I had to admit he had something there. People do attach a lot of importance to an unidentified body. Especially if it's theirs.

"Besides, the head mortician was knocked unconscious, don't forget!" Lavers added sharply.

"So somebody slugged Charlie," I agreed impatiently. "He has that effect on everybody. Every time I get near I feel like slugging him myself."

"You don't like him?"

"I hadn't thought much about it either way," I said honestly. "All I know is that when I get within striking distance, the palms of my hands begin to itch. It's an automatic reflex. Be honest, Sheriff, Charlie is a creep."

"But employed by the County, and therefore our responsibility," Lavers grunted. "I think that first corpse is significant."

"The first corpse died of natural causes," I said. "No beef for a cop. The second one died of a .38 slug in the chest—and that means trouble for a cop."

"Has anybody identified the second corpse yet?" Lavers asked.

I shook my head. "Nobody. All we know about that cadaver is that it's male, aged around thirty-five, and was shot dead. I'm glad I don't have to write the obituary notice."

"The papers have done that this morning," Lavers said sourly. "Right across the front page. Didn't you find out anything last night?"

"This morning," I said heavily. "The body was discovered at 1:10 A.M. I quit around three-thirty and went home. It is now nine-thirty of the same morning, and—no, I didn't find out anything this morning."

Lavers took the pipe out of his mouth, looked at it disgustedly for a moment, then tossed it onto his desk. Knowing what came next, I lit myself a cigarette in self-defense, just about ten seconds before he lit the inevitable cigar. "The corpse couldn't have walked into that coffin!" he said.

"Somebody pulled a switch," I said. "Up to half an hour before the show went on the air the coffin was in the property room, complete with one small, papier-mâché monster. When the lid came off, the corpse was there. They found the prop in the property room afterwards, stuffed into an old trunk."

"All right," Lavers said in a resigned voice. "Who could have substituted the corpse for the dummy; who had the opportunity?"

"Everybody inside the studio, and anybody from outside who cared to walk in," I said. "That's as far as I can figure it, and it's far enough. They keep a minimum staff working at that hour because they have to pay them overtime. So they had one doorman on duty out front. The back doors to the studios were unlocked and the property room is situated at the back of the place. Anybody could have carried in that corpse and left it there."

"You didn't uncover any motive?" the Sheriff asked.

"Motive—for killing a guy that nobody even knows?"

Lavers grunted and puffed a cloud of smoke at me. "You don't seem to have made any progress at all, Wheeler."

"Check."

"Well, don't just sit there. Haven't you got any ideas at all?"

"Yes, sir," I said. "I'm going outside right now and scream, 'Help!'"

"This is County business."

"That doesn't stop us asking Homicide for help, sir." I said, "and right now that's just what we need."

"Is this the Wheeler I knew?" he asked wonderingly.

"It's the Wheeler you know now," I said. "We don't have anything to lose by calling in Homicide. The way things are it might take them a week to identify the corpse. It could take us a couple of years ..."

"You can have Sergeant Polnik from this office to help."

" ... Five years!" I said bitterly. "No, sir. Leave us call Homicide."

The Sheriff grunted and settled further back into his chair. He folded his hands across his paunch and just looked at me. There was a speculative glint in his eye that I didn't care for much.

"Well, well!" he said happily. "I can't help remembering the times when I desperately wanted to call Homicide in on a case, but you overruled me. 'We can handle it,' you used to keep on telling me—and that left me sitting around here sweating it out, squaring off with City Hall, the Bureau, the prominent citizens—while you went your own unorthodox way."

"Yes, sir," I said cautiously.

A nasty grin split his face, making him look like a gargoyle that's just been goosed. "You're forgetting a couple of things, Wheeler," he said politely. "As I remember, you were a homicide lieutenant before I had you attached to my office?"

"Yes, sir."

"And why did I have you attached to this office? To take care of any homicides that might come my way. Right? What's the matter, Wheeler, don't you want to earn your pay check?"

"Not if I can get it any other way," I said. "But I catch the drift."

His grin had become malicious, but malicious. "This is your homicide, Wheeler," he said generously. "I'm making you a present of it. You go and sweat it out and I'll sit here and smoke cigars, just for a change." His face was suddenly wreathed in hope. "Who knows?" he said hoarsely. "Maybe I'll pick up a blonde or two, just sitting here!"

"Not unless you go on a diet," I told him. "You want me to report in regularly?"

"I'm giving you an entirely free hand," he said happily.

"Just watch I don't bite it off at the wrist," I snarled, and got to my feet.

"Don't bother your unorthodox little head about reports, Wheeler," he cackled. "I'll wait till you bring in the murderer and then you can surprise me. I like surprises."

"Sheriff," I said. "Something's come over you and whatever it is, frankly, I don't like it."

"For once," he said contentedly, "we have a murder in which I am not immediately involved. I have no personal interest—no one is accusing me of conspiracy or corruption that led to the murder—no one, not even the papers, is putting the heat on me to solve it. Why? Because nobody knows who got murdered. But if I turn the case over to Homicide a few days from now because you haven't been able to even make a start, Wheeler ... guess who is going to look stupid?"

"Me," I said. "But then it'll be my first time, Sheriff, and I guess you're about due for a break."

Lavers still grinned his gloating grin. "If you get in real trouble, Lieutenant, you can always call Dick Tracy," he suggested helpfully. He thought about it, found it very funny and chuckled happily.

"Thanks," I said. "And don't think we won't need him. Not to take care of the homicide—but the Calthorpe sisters."

"What do you mean?"

"I always remember Prudence's king hit," I said soberly. "One of the Miami resort hotels. Somebody hired the Skyline Room for a private party and she wasn't invited. Just after midnight she let off half a dozen of her favorite smoke bombs in the corridor outside, set fire to a wig she wore for the occasion, then rushed into the room screaming, 'Fire!' at the top of her lungs."

"It finished the party?" Lavers asked.

"It finished a couple of the guests permanently," I said. "They jumped out the window."

Lavers had lost his smug look. "I have to admit, I was forgetting about them," he said thoughtfully. "You think they're mixed up in the homicide?"

I looked at him carefully. "Right now," I told him gravely, "I'm trying to make up my mind whether you're really Sheriff Lavers or Prudence Calthorpe dressed up to look like Sheriff Lavers?" I shrugged my shoulders. "Of course, there's one sure method you can prove it either way."

"Get out of here!" he yelped furiously.

I went out of his office, leaving the door open so he'd have to get up and close it. The desk in the outer office was occupied by a female monster who looked like she could audition for Bruno without make-up. I stopped at her desk, braced myself, and looked at her. "Where is the flower of the South?" I asked in a severe voice.

"If you mean the yellow rose of Texas, Lieutenant," the Face said in a hard, masculine voice, "she's on vacation."

"Annabelle Jackson on vacation?" I said. "Why doesn't somebody tell me these things?"

"I imagine because nobody considers that it's any of your business, Lieutenant," she said, stroking the heavy mustache on her upper lip. "But just for your information, for the next three weeks, I'm filling in as the Sheriff's secretary."

"If you're going to fill in for Annabelle Jackson, honey, you need to put another six inches on your bust," I said coldly.

Her typewriter banged away at frightening speed. "They told me about you in City Hall, Lieutenant," she said frigidly. "Cold baths might help!"

I went over to my desk and sat down. Life without Annabelle was going to be bleak. In fact, Life was bleak all around what with an unidentified corpse and the prospect of working with Sergeant Polnik. Even the passionate blonde had departed some time before I got back to my apartment in the early hours of the morning. She'd left me a note though; it said two words and somehow, written down, they looked even worse than they sound when somebody says them.

"Hey!" I said to the monster. "Today's Sunday. How come you're in here?"

"Urgent work for the Sheriff," she said. "I'm on overtime, Lieutenant. Please don't interrupt me again, it's so expensive for the department!"

The phone rang and I picked it up idly.

"I would like to talk to Lieutenant Wheeler," a cultured male voice said.

"This is Wheeler," I told him.

"I have a message for you, Lieutenant," the voice said politely. "I'm worried."

"So am I," I said. "Just who the hell is this speaking?"

"A fellow who likes to keep things neat and tidy," he said. "I'm puzzled, Lieutenant, because I can't understand how a girl could forget a husband so quickly."

"Why don't you write Dorothy Dix?" I snarled.

"Even if he is an ex, you'd think she'd remember him," he went on imperturbably. "Of course he was a bum; a tennis bum, to be accurate. But you'd think she would at least remember his face, his name— something about him."

"Go on," I told him.

"I won't waste your time, Lieutenant. You must be a busy man right now from what I read in the papers. Your corpse, so cute in its coffin, is that of a man named Howard Davis. He was a pro tennis player, but not good enough to be generally known. You know the type, always prepared to give the ladies of the club special and private tuition."

"And what's your name?" I asked without any real hope.

"Of no significance, Lieutenant; just look upon me as a friend. If I may offer a word of advice: why don't you ask Penelope Calthorpe just how it was she didn't recognize her ex-husband?" There was that click in my ear again as he hung up.

I put the phone back on the cradle and stared at it moodily for maybe a minute. No dice. I tried like hell to think of something better to do than do as the man said, but I couldn't. If my friend called again with another message, I figured I'd better start calling him, 'sir.' He had it coming; he was the only guy around the office who was doing any detecting.

Chapter Three

Penelope Calthorpe was staying at the Starlight Hotel. I stopped to check her room number with the desk clerk. She didn't have a room of course, she had a suite.

"I'm afraid you can't see her, Lieutenant," the clerk said firmly. "She left strict orders that she wasn't to be disturbed. No phone calls, no visitors. Miss Calthorpe is resting."

"Into each life some cop must fall," I said sympathetically. "Have you checked your conscience lately?"

"I'm afraid," he said even more firmly, "that I shall have to insist!"

I leaned my elbows on the desk and looked at him interestedly: "O.K.," I said. "Go ahead—insist."

He made a gobbling noise that reminded me of Thanksgiving; then he was saved by the bell. There was a grateful look on his face as he lifted the phone. I wandered away toward the elevators and rode up to the tenth floor. Three polite knocks got me no answer, so I started knocking out "I Got Rhythm," using both hands and my right foot against the bottom of the door as a bass drum to keep the beat.

I was just working up to a nice, breakaway roll when the door opened suddenly and Penelope Calthorpe stood there, her mouth wide open. "My God!" she said bitterly. "I thought it was a fire or something."

"You remember me?" I asked hopefully. "Lieutenant Wheeler, from the Sheriff's office."

"After this I'll never forget you," she said. "I was sleeping."

"So I see," I said gratefully.

And I did take a good look. Her hairdo was strictly Oriental, with a fringe, and she used an eyebrow pencil to give her eyes a slanted look. The flaming red hair wasn't exactly a Far Eastern trademark, but then you can't have everything even if you're one of the Calthorpe sisters.

She wore a pair of tailored, white Fuji silk pajamas which draped her shape with revealing intention. From high on her right shoulder, a diagonal line of tiny blue Japanese sandmen marched determinedly toward her left breast. You learn something new every day—I'd never thought of throwing sand in a dame's eyes before.

"What do you want?" Penelope asked impatiently.

"Is yesterday a blank in your memory?" I asked soothingly. "Do you put things down and never pick them up? On Main Street, does a sudden breeze remind you you've forgotten to put anything on underneath? The Wheeler Memory Refresher course guarantees in ten easy lessons you'll have achieved total recall from now back to your birth, if not further."

"You must be crazy," she said, "and there's nothing wrong with my memory!"

"Then how come you didn't recognize your ex-husband when his corpse was staring you right in the face?" I asked sadly.

A dull film seemed to glaze over her eyes like a veil. "Maybe you'd better come inside," she said.

I followed her through to the living room of the suite and stood waiting politely while she lit herself a cigarette. She said to sit down and I did. She sat opposite and inhaled deeply. Did you ever see a Japanese sandman rock and roll? Well, it's ... sexy.

"I'm sorry, Lieutenant," Penelope said finally in a tight voice. "You see, it was such a shock because I hadn't seen him in six months, not since the divorce. When I opened the coffin and saw Howard was inside— dead! Well, I—"

"You knew he was dead?"

"I could see the bullet hole," she answered promptly. "I thought he must be dead, he didn't look as if he was breathing at all. The shock was so terrific, you see, I just ..."

"Lost your memory?" I was still sympathetic, the friend of the family at the funeral, who came to laugh but stopped to grin. "For just how long did you lose it?"

Her back stiffened. "I didn't say anything about losing my memory; that was all your idea. I was so upset, I wasn't thinking coherently, that's all. I was confused."

I shook my head sadly. "You'll have to do better than that, Penelope."

"What do you mean?"

"You'll have to find a better reason for lying about not recognizing your ex-husband."

She stubbed out her cigarette with a nervous intensity, then got to her feet and walked over to the window. "All right!" she said finally, her back toward me. "I was frightened of the publicity."

"I would've figured it was great publicity," I said.

"You don't understand!" She turned toward me again, her eyes blazing, her red hair about to catch fire. "As far as the newspapers are concerned, I'm one of the crazy Calthorpe twins with no morals and too much money! If they get hold of the story that my ex-husband's corpse turned up on my first TV program, it would finish me."

"Why?" I asked blankly.

"Because, believe it or not, television executives are very morals conscious. They're sensitive to all the no-joy pressure groups. Howard's corpse would be a little too much for their rating-sensitive stomachs!"

"I hear tell you're one of the ten richest women in the country," I said. "The money you're getting out of this television deal must be less than peanuts. Why are you so worried about it?"

"Because this is my big chance!" she said fiercely. "If Bruno and I can make a hit on the local station, then maybe one of the major networks will pick us up and we'll be made."

"Why is it so important?" I said.

"Because I'm going to prove to somebody that I can achieve something in my own right," she said harshly. "Something that's got nothing to do with my money."

"Somebody in particular, or just anybody?"

"Somebody in particular," she said. "Now, can you understand why I didn't want to say it was Howard in that coffin?"

"No," I said honestly. "Do you have any idea who might have murdered him?"

Penelope shook her head. "None."

"Any idea why he might have been murdered?"

"Not really. But I wouldn't put it past Prudence to have had him murdered and his corpse put into that coffin just to ruin my television career!"

"Prudence?"

"My twin sister. We're complete opposites."

"You said you haven't seen Howard since your divorce six months back?"

"That's right."

"Were you paying him a lot of alimony? That's the new chivalry isn't it?"

"Not a dime!" she said with immense satisfaction. "Not one single, solitary dime!"

"There goes a nice solid motive in one strike," I said miserably. "Where would I find your twin sister?"

"In the penthouse suite," she said. "She beat me to it by three minutes, the bitch!"

"Maybe I should go talk to her," I said.

"A good idea, Lieutenant, and I can try and catch up on my interrupted sleep!"

"Why not?" I said. "Those sandmen are getting to look frustrated again." I got up and walked toward the door. "What's your relationship with Bruno?" I asked, looking back at her.

"Strictly business," she said. "Japanese flower arrangements are his hobby, Lieutenant. He's just too red-blooded for me!"

"That I can believe," I said politely. "You did say the penthouse suite?"

"I did," she nodded. "Just watch out Prudence doesn't add you to her collection, Lieutenant?"

"Of what?"

"You'll find out!"

There was a massive bronze Buddha who sat cross-legged on his pedestal beside the door. I stopped for a moment beside him and rubbed his enormous belly with my fingers. "You got him on a diet again?" I asked her.

I let myself out into the corridor again and walked down to the elevators. Half a minute later I arrived at the penthouse suite, which had a front door complete with knocker. I knocked, and the door was opened almost immediately by a luscious brunette. We looked at each other with mutual interest. "I've seen you somewhere before," I said.

Her overfull lips curved in a slow smile. "With an original line like that, what are you selling—shoelaces?" she said in a dry voice.

It hit me. "You were the exotic-looking brunette in the bunch of rubbernecks watching Bruno and Brunhild at the television studios last night," I said. "And you must be Prudence Calthorpe."

"Maybe," she said. "But I'm still not buying anything."

"I'm Lieutenant Wheeler," I told her. "From the Sheriff's office."

"How nice for you," she said. "Don't stand out in the rain too long, Lieutenant. You look the anemic type that catches cold easily." She started to close the door, but I used my streak of original audacity and stuck my foot in as a wedge.

She shrugged her shoulders. "All right, you talked me into it." I followed her inside the apartment until we stopped in front of the well-stocked bar. "Can I make you a drink, Lieutenant?" she asked.

"Scotch on the rocks, a little soda," I said.

I watched her while she made the drinks. Her dark hair was parted in the center and came down to just below her ears in soft waves. She had an intelligent, almost beautiful face, but the hard green eyes belied the full softness of her lips. She wore a black silk shirt over tapered white pants, with a crimson sash around the waist. Her figure was as good as her twin sister's, maybe a little better. There was something almost ruthless about the thrust of her high breasts against the silk of the robe—but then I wasn't about to be hypercritical.

"I've just been talking to your sister," I said.

"And little Penny said nothing nice about me," she said easily. "Why don't we sit down, Lieutenant? On that couch over there. I'll bring the drinks and you take yourself."

We sat on the couch and she handed me my drink. "Now let me guess. You've come to ask questions, Lieutenant. You're going to shock me into making some damaging admissions. Like, did I know the deceased?" She grinned at me. "Of course I did, he was Penny's ex. A slob by the name of Howard Davis who had two rackets and only one for tennis. The other was lame-brained little rich girls like my delicate sister. Why didn't I tell you all this last night? Simple, Lieutenant. You never asked me."

"What made you sure I was going to ask you now?"

"Female intuition," she said. "Besides, it'll all be in the morning papers anyway."

"They aren't on the street yet, so how can you be so sure?" I asked her.

"Female intuition again." She smiled lazily. "Added to the fact that I called them and gave them the information."

I drank a little of my drink. "I hate to be sordid," I said, "but Howard was murdered, and I am a cop. You can get yourself into a lot of trouble doing something like that."

"Now you're beginning to frighten me," she said. "What will you do, Lieutenant? Handcuff me, then take me downtown and beat me all over with a rubber hose?"

"That's not very amusing," I told her.

"It might be," she said idly. "As long as the bruises didn't show."

I drank some more of the Scotch and looked at her reflectively. "I'd heard of the Calthorpe sisters but never met one until last night," I said. "Tell me about them?"

"You've already met Penny," she answered. "Did she take her clothes off for you?"

"Not that I noticed." I considered for a moment. "I'm sure I would have noticed."

"You couldn't have stayed very long," she said complacently. "Penny drinks too much, drives too fast, and takes off her clothes whenever there's a man in sight; right now she's on an oriental kick. Maybe you didn't come under that heading, Lieutenant?"

"We were talking about the shortcomings of the Calthorpes.

Remember?"

"Our father died just over a year ago and we shared his estate 50-50, with no strings. Penny is a lamebrained doll with a crazy ambition to become an actress, but strictly a no talent gal. The only smart thing she ever did was to take advice about how to dump Howard Davis without having to pay him off, which was what finally happened."

"That takes care of Penny," I said. "How about Prudence?"

"I'm afraid you'll have to ask Penny about her," she said with a smile. "I could be biased."

"Penny says she hadn't seen Howard since the divorce," I said. "Had you seen him since then?"

"No." She shook her head firmly. "Not interested. Penny said he might be O.K. on a tennis court, but in a boudoir he was strictly a double-fault guy. Just one love game meant set and match."

"You know anyone who'd have reason to murder him?"

"Penny maybe," she said. "She's just stupid enough to do something like that. Outside of Penny, I can't think of anyone else. The Howards of this world aren't worth killing, Lieutenant; they should be left for the garbage men to take away."

"Do you mind if I make a note of that?" I said earnestly. "Philosophy always thrills me."

"Don't you have some other place to go now?" she asked coolly. "You've finished your drink and you won't get another one here. Also, you're beginning to bore me, Lieutenant."

"I can see a delicate hint when it gets up and sinks its teeth into my shinbone," I said. "So, all right, I'll go."

I stood up and looked down at her regretfully. "I can't help thinking I haven't made a hit with the Calthorpe sisters," I told her. "Penny didn't take her clothes off for me, and you haven't even offered to show me your collection."

A spark of faint interest showed in her eyes. "I guess Penny told you about that? What else did she tell you?"

"Nothing else, she just said something about being careful you didn't add me to your collection, but she didn't say of what. Men? Do you mount their heads and decorate your walls with them the way the big-game hunters do?"

"If I did, I'd have to buy up Madison Square Garden to house them," she said easily. "My collection is much more interesting than that, Lieutenant. Of course, I only have a few of the choicest items with me when I'm traveling. Would you like to see them?"

"I'd love to," I said. "I always wondered what the fabulously rich people did with their money, besides buying other people with it."

Prudence Calthorpe led the way into the bedroom. It was furnished the same anonymous way as the other ten million hotel bedrooms throughout the country. But as this was the penthouse suite, the furniture wasn't scratched—and Prudence had added some of her own personal touches.

A pair of black lace panties sat astride the bedhead, communing silently with the left cup of a satin brassiere which was perched precariously beside it. At the foot of the bed, a blue mink stole richly caressed an ancient human skull.

Four shrunken heads perched in a straight line on top of the bureau looked like income tax examiners who had just finished looking over my returns. Beside them, a crumbling brick stood on end, with an almost faded sign painted on it. The sign was red painted—a cross surmounted by a cedilla.

Giving the final, homely touch, was the shriveled, mummified hand that looked more like a claw, as it clung to the folds of a shabby, stained dress of rusted black satin which was draped across the mirror.

"How do you like my little treasures?" Prudence asked.

"Where did you buy them?" I asked. "One of those trick shops on Broadway?"

Her face flushed a little: "The shrunken heads are genuine, little man, just like yours! The skull belonged to a Mary Miles who was burned at the stake as a witch in New England in the year 1692. The mummified hand is supposedly that of Kubla Khan; I can't guarantee it, but it was very expensive. The dress is genuine; Lizzie Borden wore it once and the stains are bloodstains, I had them analysed. Of course," she added thoughtfully, "the man who sold it to me couldn't swear they were *the* bloodstains."

"What about the brick with the, 'God Save Us,' sign?" I queried.

Her eyes showed faint surprise. "I didn't think you'd recognize it, Lieutenant."

"I spent three years with Army Intelligence in London once," I said. "I was the exception to the rule. I saw that sign a couple of times chalked in the bomb ruins of Berlin just after the war finished. It's older than Christianity."

"That brick is pretty old, too," she said. "It also came from London. The sign was painted on it during the year of the Great Plague."

"You have any more treasures with you?"

She shook her head. "I always travel light, so I only brought my special favorites with me. Don't you just love those shrunken heads. I call them my barbershop quartet —Eeny, Meeny, Miny and Mo."

"What do you do nights?" I asked her. "Write dirty words in the sky with the fiery end of your broomstick?"

"I'm not a practicing witch, Lieutenant," she said with mock solemnity. "Maybe my sense of humor is a little different, that's all, a taste for the macabre. I think it must run in the family. I collect these things—Penny collected things like Howard Davis!"

I lit a cigarette and took another look around the room. "How about the bra and panties? Do they have any macabre significance?"

"Only erotic—by the gleam in your eye," she answered casually. "I think you really have to go now, Lieutenant."

"Can't you just dematerialize me?" I asked hopefully. "It would save waiting for the elevator."

Prudence Calthorpe looked me up and down, slowly and carefully. Then those green eyes flickered again. "Come back tonight, around eleven, Lieutenant," she said softly. "I'll see what I can do for you then."

Chapter Four

After I left the Starlight Hotel, I had some lunch, then went back to the office. It was a little after three in the afternoon when I got there. Sergeant Polnik was waiting for me at my desk, an expectant grin on his face. "The Sheriff tells me I'm working with you on this new homicide, Lieutenant," he said. "So when do we start?"

"Right now," I told him. "The corpse's name was Howard Davis. Maybe he was knocked off right after he arrived in Pine City, and maybe he wasn't. If he wasn't, he was staying some place, so let's start in finding out."

I ignored the blank look on his face and pointed to the phone on the female monster's desk. "You take the motels, I'll take the hotels—and I'll be in the nuthouse afore ye!"

"Huh?" Polnik grunted.

"Motels," I said impatiently. "You know—sawed-off hotels where you get parking space instead of a living room. Passion pits with television. You know?"

Polnik grunted disgustedly and waddled over to the phone, his rear view looking like the departing end of some prehistoric mistake. I picked up the phone book and thumbed through to the hotel listings and started with the first one.

It was around twenty minutes later that Polnik looked across at me with triumph on his face. "I got it, Lieutenant!" he said excitedly. "The Paradise Motel, it's about five miles out on the San Bernardino Freeway. Guy who owns the place said Davis was there a couple of days but he hasn't been back since yesterday afternoon."

"Fine," I said. "We'll go take a look."

We went out of the office and Polnik squeezed himself painfully into the passenger's seat of the Austin-Healey. "I guess this is just the routine, huh, Lieutenant?" he said confidentially.

"I guess so," I said blankly.

"That's the way I had it figured," he said, satisfied.

I moved the Healey out from the curb in back of a new Lincoln and tried to ignore the sneer of its tail lamps looking down at me from a great height.

"Yeah," Polnik said suddenly. "We take care of the routine first, huh, Lieutenant? After that we get to the dames!"

"What dames?"

"I don't know what dames, Lieutenant." A look of simple faith spread over his face. "But I know if you're handling a homicide, there's going to be dames!"

"One of these days I'm going to tell your old lady about you," I said coldly.

"She already knows," he said sourly. "And she knows it don't do me any good, either."

The Paradise Motel was half a mile off the freeway, along a dirt road that led to the end of the world and by the time you got there you'd be glad they were doing away with the dump. The neon sign outside said, "Vacancy." I stopped the car just inside the entrance and thought if this was Paradise, I'd stop worrying about missing out.

There were a dozen cabins grouped around a dustbowl. The paint had long since blistered and peeled from the boards, but outside the nearest cabin was a freshly painted sign which said, "Manager." We got out of the car and walked across to it. The manager came out onto the top step to meet us. He looked like a refugee from the "Keep Your City Clean" campaign and I figured he'd found the perfect hideaway.

He wore a faded denim shirt and faded denim pants held up by a pair of dilapidated suspenders with oversize nickel clasps which proudly said, "Fireman." A mane of white hair sat on top of a thin pointed face, and when he smiled you wished he hadn't. His name was Walnut, he said, and if he wasn't cracked already, the pressure was getting too much for him fast.

"Knew there was something wrong with that Davis guy," he said in a shrill falsetto as soon as Polnik told him who we were. "Picked him right away, yessir!"

"The way he looked?" I asked, interested. "Something he did?"

Walnut shook his head. "He come here by himself," he said simply.

"What's wrong with that?"

"No girl."

Polnik gave me a sympathetic look and tapped the side of his head with one finger significantly. I couldn't let it go at that, even if it did make me a masochist.

"No girl?" I said to Walnut persistently. "It has social significance?"

"Look, Lootenant," he answered patiently. "The only people whoever want to rent a cabin from me are guys with girls. Old guys with young girls, middle-aged guys with young girls and sometimes I even get a young guy with a young girl. But they all got a girl with 'em. Why else would they come way out here to a broken-down dump like this?"

He cackled sharply and dug me painfully in the ribs with a sharp elbow. "Nossir! I picked that Davis for a phoney the first time I saw him—no girl!"

"You shouldn't think about girls so much," I told him reproachfully. "An old man like you."

He cackled again, but this time I saw the elbow coming and dodged it neatly. "I ain't so old," he said triumphantly. "You don't believe me, you ask Widow Smee who lives down the road apiece from here. Weren't for me, I don't know what she'd do all through them long winter nights, nossir!"

We waited outside the end cabin while he unlocked it for us, then we went inside. Polnik peered over Walnut's shoulder and seemed disappointed that there wasn't another corpse inside. I gestured to Polnik who shrugged his shoulders manfully and managed to shrug Walnut outside the door at the same time.

"That guy is a nut, Lieutenant," he said heavily.

"Sure," I winced, "a Walnut."

It didn't take long to go through the cabin. Howard Davis had left one suitcase behind, containing a suit, a couple of shirts, a change of underwear and some socks. One of the bureau drawers had a letter in it, postmarked San Francisco and addressed to Davis at a San Francisco address; the date was a little over a week old.

I took the letter out of the envelope and it read:

> Dear Howard,
>
> You now owe me nearly six months back alimony and I'm not going to believe your lies any longer. Unless you pay the amount owing in full within the next three days, I'm going to put you right where you belong—behind bars.
>
> Don't bother calling me to tell me some more of your lies because I won't listen. You can talk to my lawyer or the police, you

please yourself. And don't try to run out on me, because I'll just follow you. You can't get away from me, so it's no use you trying!

Yours faithfully,

(sgd) Thelma.

Polnik was breathing heavily into my ear with the effort of reading the letter over my shoulder.

"I like that 'Yours faithfully' touch," I said. "I wonder just how many wives this guy had?"

"You figure this dame knocked him off, Lieutenant?" He sounded smug. "I told you we'd get around to the dames sooner or later!"

"I wouldn't know," I said. "Take a look through the rest of the drawers and see what you can find."

I lit a cigarette while Polnik went to work. He came up triumphantly with a sheet of notepaper half a minute later. "Look, Lieutenant. Another letter!"

The address at the top of the sheet was the Paradise Motel, Pine City. It started off:

Dear Thelma,

You'll see where I am by the above address. I'm onto a really big deal here, so please be patient and hold off the wolves just for a few days, Thelma. After that everything will be O.K. and you can collect all your back alimony and maybe a bonus. But please don't do anything stupid like you threatened in your letter because it will ruin this big deal I ...

The letter had never been finished. The date at the top was three days old. One thing was for sure, Howard Davis didn't have to worry about paying alimony anymore. I put both letters in my pocket carefully. Another couple of minutes and we'd finished searching the cabin without finding anything more of interest.

Walnut followed us eagerly back to the car, skipping along behind, the clasps of his suspenders flashing wildly in the sunlight. "What did you find out, Lootenant?" he kept on asking with painful curiosity. "You find out what happened to him—what is he, one of them big racketeers or something?"

"He's been murdered," I told him as we got into the car.

"Murdered?" He cackled with delight. "You got any idea who did it, Lootenant?"

"Sure," I said as I started the motor. "It was a girl."

"Like I always said, women are nothing but trouble, yessir!" He breathed heavily. "You got any idea who she is?"

"Naturally," I said in an official-sounding voice. "Where did you say the Widow Smee lived?"

"Down the road apiece." Walnut blinked at me for a moment; then the enormity of my question hit him straight between the eyes. "Hey!" he said in a strangled welp. "You don't mean ..."

I put the car into gear and tramped on the gas pedal. When we hit the road I looked back for a moment, but there was only a dense cloud of whirling dust to be seen. I thought that would teach him to mind his own business and wear respectable suspenders the next time he talked to a cop. Fireman yet!

It was around five-thirty when we got back to the office. I dropped Polnik there and told him to put through a request to San Francisco and have them check whether Thelma Davis was still there and to see if they could pick up her movements the day before. Then I drove on home to my apartment.

I knocked with the knocker on the front door of the penthouse suite at exactly eleven o'clock that night. Prudence Calthorpe opened the door and smiled. "I see you're punctual, Lieutenant. Is that what police training does for you?"

"That, and your invitation," I agreed.

"You'd better come in," she said. "You're only creating a draft standing out there."

I followed her obediently into the living room. She was still strictly high voltage in a high-necked, tight-fitting white sheath which came down to an inch below her knees. Two black panthers stalked around her shoulders, and the gown was split up one side from knee to hip.

As she walked, I caught the flash of her rounded thigh for a fraction of a second. Either she had a very long thigh or that split went even further than I'd thought. It made me wonder if she wore anything at all underneath, and that gave me all the zeal of the scientist, on the threshold of a new discovery, for bare, unadorned fact.

I sat down in a comfortable armchair and watched Prudence build us a drink, but I got tired of watching after a few seconds. I could see her only from the waist up, the rest of her being hidden behind the bar. It was interesting, but not absorbing the way that now-you-see-itnow-you-don't thigh was. A Manhattan brunette I knew once told me I thought too much about sex, but she was wrong; I only react.

There was a framed photograph on the small table beside me, so I picked it up and took a closer look. A guy who was maybe forty, with a fullback's shoulders and look of grim determination. Fair hair, cut short and parted on the side, then brushed straight across his head. His eyes wouldn't give a blind man begging room on a street corner, and his mouth was set hard in a thin line above a square jaw. A comic strip hero come to life, except for those eyes; they worried me.

"Next time I bring you a drink," a soft voice said in my ear, "should I ring a bell?"

I looked up to see Prudence standing directly in front of me, and took the glass out of her hand. "Thanks," I said

"You find the photograph fascinating?" she asked.

"Sure," I said. "Your mother?"

"My ex-husband," she said in a casual voice. "Jonathan Blake. Him big white hunter, bang-bang! Him also blue-nosed slob with big idea of fun—clean elephant gun!"

"Where is he now?"

Prudence shrugged her shoulders. "In Africa again for all I know—being eaten by a lion, I hope."

I looked around the room carefully. "You have a current husband?"

"One was enough," she said shortly.

"You make me breathe easier," I told her. "I was all set to go into my hotel-manager-investigating-a-mysterious-noise act."

"You don't have to worry, Lieutenant," she said confidently. "We won't be disturbed."

"Fine." I raised my glass. "Here's to an interesting friendship, just so long as I don't wind up on top of your dressing table with you calling me, 'Teeny.'"

"I'll have to call you something," she said. "Calling you 'Lieutenant' sounds so formal I feel I should be wearing a bra."

"You can call me Al," I offered generously. "It has two advantages, it's short and also my name."

"Short for what?"

"That's a secret between me and my mother," I said firmly. "What should I call you? Prudence, Lady Macbeth or Fly-by-Night?"

"Just make it Pru," she said. "It has the same twofold advantage that 'Al' does."

"So now we know each other," I said.

She turned away from me fractionally, then plopped herself down gracefully on my lap. The sheath parted company both sides of the slit and I closed my eyes against the dazzling whiteness of her thigh and flawlessly curved hip. Then I opened my eyes again quickly, but it was O.K.; she hadn't made any adjustments to the gown at all.

Her green eyes were faintly amused as she looked at me, "I bet you think I'm trying to seduce you," she said.

"If you're not, my ulcer is going to hemorrhage," I said morosely.

"I also bet you think it's your fatal charm, your irresistible masculinity, as well?" she added.

"I never question these things," I said modestly. "If I get a swollen head, I have to buy a new hat."

"With the sort of money I've got I don't have to make much of an effort at seduction," she went on conversationally. "I have a choice of around ninety per cent of the male population as a sleeping partner, whenever I'm in the mood."

"If I'm not unique, at least I'm here," I said hopefully.

Pru shook her head gently: "You don't know it, Al, but you've got something I want—and don't guess what, because you'd be wrong." She paused for effect. "I want you to help me add to my collection."

"You light a fire, I'll shrink right out of here!" I warned her hastily. "I'm not spending the rest of my life sitting around with that barbershop quartet—I bet they don't even play poker."

She took the glass from my hand and put it down on the table, then took my hand and placed it high on her thigh, her own hand pressing down firmly on top of mine. "Just listen," she said gently. "This is a golden opportunity and I'm not going to miss it. I want something of Howard's, to add to my collection, and you can get it for me."

"I can?"

"Of course!" she said impatiently. "You're a law officer and you're investigating his murder. You could get it for me easily without any trouble."

"Did you have anything special in mind?" I asked her. "A left shoe or a lock of his hair or something?"

"His heart."

I started to grin, then stopped abruptly when I saw she was deadly serious. "You're crazy," I said flatly.

"They have to do an autopsy, don't they?" she said. "The doctor can take care of it for you. I'll go as high as five thousand dollars for that heart—immersed in formalin and sealed in a nice airtight bottle. I'll provide the bottle." She considered. "I think Howard should have something rather special, Venetian cut glass perhaps, or I could have something specially blown in the shape of a tennis racket."

"If you think I'm going to play Hyde to the coroner's Jekyll, you're still crazy," I told her.

She got up off my lap smoothly and walked toward the door. "Too bad, Al," she said coldly. "I thought you were a man with some imagination."

"But I am," I said. "Or I was. The trouble is you didn't leave anything to my imagination with that split in your gown, so it withered and died right while I was just sitting here with you on my lap."

"Good night, Lieutenant," she said, and opened the door.

"What makes you think I'm leaving?" I asked politely.

"Don't be a boor," she said shortly. "But if you insist I can call the desk and have them throw you out."

"You're forgetting something, Lucretia," I said, smiling unpleasantly. "I'm a cop. They don't throw cops out of hotels even if a guest insists. But if you don't believe me, try it."

She bit her lip for a moment, then slammed the door shut and walked back into the center of the room. She slumped into an armchair and this time she adjusted her gown very carefully indeed, so that even her knees didn't show. "All right," she said. "What happens now?"

"I've got a secret," I said, "but you don't need to go through the twenty-questions routine—I'll tell you. I came back tonight for a couple of other reasons besides your gorgeous body. I wanted to know what you wanted from me, and I freely admit the answer was a pip. I also wanted a little more information and I figured you were just the girl to give it to me."

"I wouldn't give you a match to set fire to yourself," she said quickly. She thought about it for a moment. "Maybe I would."

"Howard Davis had a wife," I said.

"But Penny divorced him."

"Before Penny, her name's Thelma. You know her?"

"Why would I? Howard was married to Penny, not me. Why don't you ask her?"

"I'll get around to it," I promised. "You sure Jonathan Blake's being chased by a lion in darkest Africa right now?"

"I don't really know where he is." She shrugged her shoulders. "Why do you ask?"

"Because there's somebody else around who knows everybody connected with the case," I said, and I couldn't stop the sour note creeping into my voice. "This guy is a mine of information but he's shy— he only talks over the phone, and he won't give any name."

"You think it's Jonathan?" Sharp interest showed in her eyes. "You think that maybe he's here in Pine City?"

"I don't know," I said. "Do you know definitely he's not?"

Pru shook her head. "I don't know where he is right now. We were divorced nearly a year ago; I haven't been interested in his activities since then."

"How long were you married?"

"Two years."

"And you didn't get along," I said. "I remember you told me, big white hunter and all that jazz. You didn't go for life in the raw."

"We both had a different idea about what the phrase meant." She smiled wickedly. "He was hard to take all the same, that Boston blood trickling through his veins, the stiff upper lip. I only went on the one safari with him and then he really reverted to type. I thought he'd start talking about the 'white man's burden' before we got out of that Godforsaken jungle again."

"So you divorced him?"

"Maybe we could have got along," she said. "But after what happened to Father, I got to the point where I couldn't stand the sight of Jonathan."

"What did happen to Father?"

She looked vaguely surprised. "Didn't you read about it? It was in all the newspapers."

"I only read the 'What's New in Hi-fi' column," I said. "Tell me."

"Father liked Jonathan," she said. "They got along fine together. I guess big game hunting is a sort of disease and if you come in contact with it, some of it rubs off. Father got mad keen to try it, so finally we did. The five of us went along, Father, Jonathan and myself, Howard and Penny. They were only just married so it was a sort of honeymoon." She shuddered. "In a tent—with all those mosquitoes!"

"So what happened?"

An innocent look came over her face. "There was that night a python somehow got into their tent and crawled up onto the bed. They didn't notice it for a long time—I had an awful long wait outside the tent. It was just like watching a ship go down, you know that 'Women and children first' jazz. Penny made the door, pulled back the flap and was just going to leap out when Howard grabbed her by the shoulders and pushed her to one side so he could get out first. As it happened, she tripped and fell back onto the bed and found herself sitting on the python."

"What happened after that?"

"The python was never the same," she said casually. "He got a thing about human beings and followed us around for weeks afterward."

"I guess it was only you and Penny it followed around, wasn't it?" I said. "I mean, there was nothing queer about that python?" I grinned at the look she flashed me. "Let's get back to dear old Dad."

"Father wanted a lion," she said. "It became a big thing with him. He wouldn't go home without one. The three men went looking for one and we spent a week running all over Africa looking for a lion, and finally they found it."

Pru looked away from me, her eyes remote. "They caught up with the lion about an hour after dawn one morning. Jonathan got the first shot, but he only wounded it, so the lion came at them. Father was closest to it and he raised his gun and fired, but the gun jammed. Jonathan killed it with his second shot but he was about three seconds too late."

"The lion killed your father?"

"They brought his body back to the camp," she said in a whisper. "It wasn't a pretty sight at all. My father was about the only person I've ever really cared for in my whole life. I couldn't stand the thought of having Jonathan around me for the rest of my life; every time I looked at him I'd think about what happened to Father. So I divorced him."

I picked up the empty glasses from the table and took them over to the bar. "You could use a drink," I said. "I've been looking for an excuse myself."

"I could use a drink," she agreed. She smiled faintly. "Wasn't I going to throw you out?"

"That was last year," I said. "Did you do as well as Penny with your divorce, or do you have to pay Jonathan alimony?"

"I was just as smart as Penny," she said. "Smarter, because I did it first. I took advice and I didn't have to pay Jonathan a dime, either. Not that he needed it, he's got plenty of money in his own right. As a matter of fact, I advised Penny to take the same advice I did."

The phone rang and she looked at it for a few seconds, then decided to answer it. I made the drinks while she was busy, and listened carefully to what she said, which wasn't much.

She lifted the receiver and said, "Yes, this is Prudence Calthorpe." Then she listened for awhile. "Not now," she said curtly, "I'm tied up. Call me in the morning." She put the phone down and walked over to the bar. "My lawyer," she said. "He keeps on worrying about my money making more money all the time. I don't understand it, but it seems to work out all right."

I handed her the fresh drink and she took it gratefully. "Thanks, I need that. Have I answered all your questions, Lieutenant?"

"All but two," I said. "Why are you in Pine City right now, anyway? I know why Penny is, because of her TV thing."

"Why, Al," she pouted. "Could I let my little sister play the biggest moment in her life all on her lonesome? I came along to cheer. Next question."

"If this mine of information isn't your ex, Jonathan Blake," I said. "Then who the hell is he?"

"I wouldn't know," she said. "Maybe he's just a figment of your overexcited imagination—and don't think I didn't feel this gown rip off my back the first time you looked at me when I opened the front door to you!"

"I get one more call from him and I'll go crazy," I said savagely. "Him and his messages!"

Her glass made a tinkling sound as it shattered on the floor. She looked at me, her face pale and her eyes flecked with something close to fear. "Did you say, messages?" she asked faintly.

"Sure—messages. Every time the guy calls he says he's got a message for me."

"Messenger John!" she whispered.

"Huh?"

She shook her head slowly. "No, it couldn't be."

"Messenger John?" I repeated. "It's a real name? Who the hell is he?"

"I just made it up," she said. "I thought it sounded appropriate—an informative version of 'Dear John,' don't you think?"

"I think you're lying," I said. "Who is he?"

"Am I?" She smiled at me determinedly. "Can you imagine anybody ever calling themselves Messenger John? It's a name out of a comic strip, Al!"

She looked at me for a long moment, then turned away and walked into the bedroom. I finished my drink and wondered if I should call information and ask them what I did next. But the problem was solved for me. "Al," Pru's voice called softly, "come in here."

I walked into the bedroom and found her waiting for me just inside the door, her back turned toward me. "Al," she said, "catch the neck of my gown in your two hands." I did as I was told. "Do you have a good grip?" she asked lightly.

"Fine," I said. "What are we playing?"

"Now rip!" she said tautly.

I ripped. The gown split down the back as far as the base of her spine, then slipped to the floor at her feet. I unclenched my fists slowly as she turned around to face me.

The pointed nipples emphasized the aggressive thrust of her breasts as they rose and fell quickly. Her hands reached out and caressed my face gently. "After that first look you gave me, I would have been disappointed if it hadn't happened," she said softly. "And I don't even get Howard's Purple Heart out of this!"

She almost took me in her arms, which was a reversal of roles I didn't care for, so I made sure she got kissed and not me—I got bitten.

We moved toward the bed and I saw the skull was still there, wrapped in its mink caress. "That Mary Miles, out of New England in 1692, making like a smoke signal?" I said. "She was a spinster?"

Pru looked up at me with wide-eyed surprise. "I think so."

"Excuse me," I said.

I reached down and reversed the skull so that the eyeless sockets stared fixedly across the room toward the barbershop quartet. "I'm sorry, Mary," I said. "But what would the Puritan fathers have thought?"

"She won't mind," Pru said. "If she smiles real nice at them, the boys might sing her something."

"They have a favorite number?" I asked.

"I Ain't Got Nobody," she said. I cut her off by pasting my mouth against hers. I could feel her lips moving, her tongue probing, then suddenly she relaxed, moaning softly in ecstasy.

Chapter Five

The persistent ringing woke me up. I reached out and lifted the receiver off the hook, taking it down onto the pillow so it could contact my ear. "Yeah?" I said harshly.

"Good morning, Lieutenant," the cultured pleasant voice said familiarly.

"Not you again!" I snarled. "What the hell do you want this time?"

"I have another message for you," he said briskly. "I hope you're concentrating, Lieutenant?"

"I am not," I said. "I am not even hearing you—but maybe you'd better tell me, anyway."

"That's what I like about you, Lieutenant. You're not too proud or stubborn to accept a little help on a homicide, are you?"

"Oh, no, John, no, John, no!" I said savagely.

There was a short silence. When he spoke again, the tone of his voice had changed slightly. "So you know my name, Lieutenant? That's interesting."

"It's a matter of opinion," I said. "For me, you belong in a comic strip and I wish you'd stay there."

"I'm only trying to be helpful, Lieutenant," he said suavely. "Do my duty as a citizen, give you what information I have."

"You've got too much information to be an honest citizen," I told him. "All right—what have you got?"

"Jonathan Blake," he said promptly. "A white hunter of some renown and the ex-husband of Prudence Calthorpe. At the present time he is not in darkest Africa, systematically denuding that continent of its wild life."

"He's not?"

"No, Lieutenant. He's staying at a dude ranch about forty miles out of Pine City. It's called, El Rancho de los Toros. I think the owner went to Tijuana and saw a bullfight once. Mr. Blake is a guest out there, has been for the last week, I understand."

"So what?"

"I thought you'd be interested to know, Lieutenant. He's going to try the other half of the Calthorpe twins too, but I expect you know about that?"

"About what?"

"He's marrying Penny Calthorpe this time," he sounded mildly surprised. "I thought you knew?" Then he hung up quickly and I remembered too late I'd sworn I'd hang up on him the next time he called.

I checked my watch and saw it was ten-thirty on a bright and too sunny morning. It had been four-thirty the morning when I got back to my own apartment from Prudence Calthorpe's penthouse suite. Six hours sleep should be enough for any man but not, I realized as I stared at my bloodshot reflection in the mirror, for me.

The shower-to-dressed-to-black-coffee routine took another thirty minutes. Then I lit a cigarette and thought if I didn't do something positive soon, the morning would be a dead loss. Come Judgment Day and they ask me what I did with this Monday morning, what could I tell them that wouldn't fuse the recorder's pen?

I called the office and recognized the brimstone overtones of the female monster. I wanted to talk to Sergeant Polnik, I told her briefly, and a few seconds later I heard the familiar whisky baritone.

"You had anything back from San Francisco on Thelma Davis yet?" I asked him.

"Sure, Lieutenant," he said proudly. "I got it right here."

"So what does it say?"

"You want me to read it?"

"Just tell me," I said wearily. It began to look as if I hadn't beaten that recorder after all.

"She lives in a rooming house," Polnik said slowly and distinctly. "She ain't been there the last couple of days, and they can't find anybody who's seen her in that time. She has a job as a stenographer, but she hasn't shown up there the last couple of days, either."

"So maybe she followed her husband to Pine City," I said. "You'd better start in on that hotels-motels routine again."

"Hotels, schmotels!" Polnik said bitterly. "When do I get to see the dames?"

"You find Thelma Davis and I'll let you see her," I said generously.

"O.K., Lieutenant," he said bleakly. "If I find her, where do I contact you?"

"I'll be out in the wide open spaces," I said, unenthusiastically. "Where men are men and the rattlesnakes don't give a damn either way."

"Sure, Lieutenant," he said in a humoring voice. "You got a phone number out there?"

"Don't call us," I told him, "we'll call you." Then I hung up.

El Rancho de los Toros was a bright, shining oasis on the fringe of the desert country. It wasn't so much the date and palm trees that made it a shining oasis, but the reflected glitter from the chrome work of the Cadillacs and stations wagons parked out front.

It was just after one when I put the Healey in a space between two station wagons, and I felt like a drink. I also felt out of place in my blue suit and vertical tie. I should have been wearing a Stetson and spurs that jingled, jangled, jingled, at the very least.

I slunk through a bevy of glittering cowboys and cowgirls who were lounging around out in front of the place, hoping I wouldn't be noticed. I wasn't. Most of them were too busy debating whether they'd take that one more martini before lunch, or whether they'd eat right now and spend the afternoon taking a look at the wide open spaces through the windows of their station wagons.

The bar was an exact replica of an adult western's conception of a pulp western's idea of what a bar looked like in the old West—right down to the sawdust on the floor. I started to feel in character and looked around for a cuspidor, but I could see this dude ranch had its own standards.

After one quick drink at the bar, I went to the reception desk. The guy behind it was really something—what, I wasn't too sure. He was a little fat guy with big rimless glasses and a drooping mustache. He wore a plaid shirt with patch pockets and a pair of tight-fitting spangled pants tucked into highly polished yellow boots. Around his waist was a gun belt with a silver buckle, and a toy forty-five with an imitation pearl handle dangled in its holster on his right hip.

I took another look at the star pinned to his chest and saw I'd read it right the first time; it did say, "Clerk." He gave me what I assumed was a friendly grin. "Welcome stranger," he said heartily. "Welcome to El Rancho de los Toros!" He held out his hand across the desk. I took my shield out of my pocket and placed it carefully in his palm

He looked at it blankly for a moment, then looked at me. "What is this, a gag?" he asked suspiciously.

"It's for real," I assured him. "You've got a Jonathan Blake staying here?"

His face brightened. "You're a friend of his, Lieutenant? Yes, sir, Mr. Blake certainly is staying here, and it's a pleasure to have him with us, if I may say so."

"You may," I assured him. "The First Amendment makes that perfectly clear."

He blinked. "But I don't think Mr. Blake is here at the moment. He left the ranch a couple of hours back."

"Ranch?" I was getting interested against my better judgment. "What do you raise here—beside suckers?"

"Really, Lieutenant! I don't think that's amusing!"

"Nobody ever does," I said. "You have any idea where Mr. Blake went?"

"I couldn't say for sure, but he often goes down to Devil's Canyon for some target practice."

"Where's that?"

"You follow the highway another three miles east, then there's a turn-off to your right onto a dirt road. Just keep going on that dirt road, Lieutenant." He smirked. "When you run out of road, that's Devil's Canyon."

"You have it air conditioned with juke boxes on the side?" I asked.

"It's virgin country out there, Lieutenant," he said stiffly.

"I'd better check this right away," I said. "Mr. Blake can't do this. Using virgins for target practice is strictly illegal."

The clerk smiled wanly. "Do you have a hat with you, Lieutenant?"

"You want me to raise it as I say farewell?"

"It gets to be pretty hot up there in the canyon at this time of day," he said. "Around a hundred and five in the shade—if you can find any."

"Thanks," I told him. "I have a hat."

"I'll consider it raised," he said happily. "Good day, Lieutenant."

"Take it easy, Windy," I told him. "Or I'll tell Wyatt Earp about you."

I went outside to the car, and had to wait for a screaming blonde to be rescued from the saddle of a motionless horse before I could back up.

Three miles further east on the highway was the turnoff, like the man had said. I followed the dirt road as it zigzagged along for no apparent reason, until I'd gone just over six miles according to the clock. Maybe the clerk had been kidding me and the dirt road went clean through to Florida. Then, as I came around the next bend, I saw he hadn't been kidding at all.

The road didn't run out—it just stopped. Instead of the dirt surface, there was broken rock, cactus and giant boulders ahead. I stopped the Healey beside a tan station wagon with three spotlights attached, as well as the usual four headlamps. I got out and took a closer look at it.

The heat beat down on me from the towering walls of the canyon on either side of me, and I realized the clerk hadn't been kidding about a single thing. The temperature was at least a hundred and five, and there was no shade in sight.

I tried the doors of the station wagon but they were locked. Inside I could see the neat gun racks which housed a private arsenal. Unless the place was overrun with mad dogs and Englishmen, the wagon had to belong to Jonathan Blake. Who else would be out in this blistering hell? Even if it did, where the hell was he I wondered, looking dismally at the unending canyon stretching ahead of me.

If I stopped much longer out in the blazing sun they were going to call me "Sahara Al" when they picked up my bones. I lit a cigarette and wondered if a hoarse scream might bring Blake out from wherever he was. Then I heard the sharp crack of a rifle somewhere up ahead of me in the canyon, and moved toward the sound.

The going got rougher with every step. By the time I'd gone a couple of hundred yards my shirt stuck to my back and my suit was limp. I stopped to mop the sweat from my face and heard another shot. Much closer this time and off to my right. Another fifty yards and I discovered the secret—there was a right-hand turn off the main canyon which ended in a natural blind alley around three hundred yards deep.

Standing with his back to me, reloading an enormous rifle, was a guy who could answer the description of the White Hunter. Perched on a boulder at least two hundred yards away from him were two black specks which could be tin cans. Blake lifted the rifle to his shoulder, took careful aim, and fired. There was a clanging noise as one of the cans disintegrated.

"Mr. Blake?" I asked politely.

He turned around slowly and looked at me. It was Blake all right, I recognized him from the photograph in Pru's suite. Except that the photograph hadn't shown just how big a man he was.

I stand a fraction over six feet, but Blake was at least four inches taller. He was powerfully built, but even so his shoulders looked out of proportion. His face was tanned the color of dark mahogany and the eyes were a very pale blue. They had a chilling effect as he looked at me. "I'm Blake," he said slowly. "What do you want?"

"To talk with you," I said. I told him who I was and he frowned slightly. "If it's my station wagon you're worrying about Lieutenant," he said curtly. "I have a license for those guns."

"It's a murder I'm worried about," I told him. "Howard Davis' murder."

"Davis?" He looked slightly interested. "He's dead?"

"If he isn't they're fixing to play him a very dirty trick. They're burying him in the morning."

"When did it happen?"

"You didn't know about it?"

"Why should I?"

"It was in all the papers."

"I don't read the newspapers," he said in a definite voice. "Tell me about it?"

"I figured if you hadn't read it, then Penelope Calthorpe would have told you," I said.

"I haven't seen her for the last three days at least," his voice was cold. "Are you trying to call me a liar, Lieutenant?"

"No," I said carefully. "I just wanted to check if your memory was functioning, that's all."

"It functions extremely well," he said. "However, if we're going to talk we might as well go back to the wagon." He looked down at the rifle in his hands for a moment, then grinned at me. "Care to try your luck before we leave, Lieutenant?"

"Why not?" I said, and took the rifle from him. I raised it to my shoulder and squinted into the sight. The remaining tin can almost leap out at me. "This is one hell of a sight you have on this gun," I said.

"A Bausch and Lomb, Balvar 24 scope," he said. "Quite good."

I took careful aim and fired. The next moment I was sitting down on a sharp rock protrusion, nursing a numbed shoulder. The rifle lay on the ground a few feet in front of me.

"Sorry, Lieutenant," Blake sounded amused. "I should have warned you about the recoil. These Winchester four-fifty-eight's are the very devil when you aren't used to them."

"Well, thanks a lot for the thought, anyway," I said coldly and dragged myself up onto my feet again.

Blake picked up the rifle and tucked it under his arm and we worked our way back to the station wagon again. "Tell me about Davis' murder, Lieutenant," he said as we walked. "I can't imagine him ever having enough significance for anyone to bother killing him." He patted the stock of his Winchester. "Murdering Davis would be like using this baby to kill a squirrel."

I gave him the details of how Davis' corpse was found in the fake coffin at the television studios. He was grinning when I'd finished. "Sounds like your murderer has a sense of humor," he said.

"He's a riot," I agreed. "When I find him we can both laugh."

"You said you had some questions to ask me," he went on abruptly. "Go ahead, Lieutenant."

"What are you doing here," I asked him, "staying at a dude ranch close to Pine City?"

"Penelope Calthorpe is something more to me than a good friend," he said slowly. "I expect to marry her, Lieutenant. She was wildly excited about this new television nonsense of hers, so I thought I should come along and stay around until it was over, give her some encouragement if I could. But I can't stand being cooped up in a hotel, so I came out here to the ranch." He almost spat the last word. "Ranch! It's more like a chrome-plated brothel, of course, but at least I can get out here during the daytime and keep my eye in."

We reached the station wagon and he unlocked it. We sat on the front seat and if anything it seemed a couple of degrees hotter than the temperature outside.

"Where were you the night before last?" I asked him

"At the ranch—I went to bed early," he said. "I can't stand the people, frankly, not my type at all. So I have an early dinner, a nightcap, and I'm in bed by nine."

"You have a room there?"

"A sort of bungalow for midgets they call a cabana," he said. "It gives me privacy, if not peace. The night air is shrill with feminine squeals from dusk to dawn. The jungle is a quiet place by comparison."

"And its jackals don't wear silver stars with 'Clerk' written across them," I agreed. "You were married to Prudence Calthorpe once?"

"I was." His voice was cold. It was obviously a topic the boys in his set didn't consider it cricket to discuss. Particularly with the police.

"You knew Penelope then, of course, and Howard Davis was her husband then."

"He was."

"Do you know of any reason why someone would want to kill him?"

"You squash a mosquito because it's a slight irritant when it bites," he said. "Davis could never be more than a slight irritant, but I can't think why someone would take the trouble to squash him."

His forehead knotted for a moment. "The way his corpse turned up on Penny's show sounds exactly like the sort of idiotic practical joke that Prudence would play. It would seem funny to her warped mind."

I offered him a cigarette which he accepted. He gave me a light from his gold-plated Dunhill.

"Any more questions, Lieutenant?" he asked finally.

I squirmed around and looked at the gun racks in the back of the wagon. "You have a beautiful collection there," I said.

He half-grinned with pleasure. "My family," he said paternally. "The Winchester is the newest acquisition. That's a Weatherby magnum beside it, and the three, double-barreled boys further down have been with me for some years. Those two are a Marlin .455 and the Higgins .270."

"Powerful?"

"Fine for a mountain goat, but don't try to stop an elephant with it. At least, not when you're with me."

"How about hand guns?" I asked him.

He reached back, snapped open a gun case. "Beauties, eh?"

He pointed with his index finger. "You can take your pick, Lieutenant. There's a Ruger .357 magnum which is a comfortable second gun to have along when you're hunting. They go all the way down to a Smith and Wesson .22. Take your pick."

"You have a thirty-eight?" I asked him.

Blake smiled thinly: "That's a subtle question, I imagine, Lieutenant? I presume Howard was killed with one, and if I say I don't own a thirty-eight it makes you immediately suspicious?"

"You're much too smart for me, Blake," I told him. "Why don't we keep it simple and you just answer the question?"

"I have a thirty-eight." He reached across the back of the seat and lifted a gun from its rack and gave it to me. A nice gun, a Smith and Wesson Outdoorsman which looked very new.

"How long have you had it?" I asked.

"About three months," he said. "I haven't used it yet, which reminds me I must try it out."

"A nice gun," I said and gave it back to him.

He returned the gun to its rack and looked at me again, a trace of impatience showing in his eyes. "It's damned hot out here," he said. "Any more questions, Lieutenant?"

"One," I said. "Do you know, or have you ever heard of a man called Messenger John?"

Blake's back stiffened. He reached out and lifted the Winchester .450 rifle from its rack and laid it across his knees carefully. His right hand stroked the butt, absently. "I've heard of Messenger John," he said quietly. "Is he mixed up in the murder?"

"Up to his ears," I said cheerfully. "My trouble is I don't get to meet him. He calls me all the time, tells me a little of this, a little of that; but I never get around meeting him. Maybe he's a retiring character?"

"You meet him, I would say you've met your murderer, Lieutenant," Blake said shortly.

"You know him well?" I asked.

"Well enough." His eyes had that remote, malignant look in them again. "You know why Prudence divorced me?"

"I heard something about it," I admitted cautiously.

"That was organized by Messenger John," he went on his voice devoid of expression. "There's a trite phrase about every man having his weakness, Lieutenant, and that's Messenger John's strength."

"Huh?" I said feebly.

"His strength is searching out another man's weakness," Blake said. "He found mine and exploited it, very successfully, too."

"Should I ask?" I asked.

"Maybe it comes from knocking around the more primitive parts of the world," he said. "When you're known as a hunter, everyone automatically thinks of Africa. I know that continent pretty well—but I've been in a hell of a lot of other places too, and most of them a damned sight wilder than the African jungle."

"This is your weakness?" I sounded confused, even to myself.

"It may partially explain it," he said. "Man needs woman most of the time, you know, Wheeler. Problem in a lot of places is to find one. Some places it's impossible to find a woman of any sort, but in most of those places it's always impossible to find a white woman!"

"So?"

"So I developed a taste for yellow women," he said with cold deliberation. "You can understand it happening can't you, Wheeler? You're a lieutenant of police, not one of those damned snotty-nosed, white-collared pimps whose idea of life comes from the stories they read in the glossy magazines?"

"I can understand it," I said hastily.

"Yellow women," Blake repeated with morose satisfaction. "To me, they're something special. Chinese, Japanese, Javanese ... the nationality doesn't matter, it's something to do with the color. Maybe one of these analysts could explain it to me, but I don't want it explained. When I'm hungry, I eat. If some damned fool tells me I'm hungry because I haven't eaten, where does that get me! I ..."

"You were telling me about Messenger John," I reminded him.

"I still am," he said coldly. "He found out my weakness. Prudence was in the scheme, of course. She made an excuse to be out of town for a week, and I was left alone in the house, except for the servants and they didn't count. On the fourth night, straight out of my wilder fantasies, a charming little Chinese girl walked into the house. I found out later she took off her clothes for a living in one of the Chinatown nightclubs in San Francisco.

"It was late, after midnight; the servants were all in bed. I answered the doorbell. Her car had broken down—that's what her voice said, but her eyes said it was going to be all right and no trouble at all—she appreciated me." Blake coughed modestly, deep in his powerful chest. "Women often do, you know," he confided.

"You take the beasts of the jungle, they take you, it gives them a superwoman complex," I said. "Or maybe it's just your muscles."

Blake looked at me suspiciously for a moment. "Anyway, by the time the situation got really interesting, in came Messenger John, complete with two photographers to record every sordid detail." He looked at me coldly. "I didn't care for it, Wheeler," he said seriously. "To put it mildly, I was bloody annoyed. Dammit, there we were in the raw, with flashbulbs popping everywhere.

"I had a Browning shotgun in the closet and it was loaded.   A beautifully-balanced gun, one of my favorites. Well, like I told you, I was damned annoyed, so I got the gun out of the closet and I was going to teach them a lesson in social behavior. Before I could pull the trigger, Messenger John took the gun, and ..." Blake nearly choked with fury. "He took it in both his hands, bent the barrel nearly to a right angle, then had the audacity to hand it back to me!"

"Tough," I said sympathetically. "So Prudence got the divorce, and you didn't get any of her money."

"I didn't want any of her damned money," he said coldly. "I have plenty in my own right, thank you! But I didn't like being made to appear the complete fool that he made of me. It's a score I have yet to settle." He patted the stock of the Winchester again fondly.

"What does he look like?" I asked.

"He's a giant of a man," Blake said. "Bigger than I am. Wears his hair far too long so it curls at the nape of neck like one of those over muscled pixies you see wrestling on television. His hair's very fair, too. It wouldn't surprise me if he peroxided it, but don't misunderstand me, Wheeler; Messenger John is no fairy. He's a dangerous and completely unscrupulous man who will stop at nothing, not even murder, so long as the payment is high enough."

"You think somebody hired him to murder Howard Davis?"

"That's obvious," he said firmly. "Messenger John would never allow himself to murder for pleasure, only for profit!"

Chapter Six

It was around six in the evening when I got back into town from Blake and El Rancho de los Toros. I went straight to my apartment and had a long cold shower, then got dressed again and made myself a drink. I put Peggy Lee's "Sea Shells" onto the hi-fi machine and let the five speakers pour her soft, soothing, perfectly phrased voice over me. She sounded cool and gentle and in no hurry, and right then that was just the way I wanted to feel.

After both sides of the record, and three drinks, I began to feel that even if life wasn't worth living, I might keep on, just for the hell of it. I also felt hungry as if I'd missed out on lunch, so I went down the street to the Coffee Inn on the corner three blocks away, which featured lousy coffee, but superb steak sandwiches.

It was a little after nine when I arrived back in the Starlight Hotel. I checked with the desk clerk and he told me Miss Penelope Calthorpe was in her suite but didn't want to be disturbed. Don't we all?

I knocked on her door twice and she didn't open it, so I started in with that "I Got Rhythm" routine again, and this time she let me make the breakway roll before she opened the door.

She stood there with that permanent flame on top of her head burning brightly—a redhead who was real mad at me and couldn't think of words nasty enough to do her feelings justice.

"You should have opened the door sooner," I told her. "That way you smooth the emotional tensions, prevent ulcers and lessen the chances of a coronary occlusion. That will be twenty dollars please, for the consultation."

"Why, you ..."

"Just call me doctor," I said benevolently, "and when you're not doing anything special, just call me."

"Are you drunk?" she asked harshly.

"No," I said, "but I can be persuaded. Are you going to ask me in, or should I just walk in?"

"You can't come in!" she said flatly, and went to close the door.

I put the flat of my hand against the door and held it open. "Never be rude to a cop," I said reprovingly. She threw her weight against the door and nearly got it closed, almost breaking my hand off at the wrist in the process.

I stopped it with my shoulder, put my weight behind it. The door opened suddenly. Penelope was sent staggering about six feet down the hall, trying to regain her balance.

"My God," she said despairingly, "You're impossible!"

I walked past her, into the living room and she followed me stormily.

She affected the Oriental motif again. I wondered if one of her main attractions for Blake was that she was trying to give him a new slant on life. The loose fitting silk pagoda jacket hung loosely from her shoulders to her waist, making slight upward and outward detours at the appropriate places. Her legs were sheathed in tapering pants that hugged well-rounded thighs and made no attempt to minimize the magnificence of her bottom. As I swept past her, I almost drowned in the heady perfume she wore. I don't know the name, but it could have been "In An Emperor's Garden" because it would make any red-blooded man want to wade around in it barefoot.

She crossed her arms under a bosom that didn't need their support, and glared at me. "What the hell do you want this time?" she demanded.

"I wanted to talk to you about a friend of yours," I said. "A reject from Western Union, a guy who calls himself Messenger John."

Penelope jumped visibly. "Who?"

"Leave us not go into the 'I've lost my memory' or 'I'm confused and it's bad publicity for my television debut' routines again," I pleaded. "I'm talking about the guy who organized Prudence's divorce so she didn't have to give Jonathan Blake a handout on his departure. The guy who organized your divorce from Howard Davis so you also didn't have to part with any of your vast fortune. Do you remember now?"

Her head nodded jerkily like somebody had pulled a string. "Yes," she whispered.

"That's great," I said. "He's a friend of mine, too. He's organizing the murder investigation for me by long distance. Where do I find him?"

"I don't have any idea!" she said quickly.

There was an armchair about two yards to my right, set facing the big windows. I moved over and sat down in it. The thick drapes were pulled tight across the windows, which was a pity; I might have enjoyed the view.

"Just what are you doing now?" Penny asked uncertainly.

"I'm sitting here until you tell me where I can find Messenger John," I said. "Comes tomorrow, comes the day after, I'll still be here—unless you tell me. I am a stubborn character when I'm roused."

"I told you I don't know!" she said. "It won't do you any good to sit there with that stupid grin on your face!"

"You disappoint me, Penny," I said soberly. "You told me to watch out that Prudence didn't add me to her collection, and she did. Prudence told me you drink too much, drive too fast and take off your clothes without any encouragement at all. So far, you're right out of character. You don't take off your clothes, you don't offer me a drink, you don't even make yourself a drink."

"Get out of here!"

"When you answer my question, honey," I said. "You don't have to worry, I brought my razor."

I settled down more comfortably in the chair and lit myself a cigarette. Behind me I could hear Penny muttering to herself and I didn't listen too hard because I guessed she was talking about me. I concentrated on the view instead—the limited view of the draped window.

Like it said in the correspondence course I never took, concentration is important. Without it you overlook things that shouldn't be overlooked: the last inch of Scotch at the bottom of the bottle, the ten dollar bill the guy in front of you just dropped, and various blondes, brunettes and redheads.

If I hadn't been concentrating on that draped window, maybe I would have missed them altogether. The two large feet that protruded beneath the bottom edge of the drape, I mean. They were encased in a pair of highly polished oxfords and I figured however forgetful a guy might be, he just doesn't leave his feet behind. So with a triumphant follow-through, I deduced that the rest of the guy was still there, behind the drape.

I got up from the armchair and walked over to the window, caught hold of the drape and pulled it back with a sharp tug. The guy was still there all right, and I was looking at his chest. I raised my eyes slowly until I saw his face.

He must have been around six and a half feet tall, with the build of a pro wrestler. His blond hair was definitely too long and curled into ringlets at the nape of his neck. I stepped back a pace and took another look at him. "Well, well," I said, "if it isn't Long Distance himself!"

His vivid blue eyes bored into mine for a moment, then he smiled pleasantly: "Lieutenant Wheeler," he said easily, "this is an unexpected pleasure—it was the feet, of course?"

"All exposed," I agreed. "If you'd stood a couple of inches in the air, the drape would have hid them."

"I would have chosen a better hiding place," he said casually. "But then I told Penny not to let anyone in here while I was with her. You must be a very persistent lieutenant."

He walked away from the window, toward the center of the room, flexing his shoulders as he walked. "I need a drink," he said to Penny. "Scotch, I think. For you, Lieutenant?"

"On the rocks, a little soda," I said. "I hope I didn't interrupt anything when I knocked on the door? Or were you making a business call?"

"It wasn't important," he said. "But I don't think you need the help of my messages any more, Lieutenant. You seem to be doing very well on your own."

Penny brought us the drinks on a tray, the glasses chattering together; her jaw was clamped tight shut so maybe her teeth were the same way. I took the nearest glass from the tray and looked at Messenger John. "I told you before your name belonged in a comic strip," I said pleasantly. "Now that we've met, I think the name fits you very well."

He sipped his drink appreciatively, then looked at me. "Have you caught your murderer yet, Lieutenant?"

"That's the exact question I'm asking myself right now," I told him. "All those messages you sent me—why?"

"My duty as a citizen." His lower lip curled slightly. "A desire for justice."

"Or a careful misdirection," I said. "Point me the wrong way and build up other suspects so I don't have time to even think about you as the chief suspect."

"You're wrong," he said contemptuously. "Try hard, Lieutenant. Use what little intelligence you have, you can't afford to waste it."

"Messenger John," I said regretfully, "I am not impressed. To be honest, I'm disappointed. I expected something much more exciting than this and what do I get? A king-sized slob in need of a haircut."

His face darkened slowly. "Take it easy, Lieutenant," he said. A note of menace crept into his voice. "I don't take that from anybody, including you!"

"Johnny," I said, "you frighten the very life out of me when you bare your teeth like that. Reminds me of Bugs Bunny on the carrot-top trail."

"Stop it!" Penny said to me in a high-strung voice. "You don't know what you're doing."

"I should let him worry me?" I asked her. "There are a lot of ways of making a dirty living, but he's hard to top. Pandering to rich women who want a cheap divorce!"

"I advised you to shut up!" Messenger John almost spat the words at me.

"So you did," I remembered. "But you forgot something, Johnny. You're not talking to poor little rich girl Penny now; you're talking to me. I'm still not impressed. I heard about how you fixed up Jonathan Blake with a girl his favorite color and then brought the photographers along to the party. Big deal! Keep this up and you'll be purse snatching next."

He took a couple of steps toward me with his fists clenched, then changed his mind suddenly. He veered off, walking with quick, light steps across the room to where a gilded horseshoe hung on the wall. He lifted it off the hook and turned back toward me again.

"Don't!" Penny cried out. "Please, Messenger John, that's my luck piece, I need it!"

He ignored her completely and stopped a few paces away from my chair, shifting his grip so he held the horseshoe in both hands. There was a gentle smile on his face as he looked down at me, then the veins corded on the backs of his hands for a brief moment.

"There is another message for you, Wheeler," he said easily a second later. Then he tossed the straightened horseshoe into my lap. "Think about it."

"So you're a big strong boy now," I said. I picked the straightened iron bar and looked at it. "Maybe I was wrong, at that. Maybe you fixed Penny's divorce from Howard Davis for her, but it wasn't enough. She wanted him murdered, so you took care of that, too?"

"You have a vivid imagination, Wheeler," he said, "but misguided. I had nothing to do with Davis' murder."

"You can prove that?"

"I don't have to," he said. "You're out of your mind!"

"It was you who told me where I could find the corpse that was stolen from the morgue," I said. "I'd find it in the television studios, you told me. When I got there, I hit the jackpot, and came up with two corpses. It's my bet you stole the corpse from the morgue in the first place and murdered Davis in the second place."

"And stumbled onto the studios as a convenient place to leave both corpses?" He laughed shortly. "You kill me, Lieutenant."

"It's something worth thinking about," I agreed. "I don't think you stumbled on the studios at all, I think your client told you specifically to leave the corpses there and to be very sure you put Davis' body into that fake coffin."

"This is an interesting, if stupid, theory," he said coldly.

"I'd like to go along with it," I said. "That's why I'm booking you as a material witness, Johnny. If you have a hat, you might as well collect it now."

"You're mistaken about one thing, Wheeler," he said. "It wasn't I who called you and told you where to find the body that was stolen from the morgue—it was someone else who used my name, to try and implicate me."

"You don't expect me to believe that?"

"No." He smiled. "But try and disprove it!"

"I'll do that," I told him. "Meanwhile we'll find you a nice comfortable cell. Material comforts are important to a material witness, aren't they?"

The smile faded slowly from his face. "You can't be serious about this, Wheeler?"

"Can't I?" I stood up quickly and started toward him. "Do you come along peaceably or should I produce handcuffs?"

He dropped his hand into his pocket swiftly and it came out holding a gun. "Just stay right where you are, Wheeler," he said softly. "Unless you'd like a third eye?"

I looked at the gun in his hand. "Thirty-eight caliber?" I asked.

Messenger John backed off slowly toward the door. I watched him go and didn't try to do anything about it. Thinking a guy with a gun in his hand is kidding can be a fatal practice any time, and I didn't think Messenger John was kidding for one moment.

He opened the front door of the suite and stepped backward into the corridor. "Don't try to follow me, Wheeler," he said, "or you'll end up in the morgue, too." Then he closed the door firmly.

I finished my drink, then looked at Penny. Her face was an ivory color, almost yellow. Tension etched deep lines around the carefully slanted eyes. She moaned softly and flopped onto the couch.

"You remember I was saying before that gun so rudely interrupted me, that Messenger John acted under specific instructions from his client in placing both corpses in the television studios?" She nodded faintly. "It's true, isn't it?" I said crisply. "That's what you told him to do?"

"Me?" Her eyes widened suddenly. "You don't think it was *me!*"

"It could be," I told her. "You might have had everything figured out all nice and neat. Not that I'm ready to say this is how it happened—yet. But it could have." I walked over, stood straddle-legged in front of her. "You wanted Howard Davis killed, so you turned to Messenger John. He handled your divorce for you and you liked the way he worked—"

"That's crazy," she protested. "Why should I want Howard killed?"

"That," I admitted sourly, "I haven't figured out yet. If I had, we'd be two characters in search of a police matron."

"You're wrong," she shook her head. "Even if I did want Harold killed do you think I'd arrange for him to show up on my show and ruin my debut?"

"That's where the clever touch comes in." I raised a hand to offset an interruption. "As I say, I'm not saying this is how it happened. But if you did arrange for Howard to shuffle off this mortal coil, you'd know the police would come looking for you as an ex-wife. So you had to have something to convince them you had nothing to do with it. Something that would make it look as though you were the injured party, that someone was conspiring against you and using Harold's remains to harass you."

"No!" she whimpered. "No, no, no!"

"So you had Goldilocks dump the corpses in the studios," I said. "You knew the layout of the place, you could tell him where to put them, how to get in and out of the place without being seen. And you told him to put Howard's body into that fake coffin. Then, when the police questioned you later, you could tell your sob story about how the publicity would ruin your television deal and they'd be convinced you'd never do that to yourself."

"It's not true," she said in a muffled voice.

"I think it might be," I told her. "I'm going to try to prove it, and if I do, you'll be on your way to the gas chamber. With Messenger John along for company."

She got to her feet slowly, her whole body trembling. I watched while she walked across to the bar and filled a tumbler with neat Scotch. She drank it in three gulps, then shuddered violently.

"You know where I can find Messenger John," I said. "Tell me."

She took a deep, shuddering breath: "He's staying out at a place called Hillside, renting a house out there. Seventy-eight Stanwell Drive is the address." She gave me the phone number.

"You'd better be right," I told her. "Or you'll wind up in that cell I promised Messenger John, as a material witness."

I watched while the deep breath abruptly stopped the pagoda jacket from lounging anymore. She dabbed her eyes a couple of times, streaking her make-up so that the Oriental look became merely coincidental. Then she tried to put a smile on her face. It slipped a couple of times but then she got it fixed.

She walked toward me slowly, a swing to her hips that wasn't normally there. Her hands reached out and gripped my shoulders tightly, "You're one hell of an operator, Lieutenant," she said huskily. "I could go for you, if you'd only believe me when I say I'm telling you the truth."

Her hands slipped away from my shoulders; she fumbled at the catch that held her trousers at the waist. She peeled the skin-tight pants down from her waist, gracefully slid them over one foot, kicked them aside with the other. Then she pulled the pagoda jacket over her head, tossed it to the couch.

She stood there, a tall, slim, breathtakingly curved figure dressed only in a white bra and candy striped briefs.

"Is this the world of Suzy Wong?" I asked wonderingly.

The fixed smile was still on her face. "Maybe you'll believe me now?" she asked softly. She turned her back to me. The view from the rear was as satisfying as it had been from the front. "Unhook me."

I prodded the last vertebra of her spine, about three inches below the waistband of her briefs, with the index finger of my right hand and she jumped convulsively.

"What is this?" I asked her. "Custer's last stand?"

"Don't you want to take off the rest of my clothes?" she asked in a shaking voice.

"When you run out of everything else, there's always sex," I said. "I guess it's what makes the world go round, but right now I'm a square."

I walked across to the front door, then stopped for a moment and looked back at her. She stood there, her whole body shaking uncontrollably, the last traces of the Oriental make-up dissolving into a tear-stained blur.

"Put your clothes back on, Penny," I said gently. "You'll catch cold."

I rode the elevator down to the lobby, and tried to relax. It had been a stimulating evening, as a female contortionist once said to me. Maybe it would have been easy to relax if I didn't keep on remembering that horseshoe Messenger John had straightened into an iron bar without even taking a deep breath.

Chapter Seven

I got into the office early the next morning, if not bright. The female monster grunted vaguely in my direction and went on with her filing. I wondered if she drank the blood of little children for breakfast.

Polnik arrived in the office ten minutes later. He gave me the sort of look a trained seal gives its master when the last piece of fish was just a little bit ripe. "You were going to call me, Lieutenant," he said reproachfully.

"I had a busy day," I told him. "How did you make out?"

"I found her O.K.," he said proudly. "Thelma Davis got into the hotel just after lunchtime yesterday." The aggrieved note was back in his voice. "I waited around all afternoon for you to call me like you said you would, sitting around on my ..."

The sudden rustle of outraged papers from the direction of the filing cabinet sounded a warning bugle.

"... chair," Polnik finished lamely.

"I weep for you, Polnik," I said politely. "And now that's taken care of, where the hell is Thelma Davis?"

"Park Hotel," he said. "It's one of those downtown fleabags in a back street, you know the kind of joint, Lieutenant. There's no park within two miles of it, either."

"O.K.," I said. "I'll go see her."

"Lieutenant—you promised!"

"Promised?" I looked at him blankly. "What?"

He looked around furtively at the woman at the typewriter, then lowered his voice. "You know, dames! You said if I found this Thelma Davis, I get to go with you and see her. All I been doing on this case is sit on my can—"

"Sergeant!" the female snapped sharply.

"Don't let it worry you," I told her. "The sergeant meant to say fanny."

We got out of the office while she was still gobbling. Half an hour later, I parked out front of the hotel and we went inside. The desk clerk told us Thelma Davis had a room on the third floor. The elevator was out of order so we walked up on carpet that had seen better days just about the time Teddy Roosevelt was a young man.

We reached her room and I knocked on the door. Polnik panted heavily beside me and I hoped it was just climbing the stairs that had caused the effect.

"Who is it?" a feminine voice called sharply.

"Police!" Polnik said hoarsely. "Open up!"

I looked at him disgustedly: "The king of the clichés. Can't you wait to get a look at her?"

"No," he said, "and ain't that the truth!"

The door opened suddenly and a woman stood there. She was in her middle thirties, a good figure, and she'd been pretty once, but she'd rubbed up against Life too often and it had sharpened her features a little too keenly. Her nose was too sharp, her lips too thin, and her eyes too suspicious. "What do you want?" she asked flatly.

"You're Mrs. Davis?" I asked.

"Miss since the divorce," she said. "But I kept the Davis; it's easier to say than Katatiker."

"I'm with you," I agreed.

"Who are you?" she asked.

"I'm Lieutenant Wheeler, from the County Sheriff's office," I told her. "This is Sergeant Polnik."

"What do you want?"

"To ask you some questions," I said. "About your husband, Howard Davis."

"My ex-husband, you mean," she said. "I divorced him a couple of years back."

"Can we come inside?" I said.

She hesitated for a moment. "I suppose so," she said reluctantly. "It won't take long, will it?"

"I don't think so," I told her.

She opened the door a little wider and we went inside the room. There was a bed, a closet, a chipped bureau. A battered suitcase stood in one corner. The carpet was frayed and there was a layer of dust and minor despair over everything.

Thelma Davis was neatly dressed in a white blouse and blue, pencil-line skirt. She was a blonde, but not the exciting type. The disappointment settled in deeper on Polnik's face as he took another look at her. She lit a cigarette and looked at me impatiently. "Make it fast will you, Lieutenant, I happen to have an appointment."

"Sure," I said. "You know your husband—ex-husband—was murdered two days ago?"

"I read about it," she said indifferently.

"I thought you would have claimed his body," I said.

"Why me? Let Penelope Calthorpe have it. She was married to him after me! She can build him a marble tomb some place with all those back alimony payments I won't get now!"

The hatred on her face was naked in its intensity. Maybe she'd hated too many people through her life and that explained the sharpness of her face. She looked like she was a good hater. I walked over to the window and lit myself a cigarette. "Why did you come to Pine City, Miss Davis?"

"Following him, of course," she snapped. "He was six months behind on his alimony payments already, then he ran out on me from San Francisco, but I found out where he'd gone from his rooming house."

"You wrote him a letter from San Francisco first," I said, "giving him three days to pay the alimony or else you were going to put him behind bars—where he belonged was your phrase—as I remember."

"Howard always did keep letters," she said. "His one streak of sentiment."

"What made you change your mind?"

"About what?"

"About putting him behind bars?"

"I didn't."

I turned around to face her again. "You wrote him the letter, then you found out he'd left San Francisco, so you followed him here. But when you caught up with him, you didn't file a complaint with the court here to have him arrested. What made you change your mind?"

"I'm a woman. Is there any law against changing my mind?" she asked tartly.

"Howard started to write you a letter, but he never finished it," I said. "I guess because you arrived here before he had time. He mentioned he was just about to make the big deal he'd been waiting for all his life. Maybe be told you about it, and that's why you didn't go to the court?"

"He never told me anything about a big deal! The only big deal he ever made in his life was marrying that Penelope Calthorpe and that blew up right in his face soon enough. He couldn't even die decently; he had to get himself murdered!"

I looked at Polnik, who rolled his eyes helplessly back at me. "I think you're lying, Miss Davis," I told her.

"If you're going to insult me, you can get out of here!" she said loudly. "I've got my rights as a citizen."

"Do you know of any reason why your husband should be murdered?"

"It'd be something to do with the Calthorpe women," she said, "you could be sure of that."

"Why?"

"They're no good, neither of them, never were. Too much money and alley cat morals. Ever since their father died, they just bought whatever they wanted, and that included Howard as far as Penelope was concerned."

"Didn't Howard have anything to do with it?" I asked.

"He never did amount to much," she said tightly. "A pro tennis player who didn't ever make the grade, but he would have done all right if it hadn't been for her. With me, he might have gotten along. Maybe we wouldn't ever do any better than a walk-up apartment and last year's car, but we would have gotten by. She ruined him."

"In what way?"

"Dazzled him with all that money. He got used to wearing three-hundred-dollar suits and living in fifty-dollars-a-day hotels. After a time he got like a pet dog; when she snapped her fingers, he jumped. When she got tired of him, she dumped him without any money at all. He couldn't take it, he was too lazy for the pro grind any more, and he wasn't getting any younger. She killed him all right, one way or the other."

"You keep on saying that," I yawned. "You have any proof to back it?"

"Don't you worry about that, Lieutenant!" she snapped. "I've got something that'll take care of the Calthorpe family all right. I haven't even started yet. When I've finished with that redheaded witch, she'll think the sky fell in on her, and then she'll wish it had. She's got it coming." Thelma Davis smiled with immense satisfaction. "And I'm going to make sure she gets it!"

"If you're withholding evidence, it's a criminal offense, Miss Davis," I said coldly. "If you know anything that has any bearing on your ex-husband's murder at all, it's your duty to tell us now. If you don't, then ..."

"Skip it, Lieutenant," she said harshly. "I'll save us all some time. That routine might have frightened people twenty years ago, but not since television. Now everybody hears some actor playing a cop say that sort of thing three times a week on six different channels. It's kind of lost its punch. You can't touch me, and you know it."

"Personally, I wouldn't want to," Polnik growled at her.

"Do you plan on staying in Pine City long, Miss Davis?" I ignored the interruption.

"That's my affair!"

"If you really know something, I wouldn't stay too long," I suggested gently.

"What do you mean by that?"

"If you know whatever it was that Howard knew, it could be dangerous for you," I said. "Look what happened to him."

"I'm not frightened of anything happening to me," she said briskly. "I'm not the sort of fool he was."

"What kind are you?" Polnik asked brightly.

She scowled at him, then at me. "What do you have him along for?" she asked. "To keep your shoes clean?"

I nodded to Polnik and moved toward the door. "Thanks, Miss Davis," I said to her. "What for, I don't know, but thanks anyway."

"You've kept me twenty minutes already!" she snapped. "Don't you have something better to do?"

"Lady," Polnik said with terrible sincerity, "if I had had a crystal ball, believe me, I would have found something better to do. Anything!"

I knocked on the door of the ninth floor suite and it was opened almost immediately, but not by Penny Calthorpe. Jonathan Blake stared at me coldly: "What do you want, Lieutenant?" he asked.

"To talk to Penny," I said, and walked past him into the living room.

Penny sat on the couch, wearing a demure, high-necked mandarin sheath which gave her a fragile look—the one touch and she'd break kind. Her eyes were heavy, red-rimmed and slanted more acutely than they had before. She looked a living image of Jonathan Blake's favorite weakness.

A heavy hand clamped down onto my shoulder and spun me around. I found myself looking at Blake's determined face. "Look here, Wheeler," he said icily. "I demand an explanation of your behavior last night!"

I knocked his hand away from my shoulder: "Just who are you to demand anything?" I asked him.

"We're going to be married in a few weeks," he said. "I regard myself as Penny's protector."

"But the law doesn't," I said. "Until you're married to her, you don't exist in her life, legally. You don't have any say in her affairs at all. I'll give you two words of advice—shut up!"

I turned back toward Penny, then felt his sinewy fingers grip my shoulder again. "Take your hand off my shoulder, Blake," I told him without turning around. "If you don't stay out of this, I'll call my office and have them send a couple of men around and book you for obstructing a police officer in the performance of his lawful duties. And I can make it stick."

His grip loosened slowly until his hand fell away. "You ready to tell me the whole story yet?" I said to Penny.

She clutched hold of the arm of the couch. "I told you last night,

Lieutenant," she said hysterically. "I didn't kill Howard. I didn't, I didn't!"

"That's just about far enough for you, Wheeler!" Blake said. He walked swiftly across the room to the couch to the redhead. Penny jumped to her feet and clung thankfully to his chest. "Protect me, Jonathan," she whimpered. "Please don't let him keep asking all those horrible questions again. I get so confused I don't know what I'm saying! He frightens me!"

The pink spots faded out of Blake's cheeks, leaving his face a dead-white color. "Dammit, Wheeler," he said in a low voice. "I'm not going to stand here and watch while you terrorize the girl. We've got a right to have a lawyer, and Penny isn't going to answer one of your questions until there's a lawyer sitting right here in this room!"

"It looks real good, Blake," I said. "Law of the jungle stuff with the Mighty White Hunter protecting the helpless female of the species. It deserves a small round of applause."

"I'm not going to stand around and listen to your cheap bloody sarcasm!" he said. "I'm calling a lawyer right now!" He moved toward the phone on the table.

"Sure," I said, "you can call a lawyer. But before he gets here, I'll take Penny down to the Sheriff's office and book her as a material witness. Your lawyer will have to get a habeas corpus writ signed by a judge to get her out again. He'll get it O.K. but it takes time. Half a day, maybe—three hours at least. Meanwhile, I get to ask her all the questions I want without any interruptions from you, your lawyer, or anybody else."

He stopped and glared at me: "All right," he said with an effort. "What do you want?"

"The same thing I wanted in the first place," I snarled at him. "To ask some questions. Will you sit down someplace now and shut up. Better still, you could make us all a drink."

"Very well," he said. "Don't think I shall forget this, Wheeler."

"I won't," I said wearily: "I promise. Is that O.K.?" I looked at Penny again. "Thelma Davis is in town," I said. "Did you know that?"

She shook her head, "No, I didn't."

"So I bring you news. I've just been talking to her. She doesn't like you."

"It doesn't surprise me," Penny said. "She was a possessive, vindictive sort of woman, as I remember."

"Vindictive is the word, I'd guess," I said. "She said she had some information that would blow the Calthorpe family sky-high, and you in particular."

Penny straightened up, looked from me to Blake and back helplessly. "What kind of information?"

"I figured you might be able to tell me," I said. "Don't you have any idea what she's talking about?"

She shook her head: "None, none at all, Lieutenant."

"That's the sort of wild threat a lot of people make under great emotional strain," Blake said. "Just the wild nonsense of a woman who's emotionally unbalanced, I would say. Not worth listening to, Lieutenant."

"Thank you, Doctor Blake!" I said. "Tune in on this program next week, folks, and hear the doctor's thesis on why leopards change their spots."

His face reddened again. "I was only trying to be helpful," he said stiffly.

"There's the pity of it," I told him. "Stick to your guns, Blake, will you? With any luck you'll blow your head off one of these days."

He walked over to the bar with slow deliberation, picked up a cut-glass bowl and hurled it across the room. It shattered against the far wall with a noise like Judgment Day. Blake took a slow, deep breath. "I'll make the drinks," he said. "Scotch for you, darling?"

"Please," Penny whispered. "The lieutenant has a little soda with his."

Blake made the drinks and handed one to Penny, then brought mine across to me. "Thanks," I told him as I lifted the glass out of his hand.

"People always remind me of animals," he said almost casually. "They assume the characteristics of one species or another. Penny now." He smiled at her momentarily. "She reminds me of a gazelle. Timid and graceful and incredibly beautiful."

Penny blushed suddenly. "Jonathan!" she said. "That's the nicest thing you've ever said to me."

"Then there's Prudence," he went on. "She reminds me of a leopard. Sleek—and deadly."

"There has to be a punch line somewhere," I said. "Me? Let me guess what I remind you of—a jackal?"

He shook his head. "To me, you're a hyena," he said easily. "That laugh of yours—if I heard it in the jungle, I'd put a bullet between your eyes without thinking."

"If your aim has improved lately," I agreed.

"You infer something, Lieutenant?" he said softly.

"I was just remembering Penny's father," I said. "Your aim was a little off that day, wasn't it? You only wounded the lion with the first shot."

A white film formed slowly over his vivid blue eyes like a veil. "You go too far, Wheeler," he said in a choked voice, then his hands closed around my throat. The steel fingers dug deep, gouging into my flesh, choking off the windpipe. I threw the contents of my glass into his face. His grip on my throat relaxed suddenly.

He pawed the white handkerchief from his top pocket and wiped his eyes free of the burning spirit. I took the thirty-eight out of my shoulder holster and rammed the muzzle into his chest the moment he started toward me again. For a timeless moment I thought it wasn't going to stop him, but the cold rim of steel boring into his skin took the edge off his fury.

He stood there, his chest heaving, and slowly the white film lifted from his eyes.

"Get out, Lieutenant!" Penny whispered urgently. "Please go—now. Or something dreadful will happen and it'll be your fault. You shouldn't have said that to him; he'll never forget it, never. He'll never forgive you for it. Why did you have to say a thing like that!"

"I'll go," I told her, "and I'll be back." I looked at Blake. "Don't be here when I come back," I said. "I've had all I'm going to take from you. Lay a finger on me again and you'll wind up in the morgue. That's a threat!"

He folded his handkerchief carefully and returned it to his top pocket. "Lieutenant," he said carefully. "I was going to say exactly the same words to you, only I meant them as a promise."

Chapter Eight

I stopped off for a late lunch on the way back to the office and had a cottage-cheese salad. Blake had provided all the red meat I needed for one day. It was just after four when I walked into the office, and the monster smiled a thin greeting at me. "The Sheriff wishes to see you, Lieutenant Wheeler," she said. "Immediately."

"I knew he couldn't get along without me," I said confidently.

"From the sound of his voice, I'd say he's made the adjustment," she said acidly.

I knocked, then walked into Lavers' office and closed the door behind me. "Sit down, Wheeler," he grunted. "What progress are you making on the Davis case?"

"Some," I said cautiously. "I thought you weren't interested? I could turn up the murderer or Homicide would take over the case. That's what you said, wasn't it?"

"That's right," he agreed benevolently, "and now I've changed my mind. The corpse has been identified, you remember, as Howard Davis. Now the newspapers are starting to take an interest. I have my public to think of, Wheeler. They're the people who put me in or out of office at election time."

"Yes, sir," I said.

He lit a cigar and looked at me. "All right, tell me about it."

"About what?"

"Your investigation, what results you've got to date." He reared up suddenly in his chair. "You have been conducting an investigation, haven't you?"

"Yes, sir," I said. "Night and day."

"Maybe I'd better not ask about the nights," he muttered. "Just give me a version that the D.A.'s office would approve."

I told him most of it, not all of it. Even a cop's entitled to a private life, if it does get mixed up with his public life.

"You're sure you didn't dream this Messenger John character up out of a fresh bottle of Scotch?" he asked.

"He's for real," I said.

"You told him you were booking him as a material witness, then let him walk out on you?" he said nastily. "You could have had him picked up at any time—why haven't you?"

"I've been telling everybody I'll book them as a material witness," I said. "It feeds my power complex."

"I am normally a very patient man, Wheeler," the Sheriff said untruthfully. "But I can feel a sudden change coming over me. Why did you let this ... Messenger John ... walk out on you?"

"I figured he'd be more interesting on the loose than he would be in a cell," I said. "Time will tell—I hope."

Lavers opened his mouth to say something but the phone interrupted him. He picked it up and said, "Lavers," curtly. Then he listened for awhile, grunting occasionally to show he was still alive. "Thanks," he finally. "Lieutenant Wheeler will be right there," and hung up.

"Right where?" I asked him coldly.

"That was the highway patrol," he said crisply. "They found a woman's body by the side of a road, ten minutes back. They've identified it as Thelma Davis, with a San Francisco address."

"Where did they find her?"

"A dirt road about six miles east of the city, on the coastal highway. There's a patrol car waiting for you at the turn-off."

"I'll get going," I said and started for the door.

"This makes it even more important we get some action, Wheeler," Lavers said soberly. "You can have another twenty-four hours. Then I'll have to call in Homicide."

"Sure," I said. "How was she killed?"

"Her neck was broken," he said slowly. "Maybe I'm starting to believe in this Messenger John of yours, after all."

I stopped the Healey behind the patrol car at the side of the dirt road and got out. Polnik heaved his bulk out the other side and sighed with grateful release. We followed the patrolman across the grass to where his partner stood waiting for us.

"It was just luck, Lieutenant," the patrolman said. "We were on a routine patrol through here. There was a sudden gust of wind and it must have lifted her skirt. I saw it out of the corner of my eye—it looked like a flag or something waving over the top of the grass, so we stopped to take a look."

We came up to the second patrolman, who pointed downward into the long grass. Thelma Davis' body lay on its stomach, but the head was twisted at a grotesque angle so that her wide-open, disbelieving eyes stared up at us mutely.

"I didn't go for her much this morning," Polnik said huskily. "But this shouldn't happen to a dog!"

"We found her purse over there." The patrolman pointed to a spot a couple of yards from the body. "You want to take charge of it, Lieutenant?"

"What was in it?"

"Not much," he said. "Lipstick, comb, vanity case. Ten dollars eighty, in cash. There was a checkbook, social security card, ballpoint pen, handkerchief—that's about all, Lieutenant. But somebody checked her purse before we did."

"You mean whoever killed her?"

"I guess so. It looked like he searched the body, too. Her skirt was over her head when we found her, and you can see where he ripped her blouse across the shoulder. He must have been in a hell of a hurry to find whatever he was looking for. Maybe he didn't find it?"

"Maybe he was one of them sex maniacs," Polnik said.

"The doctor can tell about that," I said. "Has he been here yet?"

"Expecting him any minute now, Lieutenant," the first patrolman said. "We called in to headquarters and they called the Sheriff's office. You're handling the Davis murder, aren't you, Lieutenant?"

"That's right," I said.

"And this is his wife?"

"Ex-wife," I said.

He shook his head. "Tough. I don't like to see a woman get murdered, especially not this way!"

"Sure," I said. "Thanks again—I've seen all I want see. We won't wait for the doctor, I can pick up his report later."

"Whatever you say, Lieutenant," the patrolman agreed politely.

Polnik squeezed himself back into the Healey and I got in behind the wheel. I made it fast back to the Park Hotel and Polnik had a look of relief on his face when we stopped. I went inside quickly and Polnik caught up with me as I told the manager who I was and what had happened.

"Miss Davis murdered?" His flabby face quivered. "She seemed so nice—a real lady."

"Yeah," I said. "I'll want the key to her room."

"Whatever you say, Lieutenant." He reached behind him and pulled the key out of its pigeonhole and gave it to me. I handed it to Polnik and told him to search the room.

"Okay, Lieutenant," he said briskly and went off at a fast trot toward the stairwell. He made six paces, then stopped suddenly and looked back at me. "Lieutenant,"—his voice was faintly apologetic—"what are we looking for?"

"I wouldn't know," I said. "But you start looking and I'll be up there in a minute to help. Just don't fall out the window before I get there."

He disappeared up the stairs and I concentrated on the manager again. "Do you know what time she left the hotel?" I asked him.

"Matter of fact, I do," he said. "I was on the desk. I'm always on the desk on Tuesdays; that's the day that Joe, the regular clerk, has off, so ..."

"What time was it?"

"Pretty close to one-thirty," he said, "give or take ten minutes."

"She have any callers today?"

"None that I saw—'cepting you of course this morning."

"I remember me calling," I said. "Did she ever have any callers in the time she's been here?"

"Far's I know, no," he said. "Now, Joe maybe, he could help you there ..."

"But not here," I said. "You know if she had any phone calls today?"

"Guess I couldn't tell you that, Lieutenant," he said regretfully. "We don't have a room phone service here, there's a pay phone on each floor."

A heavy thumping sound made me look around in time to see Polnik's purple face as he came down the last three steps into the lobby. "You forgot what you went up there for?" I snarled at him.

"We're wasting our time, Lieutenant," he panted. "That room's in one hell of a mess—somebody's been through it already."

It just wasn't my day. I lit a cigarette and looked at the manager without any real hope. "Did anyone come in and ask for Miss Davis? You see any strangers go through the lobby?"

He shook his head. "No, sir, I didn't. But the fire escape runs right past the window of that room. Anybody could walk up it from the alleyway behind the hotel."

"Yeah," I said. "Well, thanks for your trouble, anyway."

"No trouble, Lieutenant," he said. "You leaving already?"

"Already," I agreed and moved away from the desk.

"Lieutenant?" he said apologetically. "I don't want to bother you ..."

"Thanks," I said, "I appreciate it," and kept on going.

"Lieutenant!" he yelled desperately. "What should I do with the envelope Miss Davis gave me to put in the safe?"

I stopped suddenly in mid-stride and so did Polnik. We looked at each other blankly for a long moment, then turned around and walked back to the desk.

The manager had an embarrassed look on his face. "I don't want to be no trouble to you, Lieutenant," he said. "But what should I do with it?"

"You could give it to me," I said carefully.

His face brightened. "Fine, then I don't have to worry about it anymore. I'll get it right away."

It took him thirty long seconds to get the heavy manila envelope with the name Thelma Davis written across the front. He handed it to me and I tore it open and emptied the contents onto the desk. An outsized cartridge dropped out of the envelope, started rolling toward the edge. Polnik caught it in his ham-like fist and looked at me hopefully. "This what we been looking for, Lieutenant?"

"I guess so," I said. "What did you expect—a plastic wrapped blonde?"

"Not on this case," he said morosely. "Not after Thelma Davis. I know when I'm licked, Lieutenant!"

I put the cartridge into my pocket, thanked the manager and went back to the Healey. I dropped Polnik at the office and told him I was going over to Homicide and he could reach me there if he wanted me.

My watch said it was four-thirty when I walked into the bureau. Captain Barker's office door was open as I went past and he yelled out to me. I stuck my head inside the doorway and said hello.

"They tell me you got a mess of murders in the Sheriff's jurisdiction." He grinned happily. "How's it coming, Al?"

"Great," I said. "Right now it looks like they're coming your way fast!"

"We don't want your leftovers, Al," he said gloomily. "You tell Lavers if you can't come up with any answers, he'd better just file them under 'Unsolved.'"

"I'll tell him," I said, "but he won't listen. That guy is a crusader for justice and besides, he's coming up for re-election in a few months."

"You ought to come back here, Al," he said. "Be an honest, hard working cop again."

"I thought you were going to offer some incentive," I told him. "Inspector Martin got himself a new secretary yet?"

"No." He shook his head disgustedly. "The same old hairpins are still around his office."

"Then I'll stay with the Sheriff," I said. "The point is, how long will he stay with me?"

I went further down the corridor and into Ballistics.

"Ah!" Ray Morris said cheerfully. "Here comes Mr. Seduction himself. I can tell right now, without even looking, Lieutenant, that all blondes are lethal."

"There seems to be an air of disgusting good humor around this place today," I said. "What happened? The Inspector take sick and die?"

"It's the springtime, Al," he said. "But I guess you're getting too old to notice it anymore?"

I took the cartridge out of my pocket and put it on the bench in front of him. "What can you tell about that?" I asked.

Ray picked it up in his hand and tossed it up in the air and caught it a couple of times. "What do you want to know, Al?"

"Anything at all."

"It sure is king-sized," he said. "You'd only need one of these to punch a tunnel through a pine plank. I'll take a look."

He pulled a stand magnifier across the bench toward as him, then held the cartridge underneath the glass. "Six hundred caliber," he said. "You could stop an elephant with one of these. Foreign manufacture, made in Belgium." He straightened up again and tossed the cartridge into the air idly. "Mostly used for Continental rifles, Al. They're imported here; this caliber in a double-barrel would cost around a couple of thousand bucks, a very beautiful gun indeed."

"And this cartridge has never been used," I said. "It's making a lot of no sense."

"You couldn't use this one anyway," he said. "It's a dummy."

"How can you tell?" I asked suspiciously.

He tossed it up into the air again. "The weight, my boy, the weight. Much too light for its size."

"You sure it's a dummy?" I persisted.

"Am I, or am I not, the ballistics expert around this joint?" he asked coldly. "So all right, don't answer the question. You want me to strip it down and prove it to you?"

"Why not?" I said. "I wasn't going any place."

It took him a couple of seconds to strip the lead nose clear and then he showed me the empty case. "Now you satisfied?" he asked idly. "I am the guy who is never wrong, Wheeler, and you should ..." He stopped suddenly, frowning down at the empty case in his hand. "Wait a minute," he said, and put it back under the magnifier.

"Well?" I demanded.

"Well, well, well!" he murmured. He looked up at me and smiled weakly. "I am the guy who was only wrong once and that was just now. It's been fired all right."

"How could it have been fired? The lead nose is still in the cartridge."

The ballistics man scowled over the cartridge, shook his head. "Someone took a lot of trouble with this shell, Al," he said as he looked up from the cartridge case. "Someone with a lot of know-how, who took a lot of time finding the exact charge necessary." He shook his head. "A real expert."

"I don't get it."

Ray Morris straightened up. "A gun this caliber takes a heavy charge of powder to expel the bullet with enough force to stop an elephant or a lion—or whatever they happen to be hunting." He pointed to the lead nose. "As you know, in order to get accuracy with any rifle, the lead nose is forced into a pattern caused by the lands and grooves of the gun barrel. So, the bullet, made of softer metal than the barrel, is slightly larger in diameter."

I nodded, as though I knew what he was driving at.

"In a gun this size it takes a pretty heavy charge to squeeze a bullet that diameter into a narrower barrel." He shrugged. "So someone operated on the cartridge, left enough powder in it to explode, not enough to discharge the bullet. It took a lot of experimentation to find that happy formula."

"So what happened when the bullet was fired."

"I just told you. It made a bang, but the bullet didn't go any place."

I considered, almost blinked at the bright light that was forming in the back of my head. Ideas often had an effect like that. "Thanks, Ray," I said. "Thanks a lot."

"My pleasure," he said. "You want this back?"

"You could do me a favor," I said. "Put the bullet back in."

"O.K.," he said. "Maybe you can do me a favor sometime. Something in a brunette, about five-two and nicely stacked and oversexed, huh?"

"I'm sorry, Ray," I said sincerely. "I don't know any girls like that."

"That's another of my illusions shattered," he said bitterly. "The way I heard it was they start taking off their clothes when the name Wheeler is just mentioned. Then when they get to see you, they—" The phone rang suddenly and he picked it up. "Ballistics, Morris speaking." He listened, then handed me the phone. "For you," he said.

I took the phone and said, "Wheeler," into it.

"Listen carefully, Lieutenant," a muffled voice said in my ear. "I have vital evidence about the murder of Howard Davis. I can't speak freely now, but I shall call you at your apartment at nine tonight."

"Who is this speaking?" I asked.

"It doesn't matter," the voice said. "But if you want proof of the murderer's identity, be waiting beside your phone at nine tonight." I heard the click as whoever it was hung up.

"Say," Ray looked at me interestedly. "Was that a guy or a doll speaking then?"

"Your guess is as good as mine," I said miserably. "You ever get messages over your phone, Ray?"

"Sure," he said. "All the time. Like, 'Drop dead!' and 'You are now three months behind in your automobile payments and while this agency is reluctant etc.' You mean messages like that?"

"No," I said. "I almost wish they were messages like that."

"You can get them—easy!" he said. "All you got to do is get married!"

"It's not my fault I don't," I told him. "It's just that I haven't found a dame yet prepared to live in an Austin-Healey. I tell you, Ray, girls aren't what they used to be."

"I don't mind," he said wistfully. "Just so long as they're girls!"

Chapter Nine

"Martha Davis and Spouse" were having themselves a ball on the hi-fi machine and it was nice to listen to a couple of people named Davis who were very much alive. I stretched out in the armchair, a drink cradled in one hand, a cigarette in the other. I should have been relaxed but I wasn't. It was almost nine and the phone was right at my elbow.

The phone rang on the dot of nine. I grabbed it and said my name into the mouthpiece.

"Lieutenant," the same muffled voice said. "If you're quick, you can catch your murderer."

"What do I do?" I said. "Advertise?"

"He's stealing another corpse from the morgue at this very moment," the voice said. "If you're quick, you'll catch him there." And clunk went the receiver in my ear.

"Ah, nuts!" I said, and dropped the phone back onto the rest.

It sounded like a nut, or maybe it was Messenger John indulging his maniacal sense of humor, or maybe ... I picked up the phone again and dialed the morgue. I listened to the steady ring, but nobody answered. I called the operator and got her to check the number. She came back onto the line a few seconds later. "The line is in perfect order, sir," she said briskly. "Maybe there's no one home?"

"There should be a whole bunch of people there, and none of them going any place," I said. "But thanks all the same."

I got out of the apartment in record time to the Healey parked out front. It took maybe ten minutes to get to the morgue by disregarding lights. I left the car about twenty yards away from the front entrance and walked the rest.

The blue lamp over the entrance cast its usual cheery glow and I had the sudden nasty thought that if it were Bruno, the professional ghoul, complete with make-up who was inside the morgue, I was going to sign my resignation with a coronary occlusion.

I pushed the swing door open and stepped inside. The door swished shut again behind me, and suddenly the world was left to darkness and to me, as the poet said.

For maybe ten seconds I stood right where I was, waiting for my eyes to get used to the darkness. Then I remembered I was probably silhouetted against the swing doors by the outside light and I was a sitting duck for anybody else inside. I eased my gun out of the holster and thumbed back the safety and took a couple of steps into the complete darkness ahead of me.

If I'd brought a flashlight with me I could have used it, but I hadn't. I took another four steps and bumped against the front desk. I felt my way around it, through the gate to the door of the refrigeration room, which was open. I stepped inside, feeling the clammy coldness settle on my face, like the touch of disembodied hands.

I could feel the short hairs at the back of my neck beginning to prickle, and then I remembered Charlie Katz. The way I felt right then, if anything—anybody moved at all in the darkness up ahead, I was going to let it-them have the contents of the thirty-eight. And if it turned out to be Charlie Katz who moved, I was going to be embarrassed, if not sorry, afterwards. Not as sorry as he'd be maybe, but sorry.

"Charlie?" I said. "Charlie? Where the hell are you?"

The silence was unbroken. I shuffled forward another six feet and felt the edge of one of the cabinets with my left hand. The cabinets, with their refrigerated drawers and their contents I didn't care to think about, ran the length of both walls.

I kept on going, shuffling forward slowly, running my left hand along the drawer fronts, so I had some idea where I was. I was getting near to the end of the refrigeration room when it happened. There was no sound, no warning.

From nowhere, a pair of powerful hands encircled my throat and a deafening explosion pounded my ears as I pulled the trigger of the gun in an automatic reflex. I struggled wildly to breathe and then my head felt as if it were being lifted from my shoulders.

My feet left the ground and I threshed wildly, dropping the gun so I could use both hands to tear at the powerful hands that were slowly throttling me. I didn't get the chance to make an impression. There was a soft chuckle close to my ear and then another painful wrench to my neck as I was swung outward and upward. The hands released their grip suddenly and I had the terrifying feeling of flying through the darkness.

It didn't last long. I stopped suddenly and the darkness exploded into an exclusive Fourth of July fireworks display, and even if it only lasted for half a second, it was still exclusive. Then I quit fighting the darkness and joined it.

I opened my eyes and a blaze of light hit them cruelly, so I closed them tight shut again.

"Lieutenant!" An agitated voice said. "You all right, Lieutenant?"

I opened one eye cautiously and squinted up at the chalk-white face that stared down at me anxiously. "I'm dead," I told him. "Put me into a drawer and let's have some peace around here."

Then I realized what I was saying and sat bolt upright. "I'm kidding," I said quickly. "I feel fine!" The walls tilted inwards to an angle of forty-five degrees, spun briskly on their axis and tilted outward way beyond the vertical. I closed my eyes again quickly and waited. When I opened them up the walls were behaving themselves again.

"You look a mess, Lieutenant," Charlie Katz said, and he just missed on keeping the satisfaction out of his voice.

I looked at the purple bruise on his forehead, surmounted by the jagged cut that was still oozing blood. "What do you think *you* look like?" I asked him. "A movie profile?"

I started a slow, complicated campaign with the objective of getting to my feet. It succeeded finally, and looked myself over. My suit was never going to be the same again, not with both knees ripped out of the pants and the long diagonal tear across the front of the coat. The more important problem was to find out if *I'd* ever be the same again. I moved my arms and legs cautiously and they resented it, but they did move. I put both hands on my neck and moved that slowly. If it didn't make a loud crunching sound, it sure felt as if it did. It was tender to the touch, and the only thing separating my head and shoulders was one big ache. But it wasn't dislocated apparently.

"Your face is a mess, Lieutenant," Charlie repeated. "I got a mirror in my locker, you want to take a look?"

"Yeah," I said. "And don't you have a bottle some place for emergencies like this?"

"All right," he said sourly. "But just don't forget rye doesn't grow on trees, Lieutenant!"

He opened his locker and took out a near-full bottle of rye and a couple of glasses. While he poured the whisky I took a look at my face in the mirror. I had to admit that Charlie hadn't exaggerated any. It was a mess. There was a cut over my right eyebrow which was trickling blood down that side of my face and onto the collar of my shirt. There was a large bump dead center of my forehead which was changing color as I watched. A half-inch of skin had been neatly scraped from the base of my chin and the graze looked red and sore.

I stopped looking before I got discouraged, and gratefully accepted the glass from Charlie. The whisky did me good. I lit a cigarette when I'd drained the glass and asked Charlie what happened.

"I quit," he said without hesitation. "Twice in one week. Lieutenant, that's too much."

"Sure," I agreed. "But what happened?"

"Same thing as last time," he said bitterly. "I hear a knock on the door but nobody comes in—so I go outside to see who it is. I get my head outside the door and—Pow!"

"You're right, Charlie," I said. "You want to quit before it gets to be a habit."

"What happened to you?" he asked, and I told him about the phone call, how I'd tried the morgue's number, then come to take a look myself.

Charlie didn't look pleased at my gallantry in attempting a lone rescue. "If you were any ordinary cop," he said, "you would've got three carloads of cops down here and surrounded the place. That way you would have got the guy cold."

"You don't have to remind me," I said. "I never think of those things till afterward."

"You take the Lone Ranger," Charlie said sullenly, "Even a guy like *him*—he's got Tonto along with him all the time!"

"You're so right, Charlie!" I said. "But you want to quit being so right, right now, because I'll slug you if you don't."

"Shouldn't you report this?" he asked frostily. "Or doesn't anybody care about me getting beaten up all the time?"

"I don't," I said. "But maybe there's somebody who does. You'd better check and see if there's anything missing first."

"I guess so," he said reluctantly.

I watched him as he opened and closed each drawer methodically in turn. There was a moment when he had his back to me and I sneaked another couple of inches of rye into my glass. Finally he came back and shook his head. "Nothing missing, Lieutenant," he said. "It doesn't make sense."

"Sure it does," I said smugly. "Wheeler to the rescue. I got here too fast, he didn't have time to do whatever it was he was going to do. I scared him off."

Charlie looked morosely at my battered face. "I'm sure glad you didn't really frighten him, Al," he said. "It might have killed you."

"Anyway," I said modestly. "It was me that stopped him."

"I don't ..." He stopped suddenly, looking at my glass suspiciously. "I thought you finished your drink a little while back?"

"Does it look like it?" I asked him coldly.

He grabbed the rye bottle and held it up to the light, peering at it closely. "You lousy bum," he said wrathfully, "You sneaked some more while my back was turned!"

"How can you tell?" I asked interestedly.

"I mark off the new level with a pencil every time I take a drink," he said. "What do you think I am—made of money or something? I can't afford to finance your alcoholism!"

"Don't be so cheap, Charlie!" I told him. "Remember, I probably saved your life. If I hadn't disturbed the guy in here so he had to run out, then maybe—"

"What time did you say you got that call?" He interrupted rudely. "Nine o'clock?"

"Sure, nine o'clock. As I was saying, Charlie, it was—"

"You didn't disturb him," Charlie said contemptuously. "I just checked what time it was when he knocked on the door, and it was just about eight-thirty. You couldn't have got here in much under a quarter-hour. That gave him forty-five minutes to do whatever he wanted to do."

"Maybe we'd better check those drawers again, Charlie," I said humbly.

"I already checked them," he said coldly. "And nothing is missing."

"How many clients you got in here?"

"Five," he said. "Been a busy week."

"I guess I could check the occupied drawers over," I said. "Point them out to me."

He pointed them out to me. The first one was the body that had been stolen and finished up inside the studios. The next one was an old man. I opened the third drawer and Thelma Davis stared at me with that wide-eyed stare of disbelief I'd seen seven hours before. I closed the drawer again hastily.

The fourth one was Howard Davis. I went to close the drawer, then noticed the stain on the sheet over his chest.

"Don't you use clean sheets for each new arrival?" I said disgustedly. "That's the least you can do, Charlie."

"Of course I do!" he said. "What the hell do think I am—a guy with no respect for the dead?"

"You goofed on this one," I told him.

"Show me!" he said angrily. I pointed out the brownish stain and he colored. "I can't figure out how that happened," he said. "That was a clean sheet all right, fresh from the laundry, when he went into that drawer." He leaned further forward. "Hey," he said softly. "There's something screwy going on here."

He took hold of the edge of the sheet and pulled it down abruptly. Then he gurgled softly in his throat. I stared down at the gaping hole in Davis' chest, then turned away quickly. Charlie leaned against the cabinet, his eyes bulging wildly, his face turning a delicate shade of green.

I slammed the drawer shut and got to the rye bottle at exactly the same time as he did. He was so shaken he didn't even argue when I refilled both glasses to the brim.

When I'd finished the rye I looked at Charlie and saw he'd also finished his, but it didn't look like it had helped him any. His face was the same color, his eyes still bulged.

"Snap out of it, Charlie," I said. "Sure, it was a hell of a shock, but you must have seen worse things than that."

He shook his head mutely and muttered something.

"For crying out loud!" I said impatiently. "I thought you were the one guy who couldn't be surprised!"

His lips trembled. "Didn't you see?" he whispered.

"Sure, I saw it. Whoever the guy is, he must be crazy to cut a hole in the chest of a corpse."

Charlie's head shook feebly. "Then you didn't see," he said. "You didn't notice what had gone!"

"Gone?" I fought down the impulse to bust him one on the nose. "What had gone?"

"The heart," Charlie whispered fearfully. "He cut the heart right out of the body—he must have taken it with him!"

Chapter Ten

Prudence Calthorpe opened the door of her penthouse suite and looked at me with mild surprise. "You should have told me you were coming, Al," she said lightly. "I would have boiled a cauldron."

"I see you're still a transparent witch," I said. "Or maybe the word is 'bitch?'"

She wore a nylon negligee over nothing and there was visible proof of that statement. "Something wrong, Al?" she asked innocently. "The police ball been postponed again—real trouble like that?"

"Did you watch when those people jumped out the window in Miami?" I said. "Or were you laughing too hard at the time. Hearing them splatter onto the sidewalk must have given you a hell of a kick!"

She smiled coolly. "You sound like you're annoyed about something." Then she took a closer look at me. "Al!" Her voice was concerned. "You've been hurt! Come right in and I'll fix it for you."

She took my arm and guided me to the nearest armchair in the living room, then pushed me down into it. You just sit right there," she said. "I'll make you a drink, and then I'll get started on the cleaning-up operations."

I got the drink in double-quick time, then she disappeared for a couple of minutes and came back looking like Florence Nightingale. At least in the supplies she carried, if not in the costume. She bathed my face, dried up the cut with a styptic pencil, and gently rubbed an antiseptic cream into the graze on my chin. She wanted to paint out the bruise on my forehead with a pancake make-up, but I told her the hell with it—she should have seen the other guy. I wished I had—just once.

Pru cleared away the surgical equipment, made me another drink, and one for herself. She sat down opposite me on the couch with a look of wide-eyed interest on her face. "Tell me all about it, Al," she said. "What happened?"

"You're cute!" I said. "I bet this appeals to that macabre sense of humor of yours. Playing nurse and cleaning off my face. You're the first Charles Addams character I ever met that stepped right out of the cartoon and slammed my head into a bucket of dirty water."

Her green eyes blinked slowly, but the spark was there, in back of them, and getting larger all the time. "Are you sure you feel all right, Al?" she asked anxiously. "You must have had an awful beating. I mean with the way your face looked when you came in, and your suit's nearly ripped to pieces!"

"I feel fine," I said, and tried not to wince as the muscles in my neck caught fire again.

I got up onto my feet and walked over to the bar and leaned against it. "Did you get it in an air-tight bottle of formalin?" I asked her. "Or are you waiting until you can have one blown in the shape of a tennis racket?"

She frowned slightly. "What are you talking about?"

"Howard Davis' heart," I said. "The prize piece of your collection. You should have seen the way he looked after the removal—it was something to keep you awake nights."

"I still don't know what the hell you're talking about," she said coldly. "You're either crazy or you got hit on the head a little too hard tonight. Why don't you go home and sleep it off?"

"Jonathan Blake told me about you and your practical jokes," I said. "And this one was a riot. You hire Messenger John to get you a new item for your collection, then call me and use a phony voice to tell me somebody's busting into the morgue and here is my big chance to be a hero."

"You're out of your mind!" she said crisply.

I finished my drink and put the empty glass down on the bar top. "You know something," I told her. "I'm mad at you, Prudence Calthorpe. I am also a very tired and very sore character—I have my bruises to prove it. Also, I am not in the mood to play games. It was Messenger John you hired to hack out your new treasure for you, wasn't it?"

"You are a slob, Wheeler," she said in a sneering voice, "and now you're becoming a tiresome slob. Crawl out of here and cry your eyes out some place else, Wheeler; you're beginning to look like the original 'Brother, Can You Spare a Dime?,' character!"

"That's all I need," I said.

I walked across to the bedroom and pushed the door open, then went inside. The medieval brick still stood on end beside the barbershop quartet on top of the bureau. I went across to the bureau and picked it up.

"Al!" Pru said tautly from behind me. "What do you think you're doing?"

"You still deny you organized the setup in the morgue tonight?" I asked. "You still say I'm out of my mind?"

"I don't know anything about it," she said. "If you think I do, then you are out of your mind!"

I raised the brick a couple of feet in the air, then smashed it down onto the bureau. Minute fragments of the first shrunken head fluttered slowly down to the floor.

"That takes care of Eeny," I said. "Now it's Meeny's turn next."

"Al!" she shrieked. "You're insane! I paid two thousand dollars each for those heads. They aren't native heads at all; they were white men, Portuguese traders who got lost in the—"

"Who cares?" I snarled. "This is the Wheeler memory-improving course. How did the first lesson affect you?"

She grabbed my arm with both hands and tried to pull me away from the bureau. I short-armed her in the midriff with my elbow and she moaned, then let go my arm suddenly.

I watched her stagger across the room, bent double with both arms wrapped around her middle. "You remember now that you did organize my night out in the morgue?" I asked. She spat one word at me, and from whatever angle you looked at it, it still didn't add up to "yes."

"O.K.," I said. "If you want to do this the hard way, it's your grief, not mine. Here goes Meeny!" I smashed the brick down on top of the second shrunken head and it powdered into a fine and faintly repulsive looking dust.

"All you have to do is admit it," I said. "And you can save some of your collection anyway. When I'm through with Miny and Mo I'm going to set fire to that old black satin of Lizzie's and then put Kubla's claw through the ice-crusher. For a switch, with the brick, I'm—"

"All right, damn you!" she said through clenched teeth.

"You see," I said, pleased. "Only the second lesson, and it's done wonders for your memory already."

"Damn you to hell and gone!" she sobbed. "I wish Messenger John had killed you tonight!"

"It wasn't his fault he didn't," I said. "Let's start at the beginning, shall we?"

"I organized it," she snarled. "I admit it. What else do you want?"

"A little cooperation," I told her, and raised the brick over Miny's unsuspecting head.

"Don't!" she yelled.

"From the beginning?" I queried.

"From the beginning," she repeated murderously. "I called Messenger John this afternoon and told him I wanted Davis' heart for my collection. I said I'd pay ten thousand dollars cash for it. He raised me to fifteen and I agreed, then ..."

"Pru," I said. "You weren't listening, I said from the beginning."

"I'm telling it from the beginning, damn you!"

"The first corpse that left the morgue and nearly became a television star," I said. "Tell me about that."

She straightened up slowly, her eyes very wide open indeed. "The first corpse?" she whispered.

"It's fairly obvious, even to a tiresome slob like me," I said. "You and your sense of the macabre, your practical jokes, your determination that your sister Penny just wasn't going to make good in television if you could do anything to stop it. So you came up with a brilliant idea. You knew one of the props was a coffin with a papier-mâché monster inside, and the climax of their act was to be when Penny removed the coffin lid and revealed the monster inside.

"So you hired somebody to steal a real corpse from the morgue and substitute it for the dummy in the coffin. From your angle, it would be a riot to watch your sister's face when she whipped off the lid and a real corpse stared her in the face—and you figured it would fix the television show, too."

"But it went wrong," she said dully. "When she took the lid off the coffin, it was Howard Davis' body inside, not the one from the morgue."

"You hired Messenger John to steal the body in the first place?" I asked.

"Messenger John," she nodded. "He'd fixed a couple of things for us. You know about them—both our divorces. Almost as soon as we arrived here, he called me to let me know he was here. If I needed any little service done, he said, he'd be happy to do it."

"O.K.," I said. "Let's get to the real interest. How did Davis' body get switched with the girl's?"

"I don't know," she said.

"Don't make me go through the brick routine again, Pru," I pleaded. "It's getting monotonous."

"Al, please!" she said desperately. "You have to believe me, I'm telling you the truth. I don't know how it happened. It's been worrying me ever since. It had to be Messenger John who did it, but I wouldn't dare ask him about it."

"Why not?"

She shuddered. "I saw him once when he got really mad about something. He punched his fist through a quarter-inch plate-glass window. He's completely different from other people; he doesn't have any conscience, any feelings toward other human beings at all. He has just one interest and that's making money; it's become an obsession with him. I think by now he's probably got all the money he'll ever need. But he keeps wanting more and more. And he'll do anything to get it."

"Sure," I said. "He scares me to death, too."

She rubbed her midriff tenderly. "Could we go back to the other room, Al? I need a drink the worst possible way."

"O.K.," I said. I tossed the brick onto the bed and followed her out of the room.

Pru got as far as the couch and collapsed onto it limply. "I'm sorry," she said tremulously. "Would you mind making the drinks. I don't think I could right now."

I went over to the bar and made the drinks and brought them back to the couch. I sat beside her and gave her a drink.

"Thanks," she said. She smiled faintly. "I guess it was me who turned out to be the slob after all."

"I'll believe you about not knowing how Davis' body got into that coffin," I said. "For now, anyway. Let's get back to the setup tonight. You really wanted his heart for your collection?"

Pru shuddered violently. "Of course I didn't. Only a maniac would take me seriously—a maniac like Messenger John. I knew if I offered enough money, he'd do it Then I called you and disguised my voice with a handkerchief over the mouthpiece. That's the way they always do it in the movies, isn't it?"

"Corny, but it works," I agreed. "What was the idea? A practical joke and if one of us got killed that made even funnier?"

"Al,"—she sounded genuinely surprised—"I never dreamed you'd go out there alone. I thought you'd naturally take a posse of police officers with you. You'd catch Messenger John in the act, and you'd put him behind bars."

"Why were you so anxious to see Messenger John under wraps?" I said.

She shivered and drank some of the neat Scotch I'd given her. "I don't trust him," she said. "He must have switched those two bodies, and I don't know why. It's been worrying me all along. I thought maybe he was trying to make me a suspect for Howard's murder. He might even be trying to pin it on me somehow. So I had to do something about him— in case he was already doing something to me."

"It makes a sort of screwball sense," I said grudgingly "Finish your drink."

"What's the rush?"

"Finish it!" I snarled. She shrugged her shoulders, then obediently drained the glass.

I took hold of her elbow and pushed her up onto her feet, then walked her toward the front door. "Al!" She struggled ineffectually. "I told you the truth, all of it. I swear it! You aren't going to arrest me now, not after …"

"Relax!" I said. "We're going visiting, that's all. Only down to the ninth floor; we'll be there in a couple of minutes."

"Penny?" she said tensely. "What are we going to see her for?"

"I'm in the mood for girlish confidences," I said. "Let's go see if she's got any."

I walked her down to the elevator and pressed the button. The door opened a few seconds later and we stepped inside.

"Nine," I said to the uniformed kid who was running the cage. He looked at Pru's negligee which showed her breasts in sharp relief with a sculptor's accuracy, then he stared open-mouthed at my face. His mouth fell open another inch when he saw the tear in my jacket and the ripped knees of my pants.

"The ninth floor is that one right between eight and ten," I told him. "And if you don't take that idiot look off your face and get this elevator moving, I'll push my hand down your throat and tear out your spleen!"

"Yessir!" he gurgled and the elevator plunged downward, then came to an abrupt stop at the ninth floor. I pushed Pru out, and I was going to follow her when I felt a nervous hand on my arm. I looked down into the kid's wondering eyes. "Excuse the question mister," he said nervously. "You on your honeymoon?"

"How did you guess?" I said confidentially. "We haven't eaten for a week."

I pushed Pru along to the door of Penny's suite and knocked loudly. Nothing happened and I gave it another twenty seconds and still nothing happened. "Rhythm and Blues" didn't fit my mood right then, so I started in kicking the door down. On the second kick it opened suddenly and I nearly dislocated my kneecap on the upswing of my leg.

Penny jumped backward with one convulsive leap and the toe of my shoe missed her right shin by six inches. I did an impromptu cha-cha step and regained my balance.

"Never a dull moment!" Pru said, then gurgled helplessly. "The Astaire of the Sheriff's office—ballet by request!"

"Very funny!" I growled and jerked her elbow so she stumbled forward into the suite.

I followed her and closed the door behind me. Penny still stood there, staring blankly at us. I returned the stare with interest and maybe we could have made a thing out of just standing there looking at each other, but Pru broke it up.

Penny looked at her twin sister with a penetrating stare. "What a coincidence, darling, here we are both in our flimsies, but at least I haven't been running around the hotel in mine."

"You shouldn't do it, darling." Prudence smiled viciously. "Although it does accentuate the Oriental influence, I have to admit. You've been collecting Chinese jade for so long you're beginning to look like one."

Two bright red spots burned high on Penny's cheeks, "I think you should cover yourself up a little, darling, but then I suppose your figure is the best practical joke you've ever had!"

"I shouldn't get mad at you, darling," Prudence said sweetly. "After all, I know you're only doing it for Jonathan's sake. You want to be his little Chinese jade, sit cross-legged on the floor and fry him some rice and hope if it burns he'll beat you with his elephant whip. Don't worry, darling—he will!"

"You lying ..." Penny dissolved into tears.

She turned and ran into the bedroom, slamming the door behind her. Pru walked over to the bar and set up three glasses in a businesslike fashion. "I don't know why we're here," she said, "but we might as well have a drink."

"Sure," I said.

Ice dropped into the glasses while she watched me the whole time out of the corner of her eyes. "Whatever it is you brought me down here for, it's not going to be pleasant, is it, Al?" she asked cautiously.

"Depends on your idea of fun," I said. "You've an original approach to that, you have to admit it."

She pulled the cork viciously from the neck of a new bottle of Scotch. "I can't stand you when you're smug like this, Al Wheeler!" she said furiously. "I'd like to have you tied hand and foot for ten minutes; I'd wipe that stupid grin right off your face!"

The door of the bedroom opened and Penny came back into the living room. She'd put on a heavy quilted robe over the nightgown, which made her look like a new bride out of the pages of one of the women's magazines.

"Jonathan isn't here," she said defiantly to me. "If he was, you wouldn't have dared force your way in here and try to kick me on your way in!"

"What are you drinking, darling?" Pm asked her.

"Anything!" Penny said in a tragic voice. "Give me something strong, darling, my nerves are in pieces!"

I slumped into the nearest armchair and lit a cigarette. Pru distributed the drinks, then perched on the arm of a chair opposite me. Penny stood with the drink in her hand for a long moment, then sat down primly on the couch, facing me. She adjusted the hem of the robe carefully so that I couldn't even see her ankles. "If there's any reason for your visit, Lieutenant," she said coldly, "would you please come straight to the point so we can get it over with quickly? I'm terribly tired; I'd just gone to bed when you started kicking the door down!"

"Right to the point," I agreed. "Pru's just been telling me some of her girlish secrets and I figured you ought to hear them."

"My God!" Pru closed her eyes. "I hope you know what you're doing, Wheeler!"

"I have a fair idea," I said.

Penny listened in stony silence while I told her how Pru had hired Messenger John to steal a corpse from the morgue and place it in the coffin instead of the dummy.

"Tell Penny why you went to all that trouble," I told Pru. "I bet she's dying to hear your reasons."

"I'll get even with you, Wheeler, if it takes me the rest of my life!" Pru said darkly.

"Sure," I said. "Are you going to tell her, or would you rather I told her?"

"It doesn't make much difference," she said wearily. She bared her teeth at Penny. "You see, darling, I was determined to wreck your television launching, one way or another. And this seemed as good a way as any."

Penny's face was a bright scarlet. "You bitch!" she said tightly. "You conniving, scheming, dirty ..."

"I wouldn't go on, if I were you, darling," Pru said softly. "Because if you do, I shall push your teeth in."

"Jealousy!" Penny said dramatically. "That insane jealousy of yours! Ever since we were kids, you couldn't stand me to do anything better than you. You used to plot against me even when we were at school together. You even tried to turn Father against me when I married Howard!"

"I didn't have to try, darling!" Pru said with vicious sweetness. "The most damning thing against Howard was Howard himself. I know how big muscles always affect you, darling, but you didn't have to marry the bum. You could have taken him to Florida, given him a hundred dollars a week spending money, and he would have been happy. All he ever wanted was a comfortable life without having to do any work for it."

"Maybe Howard was ... what you say," Penny said, her voice shaking. "But I got rid of him. You were lucky enough to marry a wonderful man and then fool enough to throw him away."

"You can't mean Jonathan, darling?" The disbelief in Pru's voice sounded almost genuine. "Not old Heap Big White Hunter bum, who went broke shooting everything in sight all over the world! Not old Jungle Jonathan, the cold-shower-every-morning-before-breakfast man? ... You're kidding, darling, of course?"

"That's what I'd expect from you!" Penny said, her voice quivering with fury. "You and your dirty little mind. You can't help lying, can you, even when you're talking about a kind and generous man like Jonathan!"

"I said nothing but the truth, darling," Pm said languidly. "Which part did you think was a lie—the cold showers? It's true—every morning he sticks that manly chest under for ten minutes exactly, no more, no less. A creature of habit, but I can tell you how to please him. Just let your hair grow out straight, dye it black and have it cut with a fringe. Get a really good suntan, wear your Oriental clothes and if you can speak with a slight lisp—well, he'll hardly notice the difference between you and a genuine Chinese or Japanese girl, will he?"

"Shut up!" Penny screamed wildly.

"Darling,"—Pru sounded concerned for her sister—"I only wanted to prove to you I'm not lying. I wasn't lying about him being broke, either. Sure, he did have some money; his father left him a very healthy pile. But safariing around the world in the style to which Jonathan accustomed himself can be awfully expensive, and he'd been doing it for years, before he met me. Why do you think I went to Messenger John to organize the divorce? I had another Howard on my hands, darling."

"You're lying!" Penny said faintly.

"Nothing but the truth, darling," Pru repeated. "But don't let it worry you. After all, you have plenty of money, enough for both of you. And if you don't want to spend the rest of your life tramping around jungles and counting up the dead animals he stockpiles everywhere, you needn't. Buy him a small private jungle somewhere and stock it with wild game, employ a couple of pretty Japanese maids, and Jonathan will be content to stay home for the rest of his life!"

Penny got up with an animal snarl and launched herself at Pru's throat. Pru screamed once as she was knocked off the arm of the chair, and there was a nasty thump as they both hit the floor.

They rolled over and over across the carpet, kicking, biting, scratching, pulling each other's hair and both of them screaming at the top of their voices. I stood it for as long as I could, but three minutes was plenty.

I went over to the bar and filled a deep jug with ice water and took it with me to where the twin sisters lay locked together, with Penny doing her damnedest to scratch Pru's eyes out, and Pru, with both hands buried in Penny's glorious auburn hair, doing her damnedest to pull the lot out by the roots. And squealing the whole time.

I aimed the jug carefully, then tipped it slowly and a steady cascade of ice water descended on the pair of them. The squeals stopped suddenly as they gasped for breath. I poured until the jug was empty.

They rolled apart and Pru dragged herself into a sitting position and looked at me balefully. I could see only half of one eye because of the hair that straggled down across her face. The negligee had been ripped clean off her back and she was naked to the waist. Four thin red lines raked across her breast showed where Penny's nails had scored.

Penny staggered to her feet and began to cry softly like a little girl.

Her hair looked like the stuff the birds build their nest with, and her right eye was swollen and discoloring quickly. The quilted robe had been ripped open down the front, and underneath, the fragile nightgown had been also ripped, down to just below her waist, leaving her perfectly-formed pink-tipped right breast completely bare. She covered it awkwardly with her right arm and hobbled back to the couch.

I walked over and stood in front of her. "O.K., Penny," I said. "The fun is over, so now let's get down to business." She looked up at me dully through her tears. "Go 'way!" she said in a muffled voice.

"Howard Davis knew something," I said. "Something about you that could stop your marriage to Blake. He followed you down here, threatened he'd reveal his secret. Maybe he wanted money—even remarriage could have been his price. You were crazy about Blake, so you'd do anything to get rid of Howard Davis. So you hired Messenger John to murder him. And Messenger John, having already been hired by Pru to substitute the morgue corpse for the dummy, had a brilliant idea. By pulling a double switch and putting Howard's body in the coffin, he solved the problem of what to do with the corpse after he murdered him, and he made it look as if somebody was trying to implicate you in the murder."

"No," Penny cried out hoarsely. "It's not true. Not a word of it."

"Maybe you can convince a jury of that," I told her. "I warned you that all I needed to take you for it was the motive. Now I have that—both for Howard's murder and for the murder of his ex-wife Thelma."

"You must be crazy. Why would I kill Thelma?"

"Because whatever Howard was trying to blackmail you with, he shared his secret with Thelma. She told me this morning that she had something that would bring the sky down on top of the Calthorpe family and you in particular. When you killed him you didn't know he'd told his first wife what he knew, did you?

"She called you sometime after I left here this morning. I'd told you about her and booked her a place in the morgue at the same time, but I didn't know it then. When she called you arranged to meet her somewhere in your car. Then you called Messenger John and had him keep the appointment for you."

Pru limped across the floor toward me. "It's not true, Al," she said in a low voice. "It couldn't be—not Penny. She's not built that way. She's weak and selfish and sometimes she's stupid. But she's not a cold-blooded killer! I don't believe it."

"It'll be the jury's opinion that counts," I said curtly. I looked down at Penny again. "You'd better get dressed."

She shook her head frantically. "No! Listen, please! Just for a minute.

I'll tell you the truth!"

"I'm wasting my time," I said indifferently. "But I'll give you a minute."

"I hadn't seen or heard from Howard since our divorce," she said, speaking rapidly, with a painful intensity in each word. "There was no secret he knew about me—Thelma Davis must have said that, hoping you'd believe it, so it would hurt me. She always hated me for taking Howard from her.

"The night of the television show, I was here alone. I was nervous about my first appearance in front of the cameras and was trying to rest before I left for the studios. It was a little after eight. There was a knock on the door and I thought it was Jonathan come to wish me luck, so I ran over to the door and opened it.

"As I opened it I heard a shot. Howard Davis was standing there outside." She shuddered silently. "I opened the door wide, and he sort of half-turned toward me, then fell into the room. For a moment I didn't know what had happened. I knelt down beside him and then I saw the bullet hole and I knew he was dead. His legs were in the way, so I pulled them to one side and closed the door."

"Your minute's up," I said. "You want to get dressed now?"

"Please!" she said hysterically. "Hear me out! I was going to call the police but then I realized what it would mean. It would be the end of the television contract and any hopes I might have of breaking into show business. I thought about it some more, and then I wondered if the police would believe me anyway. Howard was my ex-husband, I was about to marry another man. They could believe that we'd had a terrific row and I'd shot him."

"So what did you do about him?" I asked impatiently.

"I ... I called Messenger John," she said. "I told him what had happened and asked him to get Howard's body out of the hotel and put it somewhere else. He said he would, for twenty thousand dollars. I agreed to the price, I would have agreed to anything, right then.

"He got here about half an hour later, and he brought a trunk with him. He put Howard inside the trunk and locked it, then he called the bell captain and said I had a trunk to be taken down to his car and would the captain send two men to carry it, because it was heavy. Then Messenger John made us both a drink and we were talking polite conversation over cocktails when the bellhops came up for the trunk."

I lit a cigarette. "Is that all?"

"There's more," she said in a small voice. "He didn't tell me he was going to put Howard's body into the coffin, and when I lifted the lid and saw it I nearly died. When you questioned me I couldn't think straight, so I denied I knew who it was. Then you came here and told me you'd identified the body and you knew I must be lying—you frightened me, Lieutenant." She smiled wanly. "You don't know just how much you frightened me then. After you'd gone, I called Messenger John and told him what had happened. I said he'd got to do something to help me; the way things were going, I thought you'd arrest me for murder at any moment."

"And Messenger John came to the rescue?" I said.

Penny nodded slowly. "He said he could take care of it for me, but it would be very difficult and very dangerous for him. He was prepared to take the risk and give me his personal guarantee that I would be freed of suspicion, for fifty thousand dollars."

"You paid?"

"I paid," Penny said limply. "I gave him a check two hours later."

The lights seemed to dim suddenly and her face went out of focus. I shook my head a couple of times, and things reverted to normal.

"Are you feeling all right, Al?" Pru asked.

"I'm fine," I said. "Could you get me a glass of water?"

There was a sudden silence. I looked across at her and she swallowed twice, "You're kidding!" she said feebly.

"The hell I am!" I said irritably. "What's with the water in this place, anyway?"

"No Scotch on the rocks, a little soda?" she persisted.

"All I want is a glass of water—iced!" I snarled. "If it's such a big deal, call room service!"

"Al," she said firmly. "You're sick!"

I watched her limp over to the bar and get the water.

"Lieutenant?" a small voice said, and I looked down at Penny again. She hesitated for a moment: "Are you still going to arrest me?" she asked in a small voice.

"I don't think so," I told her.

Her shoulders slumped in relief. "You believe I told you the truth?"

"Yeah," I said. "It figures."

Pru put the glass of water into my hand and I drank it gratefully and gave her back the empty glass. She still looked at me steadily. "It's quite a technique you have, Lieutenant!" she said coldly.

"Technique?"

"Strictly terrorist," she said. "You got the truth out of me by smashing the only thing I value—my collection. Then you dragged me down here and used me as bait to trigger off Penny into an emotional frenzy. And when that was done, you had her in just the right state of nervous tension to let loose your broadside. You said you were booking her for both murders and you played it as if you really meant it. You had me fooled! So the only thing left that she could do was tell you the truth, and that was all you wanted in the first place!"

"You're just too smart for me, Prudence Calthorpe," I said. "Thanks to both of you for everything. It's been a most exciting evening, and I *did* enjoy the wrestling. Now, if you'll excuse me, I have to go see a man about a message."

I turned to walk to the front door and had taken three steps when for no good reason my knees buckled underneath me suddenly and I sat on the floor.

"Al!" Pru ran over and knelt beside me. "You are sick!"

"I'm fine," I said. "A little overtired maybe. I'll just sit here for a while, then ..." I peered at the dim veil she'd suddenly tossed over her face. "Will you keep your head still while I'm talking to you!"

"I didn't move, Al."

"Yeah?" I said scornfully. "And I guess those walls aren't bending outward, either?"

Her face disappeared completely and I felt a gentle bump on the back of my head—now they couldn't even keep the floor still! A wave of blackness floated gently by and I dived into it happily.

Chapter Eleven

I opened my eyes and blinked at the bright sunlight that poured into the room. I looked around slowly. It was a bedroom, that was sure because I was sleeping in a bed. But I didn't recognize the bedroom.

The watch on my wrist said ten after nine, and for a moment it didn't register. Then it did—I must have slept for at least eight hours. I pushed back the covers and leapt out of the bed onto the deep-piled rug.

Directly in front of me stood a wild-eyed guy, stark naked, with a deep scowl on his face. I backed off instinctively and he did exactly the same. Then I grinned encouragingly at him and got an answering grin.

"Wheeler," I said. "This is a full-length mirror and that's you in there I'm talking to. And what the hell happened to my clothes!"

I looked around but there was no sign of them in the room. A door opened behind me and Pru's voice said brightly, "Good morn ... oh!"

One convulsive leap took me back under the covers again. I clutched a sheet to my chin and scowled at her. "What the hell goes on around here!"

"You don't remember," she said. "I can understand that. You just passed out last night, Al. I think you didn't realize just how bad a beating you took in the morgue, and then you drank a lot of whisky afterward, and I guess even you picked up some of that high-charged nervous tension that was being kicked around."

"So I passed out," I said. "How did I get into this bed?"

"We put you there," she said. "You were obviously exhausted and sleep was the one thing you needed."

"We?"

"Penny and myself," she said.

"What happened to my clothes?"

"You couldn't go to bed fully dressed, could you?"

"I didn't have to go to bed stark naked, either!" I snorted. "Who took my clothes off—Penny and you?"

"Penny was much too modest," she said easily. "So she left after the shoes were removed. But I'm just a nature girl and natural things always interest me. You have the cutest mole in the silliest place! Did you know that, Al?"

"I want my clothes!" I bellowed. "I want to get out of here—now! I've got things to do I should have done last night. Bring me my clothes, damn you!"

"That's a charming way to express your thanks," she said coldly. "You couldn't wear that suit again in any case—it was hopelessly torn. I threw it away."

I choked. "You—what!"

"Don't give yourself an ulcer," she said calmly. "The keys to your apartment were in your pocket, so I went over there early this morning and picked up a change of clothing for you. I even remembered the razor and toothbrush."

"Well, thanks," I mumbled. "Why didn't you say so in the first place?"

"Terrorist tactics." She smiled happily. "You taught me, remember?"

She went out of the room and came back a few seconds later with a bundle of clothes in her arms, which she dropped at the foot of the bed. "The bathroom is right next door. What do you want for breakfast?"

"I don't have time for breakfast!" I said sourly. "Well—a cup of coffee."

"You'll only fold up on somebody else's floor," she said sternly. "Fresh fruit, scrambled eggs and toast for you!"

"I never eat breakfast," I said. "It's a disgusting habit to get into. You start eating breakfast and before you know where you are, you're getting up two hours earlier and doing exercises to work up an appetite for the breakfast you don't want anyway!"

"I'll call room service," she said, unconvinced, and walked out of the bedroom again.

I got out of bed and checked the clothes she'd brought me. The tie could have been better matched, but otherwise she'd done a good job. I pulled on the pants of the fresh suit, picked up the razor and toothbrush and scuttled through to the bathroom.

Twenty minutes later I took another look in the full-length mirror and thought there was an improvement. The cut across my forehead didn't look too bad—the purple egg underneath it didn't help any though. The square of grazed skin looked red and tender, but it felt O.K. My neck still ached and was stiffening rapidly, but the fierce pain there had been the night before was gone.

I walked out into the living room and realized this was still Penny's suite; it was the bedroom that had me fooled.

Room service had been and gone. A small table was set for three in the center of the room and when I saw the fresh peaches waiting for me, suddenly I realized I was hungry.

Pru and Penny were sat opposite each other at the table, leaving a vacant space for me in between them. Penny smiled at me as I sat down. "How do you feel this morning, Lieutenant?"

"Fine," I said. "Where did you sleep last night?"

"I shared Pru's bedroom," she said. "You take cream in your coffee, Lieutenant?"

"No, thanks," I said.

I ate the fruit, the scrambled eggs, three slices of toast. Prudence looked at me across the table. "For a man who doesn't eat breakfast, you sure could have fooled me!" she said.

"You went to all that trouble," I said. "I couldn't not eat it and besides, I was hungry. Excuse me." I got up. "I have to catch up on a few things," I said. "Thanks again."

"It was a pleasure," they said simultaneously, then looked at each other and smiled.

"What gives with this sisterly accord?" I asked suspiciously. "Last night it was a fight to the death!"

"That was nothing," Pru said calmly. "We always have fights, but they don't mean anything."

"Not a thing," Penny echoed.

"Well, thanks again," I said and headed for the door.

"Wait a minute, Lieutenant!" Penny said anxiously and ran into the bedroom.

She came out again a moment later, holding my shoulder harness gingerly between two fingers, with the thirty-eight sagging in its holster. "You mustn't forget this!" she said playfully. "I put it away in one of the bureau drawers last night."

"Thanks," I said and took it from her. I took my coat and Pru's fingers whisked it away from me. "Let me hold that," she smiled.

"O.K.," I grunted. I put on the harness and adjusted it carefully, then she handed me back my coat.

"You don't want to be without that gun, Lieutenant," Penny said brightly. "Not today!"

"He certainly doesn't!" Pru agreed. "And you be careful, Al Wheeler, won't you? Don't take any chances—if you feel just one little doubt, you let him have it!"

I shrugged my shoulders back into the coat, then stopped and took another look at them. They stood shoulder to shoulder, united in their beaming approval of me. For some reason I was their pinup boy this morning. They'd sank their differences in the sea of common admiration—for me! Maybe it was that mole, I thought. Then I got it.

"You darling girls," I said. "You've taken all this trouble over me this morning and I've been plain damn rude in return. You got my clothes for me, you ordered my breakfast, you made sure I had my gun before I left—you couldn't have been nicer."

"Don't give it a thought, Al," Prudence smiled warmly at me. "It was nothing."

"Nothing at all," Penny echoed modestly.

"It's just like olden days," I said. "The knight setting forth into battle and his fair ladies preparing everything for him. A good meal, shining his armor, grooming his horse. I think it's wonderful."

"I don't exactly get the point, Lieutenant?" Penny frowned at me. "What do you mean?"

"You both know exactly what I mean," I said coldly. "You know when I leave here I'm going to see Messenger John. Behind those innocent eyes, both of you are praying that I'll blow his head off—so you've done your best to help. You've done your best to ready the knight for battle— or the lamb for the slaughter!"

"You will be careful, Al?" Pru said earnestly. "I mean what I said before. If he even looks like he might do something suspicious—you let him have it!"

"Right between the eyes!" Penny said eagerly.

"You wouldn't like to go along in my place?" I said nastily. "You can take my gun with you and I'll stay home and do some knitting on the side."

"You'd better hurry, Al!" Penny said urgently.

Pru opened the door and caught hold of my sleeve, pulling me toward the open door. "You wouldn't want to miss him?" she said.

"Don't ask me that question again!" I said.

"When it's all over, you must come back and tell us about it," Penny said, giving me a sudden shove in the ribs which sent me staggering out into the corridor.

"Yes indeed," Pru said. "We want to hear every little detail. You know ... how you shot him ..."

"And where!" Penny added.

"If he died right away or did it take a little time," Pru said in a tinkling voice.

"If he screamed or anything," Penny said demurely. "We'd like to know that, wouldn't we, Pru?"

"We surely would," Pru agreed.

Penny gave me another unexpected shove in the ribs which sent me lurching down the corridor. "You're going the right way for the elevators," she said encouragingly. "Good hunting, Lieutenant!"

"Don't forget, Al," Prudence called after me in lazy voice that was suddenly deep and husky and fingered my spine like the point of a red-hot-needle. "Come back to the penthouse; I want to hear every detail. Better bring your toothbrush, and I'll have my 'all' ready and waiting!"

I reached the elevators and pressed the button. A short while later the door opened. I looked back down the corridor for a moment before I stepped into the elevator, and both sisters waved prettily.

That guy Bruno, I thought moodily on my way down to the lobby, wasn't so much after all—not even in his make-up. He was only a beginner in the ghoul stakes compared with the Calthorpe twins!

Hillside was the swank residential district of Pine City, the sort of place I'd live in if I could knock over a bank. Number 78 Stanwell Drive sprawled behind a barrier of ornate shrubs with all the calm assurance of a six-figure investment. I ran the Healey up into the driveway and parked behind the green Cadillac that stood in the four-out and walked up onto the porch and pushed the buzzer. Somewhere inside the house chimes tinkled melodiously. I lit a cigarette while I waited, and then the front door opened and Messenger John looked at me with an expression of quiet inquiry on his face. "You wanted something, Lieutenant?" he asked easily.

He fitted in with the house very well. The dark blue sports jacket, in silk, naturally; the conservative touch of the gray flannel pants and the white silk shirt, were the Hillside badge of exclusive togetherness. The added touch of the white polka-dotted cravat knotted loosely around the neck gave him just that extra little something. It took him out of the merely loaded class into the even more exclusive world of the small but staggeringly expensive clubs.

I stared.

"I said did you want something, Lieutenant?" he repeated.

"A talk," I said. "You have the time?"

"Of course." He opened the door wider. "Won't you come in?"

He led the way through the house to the bar that overlooked the pool at the back, and that was a safari in itself.

"A drink, Lieutenant?" he asked as I sank into a cane chair.

"Thanks," I said, and told him the formula.

He made the drinks, then sat down opposite me. "I do hope you're not going to bring up that silly business about material witnesses again," he said with a smile.

"That was strictly for laughs," I said. "I was going to tell you, but you didn't stay long enough to give me the chance. You left in a hurry, as I remember?"

"The pressure of business," he said vaguely.

"Did you hear about Thelma Davis' body being found yesterday?" I said. "Her neck was broken."

"I heard," he said. "A shocking thing, Lieutenant. And you look as if you've been in some trouble yourself. Your face—there seem to be a few pieces missing here and there."

"Have you delivered the heart yet to Prudence?" I said casually. "Or did you just put it into the mail—collect?"

He finished his drink and twirled the glass slowly in his powerful fingers. "All right, Wheeler," he said. "There are just the two of us here, so I guess we can stop playing games. What's on your mind?"

"You—and two murders," I said.

"Go on."

I told him what I knew. He'd taken the first corpse from the morgue to the studios. He'd removed Howard Davis' body from Penny's hotel suite in a trunk and taken that also to the studios. He'd made the switch of putting Howard's corpse into the coffin.

"You seem to be very well informed," he said.

"It took me a long time to figure out why you bothered to call me and give me all those messages," I said. "You identified the body for me. Gave me a detailed background on Howard's association with Penny. You wanted me to put pressure on her, of course. Enough pressure to make her panic and think I was going to book her any minute for murder.

"Then you could step gracefully into the breach and guarantee her immunity—for a mere fifty thousand dollars. You had already collected twenty thousand from her for the removal of Howard's corpse. I'd hate to pay your taxes, Messenger John!"

"I get by," he said. "The thing is to keep moving and place your faith in the Swiss banks. I recommend it, Lieutenant."

"I'll trust the Fifth National with my nine hundred and fifty bucks capital," I said. "Let's get back to the messages you so kindly sent me.

Once you'd collected from Penny, you wanted suspicion diverted from her, so you put me on the western trail all the way out to El Rancho de los Toros and the white hunter."

"I'm glad to see you've caught up with events, Lieutenant," he said. "Congratulations. For a hick cop, it was a good effort."

"You go on like that, you'll make me blush," I told him. "And I'm still feeling the exhilaration of the whirl you gave me in the morgue last night."

"You were in my way," he said mildly.

I got up from the cane chair and walked to the edge of the terrace. I looked down through the plate-glass screen at the blue-tiled, kidney-shaped pool sparkling in the sunlight.

"It's a nice place you have here, Messenger John," I said.

"Comfortable," he agreed.

"Penny thinks you're renting it, my bet is you own it."

"Is that so?" His voice sounded as though he didn't care what I thought one way or the other.

"Pru thinks money is your fetish," I went on. "She thinks making money is a compulsion with you. That you have to amass an enormous amount of it, purely for its own sake. I don't buy that."

"You think a lot, don't you, Lieutenant?" he said acidly.

"Oh, you know how it is," I said modestly. "Now and then on a Saturday night if I don't have much else to do, well, I might sit around and think a little."

"We seem to have lost the thread somewhere, Lieutenant," he said. "You were talking about messages?"

"I think you make a lot of money because you need it," I said brightly. "I think that while you're making your money, you live in your own business world and your name is Messenger John and you're a very dangerous man indeed."

I took time out to light a cigarette. "But when your business is finished, the way I figure it, you step into another world—this one. And you're a man of substance with a number of very shrewd investments, and your name in Hillside isn't Messenger John at all but something like J. Berkely Addingham, and everybody in Hillside knows that if you've got a worthy cause, good old J. B. will be the first to write you a substantial check."

I turned back from the view of the pool and smiled across at him. "I think lots of thoughts on Saturday nights," I confided. "That's just one of them."

Messenger John got up from his chair slowly, checking the gold Rolex on his wrist with careful ostentation. "It's been pleasant, Lieutenant, but

I'm afraid you'll have to excuse me, I have an appointment. Unless there's something more ...?"

"There was one more point," I said. "From the time you called and gave me the first message, right up to now, wherever I've probed in this investigation, I finished up with you. You are the one person who comes out of the whole thing with a very handsome profit indeed. Seventy thousand dollars is a lot of money, Messenger John, and you took Penny Calthorpe for that sum. The one thing you needed to trigger the whole deal was a corpse to fall into Penny's suite when she opened the door. You're an organization man, Messenger John, if not in the usual sense of the word—you wouldn't let a little thing like the need to murder Howard Davis stand in your way, would you?"

His hands hung down at their sides, the fingers flexing gently, and my neck started screaming and looking for some place to hide. His face darkened slowly and I wasn't conscious of his sartorial elegance any more, but only of the malignant strength of his personality. It looked like Messenger John was back in business.

"Do I understand, Wheeler," he said softly, "that you're saying I murdered Howard Davis because I needed his corpse to make a profit?"

"Check," I said.

"Thelma Davis was murdered, too," he said. "May I ask my motive for killing her?"

"I think you planned this deal from some time back," I said. "It wasn't coincidence that Howard arrived in Pine City at the right time. My guess is you brought him here, sold him a story about a big deal with a lot of money in it for him. I think he told Thelma what it was all about when she caught up with him here. He would have been desperate, thinking he was on the verge of making a quick fortune in association with you, and then the whole thing could be ruined if Thelma had him tossed into jail for a few hundred dollars back alimony.

"After he was murdered, she made the fatal mistake of letting you know she knew Howard had come to Pine City at your invitation and was involved in some deal with you. If she told somebody like me the same story it could have been the last link in a sequence leading from Hillside to the gas chamber. So you killed her to keep her quiet. The job had all your trademarks, of course. A broken neck, the enormous strength needed to twist the head around the way it was."

"You're so wrong, Wheeler!" he said, clipping his words short. "I never killed either of them, but I appreciate your analysis; it's made me see something I missed. One can usually judge intelligence fairly accurately, and when intelligence is lacking, one forgets there are other things— shrewdness and cunning."

"I resent that," I said mildly.

"I wasn't thinking of you, Lieutenant," he said. "Your standard of intelligence is rather high, I must admit. You hide it very successfully under a rather crude veneer. I suspect an inferiority complex somewhere?"

"I always wanted to be a bartender," I admitted, "but I never got the right education."

He smiled. "You see what I mean by the crude veneer, Lieutenant?"

"That takes care of me," I said. "How about this other guy you were talking about?"

"I shall take care of him immediately," he said. "I feel chagrined to think he's put in one or two almost clever touches—to set me up as the murderer that he really is. I shall deliver him a message right away—a final message."

"You're forgetting one thing, Messenger John," I told him. "You aren't going anywhere right now—except with me. I came to take you downtown and book you for murder."

He laughed easily. "I'm sorry, Lieutenant. I'd like to oblige, but this other message is urgent. It won't wait."

"You don't think I'm going to let you walk out on me a second time?" I asked him.

Unconsciously he drew himself up to his full height, then looked down at me with a sneer on his face. "Little man," he said softly. "Do you think you can stop me?"

"No," I admitted. "But this might be a help." I slid my right hand inside my coat and brought out the thirty-eight.

"That won't stop me, either," he said.

I held the gun pointed at his chest and thought about it. I hadn't removed the safety catch yet. There was free choice—entirely up to me. If I guessed wrong I'd be dead, and if I guessed right there was no guarantee it would work out. The hell with it, I thought, if I think about it too long I'll ball the whole thing up, either way.

Messenger John came toward me slowly, walking with the feline grace of a member of the cat family—from puss to tiger. His shoulders were hunched forward slightly, and his fingers flexed more rapidly now. "You can't stop me, Wheeler," he said confidently. "You don't have what it takes to kill an unarmed man in cold blood."

"You're going to find out the hard way, if you come any closer," I told him.

He kept on coming, not hurrying, until one more step would bring him within striking distance.

"O.K.," I said tensely. "You asked for it!"

He reared forward on the balls of his feet and his huge bulk obliterated everything else from my view. Suddenly the whole world was Messenger John. I pulled the trigger of the thirty-eight and there was a metallic click.

His wild shout of laughter nearly stove in my eardrums.

"You poor fool," he said contemptuously. "You're not worth killing. Just move out of my way!"

He raised his right arm and brought it down at an angle, with his hand held open, in an almost lazy imitation of a man swatting a fly.

The back of his hand hit the side of my face with brutal, paralyzing force and I felt myself lifted from the ground and slammed backward helplessly. There was a momentary check, then the glass partition shattered as I went through it. I landed on my back on the tiled edge of the pool and blacked out.

I couldn't have been unconscious for more than half a minute. The first thing I heard was a motor start, the sound steady for a few moments, then gradually lessening as it moved down the driveway, until it faded into silence.

My left hand was dangling in the pool, I realized, and I pulled it out of the water and slowly eased myself up into a sitting position. The fall had driven the air out of my lungs when I landed, which was maybe why I'd blacked out. Sitting up proved my spine wasn't broken, I hoped. After a little while I got up and hobbled slowly back up the steps which led onto the terrace. I found my gun under one of the cane chairs and returned it to the shoulder holster.

Inside the house I found a phone extension in the kitchen. I pulled up a chair and sat down beside the phone and looked at it for awhile.

Both Pru and Charlie Katz had pointed up to me the obvious fact that if I'd been an orthodox cop I wouldn't have gone alone to the morgue. I would have organized a couple of patrol cars, full of cops equipped with floodlights, tear gas and anything that might be needed. And if I'd done that, Messenger John would have been trapped inside the morgue and I wouldn't be wearing the face I had right then.

They were right, of course. Now I had the same problem. If I lifted the phone and called the highway patrol, I could give them an accurate description of Messenger John, an accurate description of the car, with the exception of the license number—and I could tell them where he was heading. They'd have him inside fifteen minutes.

Then I remembered the safety catch I'd deliberately left on, and the aching face and back I'd gotten as a direct result. I wasn't going to suffer them for nothing. I picked up the phone and called the dude ranch, El Rancho de los Toros, and waited.

It took a long two minutes with the voices of the operators seeming to talk without getting any place. Then a new voice said loudly in my ear, El Rancho de los Toros.

"This is Lieutenant Wheeler of the County Sheriff's office, Pine City," I said harshly. "I want to speak to Mr. Jonathan Blake and this is a matter of life and death, so get him to the phone fast!"

"Yes, sir!" the startled voice said. There was a thump in my ear as he dropped the receiver onto the desk.

I lit a cigarette while I waited. It seemed a hell of a long wait but couldn't have been more than a minute, then a cold voice said, "Jonathan Blake speaking."

"This is Lieutenant Wheeler," I said.

"Yes, Lieutenant?" There was no change in the tone of his voice.

"Messenger John is wanted for the murder of Howard and Thelma Davis," I said. "I came to his house to arrest him, but he got away from me. He says he's going to kill you, and we think he's headed your way. You'd better disappear somewhere, hide for a couple of hours. By that time we'll have the whole area blanketed off, and we'll get him."

"Hide?" He laughed shortly. "That's not a serious suggestion, Lieutenant?"

"I was never more serious in my whole life!" I snapped. "This man is a dangerous maniac, and he's already killed two people, and he's sworn he's going to kill you. You find a hole and hide in it."

"I was just about to leave for Devil's Canyon," he said. "I see no reason to change my plans."

"Look," I said. "I'll be there myself just as soon as I can; I'm leaving once I've finished this call to you. Hide some place, even if it's only till I get there."

"If Messenger John has this effect on you, Lieutenant," he said tersely, "I suggest you stay right where you are and crawl under the nearest table. I'm perfectly capable of looking out for myself!" He hung up almost before he'd said the last word.

I had a look under the kitchen table, but the floor looked a little too hard for comfort. So I walked slowly and painfully through the house to the front door and theme out to the Austin-Healey.

Chapter Twelve

I held the Healey at a steady eighty down the dirt road and hoped I didn't hit a patch of really loose stuff. As I came around the next to last curve I lightened my foot on the gas and cut her down until I was doing a modest forty-five around the last curve. The road stopped suddenly the same way it had before, and I hit the brakes and came to a stop beside the tan station wagon and the dark green Cadillac, which were both empty. I switched off the motor and a moment later the silence crept up all around me.

I sat there for a moment listening. Exactly what I'd expected to find when I got to Devil's Canyon I wasn't too sure myself. The sound of rifle shots, the scream of a ricochet from one of the rock walls of the canyon—in my wilder fantasies I saw two gigantic figures wrestling on top of the spur two hundred feet over my head. I certainly hadn't expected to find nothing.

The sound of the car door opening as I got out sounded like thunder. I slammed it shut, lit myself a cigarette and walked to the front of the cars to look down the canyon.

"Hello, Wheeler," a casual voice said, and if my feet didn't leave the ground, the rest of me jumped three feet into the air.

I spun around and saw Blake sitting on the front bumper of his station wagon. There was an ancient, broad-brimmed hat shading his face and he puffed on an equally ancient thick-stemmed briar pipe. He wore an olive green shirt, open at the neck, and a pair of thick whipcord pants which were tucked into a pair of high, immaculately polished boots. The white towel wrapped loosely around his neck made a startling contrast to the deep mahogany tan of his skin. He held the Winchester .458 with its gleaming telescopic sight comfortably across his knees.

"You made it out here in very good time, Wheeler," he said, sucking gently on the pipestem. "On your own?"

"On my own," I agreed. "Where's Messenger John?"

Blake lifted his right hand and waved it casually toward the canyon. "In there somewhere," he said.

"What the hell happened!" I said tautly.

"If I'm being hunted, I like to pick the country for it," he said easily. "I've gotten to know this canyon pretty well the last week or so. That's why I came here—I left word at the desk at the ranch that if anybody asked for me, the clerk was to be sure to tell them I'd be in Devil's Canyon, and how they could get there."

"I can see Messenger John got here—that's his car." I nodded toward the Cadillac. "Will you tell me what happened, for Pete's sake!"

"Not much to it," he grunted. "I hung around here until he showed up, then I pretended to panic and ran into the canyon, and he jumped out of his car and came tearing after me. He's got a rifle with him, sounds like a .300 Savage, but I wouldn't swear to it."

"I'll accept the fact he has rifle with him, the hell with the caliber!" I said. "Go on with what happened."

"I led him around to my target-practice area," he said. "Where you found me the other day."

"Sure, I remember it."

"I'm an old hand at this," he said easily. "It was really child's play. I made sure he saw me go in, then I used the natural cover and as far as he was concerned, I'd vanished. He naturally thought I must be further into the place than he'd realized. So he goes charging along getting further and further away from the main canyon, while I'm quietly working my way out to the main canyon."

I lit a cigarette. "So?"

"It's very simple, old man. You have the hunter and the hunted. In five minutes the roles are reversed. Messenger John reaches the end of the gully and finds a two-hundred-foot wall of sheer rock staring him in the face. He's trapped unless he turns around and makes his way back to the main canyon again. But by that time I'm waiting for him in the entrance to the gully, and all the advantage is mine."

Blake chuckled contentedly. "Poor bloody fool," he said almost compassionately. "He must have felt like blowing his own brains out when he realized what had happened. I waited for him to come out, I wasn't in any hurry, there was plenty of time. Had him lined up in the scope from three hundred yards on in, but I let him get to two hundred before I fired."

He frowned slightly. "Don't know what went wrong. He should have been a sitting duck—but I must have been overanxious."

"You missed him?"

Blake looked up at me, appalled: "Great Scott, no! But I only winged him. He jumped into the air and I heard him scream as he fell to the ground. But a couple of seconds later he was shooting accurately at me, too damned accurately for comfort, so I got out and came back here."

"You mean Messenger John's still in there somewhere with a rifle," I said.

"That's right," he said complacently. "Still there." He glanced at his watch. "But if he doesn't show up within the next half-hour, he's dead."

"What makes you say that?"

He patted the stock of the Winchester affectionately. "These babies punch a pretty big hole in anything they hit, old man," he said. "I think I either got him in a leg, high up, or in the belly. Wherever it was, he'll be losing blood fast, a lot of blood." He squinted up at the sky. "And don't forget the sun, Wheeler. The temperature in that gully right now will be something better than a 110 degrees. He can't last long in that, not with a hole in him somewhere."

"Why don't we go in and bring him out," I said. "You can't leave a man to die like that, whoever he is."

He shook his head firmly. "Too dangerous—you can take it from an old hand at this game. Wounded man's like a wounded rhino—goes crazy-mad with pain and takes a hell of a lot of killing. Better wait another half hour and be sure."

"How about a wounded lion?" I said. "They take a lot of killing?"

"What's that?" he said vaguely.

"I didn't know how well supplied you were with ammunition," I told him. "So I brought this along."

I took the king-sized cartridge out of my pocket and dropped it into the palm of his hand. He looked down at it for what seemed to be a long time before he spoke: "Six hundred Continental," he said finally. "Magnificent gun. Where did you get this?"

"Out of a manila envelope," I said easily, "left in the safe of the Park Hotel."

"Interesting," he murmured.

"Thelma Davis left it there," I told him. "She got it from her ex-husband, Howard Davis, of course."

His strong white teeth took a firmer grip on the pipestem. "If Messenger John is ever coming out, it will have to be very soon now," he said.

"That's a most interesting cartridge," I said. "I had it checked by a ballistics expert yesterday. Somebody went to a lot of trouble to empty most of the powder from the cartridge and then replace the bullet."

"If I were you, Lieutenant," he said deliberately. "I'd concentrate on that canyon, if you want to catch your murderer."

"Messenger John sure confused a lot of issues," I said firmly. "But once he's removed, a lot of other things come into sharp focus."

"Really don't know what you're talking about, Wheeler," he grunted.

"I'd be happy to lay it on the line for you, Blake," I told him. "How about that?"

"Why not?" he said. "Might as well listen to you talk as just sit here, while we have to wait."

"O.K.," I said. "Let's start with Howard Davis, because he was the first

Davis to be murdered. He'd been married to Penelope Calthorpe for a time, then she divorced him without him getting a penny of her money. He'd been a third-rate tennis pro and he was too old and too lazy to go back to that game. He was also being hounded by his first wife, Thelma, for back alimony payments, with the threat of jail if he didn't meet them."

"Howard Davis was no good," Blake said dispassionately, "Always said so."

"He was desperate for money," I continued. "He wanted money and he didn't care how he got it. So he decided to blackmail for it. Prudence Calthorpe had been married to a white hunter, a man named Blake, and she had also divorced him, without having to give him a penny, either. But in Blake's case it was different—he was blue-blood Bostonian stock with inherited wealth behind him, at least that's what everyone believed."

Blake grunted: "Go on."

"That was where everyone was wrong," I said. "The safari-styled life Blake led was a most expensive one and he ran out of money. Prudence knew this; it happened while they were still married, while her father was still alive."

I stopped to light another cigarette, while Blake sat with the Winchester across his knees, his eyes steadily searching the canyon in front of him.

"I'll make it fast, Blake," I said. "Old man Calthorpe was killed by a lion on safari with you. An accident—with a couple of odd overtones, but nothing anyone could put a finger on. You missed with your first shot and only wounded the lion, which for you was unusual. Then you didn't kill it with your second shot until it had already killed Calthorpe. The old man's gun misfired.

"Howard Davis was along at the time," I said. "He wouldn't mourn the old man any more than you would. You were both broke—now the two girls, your respective wives, would inherit the fortune between them.

"The way I see it, after it was over and the old man was dead, Howard saw you remove some cartridges from the old man's gun and throw them away, or hide them somewhere. So Howard, ever curious, got hold of them, and then realized what had happened. You'd loaded the old man's gun with tampered bullets—when he pulled the trigger, there was enough powder to make a noise but not enough to expel the bullet. In the general excitement only a trained ear would pick out the difference—and ear like yours.

"Howard kept the cartridges, and when things were desperate, he decided to use them to blackmail you. The one thing he didn't know was that you hadn't any money of your own anyway—that you were relying on marrying Penny to re-establish yourself."

Blake moved his pipe from one side of his mouth to the other. "Are you trying to accuse me of murdering Howard Davis?"

"And his first wife, Thelma," I agreed.

"What sort of proof do you have?" he asked mildly.

"The cartridge," I said. "It proves that if you didn't murder old man Calthorpe, you did your very best to engineer his death. I think that when Howard threatened you and showed you one cartridge—there would be two, I imagine—you laughed at him and asked who would believe him now. He said Penny, his ex-wife would. You couldn't take the chance.

"That was when you had to do something drastic about him. If he told Penny you had murdered her father, she would never marry you, and your last hope of continuing the life of a gentleman white hunter was gone. I think you followed Howard to see if he was serious about telling Penny. You followed him to the hotel, up to the ninth floor and when he knocked on the door of the suite, you shot him, panicked and ran.

"Unfortunately for Thelma Davis, Howard had told her about it. She had the one remaining cartridge and she intended carrying out the blackmail scheme. I tipped you off about that in Penny's suite when I told you about Thelma's threats. Some time later that day she called you and you agreed to meet her, said you would bring the money and she was to bring the cartridge. You of course didn't have the money, and she didn't bring the cartridge, but you didn't know that then.

"You picked her up in your car and drove out along the highway and then turned off onto a dirt road. Once it was safe, you stopped and murdered her. Broke her neck and threw her into the tall grass beside the edge of the road. You searched her purse, you searched her clothes and couldn't find the cartridge. You drove back to her hotel, went up the fire escape to her room and searched that, but still no cartridge.

"Then I called you a couple of hours back and told you Messenger John was heading in your direction, intent on killing you, which was true, and that he was wanted for both murders, which was false."

The vivid blue eyes searched my face for a moment. "You didn't care for Messenger John much either, did you?" he murmured.

"He's been a nuisance," I said carefully. "He beat me up in the morgue last night, threw me through a glass partition this morning and nearly broke my spine. No, I'd say I didn't go for him very much."

"So you set the two of us to fight it out in the canyon," he said. "While you're on hand to claim the victor. If it's me, the charge is murder, if it's Messenger John, there are many less serious charges, but serious enough in themselves. Very clever of you, Lieutenant."

"I also figured there was a reasonable chance that you might kill each other," I said.

"You realize that now I shall have to kill you?" he said curtly.

I took the thirty-eight from the holster, this time being very careful to release the safety catch. "You can try," I said. "I have a gun."

"You also have a very complicated situation," he said. "At any moment Messenger John may reappear to complicate it further. He is an ever present potential threat. You also have to take me back with you to Pine City. This is my country out here, Wheeler. I'm sorry, but you don't stand a chance."

"There is a way of simplifying the situation, Blake," I said and stepped back a pace. Then I rammed the muzzle of the .38 into the center of his spine. "We'll go and take a look in the canyon and see what's happened to Messenger John."

"It will be a very stupid thing to do," he said.

"Maybe," I said. "Let's find out. Get up, Blake."

He made no effort to move himself, and I pressed the gun a little harder into his back. "Don't tempt me to make the situation real simple again by shooting you in the back," I said softly. "Who would ever know the difference?"

Blake got up slowly, holding his rifle in both hands.

"I'll tell you how it will be," I said. "We go into the canyon, but you go first, and I'll be right behind you. If you even turn your head back, I'll shoot you."

"What happens if Messenger John is alive?" he asked coolly.

"I guess he gets the first shot," I said mildly. "And then it's every man for himself."

"You're giving me a sporting chance, Wheeler," he said with heavy sarcasm. "If Messenger John doesn't pick me off from the gully, you shoot me in the back!"

"Howard Davis I didn't mind so much," I said conversationally. "But Thelma—that was different. I didn't like the way you left her in that long grass, Jonathan. I didn't like the way you broke her neck, the way you twisted her head around. If I had to take a choice between the two of you, I'd take Messenger John—at least he takes some chances of his own. But you sit around with a highly scientific instrument in your hands like that Winchester there and think you're a hell of a male specimen because you can kill wild animals at two hundred yards without soiling your nice clean shirt."

I pushed the gun into his spine again. "What the hell?" I said. "Let's see you stand up to a really wild human being with a rifle in his hands.

I hope Messenger John is still alive somewhere in that gully. For the first time in your life you're going hunting game that's meeting you on equal terms!"

We went slowly into the canyon. When we reached the entrance to the gully, Blake slowed to a standstill. "I tell you this is madness!" he said. "He could be anywhere in there now—maybe only ten yards away from us right now, and we'll never see him until it's too late!"

"What's the matter, Jonathan?" I asked him courteously. "Losing your nerve?"

"There's a difference between nerve and idiocy!" he said savagely. "This way, we have no chance."

"You've still got a better chance than you gave Howard or Thelma Davis," I said. "You can have a choice—you go into the gully or I'll shoot you here."

He wiped the sweat from his face with one end of the white towel around his neck. "Five seconds, Blake," I said. "Please yourself."

For three seconds he stood motionless, then he walked forward again slowly into the gully. We had gone about fifty yards into the gully when it happened.

There was the sudden sharp crack of a rifle shot, then Blake screamed thinly and pitched forward, his rifle clattering on the rocks as it dropped from his hands.

I stood there for a moment, feeling I was ten feet tall and six feet wide. Then I dropped to my knees beside Blake.

He lifted a pain-distorted face and looked at me with naked hatred shining in his eyes. "My thigh," he said desperately. "Smashed the bone; I can't walk. Do something, Wheeler; you've got to get me out of here!" He dragged the towel from his neck, mopped the streaming sweat from his face, then tied the towel around the top of his right leg. A bright stream of blood ran down his leg and into the top of his boot.

A second shot re-echoed down the gully and chips of rock stung my face. The slug had hit almost at my feet.

"Wheeler!" a harsh voice yelled. "I'm only fifty yards away from you. I've got your head lined up in the sights now. You do as you're told or the next shot will be right between your eyes!"

I didn't think he was bluffing; that last shot had been warning, and much too close to be ignored. "What do you want?" I called back.

"Walk straight ahead until I tell you to stop," he said. "Bring Blake's rifle with you and hold it by the barrel in your left hand, and carry your own gun by the barrel in your right hand."

"O.K.," I said.

"You can't do it!" Blake screamed suddenly. "You can't leave me here.

He'll kill you when you get up close and then I'll be all alone, die like a jackal!" The sob broke in his throat and he beat his fists against the ground in frenzy.

I picked up the Winchester by the barrel and held my own thirty-eight by the barrel in the other hand. Then I started walking. It was the longest fifty yards I'd ever walked in all my life.

"All right, Wheeler," a thick voice said from almost under my feet. "Stop right there."

I stopped and looked down. Messenger John lay behind a wedge-shaped boulder, a rifle cradled in his hands. His face was a fiery brick red that seemed to radiate its own heat and his eyes were slits in the puffed and swollen skin. The dry, cracked lips parted a fraction. "Throw Blake's rifle as far as you can up the gully," he said in a dry whisper. He waited until the rifle landed some thirty yards away and disappeared in the rock-strewn floor.

"Take the shells out of your thirty-eight and do the same with them," he said. "Make sure you get the lot—I'll be counting them, too." Again I did as I was told—the barrel of his rifle pointed unwaveringly at my chest the whole time.

"That's better," he said. "You can put that gun away now, Wheeler."

I slid the empty gun back into its holster and looked down at him. "You wouldn't have any water with you?" He shook his head slowly. "Stupid question—of course you haven't. I've been baking here for the last couple of hours, gives you a thirst."

"Why didn't you come out before?" I asked him.

"Blake would have told you," he said hoarsely. "He lured me in here, then doubled back to the entrance. Never fully lose your temper, Wheeler. It's a luxury no man can afford."

He coughed violently. "Blake got me in the hip, so I couldn't walk, but that doesn't matter now. Then he ran out and left me here to die, but I didn't. I wasn't going to let myself die until I'd given back that bastard what he gave me." The lips twisted further. "He was a sitter right then and I could have put that slug through his head just as easily, but I didn't. It was your idea to bring him back in here?"

"My idea," I agreed.

"You knew he was the real killer of course," Messenger John said slowly. "But you didn't want me walking out of the picture and taking all my profit with me. So you put on an act to convince me I was going to be convicted for two murders anyway and it was all Blake's fault, so whatever I did made no difference then. You wanted me to get so mad at Blake that I didn't care what happened so long as I got him. You did that all right!" He coughed again. "You had no intention of booking me for the murders, did you?"

"No," I said.

"And you knew the safety catch was on when you pulled the trigger—it was the last convincing touch you needed. You weren't far out in guessing about my double life, either. Sure, I lived like a gentleman, not in Hillside—but in Connecticut. The Hillside house was only rented—doesn't do to mix business and pleasure in the same town where you live. One question more, Wheeler—are you taking Blake out of here?"

I looked down at him without answering.

"Don't do it!" he said. "He left me here to die while he sat some place in the shade. Don't ..."

The rifle clattered from his hands and his head dropped forward onto the blistering rock. From where his face touched the rock there was a faint frying sound, but he never moved.

Blake had stopped swearing when I got back to him. He looked tired, drawn.

"Wheeler!" He looked up at me eagerly. "Messenger John—what's happened?"

"He's dead," I told him.

"Ah!" he said excitedly. "So I did hit him all right, eh?" He grinned up at me, but his eyes were still cold and never left my face. "Now," he said. "How are you going to get me out of here? I can't walk, you know, old man."

"I have no intention of getting you out of here," I told him sincerely.

I saw the sudden hopelessness spread across his face. "What am I going to do?" he whimpered. "I can't stop it bleeding, I'm weakening all the time, and the heat is drying me up. You can't leave me, Wheeler!" He pushed himself up on his hands. "You've got to help me!" he screamed at the top of his voice.

"O.K.," I said. "I'll give you a break, Jonathan."

"I knew it!" He relaxed. "I knew you couldn't leave me to die here, all alone."

"Messenger John's body is not more than fifty yards up ahead of you in a straight line," I said. "You can crawl; it might be tough going, but you can make it."

"What do you mean?" he whispered.

"His gun is right beside him," I said.

I walked toward the entrance into the main canyon, and after a time his screams and curses grew fainter and fainter until suddenly I couldn't hear them anymore.

I got back to the cars and slumped onto the front bumper of the station wagon. My clothes were soaked right through with sweat and clung to me limply. My throat was a dry furnace and I could feel my face burning like a beacon.

After a while I got up and walked over to the Healey and sat behind the wheel. It seemed a long time, maybe it was only a short time. I didn't check it by my watch.

Then it came, shattering the silence brutally, its echoes rolling down the canyon. The sound of a lone rifle shot from the gully. After a short time the silence came back and took possession again.

I started the Healey and backed out from between the two bigger cars, made a U turn and headed back down the dirt road. I looked back once before the bend in the road hid them from sight. They were two shimmering silhouettes in the heat and they looked large enough to be monuments of some kind.

Maybe they were, at that. The station wagon, a monument to a white hunter and gentleman; the glossy sedan, a monument to a businessman and gentleman.

I wondered what the hell I was going to tell Lavers.

THE END

Alan Geoffrey Yates Bibliography
(1923-1985)

As Carter Brown/Peter Carter Brown

Series:

Al Wheeler (no U.S. edition unless otherwise stated through to Chorine Makes a Killing)

The Wench is Wicked (1955)
Blonde Verdict (1956; revised for the U.S. as The Brazen, 1960)
Delilah Was Deadly (1956)
No Harp for My Angel (1956)
Booty for a Babe (1956)
Eve, It's Extortion (1957; revised as Walk Softly Witch!, 1959, and further revised for the U.S. as The Victim, 1959)
No Law Against Angels (1957; revised for the U.S. as The Body, 1958; 1st U.S. Wheeler)
Doll for the Big House (1957; revised for the U.S. as The Bombshell, 1960)
Chorine Makes a Killing (1957)
The Unorthodox Corpse (1957; revised for the U.S., 1961)
Death on the Downbeat (1958; revised for the U.S. as The Corpse, 1958)
The Blonde (1958; reprinted in the U.S., 1958)
The Lover (1958)
The Mistress (1959)
The Passionate (1959)
The Wanton (1959)
The Dame (1959)

The Desired (1959)
The Temptress (1960)
Lament for a Lousy Lover (1960) [includes Mavis Seidlitz]
The Stripper (1961)
The Tigress (1961; reprinted in the UK as Wildcat, 1962)
The Exotic (1961)
Angel! (1962)
The Hellcat (1962)
The Lady Is Transparent (1962)
The Dumdum Murder (1962)
Girl in a Shroud (1963)
The Sinners (1963; reprinted in U.S. as The Girl Who Was Possessed, 1963)
The Lady Is Not Available (1963; reprinted in U.S. as The Lady Is Available, 1963)
The Dance of Death (1964)
The Vixen (1964; reprinted in the U.S. as The Velvet Vixen, 1964)
A Corpse for Christmas (1965)
The Hammer of Thor (1965)
Target for Their Dark Desire (1966)
The Plush-Lined Coffin (1967)
Until Temptation Do Us Part (1967)
The Deep Cold Green (1968)
The Up-Tight Blonde (1969)
Burden of Guilt (1970)
The Creative Murders (1971)
W.H.O.R.E. (1971)
The Clown (1972)
The Aseptic Murders (1972)
The Born Loser (1973)
Night Wheeler (1974)
Wheeler Fortune (1974)

Wheeler, Dealer! (1975)
The Dream Merchant (1976)
Busted Wheeler (1979)
The Spanking Girls (1979)
Model for Murder (1980)
The Wicked Widow (1981)
Stab in the Dark (1984;
  Australia only)

Larry Baker

Charlie Sent Me (1965; revised
  from Swan Song for a Siren,
  1955)
No Blonde Is an Island (1965)
So What Killed the Vampire?
  (1966)
Had I But Groaned (1968;
  reprinted in the UK as The
  Witches, 1969)
True Son of the Beast (1970)
The Iron Maiden (1975)

Barney Blain (no U.S. editions)

Madam, You're Mayhem (1957)
Ice Cold in Ermine (1958)

Danny Boyd

Tempt a Tigress (1958; no U.S.)
So Deadly, Sinner! (1959;
  reprinted in the U.S. as Walk
  Softly, Witch, 1959, 1st U.S.
  Boyd; different version of the
  Wheeler title)
Suddenly by Violence (1959)
Terror Comes Creeping (1959)
The Wayward Wahine (1960;
  published in Australia as The
  Wayward, 1962)
The Dream Is Deadly (1960)

Graves, I Dig (1960; revised from
  Cutie Wins a Corpse (1957)
The Myopic Mermaid (1961,
  revised from A Siren Sounds
  Off, 1958)
The Ever-Loving Blues (1961;
  revised from Death of a Doll,
  1956)
The Seductress (1961; published
  in the U.S. as The Sad-Eyed
  Seductress, 1961)
The Savage Salome (1961;
  revised from Murder is My
  Mistress, 1954)
The Ice-Cold Nude (1962)
Lover Don't Come Back (1962)
Nymph to the Slaughter (1963)
Passionate Pagan (1963)
Silken Nightmare (1963)
Catch Me a Phoenix! (1965)
The Sometime Wife (1965)
The Black Lace Hangover (1966)
House of Sorcery (1967)
The Mini-Murders (1968)
Murder Is the Message (1969)
Only the Very Rich (1969)
The Coffin Bird (1970)
The Sex Clinic (1971)
Angry Amazons (1972) [includes
  Randy Roberts]
Manhattan Cowboy (1973)
So Move the Body (1973)
The Early Boyd (1975)
The Savage Sisters (1976)
The Pipes Are Calling (1976)
The Rip Off (1979)
The Strawberry-Blonde Jungle
  (1979)
Death to a Downbeat (1980)
Kiss Michelle Goodbye (1981)
The Real Boyd (1984; Australia
  only)

Paul Donavan

Donavan (1974)
Donovan's Day (1975)
Chinese Donavan (1976)
Donavan's Delight (1979)

Max Dumas (no U.S. editions)

Goddess Gone Bad (1958)
Luck Was No Lady (1958)
Deadly Miss (1958)

Mike Farrel

The Million Dollar Babe (1961;
   revised from Cutie Cashed His
   Chips, 1955)
The Scarlet Flush (1963; revised
   from Ten Grand Tallulah and
   Temptation, 1957)

Rick Holman

Zelda (1961; 1st U.S. Holman)
Murder in the Harem Club,
   1962; reprinted in the U.S. as
   Murder in the Key Club, 1962)
The Murderer Among Us (1962)
Blonde on the Rocks (1963)
The Jade-Eyed Jinx (1963;
   reprinted in the U.S. as The
   Jade-Eyed Jungle, 1964)
The Ballad of Loving Jenny
   (1963; reprinted in the U.S. as
   The White Bikini, 1963)
The Wind-Up Doll (1963)
The Never-Was Girl (1964)
Murder Is a Package Deal (1964)
Who Killed Doctor Sex? (1964)
Nude—with a View (1965)
The Girl from Outer Space (1965)

Blonde on a Broomstick (1966)
Play Now... Kill Later (1966)
No Tears from the Widow (1966)
The Deadly Kitten (1967)
Long Time No Leola (1967)
Die Anytime, After Tuesday!
   (1969)
The Flagellator (1969)
The Streaked-Blond Slave (1969)
A Good Year for Dwarfs? (1970)
The Hang-up Kid (1970)
Where Did Charity Go? (1970)
The Coven (1971)
The Invisible Flamini (1971)
The Pornbroker (1972)
The Master (1973)
Phreak-Out! (1973)
Negative in Blue (1974)
The Star-Crossed Lover (1974)
Ride the Roller Coaster (1975)
Remember Maybelle? (1976)
See It Again, Sam (1979)
The Phantom Lady (1980)
The Swingers (1980)

Andy Kane

The Hong Kong Caper (1962;
   revised from Blonde, Bad and
   Beautiful, 1957)
The Guilt-edged Cage (1963;
   revised from That's Piracy, My
   Pet, 1957; published in
   Australia as Bird in a Guilt-
   Edged Cage)

Ivor MacCallum
(no U.S. editions)

Sweetheart You Slay Me (1952)
Blackmail Beauty (1953)

Randy Roberts

Murder in the Family Way
(1971)
The Seven Sirens (1972)
Murder on High (1973)
Sex Trap (1975)

Mavis Seidlitz

Honey, Here's Your Hearse (1955;
no U.S.)
The Killer is Kissable (1955; no
U.S.)
A Bullet For My Baby (1955; no
U.S.)
Good Morning, Mavis! (1957; no
U.S.)
Murder Wears a Mantilla (1957;
revised for U.S. as same title,
1962)
The Loving and the Dead (1959;
1st U.S. Seidlitz)
None But the Lethal Heart
(1959; reprinted as The
Fabulous, 1961)
Tomorrow Is Murder (1960)
Lament for a Lousy Lover (1960)
[includes Al Wheeler]
The Bump and Grind Murders
(1964)
Seidlitz and the Super Spy
(1967; published in the UK as
The Super-Spy, 1968)
Murder Is So Nostalgic (1972)
And the Undead Sing (1974)

Unrelated Novels/Novelettes (all
non-U.S. unless otherwise noted)

Death Date for Dolores (1951)
Designed to Deceive (1951)
Duchess Double X (1951)
Forever Forbidden (1951)
The Lady Is Murder (1951;
reprinted as Lady is a Killer
with Murder by Miss Take,
1958)
Three Men, One Love (1951)
Uncertain Heart (1951)
Your Alibi Is Showing (1951)
Alias a Lady (1952)
Blackmail for a Brunette (1952)
Blondes Prefer Bullets (1952)
Hands Off the Lady (1952)
Kiss Life Goodbye (1952)
Larceny Was Lovely (1952)
Meet Miss Mayhem (1952)
Murder Sweet Murder (1952)
She Wore No Shroud (1952)
Sssh! She's a Killer (1952)
Chill on Chili/Butterfly Nett
(1953)
Cyanide Sweetheart (1953)
Dead Dolls Don't Cry (1953)
Dimples Died De-Luxe (1953)
Judgement of a Jane (1953)
Kidnapper Wears Curves (1953)
The Lady Wore Nylon (1953)
The Lady's Alive (1953)
Lethal in Love (1953; reprinted
as The Minx is Murder, 1956)
Madame You're Morgue-Bound
(1953)
Meet a Body (1953)
The Mermaid Murmurs Murder
(1953)

Model for Murder (1953;
  different from 1980 Al Wheeler
  title)
Moonshine Momma (1953)
Murder is a Broad (1953)
Penthouse Pass-Out (1953;
  reprinted as Hot Seat for a
  Honey, 1956)
Rope for a Redhead (1953;
  revised as Model of No Virtue,
  1956)
Slightly Dead (1953)
Stripper You're Stuck (1953)
Widow is Willing (1953)
The Black Widow Weeps (1954)
Felon Angel (1954)
Floozies Out of Focus (1954)
The Frame is Beautiful (1954)
Fraulein is Feline (1954;
  reprinted with Moonshine
  Momma & Slaughter in Satin,
  1955)
Good-Knife Sweetheart (1954)
Honky Tonk Homicide (1954;
  reprinted with Chill on Chili &
  Butterfly Nett, 1955)
Homicide Harem (1954;
  reprinted with Good-Knife
  Sweetheart & Poison Ivy, 1955;
  with Felon Angel, 1965)
The Lady is Chased (1954;
  reprinted as Trouble is a Dame,
  1957)
A Morgue Amour (1954)
Murder—Paris Fashion (1954)
Murder! She Says (1954)
Nemesis Wore Nylons (1954)
Pagan Perilous (1954)
Perfumed Poison (1954)
Poison Ivy (1954)
Shady Lady (1954)
Sinsation Sadie (1954)

Slaughter in Satin (1954)
Strip Without Tease (1954;
  reprinted as Stripper, You've
  Sinned, 1959)
Trouble is a Dame (1954)
Wreath for Rebecca (1954)
Venus Unarmed (1954)
Yogi Shrouds Yolande (1954;
  reprinted with Poison Ivy, 1965)
Curtains for a Chorine (1955)
Curves for a Coroner (1955)
Cutie Cashed His Chips (1955;
  revised for U.S. as The Million
  Dollar Babe, 1961, as Farrel
  series)
Homicide Hoyden (1955)
Kiss and Kill (1955; reprinted
  with Cyanide Sweetie, 1958)
Kiss Me Deadly (1955; reprinted
  as Lipstick Larceny, 1958)
Lead Astray (1955)
Lipstick Larceny (1955)
Maid for Murder (1955)
Miss Called Murder (1955)
Shamus, Your Slip Is Showing
  (1955; reprinted with A Morgue
  Amour, 1957)
Shroud for My Sugar (1955)
Sob-Sister Cries Murder (1955)
The Two Timing Blonde (1955)
Baby, You're Guilt-Edged (1956;
  reprinted with Pagan Perilous,
  1959)
Bid the Babe Bye-Bye (1956)
Blonde, Beautiful, and – Blam!
  (1956)
The Bribe Was Beautiful (1956)
Caress Before Killing (1956)
Darling You're Doomed (1956)
Donna Died Laughing (1956)
The Eve of His Dying (1956)
Hi-Jack for Jill (1956)

The Hoodlum Was a Honey (1956)

The Lady Has No Convictions (1956; reprinted with Slightly Dead, 1959)

Meet Murder, My Angel (1956)

Murder By Miss-Demeanour (1956)

My Darling Is Deadpan (1956)

No Halo For Hedy (1956)

Strictly for Felony (1956)

Sweetheart, This is Homicide (1956)

Bella Donna Was Poison (1957)

Cutie Wins a Corpse (1957; revised for U.S. as Graves, I Dig!, 1960, as Boyd series)

Last Note for a Lovely (1957)

Lethal in Love (1957; different than 1953 title)

Sinner, You Slay Me (1957)

Ten Grand Tallulah and Temptation (1957; revised as The Scarlet Flush, 1963, Farrel series)

That's Piracy, My Pet (1957; revised as Bird in a Guilt-Edged Cage, 1963, as Kane series)

Wreath for a Redhead (1957)

The Charmer Chased (1958)

Cutie Takes the Count (1958)

Deadly Miss (1958)

Hi-Fi Fadeout (1958)

High Fashion in Homicide (1958)

No Body She Knows (1958; with Slaughter in Satin, 1960)

No Future Fair Lady (1958)

Sinfully Yours (1958)

A Siren Signs Off (1958; with Moonshine Momma; revised for U.S. as The Myopic Mermaid, 1961, as Boyd series)

So Lovely She Lies (1958)

Widow Bewitched (1958)

The Blonde Avalanche (1984)

As Tod Conway (western stories)

As Caroline Farr

The Intruder (1962)

House of Tombs (1966)

Mansion of Evil (1966)

Villa of Shadows (1966)

Web of Horror (1966; reprinted in the U.S. as A Castle in Spain, 1978)

Granite Folly (1967)

The Secret of the Chateau (1967)

Witch's Hammer (1967)

So Near and Yet... (1968)

House of Destiny (1969)

The Castle on the Lake (1970)

The Secret of Castle Ferrara (1970)

Terror on Duncan Island (1971)

The Towers of Fear (1972)

A Castle in Canada (1972)

House of Dark Illusions (1973)

House of Secrets (1973)

Dark Mansion (1974)

Mansion Malevolent (1974)

The House on the Cliffs (1974)

Dark Citadel (1975)

Mansion of Peril (1975)

Castle of Terror (1975)

The Scream in the Storm (1975)

Chateau of Wolves (1976)

Mansion of Menace (1976)

Brecon Castle (1976)
The House of Landsdown (1977)
House of Treachery (1977)
Ravensnest (1977)
The House at Lansdowne (1977)
Sinister House (1978)
House of Valhalla (1978)
Heiress Of Fear (1978)
Room Of Secrets (1979)
Island of Evil (1979)
A Castle on the Rhine (1979)
The Castle on the Loch (1979)
The Secret at Ravenswood (1980)

As Raymond Glenning
(stories)

Ghosts Don't Kill (1951)
Seven for Murder (1951)

As Sinclair Mackellar

Prompt for Murder (1981)

As Dennis Sinclair

Temple Dogs Guard My Fate
  (1968)
Third Force (1976)
The Friends of Lucifer (1977)
Blood Brothers (1977)

As Paul Valdez (stories &
  novelettes)

Hypnotic Death (1949)
The Fatal Focus (1950)
Outcasts of Planet J (1950)
Jetbees from Planet J (1951)
Escape to Paradise (1951)
Fugitives from the Flame World
  (1951)

Kidnapped in Chaos (1951)
Killer by Night (1951)
Suicide Satellite (1951)
The Time Thief (1951)
Flight Into Horror (1951)
Murder Gives Notice (1951)
The Corpse Sat Up (1951)
The Maniac Murders (1951)
Satan's Sabbath (1951)
You Can't Keep Murder Out
  (1951)
Kill Him Gently (1951)
Feline Frame-Up (1951)
Celluloid Suicide? (1951)
The Murder I Don't Remember
  (1952)
Kidnapped in Space (1952)
There's No Future in Murder
  (1952)
The Crook Who Wasn't There
  (1952)
Maniac Murders (1952)
The Mad Meteor (1952)
Operation Satellite (1952)

As A. G. Yates

The Cold Dark Hours (1958)

As Alan Yates

Novel:

Coriolanus, the Chariot (1978)

Stories & Novelettes:

Client for Murder (*Leisure
  Detective* #7, 195?)
The Corpse on the Carpet
  (*Leisure Detective* #8, 195?)

Farewell, My Lady of Shalott! (*Action Detective Magazine #6*, 1952)
Hush-a-Buy Homicide (*Leisure Detective #9*, 195?)
Margie (*Action Detective Magazine #5*, 1952)
Merger with Death (*Leisure Detective #12*, 195?)
Murder in the Family (*Leisure Detective #11*, 195?)
Murder Needs Education (*Action Detective Magazine #2*, 1952)
Murder! She Says (*Detective Monthly #2*, 195?)
My Love Lies Murdered (*Action Detective Magazine #7*, 1952)
Nemesis for a Nude! (*Leisure Detective #10*, 195?)

Genie from Jupiter (*Thrills Incorporated #14*, 1951)
Goddess of Space (*Thrills Incorporated #20*, 1952)
No Pixies on Pluto (*Thrills Incorporated #22*, 1952)
Planet of the Lost (*Thrills Incorporated #17*, 1951)
A Space Ship Is Missing (*Thrills Incorporated #16*, 1951)
Spacemen Spoofed (*Thrills Incorporated #23*, 1952)

Autobiography

Ready when you are, C.B.!: The autobiography of Alan Yates alias Carter Brown (1983)

Follow the previous capers of Al Wheeler from the irrepressible...

Carter Brown

The Wench is Wicked / Blonde Verdict / Delilah Was Deadly

978-1-944520-33-5 $19.95

Al Wheeler #1-3.

"All fans of crime fiction should take this opportunity to rediscover Brown and Al Wheeler, and experience what kind of stories kept readers happily turning pages when paperback originals first ruled the market."
—Alan Cranis, *Bookgasm.*

No Harp for My Angel / Booty for a Babe / Eve, It's Extortion

978-1-944520-44-1 $19.95

Al Wheeler #4-6.

"These three novels are testaments to Brown's authorial leanness... With succulent descriptions of succulent women, two-fisted action, twists and turns, and Wheeler's irrepressible attitude, there's nothing *not* to like in Brown's series about this rakish police officer."
—Kristofer Upjohn, *Noir Journal.*

No Law Against Angels / Doll for the Big House / Chorine Makes a Killing

978-1-944520-70-0 $19.95

Al Wheeler #7-9.

"...a gripping short read...Al Wheeler is hilarious with his endless sarcasm, never completely in control but somehow being three steps in front of the bad guys and the reader. This is absolutely entertaining and a must read."—*Paperback Warrior*

The Unorthodox Corpse / Death on the Downbeat / The Blonde

978-1-944520-91-5 $19.95

Al Wheeler #10-12.

"These are all tightly written tales...plenty of action and the plots are straightforward fast reading, laced with humor..."
—Ted Hertel,
Deadly Pleasures.

STARK HOUSE PRESS
1315 H Street, Eureka, CA 95501
griffinskye3@sbcglobal.net
www.StarkHousePress.com

Available from your local bookstore, or order direct or via our website.

CPSIA information can be obtained
at www.ICGtesting.com
Printed in the USA
FSHW020147060421
80177FS